NOEL HYND
COUNTDOWN IN CAIRO

Also in the Russian Trilogy Series

Conspiracy in Kiev

Midnight in Madrid

NOEL HYND
COUNTDOWN IN CAIRO

THE RUSSIAN TRILOGY — BOOK THREE

ZONDERVAN.com/
AUTHORTRACKER
follow your favorite authors

ZONDERVAN

Countdown in Cairo
Copyright © 2009 by Noel Hynd

This title is also available as a Zondervan ebook.
Visit www.zondervan.com/ebooks.

This title is also available in a Zondervan audio edition.
Visit www.zondervan.fm.

Requests for information should be addressed to:
Zondervan, *Grand Rapids, Michigan 49530*

Library of Congress Cataloging-in-Publication Data

Hynd, Noel.
    Countdown in Cairo / Noel Hynd.
       p.   cm. — (The Russian trilogy ; 3)
    ISBN 978-0-310-27873-3 (softcover)
    1. United States. Federal Bureau of Investigation--Officials and employees--Fiction.
2. Americans--Egypt--Fiction. 3. Cairo (Egypt)--Fiction. 4. Conspiracies--Fiction. I.
Title.
PS3558.Y54C68 2010
813'.54--dc22   2009026826

Any Internet addresses (websites, blogs, etc.) and telephone numbers printed in this book
are offered as a resource. They are not intended in any way to be or imply an endorsement
by Zondervan, nor does Zondervan vouch for the content of these sites and numbers for
the life of this book.

Cover design: *Laura Maitner-Mason*
Interior design: *Christine Orejuela-Winkelman*

Printed in the United States of America

09 10 11 12 13 14 15 • 23 22 21 20 19 18 17 16 15 14 13 12 11 10 9 8 7 6 5 4 3 2 1

For Andy Meisenheimer and Bob Hudson at Zondervan.
Thanks, guys. Let's do three more.

Whoever does not miss the Soviet Union has no heart. Whoever wants it back has no brain.

Vladimir Putin

Beware: Some liars tell the truth!

Ancient Arab proverb

PART ONE

ONE

On a scorching afternoon, a few kilometers south of Cairo, a black bullet-resistant Land Rover pulled to an abrupt halt in front of the wide glass doors that marked the entrance to the Islamic morgue in the "new city" of Bahjat al-Jaafari. The morgue was a loathsome place, filled with the messy ugly detritus of death: foul stench and raw misery, oppressive heat and the sounds of unvarnished mourning, the cries of relatives and friends echoing down the narrow fetid corridors. It was in a separate wing of the pale redbrick medical center where the local police and doctors kept their records. So many dead bodies arrived here daily that piles of human remains were stacked on top of each other, separated by canvas wrappings or stained linen sheets. The morgue was located next to the hospital emergency room. The distinction was vague.

The vehicle was a relatively recent model, though not without its share of dents, and had a license plate that said it was on official business. It began and ended with robust, combative bumpers and spiked hubs that looked like weapons from a Bond film. Its windows were made of thick tinted glass, three radio antennas pierced the air, and there were enough red and blue lights on the dashboard to mark the runway of an airport.

Three men jumped out, almost before the vehicle had stopped rolling. One was Gian Antonio Rizzo, an Italian in a suit, reflective sunglasses, and a grim face. He carried his jacket over his arm, revealing an automatic pistol on his belt. Rizzo was on a black assignment from the Americans, though he would never admit that he worked for them. He still carried the documents of the Italian intelligence service, the *Servizio per le Informazioni e la Sicurezza Militare*, and actually did drop by their offices a few times a year.

The second man was a metropolitan Cairo policeman named Colonel Amjad, a pudgy but muscular man with a moustache and dark glasses. The third was an adjunct officer named Ghalid Nasri from the US Embassy in Cairo. Ghalid was acting as an intermediary—a diplomatic liaison and an interpreter for the haggard Rizzo—and was trying not to get shot while doing it. Both men carried pistols under their outer garments, as did their driver. They were all in that line of work.

The "new city" of Bahjat al-Jaafari had been built after the Six Day War of 1973, so it was now old enough to have fallen into decay. Gangs and death squads roamed its streets and the endless dunes of the desert beyond, areas that were supposed to be under the control of the central government in Cairo but were not. The area was in anarchy, and the anarchy went unnoticed until it touched upon Western visitors, who were frequent victims if they wandered off the tourist paths. Even then, however, as long as the bulk of the tourists kept coming, the dead did not count. An old Egyptian proverb has it that the dead have no voice, and this was never truer than here.

Rizzo bullied his way through the front doors of the medical complex, bumping shoulders with anyone who didn't give way. The other two men accelerated their pace to stay with him. Then they entered the dilapidated lobby that was only marginally cooler than the broiling outdoors. Rizzo spotted a front desk that served as a registry and information booth. A middle-aged man in traditional Arab clothing looked up and greeted him politely. *"Ahlan wa sahlan."*

"Ahlan bik," Rizzo answered sharply. He was having none of the politeness.

"La ilaha illa Allah," said the man.

"I'm here to see a Dr. Badawi," Rizzo said, "your medical examiner."

"For what purpose?" the man asked.

Rizzo looked as if he were about to explode. What did it matter to this fool *why* he was here? All that mattered was that he *was* there.

Amjad, the Cairo policeman, interposed himself. "We're here to view a body," he said in Arabic.

"View or identify?" the man asked.

Rizzo seethed. "Is there a bloody difference?"

"Both," Amjad said, trying to sooth Rizzo. "And with extreme urgency."

The Cairo detective flashed an array of police identifications. At first the Cairo police IDs flustered the man at the desk, but quickly they accelerated everything. The clerk wrote out a pass — Room 107 — and indicated the direction. Rizzo snatched the pass from the clerk's hand.

"There is no God but Allah, and Mohammed is his messenger," the clerk said in Arabic. The Cairo cop gave him a nod. Rizzo snarled something profane and took off. He forged across the lobby and down a shabby overheated corridor, where two bodies were stacked up on a single gurney. It was so hot that there was condensation on the walls.

They passed a door. Rizzo glanced in. Two young doctors, both of them Western women, conversed in English with what Rizzo recognized to be British accents. They were frantically trying to resuscitate premature babies while other infants wailed in the background. There had been one of the frequent power cuts in this area earlier in the day, Rizzo knew. The Egyptian health care system was a national calamity, a system suffering from underfinancing, overpopulation, and a long history of mismanagement and corruption.

Rizzo strode toward Room 107. He had been in morgues in the Middle East before and they were all awful, much worse than the ones in Europe. Many times in the past Rizzo had been called to identify remains that had been ripped apart by gunfire or explosions, sometimes by suicide bombers. Other times he had come to identify victims who had been deliberately disfigured by their killers. He had never ceased to be appalled at the sadism inflicted on the dead. He had seen many who had obviously been tortured, mostly men, often with terrible burn marks on their faces, hands, feet, or other parts of their bodies.

Then there had been the executions, both political and gangland. Some of these victims had had their hands fastened behind their backs with handcuffs and their eyes had been bound with tape. They had been shot in the back of the head or in the face or in the temple. The cruelty in this part of the world, fanned by centuries of religious hatred, could be unspeakable.

Through his career in police work, crime reports — words on paper — had led him to understand intellectually what had happened.

But visits to morgues were the images that haunted him, that some-times caused him to bolt upright at night from sleep, howling.

Rizzo led Amjad and Ghalid into the room marked 107.

The room was plain and sterile, light green paint peeling off the walls. There were a few chairs, an empty space in the middle of the chamber, and a dented steel door that led somewhere else. Rizzo turned to Ghalid, his aide from the American embassy.

"Now what?" Rizzo snarled.

"We wait for the body," Ghalid said, indicating the steel door.

"For how long?"

"Until it arrives," said Ghalid.

"In this part of the world, Signor Rizzo," Colonel Amjad began, "we must observe — "

"Go to hell!" Rizzo snapped. His eyes found Amjad's gaze trying to penetrate his. He returned the gaze with a glare filled with dislike, bordering on hatred. "Your country is the hellhole I remember it to be. It suits you perfectly."

"And I visited Italy once," said Amjad, "and found it to be a filthy, degenerate place. A civilization that has fallen to ruin."

"You? An *Egyptian*, are saying that to *me*? A *Roman*?" Rizzo said, turning fully toward him.

"Would you prefer that I say it again?" Amjad asked. "Slowly, so that you will better comprehend?"

"You do and I'll see that you're lying on your very own slab by the end of the day. How's *that*?"

"Gentlemen ...," said Ghalid, attempting to defuse them. He clearly used the term loosely.

The steel door swung open with a sharp rattle. An attending clini-cian in whites and a sterile mask pushed a gurney into the room. The apparatus was old; the wheels squeaked. On the gurney was a body bag in dark beige canvas.

Rizzo's eyes darted to the gurney as it arrived in the center of the room. A long zipper ran the length of the bag. He searched it for little details. There was a section unzipped near the head of the body within.

Dr. Muhammad Badawi followed the gurney. Badawi was small

and thin. He had sad brown eyes, a hooked nose, and a face like a ferret.

Rizzo looked at him.

The clinician stepped back and kept his distance.

The doctor spoke in English. "Which of you is —?" he began.

"I'm Rizzo."

The interpreter from the embassy explained who everyone else was. He said his piece in Arabic and English so there would be no confusion.

"Who will do the identification?" Dr. Badawi asked.

"I will," said Rizzo. "So let's get it done."

"As you wish."

The doctor gently pulled down the zipper and revealed a female body. He stopped just past the breasts and lifted a thin gauzy fabric away from the face. Rizzo gasped and felt the eyes of the other men in the room upon him. He steadied himself by placing a hand on the edge of the gurney.

"Oh, my dear Lord," he muttered in Italian. "Oh, no . . ."

His hand went to his own face. He looked upward, his eyes trying to beseech heaven but instead finding a ceiling with peeling paint. He shook his head.

"This is the woman you were working with?" the doctor asked. "The American woman who was missing?"

Rizzo nodded. Finally, he spoke. "Yes, it is," he said, fighting back real emotions. "I'm certain."

The face was so familiar to Rizzo. And yet now the face was so whitened, still, and lifeless. The woman for whom he had so much affection and admiration now looked so ghostly in the artificial light. Rizzo shook his head.

"Cause of death?" Rizzo added.

"Poisoning," the physician said. "Lethal dose of an industrial chemical. Radioactive. She never had a chance once the poison was absorbed."

Rizzo cursed violently.

The doctor replaced the filmy gauze that covered the woman in the body bag. Colonel Amjad, the irritating Egyptian cop, reached toward the body as if to feel the coldness of the corpse, or to see if the body flinched to his touch.

Rizzo intercepted the grasp. He yanked Amjad's arm upward and thrust it back toward the policeman so fast that Amjad was propelled several paces in reverse.

"Have some small amount of decency, would you, you pig," Rizzo said. "Keep your filthy hands to yourself or I'll rip your arms out of their sockets." He followed this with a withering torrent of obscenities. Amjad looked frightened enough to keep his distance but was secretly pleased at the same time.

"I was only making sure," Amjad said.

"What more do you want? A severed head? A bullet hole you can stick your fist in?"

Rizzo looked as if he were about to take out his rage violently on Amjad. Again Ghalid interposed himself, this time physically stepping between the two men. Rizzo was five inches taller than Amjad and half again as wide at the shoulders. He could have torn the smaller man apart if he'd felt like it, and everyone in the room knew it.

"All right," Amjad finally said.

"Too bloody true, 'all right,'" Rizzo said. "Let's get out of here."

The clinician rezipped the bag.

"I'm afraid there is some paperwork," Dr. Badawi said to his visitors.

Rizzo spoke softly. "Of course," he said. "Paperwork. Always. The world could come to an end, but there would be paperwork, even if no one were left to complete it."

The doctor turned to his assistant. "I'll take it from here," he said in Arabic, dismissing the technician.

"You've done a good thing by coming out here," Dr. Badawi said, handing Rizzo a file while Amjad continued to keep a distance and stare at the body bag. "A quarter of the deceased out here are never identified. The medical authorities tell me they had to bury six hundred unknowns since January of this year, unidentified and unclaimed. Eventually they're buried in the desert without a marker."

"Typical," Rizzo mumbled, along with something obscene. He

opened the folder and began to sign. There were a dozen pages and more than one place to sign on each page.

"The United States Embassy in Cairo has started procedures to retrieve her body," Ghalid explained softly. "However, it might take several days. So — "

"We're taking the body with us today," Rizzo said. "I'm not leaving without it."

"That would be quite impossible, sir," the doctor said.

Rizzo signed a final page. "Nothing is impossible," he said. "Walk on water if you have to. I'm acting on behalf of the Italian government and the government of the United States. I'm not leaving without her," he said again. "So let's get this done. Mr. Ghalid here from the American Embassy has brought the proper paperwork."

Dr. Badawi glanced to Ghalid. "True?" he asked.

Ghalid handed him an envelope containing several official documents. "True," he answered.

The doctor glanced quickly at the documents and nodded.

"All right," he said softly. "This would seem to be in order. Will you call for the proper van to transport her?" the doctor asked.

"Already done," Rizzo said. His eyes were moist.

"Under the circumstances then," the doctor said, "I'll see that the body is ready to move today."

"Grazie," Rizzo said. *"Choukrn."*

"Âfowan," the doctor answered.

"I'll remain with the body," Rizzo continued.

"You do not have any reason to think — ," the doctor began.

"I have *every reason* to think something could happen," Rizzo retorted sharply. "I said I'd stay with the body! What language do I have to say that in so that you'll understand?"

"Very good, *ya-effendim*," the doctor said. "If it pleases you, you may wait here in this chamber. Over there, perhaps."

Dr. Badawi nodded to an array of wooden chairs ill-arranged against the wall. Then he took his leave.

Rizzo turned back to Ghalid and Amjad.

"Should we wait with you?" Ghalid asked.

"No." Then with an angry nod, Rizzo indicated Amjad. "Get *him* out of here before I shoot him. We're already in the morgue, and I'm starting to think it's just too convenient to pass up."

Amjad looked to Ghalid. Ghalid interpreted. Amjad shot Rizzo an angry glance and headed to the door.

"I'll be at the embassy if you need anything else," Ghalid said to Rizzo. "Be advised, transport for the body back to the US will probably have to go to Frankfurt first, then New York or Washington."

"Just get the paperwork done," Rizzo said, exhausted.

Ghalid nodded. Amjad was already out the door.

The two men who remained exchanged an extra glance. Then Ghalid turned to follow Amjad and start the trek back to Cairo.

Left alone in the room, Rizzo exhaled long and low. He let himself calm slightly. His sweat glands were in overdrive, but he felt them slowing down now. He went to the door where Amjad and Ghalid had exited. He opened it, looked out in both directions to make sure no one was returning, then he closed the door and bolted it from within.

He walked back to the body bag, his steps falling heavily on the concrete floor. He stood above the body bag for a moment. He placed a hand on the bag and gave it an affectionate touch, almost a caress, on the shoulder of the body. Then he reached to the zipper and pulled it down again.

With a stoic expression, he stared down at the closed eyes of Alexandra LaDuca.

TWO

TWO MONTHS EARLIER

Hand in hand, Carlos and his fiancée, Janet, walked the streets of the Egyptian capital, the most densely populated city in the world. They were on what they called their "pre-honeymoon." They had been working together in Washington, DC, for more than two years as techies for one of America's more nefarious national security agencies. They had also been living together for a few months, though Janet still retained her own apartment. But this one-week trip to Egypt and the Holy Land was something special, their first trip together out of the United States. So far, it was going just fine.

They would visit Egypt and see the Great Pyramids and antiquities of the Nile, then the ancient cities of Alexandria, Jerusalem, and Palestine. They had always wanted to take this trip together ever since they had discovered a joint interest a year earlier. Their plans for a honeymoon, the following year, would be more prosaic: sun and surf in Maui. What was not to like?

Today was their first full day in Egypt. They visited the ancient quarter now known as Old Cairo, which had grown up around the Roman fortress of Babylon. They wandered through the old town, a largely Christian neighborhood of narrow, winding streets bordered by low beige buildings of sandstone. They passed quiet homes and shops and the occasional café filled with Christian Arabs sipping walnut-colored tea and eating small sandwiches and pastries. They came to the Coptic Church of Saint Sergius, one of the oldest houses of Christian worship, which was built like a fortress, and paid the admission to enter and admire it from within.

When the old church had been built, three centuries after the time of Christ, churches were exactly that — fortresses. Entrances were often walled and bolted against attack. There was no large entrance door like modern churches have, just a small door in a bare façade. In the Middle Ages the Coptic Church of Saint Sergius had been a destination for many Christian pilgrims because of its association with the flight into Egypt.

Steps within the church led down past the altar to a refuge and a crypt where, according to legend, the Holy Family found shelter after fleeing from Herod. Christianity had been the religion of most Egyptians from the third to the tenth century after Christ. Egypt had settled into the Muslim world thereafter.

Carlos and Janet continued their walking tour in the afternoon and visited the ancient Synagogue of Ben Ezra. It bore a resemblance to the Coptic Church because it had once been one too. The Church of St. Michael had stood here during the first ten centuries after Christ, but the Copts sold the structure to the Jews to pay a tax by Ibn Tuylun for the erection of a mosque.

The building, which contained some of the original structure from almost two thousand years earlier, remained a temple, but its parish had long since dispersed. Most of Cairo's Jews had been forced out of the country after the modern wars with Israel. Today, the building remained a historical oddity, a reminder of the two pasts, near and distant.

In the late afternoon, exhausted and with feet sore from their first day of sightseeing, they went back to their hotel and refreshed themselves. Then they settled into the hotel bar and restaurant.

It was a very comfortable modern bar in a splendid hotel, the Grand Hyatt of Cairo, a towering modern edifice located at the edge of the old city where the fortress of Babylon had once stood. But there was one problem. Right now, all that was on Carlos's mind was that they were in the capital of a Muslim country and the bar served no alcohol, even though alcohol was readily available at other locations in the city. At the end of a hot day, Carlos would have chucked the whole journey to be able to knock back a couple of cold brews.

"Who ever heard of a bar with no booze?" Carlos grumbled. "That's like an airplane with no wings."

Janet laughed slightly.

"You know that Bon Jovi song 'Dry County'?" he continued. "That should be the national anthem here. It's like driving through western Kansas, only worse."

"Carlos," she said, "zip it, would you? There's beer in the cafés. We'll go to another place, okay?"

"I should be able to get a brew *here*."

Selections of European and American pop music played on the sound system, covering their conversation. Soon something played in Italian, and it was incomprehensible to them.

"Budweiser. Coors. Schlitz," Carlos continued. "Iron City. Lone Star. Did you know there's a beer in Connecticut named Hooker? Their slogan is 'Get caught with a Hooker.'"

"Carlos, honey . . ."

"Or how about Pabst's? Yeah, Pabst's. I'd kill for a 'PBR' right now, know that? You know what else? I'd pay fifty bucks for a lukewarm can of Bud Ice with a slice of lime in it. That's how desperate I am."

She held his arm, squeezed it hard, and shook it. "Okay, okay! Let's go somewhere else," she said.

"Sold!"

They took off for a downtown beer garden named the Royale, located in one of the more artsy neighborhoods. The guidebooks had told them it was akin to the Left Bank in Paris. Neither of them had ever been to the Left Bank, but they had an idea what that meant.

The Royale was anything but royal. It was a narrow noisy bar on a backstreet. It evoked the air of a sordid 1920s speakeasy, complete with a paunchy one-armed barman and another barman who had an ear missing. The waitresses dressed as belly dancers. They had nice yummy flat bellies, Carlos noticed, but they did no dancing.

And that was just for starters.

Behind the bar was an array of bottles, mostly local brands that ripped off better known European products: Golden's Dry Gin in recycled Gordon's bottles, with the head of a dog replacing the boar's head of the authentic logo; Tony Talker Black Label in bottles that looked suspiciously like Johnny Walker castoffs. There was another suspicious-looking scotch concoction called Chipas Renal.

"Let's stick to the beer," Carlos said on arrival, "from closed bottles."

The Royale was crowded, filled with pungent smoke from Cleopatra cigarettes and the nasty stench of spilled Egyptian beer — Stella and Sakara, the two liquids that seemed to fuel most of these cafés. Underfoot, the floor was crunchy from cigarette butts and lupin shells from the trees on the block outside. But at least the Stella made Carlos happy when he finally got a couple of them, and if Carlos was happy, Janet was too.

They hunched together on small wooden chairs at a small wobbly table with a zinc top. Carlos wandered off after one hour and three beers to find a men's room, and Janet scanned the room, warding off the smiles and eye-contact of local young Arab men who had been waiting for Carlos to get lost.

Suddenly Janet's eyes went wide, as if she had seen a ghost.

Carlos returned. He slid easily into his narrow chair, bumping elbows with some irritable Arab men sitting next to him. Janet looked to Carlos in disbelief and urgently placed a hand on his arm.

"What?" he asked, slightly drunk.

"That man at the bar!" she said in a loud whisper.

"*What* man?"

She motioned with her eyes in quick hard glances, agitated enough not to move her head, directing his attention across the smoky room to the end of the bar.

Carlos looked. He saw the man she had indicated, a moderately sized man with thinning hair in a rumpled dark brown suit. Carlos could only see him from the rear. He was chatting with two other men.

"*That* guy?" Carlos asked.

"Him!" Janet said.

"What about him?"

"That's Michael!" she whispered in urgency.

"Michael who?"

"The Michael we used to work for in Washington," she said.

"*Michael Cerny?*" he asked.

"Yes! *That* Michael!"

Carlos looked again, then looked back to her.

"No way!" he scoffed. "You're toasted."

"Yes, way. I'm not toasted."

Carlos looked again. No recognition. "Michael Cerny's dead," he said.

"Sure. That's what they *told* us," she said. "The CIA people."

"He was shot, remember? In Paris. He died," Carlos continued. "When you die you become dead and tend to stay dead."

"I know," Janet answered again. "But that's Michael Cerny over there!"

"It might look like him, but it *can't* be!"

She leaned back and folded her arms. "Then *you* go look," she insisted.

Carlos waited for a second, as if to reject the entire notion. Then he gave her a glance of exasperation and stood again. He was tipsy. He squeezed out from the table onto the floor of the bar and wound his way through the crowd toward the bar.

He neared the man Janet had indicated. He jockeyed for a position to get a good look. He moved into eavesdropping range. Janet saw Carlos's expression freeze. He stared for a moment. Then the man they were watching turned his attention away from his friends at the bar and stared directly at Carlos. Janet saw their eyes lock for a moment.

Then Carlos raised a hand to conceal his own face, quickly turning away. Carlos fled in her direction, and Janet watched as the man kept Carlos in his sights. Janet grabbed a battered menu and raised it to hide her own face. Carlos returned and slid awkwardly back into his narrow seat.

"It's him," Carlos said in an astonished tone.

"He recognized you too," Janet said.

"I know," Carlos answered. "And they were talking in some funny language."

"Arabic?"

"No. It was something else. It sounded Slavic. And one of his friends' names was Victor. I heard him call him by name."

She worked up the nerve to glance over the top of the menu. The man was still at the bar, looking hard in their direction. Then he looked away.

"So I was right?" Janet asked.

"I ... I don't know. I don't know if you're right or not, but this guy looks exactly like Michael Cerny. It's incredible!"

"It's him!" Janet insisted.

They both looked back to the bar. But now the man they had spotted lifted a drink from the bar and went over to a corner table, where he sat down. Within a few minutes, the two men who had been with him at the bar moved over and joined him.

They fell quickly back into an animated conversation. Both of the other men wore Western suits and white *keffiyehs*, the traditional headgear with two rope circlets. At one point, one of the men in a *keffiyeh* turned and glanced at Carlos.

"I want to have another look," Carlos said.

But Janet was starting to turn against the intrigue. "I don't like this," she said. "I don't like this *at all*. Let's get out of here. You know what type of work Michael Cerny did. He was a CIA guy. Let's blow out of here."

"No, no. I want to have some fun," Carlos said.

"Fun? This isn't fun!"

"It could be," Carlos said. "It could also be a big career break for us, you know? They'd trust us because of the work we've done in DC and Virginia. So maybe we can get worked into something over here. Or Europe. Maybe they'd send us to Europe for free. Wouldn't that be great?"

"The system doesn't work that way."

"It does if you make it work that way. Don't fight me on this."

She sighed. "Why did we ever leave the hotel? A couple of lousy beers, that's why! Sheesh!"

They argued the point for several minutes, keeping the man in view with sidelong glances. Finally the three men at the table they were watching stood up. It looked as if they were preparing to leave. But instead, the two men in Arab headgear sat, and the man they were watching — who either was or wasn't Michael Cerny — made his way toward the men's room.

"Here's my shot! I'm going to go talk to him," Carlos said.

"Don't do it, Carlos!"

"No, this'll be cool. Know what I think? I think he's under some 'deep cover' of some sort. Well, we spotted him. We've been dealt a hand. I'm going to go play it."

"This is *so* not good," she moaned.

Carlos was on his feet again, to the irritation of the people at the next table, whom he again jostled. Janet sat, even more irritated, wishing she had kept her mouth shut. She watched Carlos weave his way through the smoky room.

The washroom was cramped and steamy. It stank of stagnant plumbing and disinfectant. When Carlos walked in, the man in the brown suit was the only other person there. He stood close to and facing the far wall at an old fashioned 1940s-style latrine. It was nothing more than a gutter at the base of a barely tiled wall. The man snapped shut a cell phone and pocketed it as soon as he knew he had company.

Carlos took a position a few feet away at the urinal. A big wooden fan rumbled overhead at the center of the ceiling. It turned slowly with old wooden rotors, and its function seemed to be to blend all of the ugly odors of the room into something that was even worse than the sum of its parts.

Carlos waited for his moment. Then, emboldened by his beer, he said, "Hello, Mr. Cerny. You know me from DC. Heck of a coincidence, huh?"

The man at the urinal slowly turned his head toward the intruder. He gave Carlos a long, smoldering look but didn't speak. Then he looked away again and faced the multilingual graffiti on the tiled wall in front of him.

"I mean, you being dead and all," Carlos said. "Then I bump into you here in a dive in Cairo, right? I guess that means you're not dead anymore, doesn't it, sir?"

The man didn't speak or acknowledge him. He was very still, hands in front of him, tending to business. He looked as if he could have stood that way all day, without moving a muscle.

"See, the thing is, Mr. Cerny," Carlos said, "I know all about secrecy and keeping things quiet. And heck, I was at your funeral, same as Janet. We're friends, you know? We're going to be here sightseeing.

But you know, we like to travel the world too. So if there are ever any assignments outside the US, you know you can count on—"

The swinging door burst open. Two young Arabs came in, laughing about something and bantering in Arabic. The man in the brown suit abruptly finished at the urinal. He stepped quickly to the wash basin.

Carlos followed. The Arabs took a place at the urinal wall and continued their loud banter, which suited Carlos just fine.

The man in the brown suit washed his hands carefully with the soap from a dispenser, which looked like a chemistry experiment gone horribly wrong. The man was lathering quickly.

Carlos pursued and took up a position at the next sink. For a moment, the eyes of the two men smashed into each other in the broken mirror above the washbasin.

"I'm staying at the Grand Hyatt Cairo, Mr. Cerny," Carlos said. "I'll be there for a few days, me and my girlfriend. If you want to talk sometime in secret, we can do that. Pick your place. I mean, I got a cheap rental car at the hotel and I could meet you—"

The could-be Mr. Cerny looked him straight in the eye. Then the man angrily shook off his hands, grabbed a paper towel, and made quick work of drying himself. He turned toward the door.

"Okay, okay," Carlos said, taken aback. "I won't tell anyone I saw you," Carlos said. "Okay? I'll be cool. No matter whether I hear from you or not. It's okay if you don't acknowledge." Then he added with a grin, "Say hi to 'Victor' for me."

A final glare, then the man was gone in a huff, the door closing sharply behind him and the two Arab men looking at Carlos and grinning.

Carlos washed his own hands and returned to his table. When he slid back into his chair, there was a new group next to him and Janet looked frightened.

"What happened?" she asked.

Carlos related the incident. He shook his head and appeared mildly shaken. "You were right," he said. "Whoever he was, I should have left him alone." Then Carlos looked around. "Where did he go?" he asked.

"When he came out of the washroom, he went straight toward the exit," Janet said. "And the men he was with left while he was in the washroom. They left together."

Carlos shook his head. "Strange, huh?"

"What did you say to him?"

Carlos repeated everything.

Janet shook her head. "I don't like any of this," she said. "Let's get out of here. I'm sorry I said anything." She paused. "Do you think it was really him?" she asked, changing her tone. "You had a good look."

"I think it was," Carlos said. "Yes," he decided, "it was him."

Janet shuddered. "I don't want any part of this," she said. "I mean, we were at his *funeral*. Old superstition of mine: don't mess with people if you've already been to their interment! Let's scram."

THREE

The next morning, Carlos and Janet hooked up with some other tourists and took the motor coach on the eleven-mile trip south of Cairo to view and the Pyramids of Giza. As soon as they were away from Cairo, the incident at the Royale began to recede, though not completely.

The highway passed across fields that historically had flooded whenever the Nile rose, but nowadays the area had been built up and the road elevated slightly. At its final stretch past the Mena House Hotel, the road wound gently uphill. Suddenly they were upon the pyramid and tomb of Cheops, the fourth-century pharaoh who ruled Egypt during the Old Kingdom, as well as the tombs of Chephren, Mycernius, and the smaller tombs of their wives. The pyramids stood, as they had for forty-six centuries, at the edge of the desert plateau.

Yet striking as the antiquities were, a small part of the specter of Michael Cerny haunted both Carlos and Janet. They looked for a way to dispel altogether what they had seen; but in the evening, almost against their better judgment and certainly against common sense, they visited the same ragged quarter of Cairo they had the previous day. They arrived again at the Royale at 9:30 in the evening. They sat at a different table and waited. But there was no sighting of Michael Cerny that evening, incarnate or otherwise. They half expected him to step out of a shadow, an alley, or a doorway in the raffish old quarter, but he didn't. They were relieved.

When they awoke early the next morning, it was as if some foul air had lifted. They began to think less of the man they had or hadn't seen and more about their trip. They fell easily back into the role of young lovers enjoying a holiday.

After an American breakfast, they took their deft little rental car to the ancient citadel, Midan Salah al-Din, the tenth-century fortress that had once been a starting point for Egyptian pilgrims to Mecca. A Crusader-era fortress. Carlos drove.

They were lucky and drew a clear day. They walked up to the esplanade that overlooked Cairo and took in the view of the city and the desert beyond. They enjoyed the journey better than had others who had made a similar trek centuries ago. It had been here that in 1811 the ruler Mohammad Ali had, behind the high walls and with the gate drawn, ordered the massacre of five hundred Mamluks who had been his dinner guests.

By evening Janet and Carlos felt their time in Cairo running out. They had made friends with some other tourists from America and joined them for drinks at a more upscale location in the early evening and then a Western-style dinner at a Tex-Mex place near the hotel. As they savored contact with other Americans, the bizarre notion of Michael Cerny's still being alive retreated from the improbable into the impossible. The whole incident in the Royale took on the aura of a strange little anecdote to tell to friends and one day to grandchildren. That, or it would be forgotten completely.

Their final full day in Cairo arrived; they had it in mind to take their car out onto the highway again and travel down to Memphis, on the Nile, which centuries ago had served as the first capital of a united Egypt.

Thirty centuries ago, the fortress-city controlled the water routes between northern and southern Egypt. The shrines and mud-brick palaces of the ancient civilization had vanished over the years, but Saqqâra, the necropolis of the ancient city, still stood and drew visitors by the thousands every year. Saqqâra would be the destination for Janet and Carlos on their final day. They planned to continue to Alexandria the next morning.

It was a buoyant late morning of bright sunshine and less humidity than on the previous days. Most of the smog had lifted from the city. Up until now, Carlos had done all the driving, but Janet was intent on having her day at the wheel, nutty Egyptian traffic notwithstanding.

They walked together to the parking lot of the hotel. Their rental car sat by a curb. Janet jumped into the car on the driver's side and asked for the keys.

"No," he said, "*I'm* driving."

"It's my day to drive," she said.

"What? You think I want to get killed?"

Janet laughed. Carlos jumped into the front seat and slid toward her from the passenger's side. Their laughter filled the car. She snatched the keys from him. Her hand pushed the keys toward the ignition, but his hand blocked hers.

Then he pressed his hand to her ribs and tickled her with intensity, causing her to squirm in the seat, laugh, and use both her hands to push him away. His reactions were faster than hers and he snatched the keys back.

"All right, all right," she finally said. "You drive out of the city traffic, and I'll take it on the highway," she said.

"Deal," he said.

"I'll come around."

The battle over, they kissed.

Carlos slid into the driver's seat. Janet circled the car in a quick trot, came to the opposite side, and opened the door.

"Hey," he said. "Where's the map?"

"What map?"

"The one that will take us down to Memphis?" he said.

"Oh," she said. She put her hand to her mouth to cover a smile. "It's still upstairs."

"How are we going to find our way without a map?" he asked.

"Duuh," she said.

"Duuh," he answered. Playfully, he swiped at her backside, and she ducked away.

"Good question," she answered. "I'll get it."

She turned and jogged back toward the hotel, a flurry of bare legs and arms.

In the lobby of the hotel, she skipped past the doorman and the amused gaze of the porters and front desk staff. Anxious to get going, she went to the stairs near the elevator and sprinted up them to the first floor, taking the steps two at a time. She felt great.

She would always remember how great she felt at the start of that day.

The door to their room was open. She walked in, startling the morning maid. They exchanged greetings.

Janet spotted the map. She grabbed it, gave the maid a courteous nod, then was down the stairs, through the lobby, and out the door again. She turned the corner. The sidewalk was quiet. Across the parking lot she saw their car. It hadn't moved. She felt a new surge of love for Carlos. This vacation had been what they needed. She was more certain than ever that he was her perfect partner and the right man to marry. She was about fifty paces from the car, and she raised her hand with the map, waving to him. Through the rear window of the car, she saw him raise his hand and wave back. The day was set to begin. Time to get going.

He cranked the ignition. The car give a little shake as the engine turned over.

A tremendous eruption roared in a firestorm out of the car's engine, then out of the chassis. It happened so fast that Janet later had a sense of first seeing it happen, then feeling the shock waves and then, with a disconnect of several seconds, hearing it.

The explosion knocked Janet backward and sent her sprawling. She whacked her face and arms hard on the hot asphalt.

The car flew up into the air and into the driving lanes of the parking lot, rocking the cars parked in front of it and behind it and setting them on fire.

Stones, mortar, and brick cascaded off the walls of the hotel and tumbled down into the street near Janet, almost burying her.

Her entire world was suddenly immersed in a silence punctuated by a profound ringing. She felt nothing, knew nothing.

Then it came to her that she was lying down on the sidewalk. Smoke billowed and flames raged from the wreckage of the car. There was something wet all over her, which she quickly realized was her own blood.

An excruciating pain throbbed through the silence. Her vision blurred. Mentally and physically, she was in shock. Prone, she moved her hands, which seemed like someone else's. She saw that all that remained of the auto in front of her was wheels and a chassis. The rest of it burned before her, the body of the young man she loved within it.

She blinked. There was hot sticky blood in her eyes. Everything in her vision had a reddish tint. Words and ideas formed in slow motion, but they formed anyway. *Carlos is dead, and in a few seconds I will be too.*

Good thing, she thought as an excruciating pain shot through her head. *At least we'll die together.*

Things went very white, and then completely black.

FOUR

In a quiet wing within the main building of the United States Department of Treasury in Washington, DC, Alexandra LaDuca leaned forward at her desk. On the screen of her main computer, Alex studied the final anatomy of a case she had plunged herself into upon her return from Spain two months earlier.

Ray Medina's clients had been his wealthy friends. He had promised them twelve percent on their investments; then, using the old technique of underselling his abilities, he had produced K-1 tax forms showing returns of twenty percent.

But Medina had also been battling a serious liver infection. His health had declined to such a degree that he had taken his wife and children to the mountain home he was having built in Aspen. He needed time to convalesce.

Medina's clients grew worried. So while he was away, several clients exercised a remote clause in their agreement with him that granted them access to Medina's office should he become incapacitated. A few hours later, the investors were phoning their friends. Office records showed that there was hardly any money in the brokerage accounts. Other accounts didn't exist. The K-1 tax forms Medina had been providing them for years were forgeries.

Two days ago, Medina had pleaded guilty to fifteen counts of theft, securities fraud, tax evasion, money laundering, and forgery. He had been sentenced to sixteen years and eight months in the Arizona state prison system, plus a restitution order of nine million dollars.

Through a default judgment in the civil case, which Alex had helped arrange, some of the victimized clients had reclaimed just over three million dollars of their missing funds.

Another "mini-Madoff," as these schemes had come to be known. With the downturn of the world economy in the first decade of the twenty-first century, there was no shortage of them. These cases were starting to depress her. She was bored to tears of white-collar frauds, mini-Ponzi schemes, and their slick-as-oil perpetrators.

A phrase came to mind from the old Woody Guthrie ballad about Pretty Boy Floyd:

> *Some will rob you with a six-gun,*
> *others with a fountain pen ...*

She was glad she had been able to help some of these people recover some of their retirement savings from one of the fountain-pen thieves.

Enough!

She sighed. She glanced at the time at the bottom right corner of her computer screen. It was past 6:00 p.m. For today, she was more than ready to blow out of the joint.

She logged out of both computers on her desk. She was conscious of the weapon on her right hip. She was overdue at the firing range and always needed to stay sharp, just in case. Not everyone she went up against robbed with a fountain pen, and increasingly she found the other type of criminal a more exciting challenge. So she wore her firearm everywhere now. There was no reason not to.

Recently, she had gone over to a new weapon for personal protection: a Glock 26, better known as the "Baby Glock." The weapon was a snub-nosed automatic that carried ten rounds. It had been developed for ease in concealing and accuracy in firing. Alex had acquired it when she returned from Spain. It fit her hand nicely and on her right hip just as well. She appreciated the perfect match.

Now if she could only get to use it ...

FIVE

Shortly before dawn the next day, in southern Ontario, a blue Volvo pulled to a stop on the road that led to the official entry point into the United States. Out stepped a Syrian named Nagib, a large bulky man, about six-four when standing. His boots crunched on the thin layer of packed snow on the edge of the roadway. Winter had come early to the region just north of the border, twenty miles east of Buffalo; then again, it often did.

Nagib looked at his driver, then over his shoulder at the southern embankment of the highway. It first sank lower than the road, then led up into a stand of trees that veered into deeper woods. He scanned the area for several seconds. He saw no one and neither did his driver. The location was quiet in the dim gray light of near-dawn. The only sound was the rhythmic flap of the windshield wipers and the rumble of the engine. Frost had turned the side and rear car windows gray and opaque.

The men spoke in Arabic with Syrian accents.

"You know where you're going?" the driver asked.

"I have it memorized," Nagib said.

"Then go with God," the driver said.

"And you also," Nagib answered.

They exchanged a hand clasp. Nagib turned and faced the quiet woods as the car did a U-turn and drove away.

Nagib lit a cigarette and began his hike. He trailed a stream of smoke and breath. He entered the stand of trees, looked up at the moon, and listened to the churning crinkle of his boots on the snow in the woods. His gloved right hand dipped into his pocket and pulled out a compass. He consulted it carefully. Yes, he was in the right spot, and, yes, he was heading in the right direction.

He saw his first marker, a blue ribbon tied around the trunk of an otherwise bare maple. He trudged past it. Nagib had slipped in and out of many countries in the past and had developed an instinct about such things. He continued due south beyond the first marker and then found another yellow ribbon about fifty meters farther into the woods.

There was a faint hint of a breeze. He continued to smoke. He found the third marker and the fourth. He came to a clearing and crossed it. By now there was a certain logic to his trek. He found a small lake and followed its bank. This was all as expected. He knew that he was now within a mile of the United States.

He glanced at his watch. Seven past five in the morning. Hurry, hurry! His next ride — the one on the American side — could only sit for so long without arousing suspicion.

Then he came upon something unexpected. A pair of men with rifles in heavy camouflage-style clothing. There was a green Jeep parked beyond them. Nagib halted and caught his breath. He didn't like this. Not at all.

The men were about fifty yards in front of him, near the lake, and they turned toward him. They seemed surprised to see him too. He had a choice now. Continue on, challenge their guns, or turn and run, which would perhaps mean challenging their ability with their guns. He wished he had carried a pistol, but his handlers insisted that he not do so. To be caught with an illegal weapon would have made things worse.

He made a choice. He continued forward. The men stared at him. Nagib moved at a quick pace.

He came within twenty feet. One of them broke into a grin and raised a hand in greeting. Then Nagib could see what they were doing. They had a bag of duck decoys that they were about to set onto the lake. They were hunters. Or they looked like hunters. Guns made Nagib nervous, especially when he didn't have one.

Nagib approached.

One of the men raised a hand in a friendly wave. "G'morning!" he called.

Nagib nodded. "Morning," he answered. He hoped his accent didn't betray him.

"Where you off to?" asked the second man.

Nagib made a funny motion with his head, pointing to where the woods picked up again on the other side of the lake.

"Yeah, well, enjoy your jog," said the first hunter.

Nagib nodded in accord. He kept going. He jogged several paces and wondered whether he was going to get shot in the back. He looked over his shoulder. The two men weren't even watching him. One of them said something to the other, probably a joke at Nagib's expense, and they both glanced back at him and laughed. They saw him looking. They gave him a friendly wave as if he were a nutcase to be indulged. Then they returned to setting out their string of decoys.

Okay, Nagib said to himself, *go ahead and kill the little birds. That's good. I have larger prey myself.* He kept jogging.

A pair of blue ribbons tied to tree trunks marked his entry point to the far woods. He traveled a path, found three more blue ribbons. The last one was a hundred feet before a chain-link fence that ran through a thick area of trees. Forewarned, Nagib spotted the trip wire at the base of the fence that might have alerted the US Border Patrol. He stepped carefully over it and climbed the ten-foot fence.

It was an easy climb, up and over the top. He spotted the trip wire on the American side and was careful to avoid it when he jumped back to the ground. The snow was brittle but cushioned his landing. A big man, he couldn't avoid hitting the ground hard.

Hurry, hurry.

He glanced at his watch again. He was right on time, but this part had to be executed with speed and care. The Americans were paranoid about their borders these days. He knew they had teams patrolling the woods, sometimes on snowmobiles, often in pairs, and frequently with rifles. The last thing he needed was a chance encounter.

He accelerated his pace. He looked again at his watch: 5:18. The trees were still thick. He continued to find the ribbons that had been left as markers for him by teams of Islamic moles within Canada and the United States.

The sky brightened. He approached a clearing. In the distance, he could hear some of those snowmobiles. He froze for a second and listened to the wind. He had a sense that he was near the final clearing.

He made a move toward it: a final zigzag route of a hundred

meters weaving around trees, following a path that might have been imperceptible to anyone else.

He came to the clearing. Down a slope below him, about fifty feet away, was the same highway from which he had been dropped off, except this part was on the American side and had gone past the immigration station.

He looked at his watch. It was time again. Five twenty-three.

He looked to his left. An old Ford station wagon approached in the Canada-bound lane, its lights on, a freezing mist still falling. That was the type of vehicle he had been told to expect. Nagib stepped from the trees and waved.

The driver cut his lights for a moment, then put them back on. That was the all clear. Then he cut them a second time, flashed twice, and accelerated.

Nagib hurried down the embankment. Across the highway the Ford slowed, eased into the slow lane, then left the road. It drove down into the deep furrow between the northbound and southbound roadways and executed a U-turn, coming up onto the southbound side.

It slowed to a stop where Nagib stood by the side of the road. He was shivering but smiling from behind his growth of rough beard. Inside the old car the driver leaned over and unlocked the door on the passenger side. Nagib opened the door and got in. The interior smelled of sweat, stale tobacco smoke, and car deodorizer.

The driver checked his rearview mirror and hit the gas. There was no suggestion of any complication.

They spoke Arabic. "Have any trouble?" the driver asked after a minute. Nagib recognized the accent as Egyptian.

"None," Nagib answered.

Another minute passed. The car moved as quickly as the icy highway would allow. "Good," he finally said. A few miles later, he added. "We're going to Brooklyn, New York, first. You'll get a weapon, some money, and some clothes. Do you know your assignment yet?"

"I know what I'm supposed to do," Nagib said. "I don't know who or where."

The driver grinned slightly. "You'll be instructed on that too," he said. He flipped a pack of Marlboros to his passenger. "There's food in a bag on the seat behind you. We'll be driving for seven hours. Be comfortable."

Nagib nodded. He grabbed a gas station sandwich from the seat behind him and a carton of juice. For much of the rest of the ride, no one spoke. A million thoughts passed through Nagib's head as they traveled, but most he thought of his wife and two young children who were back in the Middle East. In Damascus. That was all part of this assignment and part of the irony. If Nagib completed his assignment, it would be his last. He would be paid a lot of money in cash. His handlers would whisk him out of America quickly and relocate him to London. After a year, when the coast was clear, his family would be smuggled into Great Britain to join him.

It all made sense.

For half of the ride, Nagib slept. He had come a long way on a special assignment and was very much on schedule.

SIX

Eight seventeen the same morning.

Alex's cell phone was yakking at her.

She was in the cold parking structure that led to her office at Fin-CEN; the structure was open, and the cold wind from the Potomac swept through like a Russian scythe. Her cell phone had come obnoxiously alive with a text message.

Her boss, Mike Gamburian, already had a burr in his butt for the morning:

```
Alex—Come see me right away this a.m. mg
```

She texted back.

```
OK
```

Seventeen minutes later Alex wandered down the corridor toward her boss's office. Mike's door was usually half open. Alex could never figure out whether that was a good sign or a bad one, the in-between nature of the door. Was it a metaphor, an omen, or a gravitational quirk in the old building?

Today, however, as she approached it, she was not in the mood to overanalyze.

She arrived at Mike Gamburian's door and used the toe of her shoe to nudge it open.

Gamburian was at his desk, leaning back.

"Ah," he said.

"You asked to see me?" she said.

"Yes. I sure did. Come in and sit down," he said.

"Will I be sorry?"

"Probably," he said. He was seated in front of his Fenway Park montage that still hung from 2004. Alex settled into the leather chair in front of his desk.

"So? What's up?" Alex asked.

"Name the most disreputable person you've ever met in your life," he said. "Aside from me, of course, I don't count."

"Hard to name just one," she said. "I've been compiling a pretty good list in recent years."

"Try for just one," he asked.

She named a former President of the United States whom Gamburian had once worked for. Gamburian laughed.

"Think closer to home," he said. "From your recent experience."

"You're steering me toward Yuri Federov," she said after a second.

"Very good. Your Russian-Ukrainian mobster. Guess where he is right now."

She shrugged. "I have no idea," she answered. "After two heavy doses of him I assumed he was out of my life completely."

"Naive assumption," Gamburian said. "He's in New York."

She was visibly surprised. "He entered the US again?"

"Yup. I suppose if I told you that he arrived here two days ago on a direct flight from Switzerland, you'd share my consternation."

"Seriously," she said. "Why is he in the US?"

"We'd like to know that too," Gamburian said.

"Aren't there warrants still out?" she asked. "Tax liens? A half-dozen or so felony indictments scattered across the northeast? A whole host of things that might deter his tourism here?"

Gamburian flew his chair back down to earth and leaned forward at his desk.

"Oh, there used to be a lot of crap," he said. "Warrants, liens, subpoenas, indictments. All that plus a few dozen old enemies hanging around who wanted to blow his head off. Normal stuff for a thug in his line of work. But he's clear with the United States government these days, and all of the state and local stuff went out the window too. That ten-million-dollar tax assessment against him went down the tubes in exchange for his help in Spain, as did just about everything else. Recall?"

"That's been resolved already?"

"Two weeks ago, and all the other stuff got washed with it. He's as clean as Mother Teresa, except he has the added advantage of being currently alive. What do you think about that?"

"Shows you what friends in the right places can do."

"Absolutely. And next thing you know, after he's got a legal green light, he's on a plane for New York. Nonstop from Geneva. First class, naturally. I refer here to the seat location, not the passenger. I still personally think he's a piece of — "

"I know what you think, Mike." She considered the situation. "I'm a little surprised at his coming to the US," Alex said.

"So are we."

"Ten million dollars was a hell of a 'fee' for his cooperation," she said.

"You helped arrange it."

"It wasn't my idea; it was my assignment. There's a difference."

"No need to stress," Gamburian said. "Uncle Sam got what he paid for, and the state and local DAs and AGs were willing to play along. No one was ever going to get an indictment against him anyway. And how much would it have cost to rebuild our embassy in Madrid? Fifty million? A hundred? Not to mention the loss of life? And you know as well as I do he was never going to pay the ten million anyway. So to some degree, it was 'funny money.' He worked for 'free' and didn't even know it."

"That's one way to look at it."

"That's the only way to look at it," Gamburian said. "But at the same time, we still might be interested in his current movements. Why *is* he visiting the US? Can't be women, can it?"

"He's got them scattered all over Europe. He doesn't need to fly here for assignations."

"What about friends or family?"

She sensed where this was going. "As far as I know, his only blood relative are two daughters who live in Canada and hate him. And as for friends, those are the people who'd probably want to kill him."

"So then maybe you can find out for us."

"Find out *what*?" Alex asked.

"Why he's here."

"How?"

"Ask him?"

She laughed. "I should just ring him up on the phone. 'Hi, Yuri, it's Alex. You alone? Can I come over and give you an evening you'll never forget?'"

"Well, not quite like that. Or maybe exactly like that if it floats the boat."

"Come on, Mike, what am I?" she asked. "Your Ukrainian gangster expert, specializing in this one?"

"Well, in a way, you *are*," Gamburian said. "Look, Alex. We could assign some FBI and Treasury teams to tail him; we could drop electronic surveillance on him; we could see if the NYPD would do some pavement work on him. *Or* we could send you up to New York, put you up in a nice hotel for a few days, have you make contact, flirt a little, and see what you come away with. Frankly, for whatever reason, he's more likely to voluntarily leak information to you over three or four martinis than he is to slip up with our surveillance teams."

She folded her arms. "Uh, huh."

"He's staying at the Waldorf-Astoria on Park Avenue along with another several billion dollars' worth of Eurotrash guests."

"I know where this is going, Mike," she said.

"Of course you do. Is there something on your desk more interesting? Don't even answer that. Look, why don't you go up to New York and see him?"

"Do you already have a surveillance team on him?" she asked.

"Didn't I just say that would be a waste of time?"

"Sure, you did. But the FBI wastes money all the time. Answer my question."

"It was suggested by the FBI, but I talked them out of it. Federov would spot them a mile away anyway. Waste of time, you're right. I nixed it."

"Is he traveling alone?" she asked. "Or is there an entourage?"

"Federov came into the country alone," Gamburian said. "Take it from there."

She thought about it for at least three seconds, plus another two to consider the tedium on her desk. "Okay. I never mind a trip to New York," Alex answered.

"Good!" he said with finality. "And it's funny you should answer that way. That's the other thing I wanted to talk to you about — New York."

"What about it? I like New York."

"FinCEN is going to open offices there," Gamburian said. "We're going to move some of our experienced people from here in Washington up to the big city." He paused. "Interested?"

"In being transferred to New York?"

"Exactly," he said.

A swarm of emotional reactions were upon her, not the least of which was a lingering disquietude over life in Washington. Yes, it was tranquil. Yes, it was comfortable. But day to day, there were still too many memories of the way things had been a year earlier before her fiancé, Robert, had died in Kiev. She was, she knew, fighting a daily round of small avoidances, dodging associations of how things had been and how things could have been.

She even knew that she had stayed on in Madrid and taken the Pietà of Malta case to avoid coming home. And since coming home, she had already started to entertain the wanderlust that was in her, a desire to be part of the action, to keep shaking things up.

Then, "I still have a brief trip to Venezuela coming up," she said.

"Any dates on that yet?"

"None yet. I'm thinking within the next few weeks."

"What's the guy's name, the philanthropist, who sends you?"

"Joseph Collins."

"That could be worked into the equation," Gamburian said. "When might you know the dates on that?"

She shrugged. "I could go see Mr. Collins when I'm in New York and see what his thinking is."

"Well, as I said, considering your service and sacrifice this year, I'm sure the powers that be can let you work Venezuela into the schedule," Gamburian said.

"Then, yes," she said, "I might be interested."

"The big bosses here see you as the third in command in New York, maybe even the second," he said. "The top job will go to someone more administrative and, frankly, older, who's been in Treasury longer. But the number two and three positions? They would be ones of senior investigators. Those positions presume youth and energy, someone willing to go out and shake the world up where it needs shaking up. The type of thing you showed you're adept at in Kiev, Geneva, Paris, and Madrid, and wherever else you've been dumping bodies." He paused. "The age thing is tricky. They look for a balance in these offices. Gray hair and wisdom combined with youth and diligence. A dash of treachery and savoir faire with both. How old are you again? Seventeen?"

"I'll be thirty on December twenty-fourth."

"Oh. Thirty. Ancient," he said.

"So this would be a major promotion also?" she asked.

"Unquestionably," Gamburian said. "Bigger title, heavier paycheck, increased oversight and responsibility. More physical risk perhaps. The assignment would start after the first of the year, and the offices will be in the Wall Street area. What better place to watch out for financial crime, right? You can just look out your window if things get slow. Oh, and I'm also told that much of the work will have to do with Central and South America, so the job presupposes fluent Spanish. Not just fluent, but so good that it could pass for an educated native speaker. What the State Department grades a 5 out of 5. Again, that's you."

"That's me," she said.

He leaned forward and wrote out a phone number. "Here's the number to call for an interview. Think about it," he said.

She took the paper and folded it away. "Thanks, Mike," she said. "I already have."

SEVEN

The car carrying Nagib was in New York City within five hours. The car traveled not to Manhattan, the city of skyscrapers, the upscale, and tourists, but rather to Brooklyn and a neighborhood known as Prospect Heights.

Prospect Heights lies adjacent to Prospect Park, between Park Slope and Crown Heights. It is surrounded by the finest cultural and recreational institutions in Brooklyn — the Brooklyn Museum, the main branch of the Brooklyn Public Library, the Botanic Garden, and the Brooklyn Academy of Music. It is a polyglot area, with a typically New York mix of everything, notably people from the Caribbean, Africa, and the Middle East. The tenor of neighborhoods change from block to block; boarded up, burned-out structures defaced with graffiti stand next to newly renovated apartment complexes with glass elevators and rooftop gardens.

Nagib's car stopped at a three-story tenement on Lincoln Place. His driver guided him inside to the second-floor home of a man named Hassan, who tearfully embraced Nagib. Hassan was Nagib's uncle, and he too had come to America illegally seven years ago.

The uncle now had a new ID and a social security card. He had married an American woman of Lebanese descent and was legal to stay. Now he ran a small store and a small cell of conspirators. The uncle's home was a halfway stop to Nagib's destination. Hassan served Nagib lunch and provided him with some changes of clothing to take with him. From a safe concealed under the floorboards of a closet, he also provided him with a Chinese-made pistol and a silencer. They went to the basement of the building where there were sandbags and concrete walls. Hassan had built a makeshift shooting gallery there. The man who had guided Nagib this far through his journey gave Nagib a nod, and the traveler took several minutes to practice with his new weapon.

Then a new driver appeared with a different car, a battered 1990 Taurus with a New York license. Nagib climbed in with his new driver, who wanted to be known simply as Rashaad. He was dark-skinned and seemed more American than the previous one. He spoke Arabic with a Saudi accent, and for that reason Nagib didn't like him.

A few minutes later they were on an expressway, going through a long tunnel. Then they were in an area of oil refineries in northern New Jersey, continuing south. They passed Philadelphia by 2:30 in the afternoon and Baltimore two hours after that. Nagib said little on this leg of the journey. Rashaad said even less. Halfway there, Nagib reached into his pocket. Folded up with some American money was a crinkled photograph of his wife, a pretty woman of twenty-four in a green prayer shawl.

The driver glanced over and spoke in Arabic.

"Put that away," Rashaad said. "You shouldn't even have that. I should take it from you and burn it."

"You try to take it and I'll break your wrist," Nagib said. "Then I'll break your neck."

Rashaad swore bitterly at him but didn't do anything. Nagib then thought better of things and put the picture away. There was an old Arab proverb: Me and my brother against my cousin, but me and my cousin against a Christian.

He spoke the proverb aloud, but the Saudi only glowered. Nagib might not have liked his partner, but there was no need to make an extra enemy either.

They continued on in silence.

There was little to talk about and little to joke about. But there was much to think about and much to plan.

EIGHT

Later the same day, as Alex tidied up some final points on the Medina securities case, she phoned one of her favorite New York hotels, the Gotham, on West 55th Street, between Fifth and Sixth Avenues. She booked herself a room for the next evening.

She followed this with a call to her FinCEN contact in New York and arranged for an interview in two days. The FinCEN offices had an address in the financial district, not too far from Ground Zero. They had a time slot open for her in the morning at 10:00 and she took it.

Then she called Joseph Collins, a philanthropist and her mentor — as much as anyone had been one. She set a meeting with him for the next afternoon at 2:00. He would meet her in his home office at Fifth Avenue and 84th Street, he told her.

Her trip, though on short notice, was taking shape.

On the computer in her office, she went to the internet and booked an Amtrak ticket for the next morning. The train was easier than the airlines from Washington, she always figured, and faster too.

She glanced at her watch. If she left work on time today, which Mike had suggested, she could catch a solid workout at the gym in the evening and still have time to pack.

Tonight was her night to join in the pickup basketball with her friends at the YMCA. She had nicely worked the games back into her Wednesday schedule. She enjoyed seeing and competing against a good group of friends, and she could more than use it this evening. The tedium of being bound to a desk was slam-dunking her. And yet at the same time, she had been putting off placing the call to Federov. She wasn't sure why. Maybe there was too much that could go wrong.

"What the heck," she finally mused to herself, pumped a bit at getting away from the office again for a few days. "I'll make the call and then I'm out of here."

So her final call of the day was to the switchboard at New York's

Waldorf-Astoria, where she asked for a guest named Yuri Federov. She waited to see if he had registered there under his real name and was partially surprised to learn from the operator that indeed he had.

"Could you put me through to his suite?" she asked.

She felt her heart race. She was under no illusions about Federov's amorous feelings for her. He was an assignment, she reminded herself. He was potentially dangerous and had to be played carefully. She often wondered if there was a shred of decency in him and had come to the conclusion that, yes, if she looked hard enough, she could find some.

Maybe not much. But some.

Then she reminded herself that the last time she had seen him was a dark night in northern Italy, and he had just executed a man who had betrayed him. Sometimes she needed to do an urgent reality check on some of the people with whom she dealt.

There was light classical music as she waited for the connection. Lord, the money that people paid for these hotels, she thought to herself, and not for the first time. How much did it cost Federov to stay in a suite in the Waldorf-Astoria? Fifteen hundred bucks a night? Two thousand? A hundred bucks an hour? Two bucks a minute?

Well, if you had stolen obscene boatloads of money you could afford to spend obscene boatloads, just as long as you didn't blow all of it. She remembered how her mother had busted a gut just to earn five hundred dollars a week in the 1980s and thought she was doing well. Even though Alex worked in financial crime deterrence, sometimes the fiduciary realties of the modern world were surreal.

The phone in Federov's suite rang twice. Then he picked up. His response was sharp and gruff. "Hello?"

Alex felt a final surge of nerves. Then she spoke into her phone.

"Hello, Yuri," she said.

A slight pause. "Who's this?" he asked.

"This is your favorite American woman, or one of them, at least." His mood changed. "Alex?"

"Alex," she confirmed.

"My goodness! How wonderful!" he said. "And your spies are so efficient! I've hardly been here long enough to unpack."

In the background, there was electronic conversation in Russian, most likely an internet television link playing in his suite. It scrambled her thoughts slightly to be speaking one language while hearing another one acting as a counterpoint.

"Consider yourself lucky to be here long enough to unpack," she said, playing along.

He laughed. "I have you to thank for that."

"Not me, my bosses," she said.

"You're in New York, I hope?"

"No, not yet. But I'm going to be in New York tomorrow night. Interested in having some drinks and some conversation?" To her abiding shame, she added a flirtatious tone. Oh, well, she reasoned. They both knew it was a game, and they both knew how to play.

He switched into Russian. "For you? I'll order iced champagne in my suite. Or vodka and beluga caviar!"

She laughed. "Let's not get ahead of ourselves."

"Let's not waste time, either," he answered. "I'm so very pleased to hear from you and would be delighted to see you." He paused. "Even though I know you phone for business probably, not pleasure or romance, right?"

"Right," she said.

"Then the vodka and seduction can come later," he said. "Maybe the next day. What do you think of that?"

"I'd say it's evidence that you're still a dreamer," she said.

"Hey," he said with a laugh. "Listen, Alex LaDucova. I'm already having dinner with a friend tomorrow. We're going down to the New York Italian Mafia neighborhood in Manhattan. What does he call it?"

"Little Italy?" she asked.

"That's it. You come here to the Waldorf, we have a few drinks, and then you would be welcome to come along."

"Who's your friend? A woman or a gangster or both?"

"Neither," he said. "Business contact in New York. He'd like to meet you, I'm sure. Very good that you called."

She was fiddling with a pen at her desk. "All right," she said. "How about this? Six thirty at the bar in the hotel lobby. Peacock Alley."

"Wear something sexy," he said. "I want to show you off."

"And you wear a suit," she said. "I don't go out with men who don't know how to dress."

"Ouch," he said.

"Yeah," she said, half amused, half revolted, fully intrigued. She clicked off, sighed, and wondered where life was leading her this time.

Ninety minutes later, she was at the Y, playing point guard in a pickup basketball game. Her friend Ben centered for her side. They played two twelve-minute halves and prevailed 37 – 32.

After a light workout with weights, she drove home. She noticed two people sitting in a battered Taurus in front of her building but thought little of it. Things like that were part of the urban landscape. No point to let paranoia get the best of her.

She parked her car beneath her building and then, wanting a little more night air, took the long way to her apartment by coming up out of the garage on the side street and walking toward her building's front entrance.

NINE

They sat quietly in the old Taurus, Nagib on the passenger side and his Saudi handler, Rashaad, behind the steering wheel. Under the newspaper on Nagib's lap, there was the Chinese pistol with a silencer on its barrel. They were like a team of military snipers. The Saudi was the spotter, the one who would identify the target. Nagib was the guy who would get paid to go in and make the hit. Rashaad was also armed, however.

The serial number had been filed cleanly from Nagib's weapon, and the weapon had never been used before. Nagib was waiting for his shot, and it thrilled him. He had previously executed successful hits in Egypt, Jordan, and Germany, twice against Israeli informants and once against an American businessman. He wasn't the smartest guy in the world, but he was effective. He had been smuggled into the country for this job and this job alone.

To Nagib's twisted mind, there was nothing quite like this — waiting in ambush for a woman. It thrilled him beyond reason. He felt so primal. He was a simple thuggish man who took great delight in life's simple pleasures and victories, eating and drinking, smoking and fighting, sex, assault, and murder. So he didn't seek to understand, especially when he was paid to do a job he enjoyed. He sought only to get the job done.

Ten o'clock came. Then ten thirty. Then ten forty-five. On his car radio, a talk radio show chattered softly, though there was nothing soft about the political content. But Nagib's mind was on the street and sidewalk beyond his car. He scanned up and down, attentively waiting. So did Rashaad.

From where he had parked his car, he could easily see the entrance of the Calvert Arms. He watched people come and go and didn't like any of them. He didn't even like the building. This was the type of residence that housed quietly genteel and educated people such as Alex LaDuca and her neighbor, the cranky, jowly old diplomat, Mr. Thomas. They lived in this building along with the usual widows, retirees, and seemingly carefree college students, mostly female.

The college students. He sighed when he thought of them. He might have been on the prowl for them — the young women around twenty to twenty-two years of age — if he hadn't been on assignment. He gave these girls an extra leer as he sat and waited. He would watch them from the time they emerged from the Calvert to the time they disappeared down the block toward 21st Street.

After all, they looked good. They also looked like his intended victim.

Nagib munched on an apple as he waited. He picked at a small box of raisins. Rashaad had explained that it was his potential victim's habit to come by this location during the hours from 9:00 p.m. to midnight, scurrying along at a quick pace to the Calvert Arms like the desirable young female that she was. Well, he told himself as he watched with narrowed eyes, the first time he had his opportunity, he would be on her like a big cat.

He would put his gun to her head and force her to come with them. Or he would stick a needle into her if he couldn't get his hand across her mouth fast enough, and he would drag her into the car. He had a syringe in his pocket. He savored the notion of tying her up and throwing her in the trunk. He fantasized about that part. His assignment was to bring her in alive to his employers if he could, but he had also been warned that there would be no second chances. If he muffed her abduction she would be on high alert in the future, and no one would be able to snatch her off the street. So if he had to kill her right there on Calvert Avenue, that would be acceptable too. But in the end he hoped to take her alive. His employers could talk to her, torture some truth out of her, find out everything she knew, and then turn her over to him for disposal.

Abruptly, Rashaad nudged him. They saw a female figure turn the corner of the side street down the block. Nagib picked up a small pair of binoculars. He steadied them, and fixed his gaze upon a nicely shaped woman approaching with a gym bag. She wore snug jeans and a light blue windbreaker. She was very pretty. Her hair was dark and wet. She looked as if she had just showered in a nearby gym and was on her way home.

Sure enough. Nagib started to breathe a little more heavily. There was no thrill like stalking a female. His hand went to his lap where it settled restlessly upon his pistol.

She was about fifteen meters from the awning that led to her building.

"Is that her?" Nagib asked in Arabic.

"I'm not sure," said Rashaad.

"Why aren't you sure? How many opportunities will we have?"

"Be patient," Rashaad said.

Nagib reached to the handle of his door. Time to get out and get a better look. Then, as he opened the door, he saw something else. There were headlights coming up behind him, a sturdy American car that had turned the corner and was proceeding slowly down the block. Nagib had a sixth sense about cars that moved at that speed.

Then Rashaad confirmed it. "Police!" he said.

Nagib closed his door again and felt his heart pound. He watched the car through his side mirror. Sure enough, there was a rack of lights on top of the car.

District of Columbia Police.

He stashed the gun under his coat.

He leaned back. So did Rashaad.

The police car came to a halt next to him on the passenger side of their car. Nagib turned and looked into the gaze of two district cops, one African American male who rode shotgun and one white female who drove. They stared at him. Slowly, his hand moved to his pistol. And yet the police car was positioned so that his own car couldn't exit if he wanted it to.

Nagib gave the police a wide smile and moved away from the pistol. He held up his empty hands and gave an engaging shrug. Then he produced the half-eaten apple and showed it to them.

"Lunch time," he said.

"Yeah," the male cop said, his window down. "Right."

"What are you fellows doing?" the female cop shouted from farther across the front seat.

Rashaad handled it. "My nephew works in that building down there," he said, pointing. "We drive him home at midnight."

"Never seen you here before," the male cop said.

Nagib's damp hand went back to the pistol and clicked off the safety catch. This was going the wrong way.

"My nephew's car broke down," Rashaad said. "What can he do? We must wait."

No smiles in return from the cops. They glared at the two Arabs. Nagib's hand broke into a heavier sweat and tightened on the pistol.

The male cop gave a little nod to his partner. Then there was movement. The police car lurched forward and eased away. The lame excuse had worked.

Nagib let an extra second go by, heaved a long sigh of relief, then looked back to the Calvert Arms. The street before the building was empty now, and the woman was gone.

A wave of relaxation spread over the car's passenger. Several minutes passed.

"Thank you," Nagib said.

"We are cousins now," Rashaad said.

"We need to get access to the building," Nagib said.

Rashaad nodded. "Maybe tomorrow. Now, we leave. We don't want to be here if the police come back."

Nagib agreed. The car pulled away from its watch a few minutes later.

TEN

The next morning Alex had a right-hand window seat on the train for her three-hour trip to New York. She had booked the seating intentionally; she wore her Baby Glock on her right side, so it would be better concealed and guarded. As the train raced northward, Alex watched the East Coast of the United States roll past her: Baltimore, Wilmington, Philadelphia, Trenton, and Newark. Old cities that seemed almost antique and quaint — old for North America anyway.

She thought of Venezuela. Earlier that year, she had gone there to investigate a problem for philanthropist Joseph Collins, who was financing a group of missionaries in a remote town called Barranco Lajoya. Their work was being sabotaged by outsiders. Alex had stayed in the village for several weeks until an unnamed armed militia attacked, slaughtering many of the residents, destroying the village, and driving survivors to other locations. The reason for the attack remained unknown and still haunted her.

Forcibly, she shifted her thoughts away from Barranco Lajoya and pondered the potential move to New York, a more pleasant development. She had already decided that, all things being equal, it would be a good move for her, both professionally and personally.

A new venue, a new chapter. New people, new challenges.

To some degree, a new life.

The train arrived punctually at 11:30 a.m. She carried only a small overnight bag, a duffel that she slung over her shoulder. She had worn good walking shoes. New York, Paris, and London were her favorite cities for walking and picking up the feel of the metropolis. So she walked easily from Penn Station up to the Gotham. She checked in and unpacked.

By 2:00 p.m. she had ventured out again on foot. Although the weather was brisk, she didn't mind the exercise and wore the proper footwear for a two-mile walk directly uptown, taking a path through

Central Park, where the trees were already bare. She noticed in passing that a few of the stores were done up for Thanksgiving but most were already well into Christmas. The holidays hit a bittersweet chord within her; the absence of a family, the loss of a fiancé. Best to keep going, keep the chin up, and not dwell upon it.

After forty-five minutes, she had arrived at the home of Joseph Collins, or, at least, his luxury apartment building at Fifth Avenue and 95th Street. There he made do with a duplex worth twenty million dollars — by the jaded estimates of Manhattan real estate.

The building had once housed several Rockefellers and a Kennedy or two. William Randolph Hearst had once bought a floor there for a mistress, and Winston Churchill had stayed there for two months with friends after being voted out of office in the late 1940s. It still housed numerous heavy hitters of the New York financial and industrial community.

The building was the work of the famous New York architect Rosario Candela, a prolific designer of impeccable apartment buildings in Manhattan between World Wars I and II. With its polished granite entrance, flanked by three doormen in subdued dark green uniforms, this was among the most luxurious apartment houses in Manhattan. The façade was sheathed entirely in limestone, and the entrance details were pure Art Deco. The front doorway told all anyone needed to know. Carved through a granite slab, topped by finials, were the letters that announced the address: 1240 PARK AVENUE.

Inside, the lobby was as Alex remembered it from previous visits: dark, lush, and wide, with comfortable sitting areas and plush carpets on marble floors. Even the elevator that brought Alex to Joseph Collins's floor bespoke old money. The elevator man wore white gloves. Alex wasn't sure whether she had walked into a time warp or a bank vault.

By 3:00 Alex was comfortably seated in a leather chair before Collins's desk. Though showing slow signs of aging, Collins still had his easy grace and charm. At seventy-six, he was a man at peace with himself and the world. He sat behind his desk in a tie and suit and spoke fondly of his son, Christopher, who was now involved in missionary work in Argentina.

"The news from Venezuela is not all bad," he said at length. "The land where the village of Barranco Lajoya stood is unpopulated now. All of the survivors moved to a different settlement. It's down the mountain a little way and near the valley. I've seen pictures. I'm told it's a beautiful area."

"What are the plans for permanent resettlement?" she asked.

"I'm not sure there will be a resettlement," he said. "The people of the village, I think there are about four hundred of them, have adapted somewhat to their new location. I've financed new housing for them. It's nothing elaborate, but it's functional. Oddly enough, the government offered no resistance when we put new buildings there, even though that dreadful demagogue Chavez is still in power. I know, I know, they criticize us as Yankee imperialists in one breath and accept our charity with the next. But the army can better keep an eye on the people of Barranco Lajoya in their new location."

"The settlement has the same name?" she asked.

"Well, the people are the spirit of the village, so why not?" he asked. He paused. "I'm thinking, assuming you can get free of your other work, maybe you could make a trip down there in the early spring. Or even February before it gets too hot."

"I might be able to do that," she said. "All else being equal."

"God willing," he said.

She agreed.

"I should mention," she said, "one reason I'm in New York is to interview for a job here."

"You're leaving Treasury?" he asked with surprise.

"No, not at all," Alex said. "FinCEN is initiating a new operation that will work out of New York. They offered me a potential promotion that would include a transfer here. I interview tomorrow."

"I'm sure they'll invite you to work with them here," he said.

"And I'm sure they have fifty qualified candidates for every job that might be open," Alex answered.

Collins snorted slightly. "Of course. You and the forty-nine runners up."

"You're too kind," she said.

"Perhaps," he said, "and now I'll be too kind again. My son asked me to continue to administer his apartment while he's out of the country," he said. "Chris will be gone for another four months, barring unseen circumstances. So if you'd be comfortable there in his apartment on 21st Street or need a place on short notice, the key is yours. Just say the word, even if it's on an hour's notice. Lady Dora will let you in and give you the key. Hotels are so darned impersonal, aren't they? I believe you were comfortable down on 21st Street."

"Very much so and thank you," Alex said. "And I was right, you *are* much too kind."

ELEVEN

That evening Alex seated herself in Peacock Alley in the Waldorf-Astoria. She selected a table for two that gave her a good view of the elegant lobby in front of her as well as the plush bar and restaurant that was to her back.

She glanced to the entrance, looking for Federov. Behind her, the bar was busy with wealthy New Yorkers and tourists, largely foreign, meeting for a drink after business, as a prelude to the theater or dinner. A waiter called on her immediately, but she declined to order until the arrival of the gentleman — she used the term loosely — who was to join her. The waiter smiled, disappeared, and returned with a small dish of nuts and pretzels. Alex scanned the lobby again. No Federov. She brought out her cell phone and riffled through the day's calls. She returned two, finished them, glanced at her watch, and saw that it was 6:32. She looked to the lobby again.

She spotted Yuri Federov before he spotted her.

Her first impression was that something had happened to him. His face looked haggard. He seemed years older than when she had seen him last. He walked without the same self-assurance that she had previously seen in Ukraine, Switzerland, Italy, and France. As he crossed the lobby, she saw that he still had a thuggish wise-guy charm about him, if there was such a thing. But he did look, she decided, worn and troubled.

Then he spotted her. His expression changed and somewhere within him the sun seemed to emerge from clouds.

He walked directly to her, smiling broadly. "Ah," he said. "The most beautiful woman in the world." He extended a hand and took hers. They exchanged a clasp.

"Hello, Yuri," she said.

He drew her close to him and wrapped her in a quick hug, then released. She went with it.

"What a pleasure this is," he said affably, sliding his massive frame into the seat next to hers. For some reason, the image flashed before her of them together the previous February at the nightclub in Kiev, Yuri on his home turf in all his overly macho glory, she in a micro-mini dress prying him for information and getting increasingly soused as the evening went along. Well, all in an evening's work.

Federov turned and signaled to the waiter.

"You have to try their specialty drink, 'The Peacock,'" Federov said to Alex.

"Named after the Shah of Iran?" she asked, making light of it. "He would have liked this place. He used to stay here, in fact, if I remember."

Federov laughed. "The place still stinks with Iranians," he said. "They're disgusting people."

"What's the drink?" she asked. "The Peacock. What's in it?"

"It's a vodka drink," he said. "Cranberry-infused vodka and apricot brandy with a sour made from scratch. The vodka is Russian."

"Sounds lethal," she said.

"It is. Russians are lethal. You know that. That's why I order it. I had three last night."

"Well, you're still alive," she said.

"Ha! Just, hey."

The waiter arrived.

"I'll take your recommendation," Alex said. "But I'm sure one will suffice for me," she said.

"Two Peacocks," Federov said to the waiter. "Make mine a double."

The waiter nodded approvingly and departed.

Federov turned to her and smiled. Now Alex got a good look, up close and personal, and he was indeed thinner than she remembered. She couldn't yet tell whether it was a sign of good health, vigor, and exercise or something more ominous. She dug through the repository of facts on Federov that she kept in her head and tried to recall his age. Given a moment's thought, she reckoned he was about forty-eight or forty-nine. Not a bad age for a man, depending.

There was an awkward moment of silence between them. "So,"

she said, quickly moving to fill it, "I thought I'd start with a basic question. Are you here in the United States legally?"

He laughed.

"Of course, I am," he said. "I wouldn't want to break any laws now that I have a clean slate."

"The tax thing," she said. "That got cleared up, I hear. Completely?"

Federov nodded. "Cleared up perfectly," he said.

"Try to keep current in the future," she said.

He made a dismissive gesture. "The future. What's that?" he said. "I'm retired, enjoying the time I have left and the money I've stashed. I don't make money anymore. I try only to keep track of what few millions I have. And you know I'm here legally. You're the government and have all the computers and the records. You know I came in on a visa, and you even know where I'm staying without me telling you."

"Touché," she said.

"I hoped you'd get in contact but didn't know if you would."

"Now you know," she said.

"Now I know, but I suspect this is business more than pleasure. Thank you, by the way."

"For what?"

"There doesn't seem to be surveillance on me. I appreciate that."

"There isn't, and it wasn't my decision," she said. "I'm not that powerful."

"You are *very* powerful," he said, "like opium."

She tried to be angry but couldn't help laughing. "I wouldn't know about that," she said.

"Opium is not good stuff, huh?" he said. "It eats the brain and destroys it. I've tried it but don't recommend."

"What *do* you recommend?" she asked, playing along.

"Vodka," he said. And as if on cue the waiter arrived with two drinks, served in the bar's signature glasses, which were sculpted in the shape of a beautiful woman. The waiter set the single before Alex and the double before Federov. Federov produced a fifty-dollar bill as quickly as some men can snap their fingers. He handed it to the waiter and declined change.

The waiter bowed most appreciatively.

Federov lifted his glass to Alex and switched into Russian. "*Za tvajó zdaróvye*," he said. To your health.

"And to yours, Yuri," she said, lifting her glass, clicking it to his, and reciprocating. "*Za tvajó zdaróvye.*"

She sipped. Federov knocked back half of his drink in one long draw. Then he set down his glass, and his gaze landed hard on her. He grinned.

"So," he said, launching one of the lightning non sequiturs that she had come to expect from him. "Why don't you marry me?"

She laughed and shook her head. "Are you still singing that note?" she asked.

"Why shouldn't I?" he said. "I've met the perfect woman. So I pursue her as I can. What can I do for you while I'm in New York? May I buy you a yacht or just take you away with me on one for six months?"

His flirtation was so outrageous that she refused to even take it seriously. "Don't you ever give up?"

"Obviously, no. Why should I?"

"My answer will never change."

"Never say never," he said. "Life changes."

"Do you know the old phrase about a snowball's chance in hell?" she asked.

"Yes," he answered thoughtfully, "and since you like to speak of philosophy and sophisticated notions, it has occurred to me that a snowball might have some small chance in hell."

"The snowball's got a hundred times better chance than you do of marrying me," she said.

"Thank you! Very encouraging."

"Encouraging?"

"Yes. This is the first time that you've acknowledged that I might have some small chance. I'm heartened."

With an overly dramatic gesture, he took her hand in his, raised it to his lips, and kissed it. These were the same hands that had pulled triggers on unarmed men and beaten several other men and women to within a few inches of their lives. Sometimes she wondered how she had the gumption to play along.

Federov finished his drink.

"A lot of women would marry me in a heartbeat," he said.

"I'm not a lot of women," Alex answered.

"No, but you're the woman who charms me and excites me. Why don't you think about it?"

"Sure. And in the meantime, why don't we change the subject?"

"To what?"

"Why are you in New York?" she asked.

"Is that what you're here to discover?"

"As a matter of fact, yes. It is. My superiors at the US Department of Treasury sent me here to find out."

"Ah."

"So why don't you tell me and then business will be out of the way."

"I'm here to see some doctors," Federov said. "Some specialists. I have a few health issues."

"Nothing serious, I hope," she said.

"American doctors are the best in the world, so I put my trust there."

"I'm sure the medical establishment will be flattered to learn that. Is that the only reason you're here?"

"If you're asking me if I'm here to do business," Federov said, "the answer is no. And why would I lie to you at this point? I've made my money; I don't live in Ukraine or Russia anymore, so I tell you again: I take my winning chips, and I walk away from the table. Is that so hard to understand?"

"Maybe," she said.

"And I have some friends here," he announced easily. "So I socialize, have dinner and drinks, and mind my own business."

"How long are you here for?" she asked.

"Don't play coy with me, Alex LaDucova," he laughed, finishing his drink and signaling to the waiter that he could use another. "I'm sure the record of my air travel has already been given to you. I'm here for ten days. And you knew that."

She smiled. "I didn't say I didn't know that."

"Then why did you ask?"

"To see if you'd tell me the truth."

Federov raised his thick hand expressively. "Again, why would I not tell the truth at this point? You have all the power here, not me."

The waiter presented Federov with his second drink, also a double. Alex was working slowly on the first half of hers.

"These 'Peacock' drinks," Federov said. "They're like a woman's breast. One is not enough and three would be too much."

"You said you had three yesterday."

"Yes, I'm a pervert and it was too much. Tonight I am a gentleman because I am with a lady."

"Tell me about your friend."

"Ah, this friend I am seeing this evening," Federov said next. "I'm glad you can come along. This is, ah, 'good fortune'—you're well educated; what is the ten-dollar word?"

"'Fortuitous'?"

"Yes."

"Is there an ulterior motive?"

"There might be," he said.

"Why don't you tell me then, or is it one of those things I have to figure out?"

"No," he said. "His name is Paul Guarneri. He is a former business associate of mine in New York. We're going to meet him at 7:00 p.m. in Little Italy."

"What sort of business?" Alex asked, suddenly suspicious.

"You can ask him that yourself. I'll tell you right now that Paul is from a 'connected family' in New York, but his businesses now are entirely legitimate. Like many people in his position, he has friends on both sides of the law."

"Thanks for the warning."

"I mentioned you to him. He's looking forward to meeting you."

"I don't date wise guys, Yuri. You know that."

"His interest is elsewhere," he said. "Come along. You won't regret, hey."

She processed a lot of information quickly. Then she decided she would go along with it and file a complete report as soon as she returned to Washington. If Guarneri was connected, could an association of this sort hurt her? As an investigator, little tidbits that she picked up at such meetings could sometimes prove of immense value.

"Okay. That's fine," she said. "I look forward to meeting your gangster pal."

He laughed again. She sipped more of her drink. The Peacock started to resemble rocket fuel, and she was on the runway. Then she realized he was looking at her very contemplatively, as if there were something else he wished to bring up.

"What?" she asked.

He reached directly to her. She held her position, not knowing where his hand was going. It went under her chin to the neckline of her blouse; she allowed it. He fingered the pendant that she wore, the one fashioned by a child for her in Venezuela. He looked at it thoughtfully.

"You still wear this," he noted.

"I do."

"You used to wear a little gold cross. I had almost forgotten. That's what you had when we first met."

She opened her mouth to remind him what had happened, but he continued the line of thought for her.

"But you lost that little cross in Kiev," he said. "The same day you lost the man you were in love with."

"That's correct," she said.

"Life is strange," he said.

"It can be. Cruel too."

He gently pulled his hand away. In doing so, he eased away from the subject. "I've done many rotten things in my life, hurt people I should not have, things I regret," he said. "Kiev. Moscow. New York." He shook his head. "Sometimes I think I should clear my ledger, like I did with the tax people. What does your religion say about that?"

"About what?"

"Forgiveness. Asking for it."

"From another person or from God?"

"Suppose it would be from you."

"If you did something heinous, and I know you have done many such things, I'd be more worried about God than me," she said.

"What if I cared more about you than God?"

"Then I'd say you had your priorities wrong," she said. "Where are you going with this?"

He shrugged, retreating from the subject. "I'm just asking," he said. There was a grave expression on his face, as if his mind had jumped to a place that was very painful.

He glanced at his watch. "Let's get a taxi," he said. "We're going way downtown. Traffic can be terrible."

"I'm ready when you are," Alex said.

Federov found another fifty-dollar bill. He signaled to the waiter that they were leaving and left the fifty on the table. Alex had the impression that the waiter would be sorry to see Federov check out. They finished their drinks. When she stood, she was mildly buzzed. Crossing the lobby, Federov took her hand to guide her to the front entrance on Park Avenue. She made no motion to object, even when he gave it an extra squeeze.

TWELVE

Yuri Federov and Alex arrived by yellow cab in front of a restaurant named Il Vagabondo on Carmine Street in Little Italy and stepped out into a light, cold drizzle that had begun on the drive downtown. Manhattan in November; the weather was typical.

If the New York restaurant critics gave an annual award for Most Sinister Atmosphere, Il Vagabondo might have been in strong contention. Three long black limousines sat outside the restaurant; once she and Yuri stepped inside, Alex saw an array of thick-browed guys at the bar, watching the entrance, watching everyone arrive. The congregation at the bar was solidly male; it looked like the waiting room in a urologist's office.

From the bar, the eyes of those assembled suspiciously jumped from her Russian escort, to Alex, then back to Federov again. She knew the routine: check out who is entering, check out the female companion, keep your eyes on the guy. Look for trouble and get a lid on it if you find it. Yuri's appearance started a few conversations. She wondered how many other Feds were in the place this evening and further wondered if anyone had dropped a wire on it. Probably, she decided.

The place was decorated in expensive Italian-American eclectic, a style that Robert used to refer to as "Early Al Capone." There were murals of Sicily on the walls and replica Roman columns at the doorway that led to the dining room. The only things missing were Mount Vesuvius and a signed portrait of Sinatra. The Italian food, however, promised to be outstanding, judging from the atmosphere.

A captain in a black jacket met them. His name was Mario and he knew Federov. Mario quickly led them to a table where a man was waiting. The captain dutifully held the chair for Alex as they sat down.

Yuri introduced Alex to his friend, Paul Guarneri.

"This is my friend, Alex LaDuca of the US Treasury Department,"

Federov said to Guarneri. "Alex, I've mentioned you to Paul many times."

"Favorably, I hope," she said politely.

"Always," Federov said.

Guarneri was fiftyish, dark, and handsome, with a little gray at the temples. He had a strong face, what some might have called a Sicilian face, but with something else mixed in. Alex, having a mixture of Italian and Spanish-Mexican blood in her own veins, was always alert to such things.

"Usually I don't like to hear from anyone at Treasury," Guarneri said with equal politeness. "Maybe tonight will be an exception."

"I'm here socially, not professionally," Alex said.

"That makes three of us," Guarneri said. "I guess it's a check-your-gun-at-the-door sort of night."

"Really?" she answered, "I didn't check mine."

Guarneri laughed. "What are you carrying?" he asked.

"If everything goes well, no one will find out."

Even sitting, Guarneri came across as tall and powerfully built. He also came across as smart.

Alex could always pick up when a man she was meeting showed some interest. There was something about the eyes on her, the body language, the tone of voice. She sensed it from Guarneri, just as she had the first night in Kiev with Federov.

"See?" Federov said. "I told you Alex was my type of broad."

"Be careful what you wish for, Yuri," she said back.

In no way did she expect to feel anything in return for this new acquaintance. If she had felt ready for any sort of new relationship, it wouldn't have been with either of these men. It would have been with her longtime friend and sporting partner, Ben, or it could have been with someone like Peter Chang, whom she had worked with in Madrid. But the bottom line was that Guarneri was an attractive man. Even though he was twenty-some years older, she picked up on something primal. And it surprised her.

"Just visiting the city?" Guarneri asked her.

"I live in Washington right now," she said. "Treasury sent me up to keep tabs on Yuri. Nothing new about that, the US government seems to think I'm his babysitter."

"Ha! We should all be so lucky," Guarneri answered.

"What about you, Mr. Guarneri?" she asked. "Yuri says you live here?"

"I have a brownstone in Brooklyn Heights," he said. "And my name is Paul, if I may call you Alex."

"That's fine," she said. "And a brownstone in Brooklyn isn't the worst thing that ever happened to you."

"No, it's not," Guarneri said. "I bought it a year ago when the market was down. I have room for my kids."

"You're married?"

"Divorced. Joint custody. Two girls, fifteen and twelve. My angels. A boy, eight. My devil."

"I get it," she said.

"I grew up on Long Island," he said. "Glen Cove. Know it?"

"I know where it is. I'm from the West Coast. So it's just a short three thousand mile walk from where *I* grew up."

Guarneri had lived in the New York metropolitan area all his adult life, he said. He added that he had gone to parochial schools in Glen Cove, "run by some of the world's toughest nuns," as he put it, and then had gone to Cornell University where he picked up an undergraduate engineering degree while nearly freezing to death for six months of each of the four years. "My old man made plenty of money," he said. "Not all of it legal, but he made it anyway. So I got sent to good schools. I try to do the same for my kids."

"That must cost you a few bucks," she said.

"Yeah. About fifty grand a year. Three private school tabs in the city."

"I'm told you used to be able to buy a house for that," Alex said.

"Now you can barely buy a judge," Federov added.

"Your father? Is he still in business or is he retired?" Alex asked, staying with Guarneri.

"Neither. He's dead. Someone shot him."

A beat, then, "Recently?" she asked.

"My father was shot to death as he walked to his car in South Philadelphia," Guarneri said. "Easter morning, 1973."

"I'm sorry," she said.

"So am I," Guarneri said, "but it was a long time ago."

"If you don't mind my asking, was anyone ever convicted of killing him?" Alex inquired. She felt Federov's squinty gaze bouncing back and forth.

"Don't be silly," he said. "Of course not. Look, he was connected to organized crime; he did what he did, and he took his risks. I loved him as a father, he was good to me, but I'm not going to sit here and say he was a good man. I'm not so sure he was. But I was provided for and so was my mother."

A waiter in a traditional white jacket brought a bottle of wine to the table and showed it to Guarneri — he must have ordered it before his guests had arrived. From what Alex could see, it was a hearty red Tuscan. Guarneri gave a nod. The waiter uncorked it and poured a glass for Guarneri, who gave another nod. Then the waiter poured wine into the other two glasses and departed.

"My father left behind the ownership to several buildings in the New York and Long Island area. So I never had to get involved in the type of business that he did. All I had to do was manage buildings. Be a landlord. Push the right papers around. I picked up an MBA at St. John's University so I'd know how to do it. But I learned more in the first month of managing buildings than I did with two years of real estate law at St. John's."

"I'm sure you did," Alex said, sipping the wine, which was excellent.

A short time later, the waiter reappeared and took their orders. A cordial conversation continued among the three diners until, after they had finished their meals and knocked back a second bottle of the Tuscan wine, Guarneri finally angled around to something he wished to discuss.

"So listen, I want to ask your opinion," Guarneri said, turning to Alex. "May I ask you how you see certain things in relation to the United States and a certain country in Central America?"

"You can ask, Paul," she said. "What country?"

"Cuba," he said.

The mention of Cuba, of all places, took her by surprise. "I'm not an expert and I've never been there. So my free advice will be worth exactly what you're paying for it."

"I was born there," he said. "In Cuba. *Mi madre fue cubana.*"

"Verdad?" she asked. *"Y habla bien el español?"*

He laughed. *"Claro que si!"* he answered.

A small exchange followed. He spoke Spanish as well as she did, which was with complete fluency. After a moment, they switched back to English for Federov's sake.

"What do you think will happen to property that was left behind fifty years ago?" Guarneri asked. "Or seized by the revolutionary government?"

"What sort of property?" she asked. "Land? Bank accounts? Real estate?"

"Any of those," Guarneri said easily. "Make it a hypothetical. All of them."

"Wouldn't a lawyer be able to tell you better than I?"

"Paul is only asking for your opinion," Federov said. "I've told him how intelligent you are. You know how your government works, and you know how the world works. And you can convey in almost any language."

"Okay, look," she said, "we'll talk as friends, how's that? Completely off the record."

"I'd like that," said Guarneri.

"Regarding property in Cuba that once was owned by Americans?" she said. "To clarify ownership there would have to be a new treaty tied in to diplomatic recognition of a new regime," she said. "Realistically, that will take several years beyond the passing of Fidel Castro and possibly Raoul Castro as well."

"I'd prefer not to wait that long," he said.

"What you'd prefer and what's going to happen are two different things," Alex said.

"Could you get legal entry into Cuba?" he asked. "Through your contacts in law enforcement?"

"Me?" she asked in surprise.

"You," he nodded.

"I've never thought much about it," she said. "And for the very reasons the United States might want me to go, the Cuban government might *not* want me to arrive. So that doesn't sound too promising."

"Would you ever be available to accompany me to Cuba?" he asked.

Again she looked at him in surprise. "What?" she asked.

He repeated. Then, "I'm trying to recover property that was abandoned by my father a half century ago," Guarneri said.

"Whose property was it?"

"I'll get to that in a minute."

"Whose property is it right now?" Alex asked.

"No one's," Guarneri said, "because no one can find it."

After a few seconds, Alex asked. "It's hidden?"

"I believe it still is, yes," he answered.

She pondered for a moment. The waiter intruded. They ordered coffee. Alex asked for an espresso to counteract the rocket fuel served at the Waldorf and the glasses of wine here.

"Okay," she said. "I'm guessing you're talking about property that you feel would have been rightfully yours if Castro's revolution hadn't happened."

"Correct," Guarneri said

"Well," she said, "I deal with international financial complications all the time. People cheating governments, governments cheating people. So I'll tell you what I know, even though you might not like it. In post-Castro Cuba the restitution of property will be the most contentious issue the new Cuban government will face. Assuming the Cuba of the future is democratic or even mildly socialist, everyone will have to take into account the hostility that many Cubans would feel toward having their national assets transferred to people such as yourself."

"What would they have against me?"

"You know the answer to that as well as I do."

"Tell me anyway."

"You and other former Cubans have been living comfortably in Miami, New York, or Los Angeles for decades. The Cuban people endured Castro and the idiotic American embargo that helped impoverish the island and kept food and pharmaceuticals in short supply."

"I thought you worked for the US government," he said.

"I do, but that doesn't mean I personally agree with all policy. A lot of it is just plain stupid. Or political. Or ill-conceived. The Cuban embargo is a great example of all three."

"Not afraid to tell me what you think, huh? I like that," he said.

"You might like it now, but you won't always," she said. "Let's get back to you. I'm guessing you have family links to the previous regime, Batista's, which was even worse than Castro."

"Why do you guess that?"

"No offence intended," Alex said, "but it's written all over you. Look where we're having dinner, for example. I feel like I'm on the set for *The Sopranos*."

Guarneri stared at her coldly for a moment, then shook his head and laughed.

"See?" Federov said to his friend. "I warned you."

But by now, Alex was intrigued.

"Okay, I'll give you some of the rest of it, Alex," Guarneri said, opening up. "My father was a part owner of a racetrack and a gambling casino near Havana. He also owned a couple of strip clubs," he said. "When Fidel Castro took over the country, my dad had to get out of Cuba fast. He was holding a lot of money at the time. Half a million dollars in US currency. But it was all in small denominations. Fifties. Twenties. Tens. Fives. There was no way that he could take it with him to the airport. The police or the army or Castro's soldiers would have taken it from him." Guarneri paused. "So he buried it."

"He buried it?"

Guarneri nodded.

"And that's the 'property'?"

"Yes."

"Hidden?"

"Yes."

"And you know where?"

"I *think* I know where," he said. "If I could get back into Cuba, I think I could find the money."

"You said, 'back,'" Alex said. "You've been there?"

"I was born in Havana in 1955," Guarneri said. "My mother was my father's mistress in Cuba. She was a dancer at one of his clubs."

Guarneri thought for a moment. He then reached to his wallet and opened it. He produced a pair of pictures, one of his mother as a leggy casino-style showgirl from a chorus line in what he said was 1957. The second was a grainy picture of himself with his mother, a faded color shot, from Long Island in 1966.

"So your mother got out of the country too?" Alex said.

"She was able to leave in 1961," Paul Guarneri said. "My father had a wife and family here, but he did the decent thing for me and my mother. He smuggled us out. I remember it happening. My mother came and got me in the middle of the night. She wrapped me in a blanket, and we were taken to a car. She told me it was time to leave, and we couldn't bring anything. We drove without headlights and went to a boat. The boat went to a seaplane, and we flew to Florida. I'm told we flew eighty miles at three hundred feet. I slept through it. When I woke up the next morning we were in an apartment in Key West. Then came the Bay of Pigs, the American invasion at *Playa Giron*. It was harder to get anyone out of Cuba after that. Years went by. My father always fretted over the thought of those greenbacks slowly rotting in the Cuban earth. But he was shot to death first and never got back to Cuba."

"I assume previous attempts have been made to recover this 'lost property,'" Alex said.

"Yes, but not by me," Guarneri said.

"Then by whom?" she asked. Guarneri glanced at Federov.

"I traveled to the island twice," Federov said. "I have a Ukrainian passport. I can go in and out whenever I want. But I was of no help."

Alex turned to Guarneri. "Taking into account the fact that much of the wealth before Castro was accumulated by friends of a repressive government with links to American gangsters," Alex said, looking him squarely in the eye, "I wouldn't think your position in Cuba would be a very popular one."

"So you're not encouraged that I'd be able to recover anything? Cash or any other assets."

The coffee arrived and so did a small tray of sweets for dessert. The espresso was scalding hot. She sipped carefully. As the caffeine hit, it was a punch in the nose. So much for easy sleep tonight.

Alex waited till the waiter had departed until she spoke again. "Generally no," she said. "And the bottom line is that restitution of property will be the sovereign decision of the new Cuban government, which can set any rules it likes."

Federov grinned to the side.

Guarneri blinked. "Is there any sort of historical precedent," he asked, "for recovery of property?"

"I remember that with East Germany and its reunification with West Germany, restitution of property led to a multitude of competing claims in the German courts as well as some Swiss, Czech, and Austrian courts. Look, Paul. Suppose a sugarcane farm was nationalized in the early sixties and the owners fled to Miami. By now, there are probably a half-dozen potential heirs who may well not agree on how the pie should be divided. You will have relatives coming out of the woodwork, second and third cousins whom you didn't even know existed, claiming that they own part of the money. And that's even if Cuban courts will award a claim to a foreigner. More likely, they will award it to people who have been on the island for most of their lives, for the reasons I already mentioned."

The discussion took a break as the bill for dinner arrived. Guarneri was treating. He peeled off some cash and laid it on the table. Over the course of the evening, Alex had now watched her acquaintance enrich the city's restaurant economy by close to five hundred dollars.

"So what you're saying, Alex," Guarneri said in closing, "is that it would be more effective for me to go directly into Cuba, grab what's mine, and get out again?"

"If it's a pile of money, yes, sure. That might work," Alex said simply. "And it might not. You might get your head blown off by local police. And you might find that the stash disappeared fifty years ago. Equally, a Cuban prison would be a pretty horrible place to spend ten years if your visit hit any snags. So be forewarned."

"I understand," he said. But he said this in such a way that it suggested more.

"Was there something else?" she asked.

The two men exchanged a glance.

"Well, there's my actual offer to you," Guarneri said.

"And what's that?"

"I'm going to make a trip into Cuba. I need to be accompanied by a woman who will pose as my wife or an adult daughter. I need a woman who is politically savvy, intelligent, able to think on her feet in dangerous situations, and is fluent in Spanish. I'm under no illusions as to how risky such a trip would be." He paused. "Yuri suggested you."

She looked back and forth between the two of them, then laughed.

"The two of you," she said, "you're *both* quite charming and completely out of your minds."

"Will you go with me?" Guarneri asked.

"No. That's a flat-out no. I don't even have to think about it."

"A woman who can handle a gun would be particularly useful," Guarneri said.

"Ask around in this room," she said. "I'm sure someone knows someone and can hook you up with a Lara Croft clone."

"Again, Yuri suggested you."

"Yuri's full of bad ideas, Paul. This would be one of them."

"Think about it," Guarneri said. "A day will come when you might want to consider my offer."

"The answer is *no*," she said. "I'm flattered, but find someone else. My answer is not going to change."

Federov smirked. "Remember what I said," he reminded her. "Never say never."

THIRTEEN

Thirty minutes after midnight, sitting again in his car on a quiet Calvert Street, Nagib had a great idea. Taking a sharp screwdriver from the glove compartment and pushing it into his belt, he turned to Rashaad and said, "Wait for me. I'll be back."

Nagib stepped out of the car and took a slow walk around the periphery of the building. The Calvert Arms took half the block on its side of the street, and there was an entrance to its garage around the corner.

He walked back and forth for about twenty minutes, keeping a wary eye out for those nosy cops who had given him a cross-eyed look the previous night. He strolled until he saw a car stop in front of the access to the parking garage. Now it was almost 1:00 a.m. The driver used a remote device to open the garage. The big steel door opened and allowed the car to enter.

Nagib drifted to the entrance door. Just when the automatic door was almost shut, he ducked inside, quiet as an eel in shallow water. There! He was in the building and the driver who had unknowingly let him in had already moved down to the lower level to park.

Perfect!

Nagib searched along the high part of the walls for security cameras. He didn't see any. That was good too. He found a remote area of the garage, ducked down between cars, and waited till he was convinced he was alone. His gun was in his belt in case he encountered serious trouble.

No one came by, no one saw him. Not a single car moved. As he waited, he pulled a pair of latex gloves from his pocket and put them on.

Toward 1:45 a.m., he rose. He circulated among some of the more remote cars and found several that were dirty and covered with dust. Obviously, these cars rarely moved. If he took something from one of these cars and did it neatly, no one might notice for a week or two, maybe even longer, judging by some of the dust.

He moved from car to car, keeping low, ever attentive for the sound of anyone intruding. He looked into various cars until he found what he wanted in an old Mercedes-Benz nestled into one of the corners on the lower of the garage's two levels. He knew his Benzes because he had been a mechanic early in his life. He had worked on old Mercedes diesels, the now-vintage 230s, 240s, and 300s, which were common where he grew up. This one appeared to be a 1980 or thereabouts, a 300 D, a dependable old Teutonic workhorse.

So this too was perfect. Judging by the dirt on the Benz's windshield, judging by the way the tires were slightly "down," this old silver-blue baby rarely moved. Nagib looked on the dashboard near the VIN number to see if there was an alarm. He saw none. God was smiling on Nagib tonight, he reasoned. This car was like an engraved invitation.

He wedged the sharp screwdriver between the driver's side doorframe and the door. He pried, parallel to the lower part of the window. He created an opening of about half an inch.

With his other hand, he took a looped strip of hard plastic from his pocket and slid it through the small passageway. He dropped the loop on the peg of the lock.

He pulled it tight. Then he pulled it sideways and upward. It fought him a little and he had to squeeze his fingers between the door and the frame. But the peg of the lock popped up. The car was unlocked.

Nagib released the screwdriver, reached to the door handle, and opened the door.

He slid in. He reached to the sun visor on the right side and removed what he had spotted from the outside: a remote clicker that he assumed operated the garage door. There was also some money between the seats. He took some of that too, but not all of it. All of it would have alerted the owner to the break-in, and he didn't want that.

He checked the glove compartment, just out of curiosity, and looked at the car registration. The car belonged to a woman who lived in the building. The name meant nothing, but he prowled through the other paperwork, one eye on the rest of the garage in case some busybody intruded.

He found a few letters and some photographs. The woman's name was Helen Jacobus, and she seemed to be a retired teacher. Good. She was older and apparently widowed. Nagib noted her name in case it might help him sometime. He stole some of the mail, just enough to have a record of the address, in case he ever wanted to steal an identity or break in again. There was also a twenty-dollar bill and two fives. Emergency money. He couldn't resist. He helped himself to that too.

The woman lived in Apartment 303. Now if anyone ever asked him why he was in the building or hanging around it, he had a name he could use immediately, enough to allow getaway time.

Helen wasn't the woman he was here to kill. A much younger, more troublesome woman held that honor. But Helen might be his unwitting accomplice.

Nagib pocketed what he needed from the car and locked the doors from within. Then he closed the car door. The damage done to the door and door frame by his break-in was almost nonexistent. It would take a close examination to tell how the break-in had occurred. And by that time, he theorized, his business at the Calvert Arms would be complete.

He pulled off his latex gloves. He walked back through the driving lanes to the garage door at street level. He pressed the button on his new remote and the sliding door opened.

This was fantastic! He now had access to the entire building whenever he wanted it. There was no doubt in his mind that this would be more productive than sitting in his car for days on end, waiting.

He was pleased with himself and his accomplishment for the evening. He went back to the old Taurus on the street where Rashaad waited.

"Tomorrow," Nagib said. "Tomorrow I'll get her."

Then they gave up their watch for the evening. By any account, however, their day had been a success.

FOURTEEN

Alex checked out of the Gotham by 9:00 a.m. the next morning and took the Lexington Avenue subway down to Wall Street. The office building where her interview would be held was in the new enclave of federal offices at Liberty Place.

She took the elevator to the fifty-sixth floor where two different representatives of the United States Treasury interviewed her, first in English and then, because it had bearing on the eventual assignment, in Spanish.

The job in question was similar to what she was already doing, but she would be a department head. Most of the anticrime and antifraud work would be against operations launched from Central and South America. Given her expertise in the field, she was a natural for the assignment, although there were currently no women holding similar "senior" posts around the country. She would be the first, an idea that attracted her. She would also be the youngest, the interviewer mentioned. That flattered her too.

Part of the job would entail fieldwork, on-the-spot investigations, and probably a good deal of travel. Some of it would be dangerous. In some instances she would be working with local law enforcement in places like Colombia, Argentina, Costa Rica, and Chile. She would be required to carry a weapon on the job if only for her personal safety. The opponents would be some very dirty people. She noted that there was nothing new about that, she was already carrying a gun. She knew the drill.

She felt drawn to the job and repelled by it at the same time. One part of her was a poet and philosopher, the part that wanted to settle into a village like Barranco Lajoya and bring peace and civilization to people who had never known it. The other part of her was the righteous warrior, the woman who could pull on jungle fatigues or navigate through a rough inner city, a woman who could carry a weapon, use it, and go after the malefactors of the world where they lived.

She was often torn as to which was the dominant part of her personality. When there was too much violence and action, she longed for tranquility. When things were too calm, like now, she longed for activity.

The interviews were rigorous. They took two hours. But afterward, Alex left feeling that she had interviewed well. Then again, as she rode the subway back uptown to Pennsylvania Station, where she would take the afternoon Metroliner back to Washington, she knew that the government was interviewing several dozen highly qualified men and women for various jobs at the New York FinCEN office. She was just one of several, she reasoned, despite Joseph Collins's high opinion. One never knew whether a personal favor or connection would pull through a long-shot applicant.

Well, that's fine, she told herself. *If the position is offered, I'm going to take it. If not, there will be something else. No point to get hung up on it.*

The express train back to DC left on time. She relaxed again into her novel on the trip back to Washington. In the evening, she went by the gym to swim twenty laps and burn off the nervous energy from the trip.

She was back home at the Calvert Arms by 10:00 p.m.

FIFTEEN

Shortly after 11:00, as the Saudi waited in the getaway car down on the street, Nagib walked down the fifth floor corridor at the Calvert Arms. The corridor was long and carpeted with thick plush runners, making his footfall all but undetectable. He had pulled the neck of a turtleneck sweater up over the lower part of his face and kept a wool cap down low.

These people who lived in this building, these wealthy Americans, he thought to himself. They all had peepholes. And who knew when some old busybody who couldn't sleep, or some young girl with a boyfriend, was going to look out into the hall.

Or, as had happened before, some night owl would step out to send a bag of kitchen garbage down the chute or go outside to smoke a cigarette. Americans were unpredictable. They were a disorderly, hypocritical population with a disorderly, hypocritical society. It was just one of many reasons why he hated them. Nonetheless, he had his assignment. He would complete it, get paid, and have his family come and join him in London.

He had his pistol tucked under his sweatshirt. It was at the small of his back with the safety catch on. He knew if someone looked out of one of those pesky peepholes and saw a man with a gun, the DC police would be called. There was a chance that the police would respond to the call, and then his whole assignment would be compromised. As it was, he was in the country illegally. They would do a background check, and who knew where he would land? So, literally, better not to show his hand until he was ready to use it.

He arrived at the apartment he wanted. Fortune smiled. The door to 506 was at a bend in the hallway where the corridor took a turn in a different direction. So he could lurk in the corner and none of the other peepholes could view him.

He stooped down and took a reading on his situation. Under the door to 505, there was darkness. Under the door to 506, the same. No music, no voices, not even the sound of a distant footfall. As he cocked his head, all he could hear was the distant steady rumble of Washington traffic.

He stood. He reached behind his back and pulled out his weapon. He wondered how much effort it would take to kick the door in. He theorized: if the young woman he wanted to kill was with a man — who knew? — maybe the man would have a gun and come out shooting.

Nagib did not know the layouts to these apartments either. If only his victim would step out quietly, Nagib could just stick his gun to her face and finish her with one pop.

But he knew better than to count on wishful thinking.

He looked at the doorknobs, first the one to 506, then to 505. They were solid-looking knobs. The building was maybe fifty years old, he reasoned, but the closing and locking apparatus was much newer.

Nagib had once killed a man in Egypt whose door could be pushed in with a steady shoulder. In Munich, he had once gone into a dissident Iranian's apartment as part of an execution team. The victim had piled furniture against the door from the inside, but the locks had given up virtually the moment Nagib and his team looked at them.

He hoped for the same here.

He put one powerful hand on the knob to 506 and gripped it. Then he turned. He held the pistol aloft in his other hand, the safety catch off. He squeezed the knob hard and twisted it. He turned it hard. He turned it with all his strength and waited for the snap that would be like music from heaven, a sign from God. He squeezed and turned so hard that the veins started to pulse on the side of his neck.

He wanted to hear the snap. Where was it?

It wouldn't come.

He cursed. The lock had held.

He released the knob from his hand.

He withdrew slightly. He looked in all directions. The coast remained clear.

He reached to his sleeve where he hid a burglar's picking pin in the material of his sweatshirt just above his right forearm. He pulled the pin out, crouched down, and went to work picking the lock. If he could just get one or two of the tumblers within the lock to cooperate, he was home free.

The sweat poured off him as he worked. The hallway remained quiet. He attempted to pick the lock for several minutes. It was so quiet that he could hear the soft rattling and scratching from within the lock. He heard a couple of faint clicks, two and maybe even a third. A good sign.

He stood and tried the knob again.

He tried with all the strength in his hand. Then he tucked the gun into his belt and tried with two hands.

Still nothing. The lock held. He sighed. He cursed to himself. He stepped back.

Then, about fifty feet behind him down the hall, a door opened. Nagib heard music and voices. Two men, two women, laughing, talking loudly, as if a social gathering was breaking up.

Then they were joined by more.

He turned away from them and away from the doors where he stood. He walked in the opposite direction, keeping his head low so no one would see his face, and one hand on his pistol in case someone did.

He arrived at the door that led to the emergency staircase. He ducked into the stairwell and hurried back down. He was sure no one had seen him. But he wasn't sure whether he'd be back again that night.

Two minutes later, Nagib was downstairs in the garage. He listened to his own footsteps echo as he walked to the automatic door. He used his remote clicker to open it and walked outside.

His assistant sat in the car, waiting, the engine running. Nagib slid into the passenger's side in the front seat. The door had been unlocked. His cohort looked to him, unable to tell by his expression whether he had killed anyone or not.

"I can't get into the apartment," he said. "Next time we see her on the street, we take her out then."

Rashaad maintained a steely expression. He let a minute pass and didn't move.

"She's there tonight," he said softly. "I saw her go in."

Nagib drew a long breath and exhaled.

"It's quiet down here; it's a rainy night," Rashaad said. "It's perfect."

Nagib eased back. "Okay. We wait a little. Then I'll go in again."

SIXTEEN

Alex was about to change and shower for bed when her doorbell rang. It gave her pause. Normally, visitors didn't show up at the door unexpectedly, and they never did this late. Her friends normally knew better to drop in on her unannounced.

She glanced at her watch. It was a few minutes past 11:00 p.m. Who was in the hall?

An emergency of some sort? She wondered. *A problem in the building?*

She stood and walked to the door. She thought of taking her weapon with her. One could never be too careful in her line of work, but she decided against it, maybe out of pure laziness.

She arrived at the door and looked through the peephole. A little wave of relief swept across her. It was her neighbor, Mr. Thomas, the older gentleman she affectionately called "Don Tomás," the retired diplomat. He was definitely a friend.

With him stood a young woman, a girl maybe a third his age.

Alex suppressed a mischievous smirk. Maybe the old boy wanted to borrow a bottle of champagne. Then she suppressed her smile, undid the latch, and opened the door.

Immediately, before Alex could speak, Don Tomás held up a finger to his lips to indicate silence. Then he spoke in a barely audible whisper.

"Good evening, Alex," he said. "I hope I'm not disturbing you." His tone was serious. She picked up on it right away.

She shook her head to indicate that, no, he was not disturbing her at all.

"I have some new music that I downloaded," he said, continuing a low tone tinged with a conspiratorial air. "I wondered if you'd like to come over and take a listen. Some of them might be of interest to you. I'd be glad to lend you a few of my bootleg CDs if you'd like to rip them."

Alex was about to open her mouth to respond softly when Don Tomás moved his firm finger from his lips to a few inches in front of Alex's. At the same time, the young woman held forth a note scrawled on the open pages of a writing tablet.

Alex glanced at it and her eyes widened. Her heart skipped as she read. The note said,

```
I used to work for the CIA
I once planted a listening
device in your apartment
I think it's still there
```

Alex raised her gaze and looked into the girl's eyes. The girl looked frightened and agitated, hunted, like a doe in deer season. Her appearance also rang a distant bell to Alex. It took a second, but Alex realized that she was Don Tomás's niece. Her name was Janet; Alex had seen her from time to time in the building and had even been introduced briefly once in the hallway.

Abruptly, Janet turned the page of the writing tablet and presented a second written message.

```
I used to work for Michael Cerny
We need to talk
```

Alex blinked in surprise and looked back up. She saw more fear in the girl's eyes.

Alex raised her own finger to indicate they should wait for a moment. She ducked back into her apartment, found her pistol, and clipped it to the right side of the belt on her jeans. Then she returned to her door and followed her neighbor across the hallway to his place.

As she crossed the hall, Alex saw no one other than Don Tomás and Janet. The corridor was as quiet as a tomb, although there was a strange scent of something cooking, or, more accurately, overcooking.

"Mrs. Rothman down the hall has gone complete daffy," Don Tomás said as explanation. "Poor old woman burns food at all hours. Puts stuff in the toaster and forgets. One of these days an onion bagel is going to turn this whole place into an inferno."

They entered Don Tomás's apartment and closed the door.

SEVENTEEN

Alex hadn't been in this apartment for some time, not since having had a pleasant brunch there almost a year earlier with Robert. Now her presence keyed the bittersweet memory. For a moment she struggled to get past it.

Don Tomás threw a second bolt on his door. Alex looked at the bolt. It was newly installed and top-of-the-line with steel plating underneath which would make a push-in almost impossible.

"I've stepped up my own personal security in here," he grumbled. "One of those blue-haired old ladies downstairs got burgled the other day, did you hear?"

"No, I didn't," Alex said.

"Or she said she did anyway," he said. "Who knows? She's as deaf as a haddock and as senile as I'll be in another few years. But at least now it will take someone a full minute to break in, as opposed to the ten seconds it probably would have taken before. You might consider doing the same."

"Thanks for the tip," Alex answered.

"Oh, I know, I'm being a cantankerous old goat," the retired diplomat grumbled, "but my niece has been staying with me recently. You never know who's hanging around the hallways these days. And the idiot doormen are usually busy getting off on *American Idol* or whatever they watch."

Don Tomás was a nineteenth-century man trapped in the small quotidian horrors of the twenty-first century. It was what Alex liked about him.

"Anyway," he continued as he trudged heavily to his living room. "Tonight's not about me; it's about my niece. You know each other?"

The two young women eyed each other as they walked.

"Alex, meet Janet. Janet, meet Alex," Don Tomás said. "There! Now you're old friends."

"I think we've passed in the elevators," Alex said.

"Well, thank God the elevator wasn't plunging from this floor to the sub-basement at the time," Don Tomás said. "I take the stairs myself. I'd take them three at a time, but I'd give myself a heart attack after one flight. Anyway, the steps are healthier."

"Healthier," Alex said as they walked past Don Tomás's ample bar and impressive collection of cigars inside an elaborate glass humidor. Janet led them to the sitting area in the living room and, with a gesture of exhaustion, eased onto the sofa.

The distinctive prints remained on the living room walls, mostly art deco originals from the twenties and thirties, stylized prints of beautiful women in most cases, including some brilliant works by the French Sapphic artist Tamara de Lempicka. In a further bizarre decorative touch, Don Tomás had added an antique print of a racehorse that bore his name, a gift, he explained, from a friend on his recent fifty-fifth birthday.

"My great-great-great grandfather was a Confederate cavalry captain in the Civil War," Don Tomás explained. "Those of his men whom he didn't get killed seemed to be rather fond of him after the war. So they named a racehorse after him."

"Apparently," Alex said, eyeing the print.

"It was a gelding," Janet said.

"It was not!" Don Tomás insisted. "And it must have been a pretty good old nag — it won the 1875 Preakness and was later put out to stud."

"A little before my time," Alex said.

"Just a bit before mine as well," Don Tomás added, "despite what you might think. I can honestly say I'm closer to sixty than a hundred and twenty-five. Would you like a drink, by the way? I have a new bottle of thirty-year-old single Malt Balvenie, speaking of graceful aging."

"I'd love a short glass," Alex said. "Where on earth did you find a thirty-year-old Balvenie?"

"Oh, I have my sources," Don Tomás said, pouring a shot of the single malt into a whiskey glass. "Plus, it's not *where* I got it; the amusing detail is what I *spent* for it. Middle range of three figures." He poured an ample portion for himself. "Janet? Can I get you something? Or would you like to stick to a carcinogen-laced diet soda or perhaps a beer, I hope?"

Janet had already retrieved a bottle of Budweiser from the refrigerator and plopped down on a chair before the sofa. She swigged from the bottle as Don Tomás and Alex savored the complexities of Caledonia. After two swigs, Janet embarked into some backstory that also had some complexity also.

"Okay," she said, turning to Alex, "I have a lot of crap that I need to bring you up to speed on."

"Then let's start," Alex said.

According to Janet, she had been one of those pretty but geeky girls in high school who had been a computer and electronics whiz. "My brain was so right-sided that the joke was that I might tip over," she said. She had parlayed her straight A's in computer sciences, physics, and math into acceptance with an academic scholarship to Georgia Tech, even though her real interests had been music and composition, the heavier the metal the better. She hung around Savannah for an extra year, picked up a master's degree in computer science, and then followed a boyfriend to Washington.

The boyfriend didn't work out and neither did her first couple of jobs. Then she answered a few newspaper ads for techie positions. One thing led to another, and the next thing she knew she was interning in the evenings at a cramped, smelly office in Alexandria, Virginia. There she was trained with surveillance equipment and how to do a quick drop in an apartment.

One more thing led to another one more thing. Janet partnered with a couple of different guys and did a string of trial drops for a local police agency.

"I got real good real fast," Janet said. "For some reason, most of the partners I worked with dropped surveillance devices in cars, offices, houses, and apartments. It was always male-female teams. The guys did the dumb work of breaking and entering and watching the street. The girls were the ones who really put our butts on the line, going into people's homes and setting up the electronic ears. It just seemed to work that way." She paused. "Once I bugged a guy's golf bag while he was putting."

"How'd you manage that?" Alex asked.

"Me and this other girl, we bribed the attendant to partner us up in a foursome where our mark played golf. The other girl never wore a bra. She kept the guys distracted with her T-shirt and size-six shorts while I put an ear into the guy's bag."

"Good work," Alex said.

The company Janet worked for was one of those incorporated-only-on-paper concerns, she continued. It was technically a private contractor. But there wasn't much doubt as to where the big boss was: Langley, Virginia.

Eventually, she partnered with a dude name Carlos, she said, first at work and then in the off hours.

Don Tomás intervened. He spared his niece the agony of plodding through the most painful part of her past history, the way Carlos had been obliterated by a car bomb in Cairo. He summarized that as quickly as possible and brought Alex up to present day on the sighting of a former boss in Cairo, Michael Cerny.

"He was kind of my everything," Janet said. "My Carlos."

"I'm really sorry. But I can relate," Alex said.

"Yeah. I know," Janet said. "Like I said, I know who you are. You just didn't know who I was."

"That seems to be changing," Alex said.

"We used to talk a lot because we worked together," Janet said. "Carlos and me. We were both interested in seeing the sights in the Middle East. You know, the pyramids, the Holy Land, Jerusalem. I didn't have anyone to go with and neither did he. But we had some vacation time. So we saved up some bread and put a trip together." She paused. "Single girl, traveling alone in that part of the world can't be too careful, can she?" she asked. "I didn't want to be sold into a harem or something. I mean, much safer to have your guy with you."

"Makes sense to me," Alex said. "Seriously. The last time I was in North Africa the whole delegation nearly got killed. I have no desire whatsoever to set foot in the place again for a good long time."

"Understandably," intoned Don Tomás. "Where exactly were you in North Africa?"

"Lagos. Nigeria."

"Ah," he said. "One of the great hellholes of the world. That area is hardly safe for any American traveling alone," Don Tomás chipped in with his usual cynical charm, based on a quarter century in the diplomatic corps. "Much less a young woman."

Alex turned back to Janet. "Here's what I'm having some initial trouble with though. I worked with Michael Cerny in Paris. The last I saw of him he was slumped low in the front seat of a car, blood on his body, with a broken windshield and a bunch of bullet holes in the glass."

"He's alive," Janet said. "Sure as I'm sitting here, he's alive and I saw him."

Following the two days she had had in New York, meeting Paul Guarneri, spending time with Yuri Federov, and interviewing for a new job, Janet's assertion had a kooky *Twilight Zone* ring to it. Alex felt a strange rumbling in her stomach and didn't know if it was nerves or fear or just outright disbelief.

"Why don't you tell me what you want to tell me, Janet," Alex said.

Janet led Alex through the story of what had happened in Egypt, how they had gone from their hotel one night to the Royale, the joint with the crunchy floors, the stinking cigarette smoke, the fake luxury scotches, and the Cerny clone with his two friends, one of them named Victor.

Then there had been the trip to the men's room, a few days of peace while they speculated on the sighting, and then the explosive device that killed Carlos.

Janet finished. Alex gave her a moment to recover. Janet used the time to fetch herself another beer. The room was silent for several seconds, aside from the refrigerator closing and the cap from a beer bottle coming off.

Alex turned to Don Tomás. "If my apartment is bugged, how do you know yours isn't?" Alex whispered.

"Janet checked," Don Tomás answered. "She has some equipment on permanent informal loan from her former employers."

"I get it," Alex said.

Janet returned and sat down.

"This bomb that went off," Alex inquired gently to Janet. "You think it was intended for *the two* of you?"

"Absolutely," Janet answered.

"Might it have been intended for Carlos alone?"

"We were with each other the entire time. If Carlos had enemies from here, why would they trail him all the way to Cairo? It was in response to what he'd seen, *what we'd seen*, in Cairo. At the Royale."

"Did the police tell you anything about the bomb? In Cairo?"

"No. They treated us like a couple of dumb young Americans who'd brought trouble on themselves. They accused us of dealing drugs and all sorts of things. I was scared. *Real* scared. I got out of the country as soon as I could."

"Janet phoned me from Cairo," Don Tomás said. "I arranged for one of the consular officers to come see her at the police station. Otherwise, they might still be holding her."

"And what happened when you returned to America?" Alex asked.

"The people I worked for debriefed me for hours," she said. "Even the evening after the memorial service for Carlos. I told them what I knew; I told them what I thought. They told me I was crazy. They told me that Mike Cerny being alive was the most preposterous thing they'd ever heard."

"That's my initial reaction also," Alex said. "But that's also a rather strange approach on their part."

"That's what I thought," Janet said, angry and defiant.

Mystified, Alex took a moment to catch up with her own thoughts. "I'm losing you a little here. Who did the 'debriefing'?"

"CIA," she said.

"CIA?"

"That's who we worked for, once removed."

"Do you have any names?"

Janet gave some. Alex was suckered in by now. She glanced around for a notepad. When she didn't see one, Don Tomás provided one, plus a pen.

"They treated me like a hysterical woman," Janet said. "It was as if they had an agenda, you know? The longer it went on, the longer they kept trying to tell me that I was mistaken, that I couldn't possibly have seen Mr. Cerny. First, they were patronizing. 'Really, Janet,' they said. 'You mustn't make up stories like that.' 'Really, you'll start all kinds of trouble if you start going around Washington saying things like that. People will think you've lost it.' I know how the head games work. They were trying to see if they could convince me that I'd been mistaken. I mean, I was traumatized and vulnerable. So they were trying to get inside my head and move the mental furniture around. Then within a few days, the tune had changed. I got another team of interrogators. The lead guy, he was almost threatening. Check that, he *was* threatening," Janet said. "He told me that Michael Cerny was buried in a family plot in Muncie, Indiana, and his wife had moved back there with a generous widow's pension. He told me that obviously I was under great stress from having lost my fiancé, but that made no difference. If I kept saying things like that, they were going to invoke one of the psychiatric codes on me and have me locked up. 'For your own good,' he said. He floated the idea of sending me back to Egypt and letting the local police take care of me. I said he couldn't do that and he laughed and said he could do anything he wanted to. Patriot Act. National security. By this time, my head was really spinning. He even claimed at one point that he was a shrink and he could have me committed to a mental cracker box on the spot and *then* sent to Egypt. Well, bull! This guy wasn't any shrink. I could tell. I've been to shrinks and they're not like this guy."

"What was this interrogator's name?" Alex asked.

"Evans," she said. "That was the name he gave. John Evans. But with those people, who knows? I figured it was a fake."

"What about the other ones? The previous interrogators?"

"The first one called himself Fisher," she said. "Mr. Fisher. Like in 'Fisher of Men.' He was a rude bastard," Janet said. "In a way the first guy wasn't as bad as the ones who followed. But probably none of them used their real names."

"Would all of those be fake names?" Don Tomás asked.

"Most likely," Alex said with a sigh. "That's how these creeps work. The scotch is excellent, by the way."

"I'm glad you like it."

"Worth every dime of the five hundred dollars."

"Let's try not to drink the whole bottle this evening," Don Tomás said. "It's always nice to have some left over for breakfast."

Janet forged on. "They kept asking if I had seen him myself, Cerny, if I could pick him out of a lineup, for example."

"And what did you tell them, Janet?" Alex asked.

"I said I could."

Alex was still processing the bulk of this when Janet sent the dialogue in a different direction. "I'd like to show you where the listening devices are," Janet said. "The ones in your apartment. I remember when we dropped them on you. Did you ever discover them?" she asked.

"No. I had no idea there was anything in there. How do you know if they're still there?"

"Most likely they are," Janet said.

"Keep in mind I've been away from Washington for several months over the last year," Alex said.

"I know. I know all about you," Janet said.

A feeling of indignation washed over Alex, first being bugged by the very people she worked for. Second that this girl, Don Tomás's niece, knew all about Alex and Alex knew nothing about her in return. And third that the devices were still there.

"How do you know they might not have been removed?" Alex asked.

"They normally send the same team back to do the retrieval," Janet said. "We never got sent. But with Mr. Cerny's disappearance, 'retirement,' death, or whatever you want to call it, assignments got confused and overlapped. But they still might have sent ..." Here her voice trailed off and cracked. "They still might have sent Carlos and me here to take the bugs out. But they didn't. Still, I hear stuff from the other teams we work with. We're not supposed to talk about it. We're not even supposed to know the people in the other teams. But we do. Most of us know each other. The bosses are careless. The whole operation is careless. And we all talk. Covering our backside, know what I mean?"

"I know what you mean," Alex said. "Exactly." She thought for a moment. "If the devices are still there do you think they're working?"

"Oh, sure. They'd be working. The audio feed is going into somewhere. I don't know where, but it's most likely being stockpiled and inventoried somewhere. Maybe by computer. They have somewhere they can download it into a written translation, and there's probably someone who reads the stuff every day. If nothing else, just for kicks."

"For kicks," Alex agreed.

Janet nodded. "You know? To see who's in who else's bedroom who shouldn't be. Never know who you're gonna catch in *that* net."

"On the taxpayer's dime," Don Tomás said. "And by the way, I'm really sorry about this, Alex."

"No, no. I just thank you that you called it to my attention."

"I just learned about this two days ago. I knocked on your door yesterday," he said.

"I was in New York."

"As you can see, Janet is quite frightened."

"Of course," Alex said.

"I've been hanging with friends," Janet said. "I've been afraid to go to work. Never sleep more than three days in a row in the same place, don't go to any of my usual stores. Nothing. They questioned me *for five days*. It was like Guantanamo North. I didn't have a lawyer there, and I never felt like I was free to go when I wanted. They kept insisting I was wrong, wrong, wrong! Like they were suggesting that I change my mind. Why would they do that if they weren't hiding something or if I wasn't onto something?"

"I don't know," Alex said.

"Then on the third day I made a mistake. I mentioned the picture I took."

"What picture?" Alex asked.

"When Carlos went over to try to take a look at the man we saw in the bar. I snapped a picture. I was tired during the interview. I shouldn't have mentioned it. But they pressed me. They asked if I still had it. I thought it might get them off my case if I admitted it. So I said, yeah, I have it, it's still on my camera. They asked if I had downloaded it onto a laptop or gotten prints. I said no."

"And?" Alex asked.

"They went over to my apartment and broke in. They took my

camera. I saw it was missing when I got home. And when I turned on my laptop, the memory was broiled. They had zapped it. Can you believe it?"

"I believe it," she said with feeling. She held a silence.

"It became the big issue for the next two days. They kept hammering me. 'Janet,' they said, 'where are the other copies? We know you must have made other copies. Where are they?'."

"But if Cerny was dead, as they said he was," Alex asked, "why on earth would they have cared about these pictures?"

"That's exactly what I was thinking," she said. "And I said that to them too, that it was pointless of them to care about the picture if they were so sure Cerny was dead. But they didn't like the situation. Next thing I know, they called in another man. Big ugly SOB with a bad haircut and halitosis. A real thug! He just sat there with his arms folded and glowered at me. Never said anything. Then I started asking if I had the right to see a lawyer."

"You did."

"They told me I didn't. They told me they could keep me locked up for weeks, and I'd do better just coming clean with them right away. They wore me down so much I started to cry."

"Got it," Alex said. She looked to Don Tomás and then back to his niece. "I want to ask you two things," Alex said.

"Sure."

"You used to work for Mr. Cerny. And you knew me from being in this building to drop a bug on me."

"Uh huh."

"But how did you know I worked for Mr. Cerny?" she asked. "I could have been just someone that he wanted to eavesdrop on."

"I kind of figured it out," Janet said sheepishly. "After that mess in Kiev in February, I saw you on the news a few times. TV, you know. I recognized you from the building here. And I recognized your name because they always had to tell us who we were dropping a bug on so we could find the right place. So Carlos and I were really following the whole Kiev case. I've known who you were since then. And there was this guy named Pete who was our supervisor. Pete talked too much when he gave out the assignments. We'd figured out his boss's name.

Pete had all these records in his office that he was supposed to keep confidential. But everything was all over his desk. So Carlos and me, we saw names. Then, follow this, we weren't in line for this assignment to bug you here, but Pete knew that I knew the building. And he made a wisecrack. He said that you'd been a lousy employee and your boss wanted to drop a bug on you. Wanted to know about your social life or something. So I put it all together. This was even before Kiev."

"My boss? Mike Gamburian?"

"No, no. Mr. Cerny wanted a special watch on you."

"Cerny?"

"Cerny. That's what Pete said."

"I see," Alex said. But actually, she didn't. Events and details seemed to float around as if in a fog, threatening to connect but failing to. Questions suggested themselves to her and then eluded rational resolution.

Had Cerny been monitoring her out of some perverse personal interest, or had there been a professional agenda? And if it had been a professional agenda, whose was it? American intelligence or something farther afield?

For the first time, Alex tried to examine the question by pulling it inside out and then apart.

"And then when everything hit the fan about a week ago," Don Tomás interjected, "I told Janet she could stay here. But I insisted that I know what sort of trouble she was in. That's when so much of this came into view."

"Of course," Alex said, finishing her scotch and putting the glass down.

"Would you like another drink?" Don Tomás asked.

"Maybe some other evening," Alex said. "I want to keep a clear head."

"You don't mind if I do?" Don Tomás asked.

"Keep a clear head or have another scotch?"

"Hopefully both," Don Tomás said, rising. "But maybe just the scotch."

Alex turned back to Janet. "Did you finally convince them about the picture? That you didn't have other copies?"

"I did," she said. "Or at least, I think I did."

Several seconds passed. "If I'm going to help you and hopefully protect you," Alex said, "you know you need to be completely honest with me. Right? You understand that, correct?"

Janet looked at her warily.

"I don't think you're foolish," Alex said. "I have a feeling you down-loaded that photo somewhere. Just for safekeeping."

Another wary pause from Janet.

"My guess is that you were, shall we say, one step ahead of them," Alex continued. "You don't have to admit it out loud. Just nod if I'm right."

Several seconds passed. Janet nodded.

"Where is it?" Alex asked. "Stored in cyberspace maybe?"

Janet grimaced and pulled a new iPod out of her backpack. She fired it up and brought up the photograph. She handed the iPod to Alex.

Alex looked down and, on a two-by-three-inch screen saw the photo from the Royale in Cairo. The figures were too small to be of any value to the naked eye. The iPod was big-screen only if the viewer was a mouse. But Alex saw a small snapshot of two men facing and one, the Cerny clone, with his back to her.

Alex looked back up. "Does anyone else know you have this?" she asked.

"Just you and my uncle."

"I need to copy this," Alex said.

"Please be careful," Janet begged again.

"I'm not going to put it through any intelligence system or com-puter network at work. If Mike Cerny is alive, who knows what's com-promised and where? I just want to run it to my own iPod. All right? Please say yes."

Janet looked to Don Tomás, who nodded. "Yes," she said to Alex.

"I have a few people whom I know I can trust. They're outside of Treasury and the CIA. They're not even American. They might be able to help me, help you, while keeping their own hands personally on an inquiry. If there's anything to this, that's the route I might have to go."

Janet trembled. "Use your judgment," she said.

Alex nodded. "Now," she said. "Let's go back into my apartment and see if those eavesdropping devices are there. If they *are* there, we should leave them. No use alerting anyone now."

"None," Don Tomás said.

"Let's go have a look," Alex said.

"Should I stay or wait?" the retired diplomat said.

Alex gave him a wink. "Join the party," she said. "No one say anything. We'll just have a look."

They went out into the hall, which remained quiet.

They crossed the hall and closed the door.

Two minutes later, Nagib emerged from the service stairs that led from the garage. He walked down the hallway, his pistol under his coat. He arrived at the doorways to 505 and 506.

He stood outside, listened, and waited. Then somewhere in the distance, he heard some sort of alarm go off.

EIGHTEEN

Janet's recall was encyclopedic when it came to devices that she had planted. She could recall all of them, where in a room she had put one, what had been the problems of location.

She had entered the apartment behind Alex, then stepped slightly ahead.

In this case, it all seemed so simple. Janet went down to her hands and knees on the living room floor, then turned slightly to an angle as she neared a coffee table that stood in front of a sofa. Alex followed her to the floor while Don Tomás was content to stand and watch.

Janet reached under the coffee table and quietly extended an index finger. Alex was next to her on the floor and positioned her head so she could see under the table. Her finger pointed to the listening device, still clamped exactly where she had put it several months earlier.

Janet turned toward Alex and said nothing. Alex nodded, not with anger but with understanding. Then Janet sprung up again and went to the bedroom. They repeated the on-the-floor guidance. Janet showed Alex the transmitter that had been wedged under the headboard of her bed.

Alex nodded. They left everything in place and returned to Don Tomás's apartment. Down the hall, they heard Mrs. Rothman's smoke alarm going off. They didn't speak again until they were inside with the door closed.

"That deaf old bat doesn't even hear her own smoke alarm," Don Tomás muttered. "Can you believe that?"

But Janet was still dwelling on the electronic snooping.

"I'm sorry," Janet said to Alex. "I had a job to do. Nothing personal."

"I understand," Alex said. "You're forgiven. You had a job to do and you did it." She paused. "Same as myself."

"Oh, and there's one other thing," Janet said. "I mentioned it to the interrogators. They laughed at me and said it was impossible. But I'll mention it to you."

Alex waited.

"The three men in the bar in Cairo," she said. "Carlos got close enough to eavesdrop. He could hear them, but he couldn't tell what they were saying. At the time he didn't know what language they were speaking. Then afterward, he realized what it was."

"What was it?" Alex asked.

"Russian," she said. "The day before he died, Carlos said he was sure. They were talking Russian."

A few minutes later Alex was at the door. She stepped out into the hallway and closed the door behind her.

From somewhere there was a noise in the hall. She turned around, looked in each direction, but saw nothing.

She reentered her own apartment. It was past 1:00 a.m.

She knew already that she was going to be sleep-deprived the next day. She would be dragging herself around as if she were dead.

On the street five stories below, Nagib and Rashaad were arguing furiously. Someone on the fifth floor had set off a smoke alarm. Around the corner from where he stood, vulnerable to view, doors began to open and a few people walked into the hall. Nagib had turned immediately and left, rather than be seen.

Rashaad was furious. The longer that it took to get the job done, the more chance that things would go wrong. They departed again, with their assignment still unfulfilled.

NINETEEN

Late the next morning Alex arrived at Mike Gamburian's door and found it half open. She knocked. Gamburian looked up from his desk. "Hey, Alex," he said. "What's up?"

"Got a couple of minutes?"

"For you, always. Two, three, maybe even four and a half."

There were a trio of hardcopy classified folders on his desk. Alex could tell by the bold red binders. He flipped all three shut as she pushed the door closed and sat down.

"What's on your mind?" he asked.

"I had a meeting in New York two nights ago with Yuri Federov," she said. "But you knew that."

"Of course. How's our old friend Yuri?"

"He's been better in his life. In fact, I can't figure out if he's got a serious health problem of some sort."

"Usually with men like that, a health problem is if someone's trying to shoot them."

"Yes, I know," she said. "We had some drinks at the hotel bar and then went for dinner at an Italian place down around Mulberry Street."

"Well! What a New York *gangsterismo* evening that was," he said.

"Seriously," Alex said, meaning yes. "And Federov introduced me to a friend."

"That's where it often gets interesting," he said. "A person of interest to us, perhaps?"

"You never know. What do you know about the Mafia in Cuba, Mike?" she asked.

"Now or in the past?"

"Either or both," Alex answered. "I've seen *The Godfather II* like everyone else, but aside from that the whole era is before my time. I assume we have files."

"*Tons* of them. You'll be sorry you asked. You might need a special access with a cosigned request form to see the top stuff. But I can get it for you if you're interested."

"I'm interested."

"Then I'll try to get you some file-archive access by later today."

"Good. I'd like to run the friend's name across the files," Alex said. "Paul Guarneri. Name mean anything to you?"

"Guarneri only means something as the patriarch of a seventeenth-century family of violin makers in Italy. I'm not up on all the current wise guys; there are too many of them, and it's not my department."

"Paul Guarnari didn't look personally that mobbed up to me," Alex continued. "Or at least not on the surface. But his father certainly was. Then again, what's he hanging around with Federov for if he's not a mob guy? The only use Federov ever had for legitimate businessmen was to shake them down."

"Where exactly was this meeting again?" Gamburian asked.

"A place called Il Vagabondo in Lower Manhattan. I did some asking around afterward. It's a mob hangout, not that I couldn't tell at the time."

"So as a Fed, if you don't mind the metaphor, you must have felt like a mosquito at a nudist colony."

"Pretty much," Alex said. "But I stuck with Guarneri. He said his family was from Cuba. His father was Italian but married a dancer who worked at one of the big hotel casinos. I think he has some major ideas about trying to get some old property back, including a pile of cash that was stashed somewhere. Does that make sense?"

Gamburian laughed. "Some," he said. "As soon as Castro is planted and pushing up daisies, all the old mob families are going to be looking for recovery of property. Then who knows what else they'll be up to. Can you keep the contact alive?"

"Sure," Alex said. "In fact, I'd like to."

"Well, you were introduced, so you'd be wise to follow it up. You never know when something small cracks something big. The 'French Connection' case was made when two cops wandered into a nightclub and spotted some hoods. 'Son of Sam' broke over a parking ticket. You could have a career case over a veal scaloppini in Brooklyn."

"It was saltimbocca, and it was in Lower Manhattan, but I catch your drift."

"Speaking of Lower Manhattan, how did the interview go? At the Federal Building?"

"Fine," she said.

"So you'll be leaving us and moving to New York."

"Let's see if they offer me anything," she said.

"Ha! They will. New York steals Washington's top employees all the time. We're used to it."

"Thanks, Mike," she said with irony. "I'll take that as a compliment."

"It was meant as one."

"I know," she said. She rose from the chair and moved to the door. As she opened the door, she turned and asked a final question.

"By the way," Alex inquired, "what do you hear about Mike Cerny's widow and family?"

Gamburian reacted with surprise. "Not much," he said. "They moved back to the Midwest somewhere from what I heard. That's all I know."

"She got her widow's benefits and pension?" Alex asked.

"Why wouldn't she?"

Alex shrugged her shoulders.

"Were you close to Mike Cerny? Did you know him well?"

"*No one* knew him very well," Gamburian said. "He was a cipher to everyone he worked with." Gamburian adjusted his glasses. "Why you asking?"

"Just curious," she said. "I'll look for the organized-crime file later."

"Enjoy them. Order out for a slice of pizza to go with them."

He flipped his classified folders back upright and returned to work as Alex's footsteps receded down the hallway.

Later, past 6:00 p.m. on the same day, Alex was sitting at her desk. She leaned back in her chair and stared at her two computers. She had read everything that had been given to her about Paul Guarneri and his father, Vito Guarneri. The files intrigued her, but increasingly they were small change. Michael Cerny was on her mind.

It was one thing that Janet claimed to have seen him, a sighting linked to the car bomb that killed Carlos. That might have been chalked up to coincidence or an overactive imagination. But why, if someone who looked like Cerny had been seen by a credible source, would there have been a failure to get a file to Alex? Alex had been an integral part of Cerny's "fatal" final mission. She should have been covered on it.

Incompetence? Maybe?

Was someone holding back because she was FBI and Treasury and not CIA?

Possible.

But overall, it didn't make sense.

She leaned to her laptop, which had a higher security access code than the desktop console. She entered her primary security clearance code and then entered her second. Both cruised.

A slight tremor came over her. To revisit Michael Cerny via the files was to revisit her personal catastrophe in Kiev and all the sorrow it had brought into her life. It had been less than a year. Was she ready to have so much of it come tumbling back?

She drew a breath. She entered her clearance for the secured site dedicated to the Kiev visit. Another dialogue box opened and asked for her name. She entered it. She remembered how in the painful first weeks after Kiev she had made this same trip and run into cyber roadblocks. More anxiety built. The dialogue window accepted her name. With two tries, it accepted her ID. Then she was back in the HUMINT, the human intelligence, leading up to the presidential visit to Kiev. Files opened. *Okay so far.*

She cringed as she read them, but unlike the previous times she had visited these sights, the files had not been bowdlerized. They seemed complete and accurate.

Okay, okay, she told herself. This might be a backdoor route to a background file on Michael Cerny. *Maybe.* Leaning forward, she attacked the keyboard with more gusto. She referenced names including her own. Robert's. Embassy personnel who had died that day. She found everyone she looked for.

Then she looked for Michael Cerny's name. Like the last time she had gone this route, she found no reference. She tried to remember.

Code names. Cover names. Cerny had had more working names

than some men have underwear. What were they? She felt as if she were fighting a battle against her own memory. Part of her wanted to recall. Another part of her remained in denial. *Wine.* One of them sounded like a German white wine.

Gewustraminer.

Garfunkle. Gerstmann. Or was it Gerstman? That was the name that had been listed as her case officer before Kiev.

She tried to access the cover names.

Cerny, Gerstman, and Gerstmann.

Nothing. The HUMINT system rejected her and returned her to START. She drew a breath. No real surprise that it should fight her. What she was searching for was not within the scope of her official duties. The system wanted to expel people on internet fishing trips. She booted up again. She laid in her codes and reaccessed her information system. She had a higher rank these days than she had had in the dark days of the previous March. So maybe she would be allowed to go farther.

Maybe. Maybe not. Well, that was the binary rule of life, wasn't it? Maybe, maybe not. He loves me, he loves me not.

She pondered for a moment. Questions expanded exponentially within her head.

What had she stumbled onto? How could Janet have seen Michael Cerny?

Logic tried to beat her up.

Michael Cerny is a dead man! You saw his body in the car on a quiet street in Paris. You were at his funeral the same way you were at Robert's. You could go visit his tombstone if you want to, you could go have dinner with his widow and say hi to the kids who don't have a father.

There was an angel on one of her shoulders, a devil on the other, and increasingly a chip of suspicion in each.

Sure he's dead. And the rotten CIA plays unofficial games with stuff like this all the time!

She kept busy at the keyboard, fingers flying a mile a minute now, trying to outflank the US intelligence system. She had a bit of conceit to her. Secretly, she felt smarter than the people who designed these infernal programs. She was sure she could outthink them.

And for that matter, Alex continued to wonder, why was her own apartment bugged? Was the bugging part of a previous operation or part of something ongoing? The bugs were intrusive and insulting. What went on in her apartment was no one's business other than her own. Where was this leading? She saw herself in Kiev with Robert again, the night before he died. She saw herself with Robert again on the last night they spent together in America as an engaged couple deeply in love. She saw herself as —

Back she was in the darkest area of her psyche. She found herself sorting through the events of the previous February, then March, when suicide was imminent until Ben grabbed her one night and pulled her out of it. Thank God for Ben. By all accounts she should have been in love with him. Her guardian angel, if she had one.

She glanced back to the monitor. The screen flickered. Then the window box reappeared again as the enemy.

ACCESS DENIED

She was ready to punch the monitor. There was information somewhere about Michael Cerny, and she now knew she was not going to get it without a fight.

She stood angrily. She folded her arms and stared at the screen. She wasn't ready to go home yet, but she was too frustrated to stay.

So this IS something! Something IS going on, otherwise I would have access! What's so secretive and important that people other than me know it and my fiancé was killed and I nearly died too?

She stormed out from behind her desk, strode to her office door, yanked it open, and — with a startled audible half-scream, half-gasp that carried down the corridor — ran smack into Mike Gamburian so hard that she drove him backward several paces.

"Mike!" she said. "Sorry! You startled me."

"Apologies," he said. "Wow!" he said, rubbing his shin. "You pack a wallop!"

"Sorry!"

"I was just coming to see you." He nodded toward her office. She picked up on the hint. They stepped in and he closed the door.

"What have you been doing in here?"

"Why?"

"My telephone practically exploded ten minutes ago. I got a call from someone named William Quintero at CIA. Do you know him?"

She shook her head. "No."

"Well, he knows you."

"How?"

"What did you try to access?" Gamburian asked, nodding toward her computer. "Within the last fifteen minutes. Were you checking the Guarneri files?"

"Yes. No problem with them," Alex said. "Then I moved on to Michael Cerny. And I got blocked."

"Uh-oh."

" 'Uh-oh' what?" she demanded.

"You got more than blocked," Guarneri said. "You just won yourself a personal invitation over to Langley to explain why you wanted access. They phoned me since you reported to me."

"Then what's going on with Cerny?"

"Alex, if I knew, I'd tell you." He paused. "Honest. Here's what I know: first, you're invited to go over to Langley tomorrow morning and view the file in person at the CIA. Nine a.m. Be there tomorrow morning, not here."

"What's the second?" she asked.

"I've been asked to clear your schedule in this department so you can travel."

"The Venezuela trip?"

"You wish," he said. "Wrong direction, Alex. From the tenor of the very angry phone call I just received, you're on your way to Egypt."

TWENTY

Victor, one of the Russians Janet and Carlos had seen that evening at the Royale, was peaceably having his dinner in a café in Old Cairo when the men in police uniforms arrived to see him. The squad of eight men surrounded him. Although apprehensive, Victor reacted calmly and asked the policemen in Arabic what he could do for them.

The alpha cop, the one with the ranking insignia on his sleeve, that of a captain, responded with equal calm. "Just a few questions, sir," the cop said. "First, could we see your identification?"

Victor drew a breath. The local police, he knew, were a nuisance that had to be indulged in order to get business done, especially these street patrols run by low-level officers. Institutionalized extortion was what it was, but it was also the way things worked in this part of the world. So Victor was sure this was a setup for some sort of bribe. Well, it was the cost of doing business, he told himself, and his own bosses back in Russia paid him well to get his job done. So there was nothing much he could do other than to indulge these local hooligans.

Victor produced his Russian passport and handed it to the head man, who looked at it thoughtfully and then returned it.

"Maybe a word with you in private?" the lead cop suggested. With his eyes he indicated a passageway that led to an alley behind the restaurant. Victor wasn't happy. His meal was only half-finished. These Egyptians were a pain beyond belief sometimes.

Victor rose. He followed the leader of the police squad. They went into a dark lattice-covered alley behind the restaurant. For good measure, Victor carried with him his knife from the dining table.

"Now, captain," Victor finally said. "Let's get directly to your business. What do you and your men want from me?"

The captain's eyes lowered and saw the knife in the Russian's hand. The Arab shook his head. "Please," he said. "There is no need for that." He held out his hand and expected Victor to turn over the utensil.

Victor gave it a long moment's thought. He held out the knife, blade forward, as if deciding what to do. For a moment, he had the mad idea to plunge it through this pest's palm. But he decided against that and gave the knife to the policeman.

The man in the captain's uniform accepted it with a smile. "Thank you for your cooperation, sir."

"Now," said Victor, "perhaps you can finally tell me what you want."

There was a strange moment when nothing happened. Then Victor realized that the police squad had blocked all the doorways to the alley so no one could intrude on their meeting. Doors to restaurants were closed and curtains pulled for the men in police uniforms. In that moment, Victor suffered a flood of hot fear, but it was too late.

From behind him a silk garrote was dropped deftly over his head. Two of the men surrounding him grabbed his arms. They held his upper body as he began to struggle. Someone else hit him in the face with a mallet, shattering his nose on impact, and then another person stuffed a rubber ball into his mouth so he couldn't scream or breathe. Behind him, whoever was working the garrote yanked the noose tight.

Victor's powerful body kicked and fought, but the grip from behind was expert. The narrow cord cut like a razor into the flesh of Victor's thick throat and severed all the important arteries. He was alive long enough to feel the excruciating pain that shot through him and the cascade of blood that burst from his wounds onto his chest.

He dug his fingers into the area where the cord was, fighting for his life, violent curses bottled up in his throat but unable to burst free.

Then he began to slump. Gradually, he stopped kicking. For Victor, there was unspeakable pain, then blackness.

The noose was held in place for an extra half-minute just to make sure the job was complete. Then the body was left on the debris of the alley as the death squad moved away.

Real Cairo police, who were not nearly as efficient as their imposters, would find the cadaver the next morning. An unmarked van would take it to the morgue and ready it for a speedy disposal.

TWENTY-ONE

At her uncle's apartment, Janet stayed indoors. Her uncle was away for the day, catching up with some old friends from the State Department.

She grew restless and depressed by the hour. She made herself a lunch and barely touched it. She watched Oprah, CNN, and a rerun of the previous night's Washington Bullets game. She didn't even like basketball. She watched anything that came across the television screen, but she wasn't really watching.

She read magazines, napped for a while, and browsed through her uncle's library, which had books in seven different languages, including ancient Greek and Latin. She wondered why the old goat spent his declining years on such stuff when he could have been out romancing some wealthy widows. She spent time staring at the prints on the wall, a series of cool but sensual Cubist portraits of women from the 1930s. They weirded her out, as did many of her uncle's tastes, even though the pop diva Madonna owned some of the De Lempicka originals. Well, if Madonna did something it was probably cool, and if her uncle did the same thing it was just terminally eccentric.

But Janet did realize his apartment was her safety island. As far as she knew, no one who was after her knew where she was. And yet, when she wasn't fighting fear, she was fighting boredom.

Alex returned around 7:30 while Janet's uncle was still out. Alex must have quickly picked up her protégée's glum mood — she phoned her friend Ben and invited him to join them for an informal dinner. Ben, working on a law degree, said he could afford a break and would join them.

After a long, depressing day, Janet was grateful for the company.

Alex switched into jeans and pulled on a bulky sweatshirt that could conceal her Glock. She never went anywhere without the gun now; she had developed an affinity for it, like a favorite bracelet.

Alex and Janet met Ben forty-five minutes later at the pub around the corner from the Calvert Arms. They started with beer and ordered burgers, all three of them. Alex's head was still reeling from the day of reading and searching files. And then there was the sudden prospect of being sent to the Middle East.

She wondered who was going to babysit Janet while she was away. She wondered if Ben could look after her a little, but she didn't want to risk setting them up romantically. Then again, Alex didn't entirely trust her own agency, and as she thought it through further, she didn't trust anyone she didn't know in the CIA at all. Not now.

She wondered: could Janet take care of herself? Was Janet's paranoia real or imagined? Could she get out of town for a while, maybe crash with her parents? But if any bad people were really after Janet, would they look there?

Okay, reality check again: even if Janet *had* stumbled across something involving Michael Cerny, it was a stretch to think people were after her. Alex tried to downplay it while she, Ben, and Janet drank beer and waited for the burgers to arrive. But some scary scenarios would not go away. Obviously, by trying to access Cerny's name, Alex had kicked over a hornet's nest.

Their food arrived. They munched their burgers. Janet obviously felt more like a human being for having gotten out and socialized. Though Alex tried to stay away from it, the subject of the Middle East came up in general and Egypt specifically, when Ben asked Alex what her next trip might be.

Janet gave Alex a strange look. Alex gave her a pat under the table as if to say, "Don't press me for details now, I'll explain later."

Ben, aware of the recent tragedy in Janet's life, was always able to reach for some comedic banter. He tried to keep the mood from getting too somber, making jokes and gestures about old 1940s and 1950s horror films involving mummies. He got both Janet and Alex laughing.

"Hey, and then there was the old Steve Martin routine, 'King Tut,'" he said. "You know? The song and dance. Check it out on YouTube if you've never seen it."

"How's it go again?" Alex asked. " 'When I die, don't want nothing fancy but, gimme a royal sendoff like they gave to old King Tut.' "

Ben laughed with them. "Something like that," he said. "I think Steve Martin had a back-up group called the 'Toot Uncommons' for that."

The laughter grew louder, along with a second and third round of Pabst. The mood grew goofier.

"How about this?" Alex said, moving her arms in the quirky parallel aloft motion of the ancient figures on the tombs. "Tell me where this is from. 'All the swell paintings on the tombs,' " she sang, splitting up the other two with her brew-inspired riff on "Walk like an Egyptian." " 'They do some silly dance, don't you know . . .' "

She rolled her eyes and gave it her best Bangles – Susanna Hoffs imitation. The people at the next table applauded.

"Oh, my gosh," said Janet. "Remember that goofy "Walk like an Egyptian" video with everyone walking around funny?"

"I was a little kid," Alex said.

"I was in seventh grade," Ben said. "I was in love with all four Bangles. Still am, actually." Ben laughed. "I should have worn a fez tonight."

They riffed on Egyptian stuff for a while, from Nefertiti to Nasser. Ben did his walking-like-an-Egyptian imitation with his arms and the women laughed again.

"When I was in Egypt, most people walked normally," Janet said with a bittersweet grin. "Until Carlos's car blew up."

"I walked normally too, until I ran into a roadside bomb in Iraq," Ben said. He tapped on his prosthesis. "But then I would never have met Alex if I hadn't been rehabbing on the basketball court."

"And I wouldn't have been leading a normal life again if I hadn't met Ben," Alex said. "God works in strange ways, right?"

They walked back to the Calvert Arms later in the evening, a slight mist falling. Ben walked along with them, and both women felt as if they had exorcised a few demons over the evening. Two hours of beer and laughter with friends, and the world didn't seem to be such a scary place. Janet felt better for being out of the apartment without incident, and Alex had calmed down a little concerning a possible trip to the Middle East.

Let's see if it even happens, she told herself.

Alex watched the street just in case. She didn't see any danger, but she continued to pay close attention to the configuration of cars on her block. That one car that she had been noticing recently, the battered old Taurus, wasn't apparent when she did a quick scan of the block. A good sign perhaps. Potential stalkers, she reasoned, were illusory after all.

They arrived uneventfully at the entrance to Alex's building. Ben said good-bye.

Janet and Alex entered the building.

"Ben's great," Janet said. "He seems like a really good guy."

"He is."

"You're lucky to have him."

"He's a friend, not a boyfriend," Alex answered.

"So he's available?" Janet asked.

"Not for you." She answered with half a laugh. "I might want to grab him for myself eventually."

"Got it. Well, you're still lucky to have him," Janet said.

Against logic, Alex felt mildly taken aback by the question of Ben's availability. "I don't know," she said. "I guess he's available. I know he's got a job, goes to classes at law school on most evenings, and hits the gym two or three nights a week too."

"Wow."

"That doesn't leave much time for dating, I'd guess."

The two young women stood for a moment in the lobby. Alex felt a little ill-at-ease with the personal topics. "Anything else you need to do?" Alex asked.

"Like what?" Janet asked.

"Any shopping?" Alex asked. "Groceries, maybe? How you doing on supplies?"

"I could use a trip to the store," Janet said.

It sounded like a reasonable request. But it was after 11:00 p.m.

"There's a mini-mart a few blocks from here," Alex said. "Would that work?"

"That'd work."

Alex held up her car keys and indicated the steps from the lobby to the garage. "Let's roll," she said.

Their car traveled up the ramp out of the garage. The mist had grown heavier and Alex flicked on the windshield wipers. She pulled into a flow of light traffic and didn't think much of the coincidence when a parked car pulled into traffic about fifty feet behind her.

TWENTY-TWO

Alex drove eight blocks and spotted an open meter in front of the small 7-Eleven. The parking spot was small, but Alex knew she could squeeze her car in.

Janet, feeling suddenly frisky, jumped out of the car before Alex could finish parking. "I'll go ahead and start getting stuff," she said. "See ya."

Alex was about to object, but Janet gave her the crazy walk-like-an-Egyptian arm movement again, followed by something reminiscent of the Steve Martin "Tut strut."

Still a little beery, they both laughed. Before Alex could suggest that she wait, Janet had walked through the automatic glass doors into the store.

Alex parked. Then, in her rearview mirror, past the wiper that cleared the heavy mist, she saw a car pull into a No Parking spot close to the mini-mart entrance. She saw a man jump out of the car, and a second man, the driver, quickly followed. They were a pair of big men in dark jeans and black hoodies. The first man, who wore an overcoat over his hoodie, took one glance in Alex's direction and forged onward into the store. The second man followed close behind. Alex felt a jolt go through her. Terrible vibes. There was something wrong with the way they were dressed, the way they swaggered, the way they went into the mini-mart on Janet's heels.

Heavy outer clothes. What were they hiding?

Alex's mind went into overdrive. In the back of her mind, she was processing something. The headlights of their car had been in her rearview mirror since pulling out from the parking garage. Under normal circumstances, she would have thought nothing of that. But these weren't normal circumstances. Then too there was something about the first man, the quick furtive nature of his movements, that Alex didn't like. She was three-quarters of the way into the parking place when she placed him. He was the man she had once seen sitting in a parked car on the block where the Calvert Arms stood. Alex kicked herself for letting Janet out of her sight for even a few seconds.

Then Alex recognized the Taurus. It had been lurking somewhere, and she had missed it. She was furious.

She ripped the keys from her ignition and threw open the door. An oncoming car blasted her with the lights and honked, splashing her as it swerved and went around her. She ducked back in the rain. The driver yelled some profanity.

Alex gestured back with the New York City turn signal, Robert used to call it, and kept moving. She turned toward the store and ran. Her hand went to her weapon, but she didn't draw it yet.

The suspicious car had left its doors unlocked but there was no one in it. *Oh, Lord protect me,* she thought. The wheels had been left pointing out and the driver had left a space of three feet between his car and the one in front. Standard smash-and-grab getaway parking position. Alex had seen it before and knew she would see it again.

She also knew what she was seeing here. Trouble with a capital T. Alex burst into the store, looking in every direction.

She didn't see Janet.

She didn't see the two men.

She looked down the first aisle, then a second. Still no one. She ran to a third, bumping into a woman with a cart. She turned a corner on an aisle and spotted Janet.

"Hey! Janet!" she yelled.

Janet turned, gave her a big smile. She had a plastic shopping basket on her arm and had already grabbed a few items.

Alex made a sharp beckoning gesture with her hand. "Come here!" Alex hissed. "We got to get going. *Now!*"

"But we just got here!"

"Now!" Alex called.

She tried to make a gesture, pointing, that suggested imminent danger. She stepped quickly toward Janet. As a precaution she pulled her Glock out and held it to her side, as concealed as possible. The last thing she wanted was a close-in gunfight.

Janet started to speak again. *"But—?"*

"We're leaving! Let's go!" Alex demanded. She walked to Janet and grabbed her wrist, pulling her.

Janet resisted. *"What the—?"*

"They're in here! People who are after you!" Alex said.

Janet gasped and swore.

"Move!" Alex said. "We got to get going."

Janet dropped her basket. The two women moved back up the aisle toward the door. Then in front of them, one of the two men from the street came around the aisle. He stopped and stared.

Alex froze first, then Janet.

The man was ten feet away, grinning, his hands in a position to indicate that under his overcoat he had firepower.

Alex looked behind her. As if by instinct, she felt the eyes on her back. She saw that the second man was behind her, about thirty feet away at the end of a long aisle.

"Just give Janet to us," the man in front of Alex said.

"Not a chance!" Alex said. She kept her Glock hard by her leg, out of sight. No point to tip them.

"You *both* want to get killed?" the man asked. He had an accent. Middle Eastern. Maybe.

"I should ask you the same," Alex answered. With her free hand, she pulled out her bureau ID. "I'm FBI. Get out of our way and get out of the store!"

The man spat at her. The spit hit on the floor three feet in front of Alex. Alex knew: it was a diversion. She wasn't falling for it.

Then, bedlam.

The man in front of Alex used both hands to swing up an automatic pistol and wheel it toward them. From behind her, she heard the second man retreat hastily for cover. Alex shoved Janet to the ground with one arm, following her into a low crouch. Once again Alex's quick reflexes saved her, along with having her own weapon already in her hand and set to fire. Precious seconds saved now meant precious decades longer to live.

Alex's right hand came up shooting. Her pistol thundered once with an enormous intimidating bang and then a second one. Her mind was lucid and her reactions crisp, as if the danger to her and Janet clarified her thoughts at the same time.

The gunman sprayed the area. But Alex's first shot hit the man in the upper shoulder. He staggered backward. His coat quickly discolored with a dark crimson. His own pistol fired wildly thanks to the impact of Alex's shot on his body. Five or six shots sprayed from the floor to the shelves to the ceiling.

Alex's second shot had ripped into the right arm of the gunman, just at the inside of the elbow where the forearm met the upper arm. The sleeve soaked with the evidence of a clear hit. The gun flew from the shooter's hand. It hit the floor hard, spun, and skidded.

The man bellowed, then followed with a long, monotonous stream of vicious obscenities. There was a slow-motion reddish explosion of blood and smashed bone from that section of his arm. It sputtered forth. The fabric of the coat had been shredded by the tumble of Alex's bullet.

More chaos. Somewhere in the store, an alarm whooped like a fire siren. From the neighboring aisles, Alex could hear the screams of other shoppers and their frenzied, panicked footsteps as they sought an exit.

Janet crouched low behind Alex. Alex knew that the danger was far from over. The man she had wounded was scrambling backward, groping for his weapon with his left hand as he flailed and knocked dozens of items off the nearest shelves. Then he lost balance and was on his knees, chest heaving, still swearing viciously, profanely vowing to kill both women if he could get to his weapon.

His partner came around the corner behind him, his weapon already out, ducking low, trying to bring the nose of his own pistol in the right direction and aim it toward their female victims.

Alex jerked her Glock toward the second assailant before he could get his bearings. "FBI! Freeze!" she screamed.

He swung around his hand that held his weapon.

Alex fired three times. At the same time, the gunman poured a volley of shots toward her.

Janet hit the floor, flat and screaming. Alex felt and heard two shots hit the floor to her right with horrible loud skidding ricochets.

Another smashed into the shelf display over her head, dispatching shampoo bottles and hairspray in every direction. But her own shots, one of them at least, had found its mark.

The second gunman staggered. Alex had hit him in the upper chest, not mortally, but enough to take him out of the fight.

He kept his weapon in his left hand and could have fired again. Instead, with his right hand he grabbed his partner and tried to hoist him to his feet.

Alex screamed again. "Freeze! FBI! Freeze!" she howled.

The gunman neither froze nor fired again. The fallen man rocked forward to his feet. If he had lunged for his gun, Alex would have shot him. Instead, the second man pulled the first man to his feet. They turned over the remaining part of an aisle candy display. They lurched and staggered toward the door, colliding with other panicked people trying to flee.

Alex whirled and eyeballed Janet, who remained curled on the floor and who was shielding her face and eyes. Alex saw no blood. Neither of them had been hit.

"You all right?" Alex blurted.

Janet gave her a terrified nod. There were tears in her eyes. Her face was white.

Alex made a decision to pursue the attackers.

"Stay here!" she said.

Alex rose to her feet and ran down the aisle. With her free hand, she dropped her FBI ID around her neck on its chain. There were customers down and cringing, and displays were turned over across the floor. Alex pushed and shoved past them.

The cashiers were still ducking low behind the counter. The footing was treacherous, but Alex ran after the gunmen.

She skidded and nearly fell. She hit the entranceway and turned the corner. The more severely wounded man had crashed into the backseat of the car and the second gunman was ducking into the driver's seat. But he held his position.

He was waiting for her. The gun was trained right at her.

Again, Alex was quick and elusive. She dropped down immediately, hit the sidewalk hard, and rolled to her right, bringing her almost parallel to the car. The bullets crashed into the brick and glass of the store structure and window.

An entire pane of glass shattered and fell behind her. The gunman ducked down into the driver's side of the front seat. She felt something cut across her left shoulder and assumed she'd been hit with a chunk of glass. It hurt like a hot knife.

On the getaway car, the driver's side door slammed. The engine roared to life and the vehicle skidded into a brutal backup.

The rain fell in torrents now. The gunman in the driver's seat took one final shot at Alex, firing through the glass. The front window on the passenger's side exploded with the impact of a shot from within the car. The bullet hit closest of all to Alex, about two feet over her left shoulder. If it had found its intended mark, it would have killed her. But it didn't.

In the distance there were already police sirens.

The tires of the escape car skidded in place. Then the car burst forward and smashed into the car in front of it. Alex had a free sight line so she fired her own weapon twice at the car's right tire, but missed. She raised the weapon and fired twice more into the car, trying to hit the driver.

She missed again. She fumbled with her own weapon and it slipped from her hand to the sidewalk.

And then, to her horror, the back door of the car flew open. The man she had wounded, blood all over his face and upper chest, his eyes alive with hatred and pain, raised another automatic weapon in her direction and prepared to kill her.

He was no more than ten feet away, the car door wide open. He lurched out, bracing himself with one leg. But the motion of the car dislodged him. He fumbled wildly, forced to use his "wrong" hand for his weapon.

The car continued to move and knocked him off balance. He fired again at her, and the bullets flew wide over her head as Alex lunged for her Glock.

She grabbed it and raised it, coming up firing point blank with the final three shots of a ten-round clip. Her volley of bullets smashed the man directly in the center of the chest. He spun wildly and fell backward toward the car. Then as the car swerved, swayed, skidded, and cut out into the street, his huge body spilled away from the vehicle for a final time. He was on one knee. There was still life in him and he tried to raise the weapon again.

Alex knew she was out of bullets. She scrambled to her feet, bolted forward and threw a vicious kick at the man's head. Her foot smashed across the lower part of his face and jaw, as if she were drop-kicking a rugby ball.

As the gunman on the sidewalk tumbled backward, the car swerved erratically a final time, careened, fishtailed and went out onto the road, its rear door flying loose until it slammed shut from momentum. The car disappeared down the block and turned the corner with a long screech of the tires as it spun out of control.

Seconds later, Alex heard a crash. Then she heard the police sirens grow louder as they approached, and she looked at the lifeless body of the man she had shot. She picked up his weapon from the sidewalk to safeguard it.

She tried to feel compassion. She felt none. She felt sick instead. Sick, and surprised to be alive.

Breathing heavily, Alex felt a pain and saw that her knee was bloody, even through the denim of her jeans. For an instant a jolt went through her like a electric shock. Staring at her injury, she realized that it was only a bad scrape, most likely from when she had hit the sidewalk outside. And her left shoulder started to sting again, this time hotter and deeper. She reholstered her own weapon.

An armada of DC police cars arrived, lights flashing, uniformed officers jumping out, weapons out.

By reflex, she reached again to her FBI ID, holding it aloft and open so the badge could easily be seen. She was shaken but alive and Janet, though terrified, was safe and physically unharmed.

But as police cars with strobelike flashing lights in red and blue continued to surround her, Alex already knew that the night would be as long as it had been violent. Then she looked at the left arm of her coat and saw that, beneath the rain, the sleeve was crimson from the shoulder down. She looked for the rip from a shard of glass from the store window but she saw none.

Instead, there was a much smaller hole, one made by a bullet. As the realization came upon her, her knees felt rubbery, then very weak.

Two DC cops were suddenly next to her, one male, one female. So was Janet.

One of the cops put an arm around her.

"We'll get you an ambulance," she said. "Or do you want to go in a sector car?"

"What are you talking about? Go where?"

Numbness was starting to sink in. Alex felt faint-headed.

"The hospital," the male cop said.

"Why?" She thought it, but didn't say it. Yet her expression must have asked the same question.

"You've been shot."

TWENTY-THREE

"You were lucky this time," the doctor said softly, looking at the bandage.

"I know," Alex said.

The physician, Dr. Christiashani, was a tall, thin man with a trim dark beard, a fastidious and fortyish Sikh in a turban, a blue tie, and an impeccable white lab coat. He had been in the emergency room when the police brought Alex and Janet in. Janet had phoned Ben, who had driven over, and the two of them now stayed quietly to the rear of the room as the doctor finished with his patient. Alex's back was to her friends.

It was 2:00 a.m. and Alex was seated upright on the edge of a bed at George Washington University Medical Center. She still wore her jeans, but on top of that, her unhooked bra and a hospital robe. Right now, the robe was only half on, as was the bra. Her upper left side was completely exposed as the doctor carefully but authoritatively inspected the bandage on her gunshot wound. A nurse stood by also.

"Ow," Alex said with a little wince.

"Could have been much worse," the physician said.

Dr. Christiashani was indulgent, smart, and calming. His accent was clipped and sounded very last-days-of-the-Raj.

"If the bullet had struck six inches lower, it would have severed a major artery under your armpit," he said. "Another few inches it would have hit you in the heart. More to the right and you get hit in the face. What can I say? You get off with a two-inch grazing to the outer muscle. God did not want you to die tonight."

"Apparently not," Alex said.

"Why do you not wear a bulletproof vest?" he scolded.

"A vest wouldn't have protected my arm. And I wasn't even on duty," she said.

"You drew your weapon. Then you're on duty. The bullet could have hit your heart as easily as your arm."

"What was I supposed to do? Go home and change and come back?"

"I am just saying," he insisted, "I am concerned. You were very lucky tonight. You can get dressed now."

She slid the robe off and rehooked her bra.

Her arm hurt when she moved it, even though an anesthetic still gave it a tingly buzz. She turned and faced her friends. Ben had gone to an all-night pharmacy attached to the hospital and purchased Alex a sweatshirt to wear home. He tossed it to her now. In a way, she felt self-conscious in front of him in just a bra and a bandage, though it was less revealing than anything she wore to the beach.

The sweatshirt was one of those gaudy red, white, and blue things for the tourists, but it fit, and at least Alex was alive to wear it. She pulled it on.

"Do you play chess?" Dr. Christiashani asked.

"I haven't played in years," she said. "Why?"

"My father was a grand master. He used to say, 'At the end of the game, the king and the pawn go into the same box.' My advice is, please be more careful."

"Right," she said.

"You are unconvinced?"

She slid off the bed. Her arm buzzed when she used it. As a counterpoint, her head pounded. She also had a bandage on her knee and various other points on her body that had obviously taken some sort of hits.

The wound to her arm would have buzzed worse but she knew she was on a major painkiller. She had a prescription to continue it, along with antibiotics against a possible infection.

"No, I'm not unconvinced," she said. "I appreciate your concern. As well as your care tonight. Thank you. And I hope your father didn't carry a gun for a living like I do so that he lived to a ripe old age."

Ben stepped forward, and Janet rose.

"He's ninety-two and lives in Mumbai," the doctor said. "He was a soldier for fifty years in the Indian National Army. He retired as a general."

"Bless him," Alex said.

"God already has," replied the doctor.

TWENTY-FOUR

Alex had phoned Mike Gamburian in the middle of the night from the hospital to bring him up to speed. She returned home by 5:00 a.m., Janet with her. Janet slept over at her apartment, the door carefully bolted.

Alex and Janet spent the better part of the next morning at the local police precinct, explaining what had happened and what they had seen. Other witnesses from the mini-mart verified Alex's testimony. The story blazed all over the local news, but without Alex's name attached to it. The public spin: a female off-duty FBI agent had intervened in a crime in progress, and a blazing "Old West–style" gun battle had ensued. The shooting was considered justified. More than justified, in fact. Yet viewers would shake their heads and wonder what was going on even in the capital's better neighborhoods. Meanwhile, Alex could already see what was going to happen. There would be a lot of sound and fury for a day, it would recede a little the next day, and gradually more immediate local stories would eclipse the investigation.

But for Alex, like the long scar on her arm and the twenty-two stitches that had closed it, the story was not likely to go away.

Alex would need to take the rest of the next afternoon to further assist the local police with their initial inquest. Her appointment with a CIA representative was pushed back a day.

The two men who had been killed had yet to be identified conclusively, though an initial investigation suggested that they were both in the United States illegally. A trace on their firearms led to a Harper's Ferry, West Virginia, gun dealer who had accepted fake driver's licenses.

Late the next afternoon, Alex slipped away and sat in a rear pew in St. John's Episcopal Church on Lafayette Square. She found the four walls of her adopted local parish again giving her solace when she needed it, an island of tranquility.

Her thoughts drifted inward. So often in life, people had reacted to her as too perfect; her easy fluency with so many languages, her mastery of so many volumes of literature, her athleticism in high school and college, her looks way above average, and her career paths that always seemed quick. Yet her father had died before she was ten, her mother when she was twenty. Her fiancé had died tragically, and now the scar on her arm was another stinging reminder of her own mortality.

But could anyone ever see the turmoil within?

She felt so vulnerable, so alone sometimes. Increasingly, she found solace in alcohol and felt a subtle attraction for men who probably ought to be locked up. She had a best friend, Ben, but only had him because she had been on the doorstep of suicide one night.

Where was it all going? Above all, as she sat in a pew in St. John's, she asked herself questions, asked God questions, and was waiting for answers.

There are moments in the life of every human being, she knew, when one had the choice to go forward or retreat, to continue on one's path or divert and choose another one. As a teenager away at boarding school in Connecticut, she had first been introduced to the poetry of Robert Frost, and she had always been fascinated by one poem in particular about a path through the woods. The poet had stopped to consider which way to go when the path diverged; he could not see where either new path led. He had chosen the one least traveled, and that choice had made all the difference.

Which path was she on? A good and righteous path? Would she be able to look back on her life in twenty years, or thirty, or fifty years, and be convinced that she had done the right things, that she had obeyed the principles of her faith and been a good and godly person?

She wondered. More and more, projects like Venezuela pulled at her — the chance to work against poverty, disease, and ignorance. And yet on a professional level, she was asked to carry a weapon, be an investigator, be a protector of the innocent. Eventually, she knew, the song became the singer, and she would become not who she wanted to be but what her job and her assignments had turned her into.

Was her path compatible with who she was, what she wanted to be? In the literature she had read, she wasn't James Bond and she wasn't George Smiley. She wasn't Jason Bourne. She wasn't even Jessica Fletcher in the old *Murder, She Wrote* reruns that she had watched as a kid.

And she wasn't akin to any of those thugs at the CIA who could always march forward no matter what the orders were. Sometimes, like now, she just plain thought about things too much.

She listened to the steady rumble of the traffic outside.

One of the church sextons came down the center aisle of the pews and gave her a friendly nod. She nodded back.

In her mind, she replayed the events of the previous evening, every horrible detail. She had a freeze-frame in her mind of how she had cut down the assailant who had aimed weapons at her from the backseat of the lurching car, and she wasn't even sure which shot fired at her had hit her. She knew she would be dead if she hadn't used her own weapon so swiftly. But that didn't mean that today she was any less traumatized.

For the first time, it sank in: she could have been killed. Her own sense of mortality was suddenly very real. It made her shiver. It made her cringe. Was her faith any stronger, or was it starting to come undone?

She wasn't sure of the answer.

She thought back to the events earlier in the year, the catastrophe in Kiev. Then there had been the investigation of the missing Pietà of Malta in Madrid.

She wondered: why was God throwing all of this her way?

Was she strong enough to handle it?

She had no answer.

In her hand was her FBI/Treasury ID and shield. She turned it over and examined it.

Keep it? Chuck it?

Should she move forward or go back? Or should she find some

other path that diverged to an unknown destination through the woods?

Could any human being answer questions like that?

Her eyes were looking straight ahead, toward the altar and the stained glass beyond. But her gaze was really upon an inner world. She was aware of her own breathing, calm and evenly paced. And she was further aware of an extraordinary stillness, almost trancelike, that overcame her.

Once again, she had killed someone. She didn't like the feeling of it.

She closed her eyes.

An old habit kicked in. She reached to her neck and fingered the stone pendant that hung there on a gold chain, the pendant that had replaced the small gold cross she had worn as a child. She held her fingers to it, gripping it between a thumb and a forefinger. It was warm from her skin. Soothing. She allowed time to flow by. She didn't know if it was a minute or five. It was as if she had a foot in two worlds, the physical and the spiritual. Then there was a sound, a clattering sound, that of a door closing. She opened her eyes and looked. She saw the sexton cleaning in the area where a side door led to the vestry and the quarters for the choir.

The trauma was still there, but she felt as if she had turned a small corner in dealing with it. She felt better. Something had changed. For the first time since the previous evening, she enjoyed an inner calm, a sense of peace.

There was no flash of light, no chorus of angels, no dramatic revelation. Rather, when she opened her eyes again, she felt as if God had wrapped himself around her and reassured her. She could live with what had happened. By all she believed in, she had done the right thing.

The question, which had been so perplexing just minutes earlier, seemed so simple now. She had acted in accordance with her faith and her interpretation of morality. She had defended herself and someone she was charged to protect. She had done what she had to do under the circumstances, unpleasant and violent as it may have been.

There then, she told herself. She would, of course, go forward.

She began to think of Egypt.

TWENTY-FIVE

Alex arrived by car at CIA headquarters in Langley, Virginia, on Thursday morning at 8:35. The meeting was in a small conference room on the third floor, west. A taciturn young assistant led her in. There was an oblong table with twelve empty chairs. The walls were bare, painted light green, with no windows. A series of prints on the wall showed embassies in various parts of the world. Near it was a valance, and next to it an American flag in a stand.

Idly, as she waited, she examined the flag. There was a small white tag on it. Made in China. Typical. She sat at the table and waited. Two minutes later the door abruptly opened and three men surged into the room. All three wore dark suits and had ID badges dangling in plastic holders across their ample midsections.

The mere sight of them reminded her of how much she disliked most of these CIA people: frequently wrong but never in doubt. Disliked, she mused, and distrusted.

"Agent Alexandra LaDuca," said the leader, extending a hand. "I'm William Quintero, Assistant Director/DCA, Middle Eastern Affairs. These are my associates who'll also be involved in this case."

He introduced them. Ronald Strauss, who was in charge of technical support for Egypt, Syria, and Jordan, and Miller Harris, whose official title suggested that he oversaw political officers and operations in the same region.

Handshakes went all around and the group of four sat down. The three men were on the opposite side of the table from Alex, with Quintero at the center.

"Well, now, Alex," Quintero said to start, "heck of an incident the other night, wasn't it? How are you holding up?"

"I'm fine."

"The arm?"

"It is what it is," she said.

"You're quite a trooper," Harris said with admiration.

"I'm more of a grouch and a sorehead today than anything," she answered. "Why am I here?"

Quintero looked at her carefully. "Are you up to a new assignment?" he asked. He continued before she could answer. "This is going to dovetail into areas where you've already done some work. So it's not entirely new."

"I'm here," she said.

"And 'happy' to be here?" he asked.

"Obviously not," she said.

"And mentally, you feel 'together'?"

"As much as any of us might," she said. "How's that?"

There was a moment, then all three men smiled.

"It's a strange line of work we do," she said. "There's stress with any assignment."

"Yes, but some more than others," Quintero replied.

"I'm all right," she said. "Tell me why I'm here."

Another short beat, then, "Okay," Quintero said softly. "We're here to talk about your ex-boss, Michael Cerny."

"He was never officially my boss," she corrected. "I was asked by my own boss, Mike Gamburian, to work with him on one particular operation. There was no name to the operation, but it involved Yuri Federov. Kiev. You have files in front of you. You know all that."

"Yes, of course," Quintero said. To his left, Harris was looking at a file that he had opened, glancing up and down intermittently, while to his right, Strauss sat frozen in place, a similar file closed in front of him, his sleek hand upon it.

"But recently you were asking questions about Michael Cerny?"

"That's correct."

"Would you mind telling us why?"

"Curiosity," said Alex.

"Curiosity?" Quintero pressed. "Or maybe something more specific?"

"Such as?"

Quintero leaned back in his chair. "Suspicion, for some reason?"

he asked. "An inkling? Some insidious rumor that you may have picked up from somewhere?"

She took a more aggressive tone in return, truthful but keeping Janet at arm's length. "I worked with Mr. Cerny on an operation that stretched from Ukraine to France and possibly incorporated a massacre in South America," she said. "Several people lost their lives, including my fiancé. It's only natural that I might want a final look at the files of some of the people involved. So I attempted to access those files."

"For what purpose if the operation is over?" Quintero asked.

"I just answered that question," she said. "That operation changed my life. Additionally, Mike Gamburian asked me once again to contact Mr. Federov. It's only natural that I would wish to review."

Quintero listened without speaking.

"Quite frankly," Alex continued, "I'm resentful that I can't access those files. I'm weighing resignation. There are a lot of other things I can do rather than put my life on the line here when I'm not getting the proper support and feedback from above." She could tell from their expressions that her feint had worked. She spoke politely and calmly. "I'm sure you understand."

Three pairs of eyes were steadily upon her.

"Of course," Quintero said. "Let's just not get ahead of ourselves."

"I wouldn't think of it," she said not so politely. "You know as well as I do," Alex added, "that operations evolve. They never completely end. But for personal reasons, I'd like some closure on this."

Quintero snorted. "Well, wouldn't we all?" he asked rhetorically.

He opened the file that sat in front of him and handed several sheets of paper across the table to Alex.

"Sorry," he said. "I have to give you these."

The papers were the confidentiality bonds. She knew the drill. She was about to be brought into a CIA operation, whether she wanted to be or not, or at least continued into an operation that was ongoing.

She looked at the documents. Alex scanned. "The usual crap, huh?" she said.

"The usual crap," Quintero agreed.

She signed and handed the documents back across the table.

"Excellent," Quintero said. He accepted the documents, made sure that Alex had signed the proper spots, and returned the documents to the file.

"Well," Quintero said, "if you're looking for personal closure, you won't find it here."

"What exactly does that mean?" Alex asked.

"Michael Cerny is alive," Quintero said.

"How is that possible?"

"He was wounded in Paris," Quintero said. "You saw right. He was hit as he sat in a car on the street. Our people did a follow-up and took him to a private medical clinic. And as things evolved, we realized, or maybe Michael realized and suggested it, that we were presented with an astounding possibility. Declare Michael dead, ship back to America a body that we bought from a local morgue, and have a cheerful funeral. Then give Mike a new identity, and he has the deepest cover that anyone in the world can have."

"Brilliant," she said, with an obvious edge. "And where did the best-made plans of men with mice-sized brains go off the rails this time?"

"What makes you think it did?"

"I wouldn't be here if things were going smoothly," she said. She glanced to the others at the table. "All four of us know that, and I have a scar in my left arm that tells me that I'm justified to think that."

"Alex, do people ever tell you that you're too clever sometimes and maybe just a bit too sarcastic?"

"Frequently. I've even told myself that from time to time. And my arm hurts this morning, and I'm still flying from the Vicodin, so I'd like some answers."

She caught Harris glancing away, suppressing a grin.

Quintero glanced to the confidentiality bonds, double checking. "You signed everything, right?"

"No. I made paper airplanes out of it. Of course, I signed everything."

Harris glanced at the papers and gave Quintero a nod.

"Michael threw the operation off the rails himself," Quintero said.

"Not with anything he did afterward. Not immediately, anyway. But with what he had done previously."

"Namely?"

"We have a spy case going on in Federal court in Philadelphia right now," Quintero said. "A military engineer has appeared in court in the US on charges of passing classified information to Israel. A man named Solomon Isaacman is charged with selling US military secrets involving information about nuclear weapons, fighter jets, and missiles to Israel in the years from 2003 to 2007. He has been charged with four counts of conspiracy to commit espionage, including disclosing documents relating to national defense and acting as an agent of Israel."

"So he's in custody?"

"He was released on $300,000 bail. His passport was taken also."

"I haven't seen anything in the press about this."

"So far, it's been under wraps because of its sensitive nature. But the Agency feels that Isaacson borrowed several classified documents related to national defense from the army's research centre between 2003 and 2007, took them to his home in New Jersey, where he would then hand over the documents to an Israeli consular official, who would photograph them in the basement. He took documents linked to modified designs for F-15 jets and several others related to nuclear weaponry. Everything was classified as 'Restricted Data.' The documents contained information concerning the weapons systems used by F-15 fighter jets that the United States had sold other countries."

"Which other countries?" Alex asked.

"Well, modified F-15s have been sold to Israel, Japan, Saudi Arabia, Singapore, and South Korea."

"So where does this come back to Michael Cerny?" Alex asked.

"Right here," Quintero said, opening a second file. "Isaacman's handler was someone operating in the United States under the code name of 'Ambidextrous.' Look at this."

Quintero pushed forward a series of surveillance photographs taken at restaurant rest stops along the New Jersey Turnpike. He identified Isaacman in the photograph. With Isaacman was the man that the FBI had identified as "Ambidextrous." "Recognize him?" Quintero asked.

Alex looked carefully. The man she saw looked like a younger version of Michael Cerny, from the years just before she had known him.

"I recognize him," Alex said. "But I don't get it. Was Cerny one of your CIA people or not?"

"Cerny worked for us as an outside contractor for many years," he said. "He was recruited in the Czech Republic during the 1990s. In previous generations he would have been a Marxist and probably a KGB snitch. But by then there was no place for a good young Red to go, so he went into capitalism. Clever mind. Well, you had experience with him so you know. He had nothing to sell so he created his own product by spying on people. His mother was an instructor at the university in Prague, and his father was a dockworker on the Danube who hated educated people. Unofficial marriage, rocky relationship as you might imagine. The son of a dedicated teacher and an anti-intellectual. Do you like that? Just think how screwed up the young man must have been."

"I think I've seen examples," Alex said.

"For the first few years he worked for us he always seemed to have an interesting bag of goods he was selling. He worked out well for many years. He had contacts all over Europe. He brought us useful snippets of gossip from embassies from Ankara to Amsterdam. Had an ear to the ground just about everywhere. So we bought a lot of what he was selling. We sent him to the FBI for a second look, and he passed their inspection too. He'd been involved in a lot of dirt, but nothing that had ever been worked against the United States. So for our purposes he was clean. Don't take this the wrong way, but he was exactly the type of man we liked to recruit."

"I'll take that exactly the way you meant it," Alex said. "And I couldn't agree with you more."

"Anyway, eventually Cerny expanded his range. He wanted his solo sessions. He volunteered to run operations against specific targets for us. Sometimes he even brought us the target and sold us on why we needed to hit it. He started getting expensive, but the yield was always good. Like Federov."

"I assume that Federov might have been a target he brought to you," Alex said. "Rather than vice versa."

"I can't really comment on that."

"That's okay," she said. "I'm assuming I'm correct."

"Should I refer back to my suggestion about your being too clever?"

"If you like."

For a moment Quintero seemed ill at ease with her assumption.

"Don't send yourself in the wrong direction," he said. "We had no reason to suspect there was any vendetta between Federov and Cerny."

"After working with him for how many years?" she asked.

Quintero glanced down for a moment at his files, as if to remind himself.

"Fifteen. And again, Federov had been convicted of felonies in US courts," Quintero said. "He was guilty of far more than we ever convicted him on. He was a tax cheat who owed the government several million dollars, and he was involved in violence in Ukraine that put US lives and interests in jeopardy. He used to run whorehouses, fake charities, and had been arrested for assaulting family members and police officers. Don't make a case for him, Alex."

"I'm not. I'm just saying—"

"Cerny was an Eagle Scout compared to Federov. Cerny wanted to run an operation to put Federov out of business. Cerny may not have been the most shining knight in our court, but matched against Federov, Cerny was a no-brainer. We'd make that same call a hundred times out of a hundred."

"And perhaps that's why the Agency is overdue for reorganization," Alex said.

Quintero sighed. He reached again into his file—his bag of tricks. More show-and-tell. He pulled out more photographs, these in color and of recent vintage.

"When Isaacson was arrested, Cerny went missing on us," Quintero said. "He probably was afraid he would be prosecuted as well. He may have been right, or maybe we would have been willing to let him walk if Isaacson copped a plea and took the fall. We'll never know. But then Cerny started turning up in another operation that we were shadowing. First he was in Beirut. Then Tel Aviv. Then Cairo. And he was meeting with Russians. The man *could not* stay away from Russians."

Quintero laid out more photographs, a nice set from each of the aforementioned capitals. In the photographs she saw Michael Cerny again, flanked by two men whom Quintero identified as Russians, known as Victor and Boris. Both men favored Western suits with open collars. They had a thuggish look about them. Boris was the larger of the two, and each time they were seen with Cerny they appeared to be in the midst of negotiating something.

"Our theory is that Cerny made off with a basketful of goodies to sell," Quintero said. "And he set up to sell them to his Russian friends. We've intercepted a few messages. He shuttles back and forth to Cairo from somewhere else in the Middle East. His code name, 'Ambidextrous,' is a self-congratulatory nod to his own abilities, I'm sure."

"Ambidextrous," she repeated. "Wonderful."

"He probably has the information on a series of memory sticks, which I'm sure he has copied. Our guess is that this is his retirement plan. He'll sell to the highest bidder, but he's starting with the Russians because he knows them. We all know that the Russians are trying to beef up their nuclear clout again, so they'd be prime customers for anything Cerny might have stolen." Quintero paused. "But here's the other disturbing thing," he added. "Cerny's Russians have links to the Mossad."

"Israeli intelligence?" she asked, surprised.

"That's the way we're reading it right now," Quintero said. Then he pushed another file toward her.

"Sit here and read this," he said. "Meanwhile, I'm going for coffee. May I bring you some?"

"I'm fine, thank you."

She accepted the files.

"I'll be back in half an hour," he said. "This should give you some background."

Quintero departed from the room. Alex broke open the seals on the set of files and began to read.

TWENTY-SIX

Alex began her journey through the hardcopy files on Michael Cerny. William Quintero had given her a selection of eighteen cases that Cerny had worked, his entire investigative file within the CIA. Cerny had brought every one of them into the Agency himself on a freelance basis.

Alex looked at the paperwork of the first case:

Case overview: Lester Chamberlain, retired from the CIA, but formerly a low-level case officer assigned to the US Embassy in Vienna. Chamberlain had a Canadian wife named Verna who liked to wander. Verna had had a brief affair with the son of a Russian diplomat during Chamberlain's final posting to Vienna. Was it a setup? A trap?

Resolution: Michael Cerny had interviewed all the principals and determined that Verna Chamberlain had passed along low-level information overheard from her husband and gleaned from unsecured documents her husband had brought home after work. Chamberlain was allowed to retire from government, but with diminished pension.

Alex closed the file and continued to the next one.

Case overview: James Thomas Barlow, Dept. of US Treasury, assigned to Boston, (2001 - 2007). Barlow approached by manager of classical Hungarian music quartet and offered cash to intercede on tax collection. Barlow accepted cash bribes of $1500 and $2500. Hungarians had connections

into political apparatus of governing party in
Hungary.

Resolution: Barlow arrested and terminated
from position with Treasury. IRS investigation
continuing. (9/2009)

Alex scanned this for a moment. Nothing monumental. She moved
through file after file. Cerny's investigations were mid-level stuff, the
type of thing the Agency might buy for inventory or keep on record
in case it became a detail from a larger picture. Alex was looking for
some such pattern to occur.

Onward she went.

She continued past four o'clock, through a take-out iced coffee.
She forged ahead through several more cases. Cerny's work seemed
to be solid. But it was not until she arrived at Cerny's penultimate case
with the Agency that something startled her. It was the case that the
man known as Michael Cerny had been involved in immediately before sending her to Kiev. It was a file that had recently been added to
the CIA's inventory and had been shared through British intelligence.

Case overview: Scotland Yard investigates
death of billionaire spy.

The body of a mysterious Egyptian billionaire
was found below his Mayfair flat just weeks
after accusations that he had spied for Mossad.
The death is part of an ongoing investigation by
a new team of Scotland Yard detectives.

The death of Dr. Ishraf Kerwidi is now being
overseen by Scotland Yard's elite Specialist
Crime Directorate. Dr. Kerwidi, 62, a chemical
engineer, businessman, and a former security
adviser to President Sadat, died on 13 December
2008 after falling from the balcony of his large
flat in Central London. He has been described by
intelligence sources as the "most infamous spy
in the Middle East." Kerwidi had worked closely

with security agencies including MI6, the CIA, the Mossad, and the KGB.

One witness has told Scotland Yard that in the moments after Kerwidi's death "two large men of Slavic appearance," both wearing suits, were seen leaning over a balcony ten flights above his body as it lay twisted and sprawled on a public sidewalk.

Several witnesses told Scotland Yard that they had observed the men seconds after Ishraf Kerwidi's plunge to death. "I saw two men standing on a balcony," said one woman, a Briton. "They were doing nothing, just gazing down. Their calmness struck me as highly suspect. An Indian lady was screaming in the garden. People were rushing around trying to help or call. But these two men were just watching. They seemed pleased, then turned and left."

Family members were highly critical of the police investigation into Ishraf Kerwidi's death. The shoes he had worn on the day he died had disappeared from the inventory of Scotland Yard detectives. The shoes were deemed to be crucial because Ishraf Kerwidi would have had to step into a plant pot and climb over an air-conditioning unit to have jumped over the meter-high patio rail. If he had done so, material such as soil from the plant pots or paint would have been left on his shoes.

Ishraf Kerwidi suffered from leg disfigurement from a previous attempt on his life (*See CIA Ishraf Kerwidi/5 - 23 - 04*; *attempt on life via car bomb*). His widow insists her late husband could not step into the bath without assistance. She also has informed Scotland Yard that her husband warned her three times that he might be murdered. Detectives from the Specialist Crime Directorate have recently been to Rome and Geneva to interview other potential witnesses.

Police have not ruled out suicide. Ishraf Kerwidi had a history of heart problems. He moved to Britain after Sadat's assassination in 1981. Yet Israeli sources maintain that he was murdered by Egyptian intelligence officers for being the Jewish state's most important agent in the run-up to the Yom Kippur War in 1973. Egyptian commentators claim he was murdered by Mossad as he prepared to expose Israel's secrets in an explosive book.

The investigation is currently headed by Rolland Fitzgerald of Specialist Crime Directorate.

Resolution: An inquest was due to be held last month but was suspended because of ongoing investigations. A spokeswoman for the Metropolitan Police admitted that the shoes worn on the day of his death had disappeared, but declined to comment on the family's complaints.

"The reason the investigation has been handed over to the Specialist Crime Directorate is because it is a complicated case and followed a review of the file in January," she said.

The door opened. William Quintero came back into the room and sat down. He sat for several minutes as Alex finished reading the final file. She made special note of the Scotland Yard investigator in charge of the case. Then she looked up from the file, closed it, and handed it back.

"So what do you want from me?" Alex asked.

"We need to apprehend Michael Cerny before he passes information on to his Russians."

"How do you know he hasn't already?"

"We don't. But our theory is that he hasn't completed his transaction yet, or he and his Russians wouldn't still be in Egypt."

"What's taking so long?"

Quintero shrugged. "Conventional wisdom? Cerny and Moscow are haggling over the price. Once they've agreed, there would probably be a cash transfer as well as a transfer of highly classified information."

"Why not exchange them both electronically?" she asked. "Isn't that how it would be done these days?"

"Not at this level," Quintero said. "There would be internet fingerprints all over anything that traveled across the web. Strange as it sounds, it's now cleaner with cash and all the information stored on a powerful flash drive. This all assumes that this is what Cerny is doing."

"And you're not sure?"

"We think," Quintero said. "It's gone as high as the director of the CIA."

"Must be a pretty fancy bit of information that he's peddling," Alex said.

"Must be," he agreed. "Questions?"

"A ton of them."

"Fire away."

"Why me?" Alex asked. "If Cerny was here at the CIA, surely he had a boss. A case officer. You have people who were closer to him to track him down. He must have worked with someone."

"Most recently, he worked with you," Quintero said again, avoiding the question.

"Not to pick out the flea feces from the pepper," she said, "but I was his subservient employee. So who was his boss?"

"He never had the same boss for any two operations," Quintero said. "It's very possibly you who knew him best."

"You fellows certainly run a sloppy operation sometimes, don't you? Eventually, you're going to need to have some woman sit on the top floor and straighten up your various messes."

"Again," Quintero said with a sigh, "I'm here to help clean it up. Same as you. None of the principals who initiated this remain with the Agency. They're all sport fishing in Florida by now. How's that for a reward for burning millions of taxpayer dollars?"

"Typical," Alex said.

"I can't say I disagree with you," Quintero said. "Look, that's why we're asking you to work with us." Quintero paused. "You're one of the few people who has actually met Michael Cerny. Cerny came to us when we wanted to act against Yuri Federov. He was a special consultant with a heavy background in Ukrainian affairs. He seemed a good risk." He paused. "Speaking of Federov, I'm told you've been in touch with him."

"That's correct. He's in New York for some sort of medical treatment," she said. "I'm not sure that he'd be of much use right now."

"But you're not inhibited from asking, correct?" Quintero asked.

She thought about it. "Probably not."

"Good," he said, with an air of conclusion. He stood up from the table. "Now, you're with us on this, correct? You're officially on this assignment?"

"I'm with you," Alex said. "As long as I have the option of calling some of my own shots while I'm in the field."

"You'll be working with a team in Cairo," he said. "We have one of our top Middle Eastern people there. A man named Bissinger, whom you'll meet at the embassy. He'll direct you to your field contact. The field contact is known only by his code name. That's all I can tell you here; you'll be thoroughly briefed when you get there. You'll have the latitude you're asking for, though," Quintero continued. "You've earned it, and you've demonstrated that you use it prudently."

"Then I'm on board. Perhaps against my better judgment."

"This whole Agency operates on people going against their better judgment. Maybe it should be called the Counterintuitive Intelligence Agency."

"What about passport? Identification? Weapon?" Alex asked.

"Before you leave here today, give us a name and birth date that you're sure to remember. We'll have new IDs operational within twelve hours. Have some new pictures taken before you leave here today. Pick them up tomorrow. You'll get a new weapon at the embassy in Cairo. I'm told they've got quite a collection."

"Cool," she said with an edge.

"Have a name that you might prefer?" he asked. "For the new IDs?"

"No," she said. "Surprise me."

"Really?" he asked. She had just surprised him.

"We're inclined to give away subconscious clues to a real identity when we choose our covers," she said. "If someone else picks a name and identity for me, I'll learn it. But at least it won't give away anything."

"Very well," he said, rising from where he sat. "How's your arm?"

"Still attached to the rest of me."

"Good. Keep it that way." He led her to the door. "Now. There's something else you should see. Follow me," he said.

"Where are we going?"

"Private TV screening," he said. "Foreign television, a special show starring one of your favorite people."

TWENTY-SEVEN

Alex and William Quintero walked down a quiet corridor of mostly closed doors, a few with names on them — but primarily numbers. Quintero spoke in a low voice.

"How much do you know about Vladimir Putin?" Quintero asked.

"I know he's the former Russian president and still pretty much running the country," she answered. "Sort of a neo-Stalin for our times."

"That would be Vladimir Putin, yes," Quintero said.

"Well, I read the newspapers and speak Russian," Alex said. "So I know more than your basic citizen but less than your experts. Or maybe I know more than your experts when they're having a bad day. How's that?"

"Pretty good," Quintero said. "And I give you an *A* for self-assurance."

"Sorry," she said.

"Don't be. I like it. Russia and the old Soviet territory are my field," Quintero said. "I speak the language okay. Could never master it, though. I read it better than I can hear or speak it. Learned it as an adult. You probably learned it earlier."

"Boarding school. University. A work-study program in Moscow," she said.

"Boyfriends in Moscow when you were studying?"

"Maybe."

"There you go," he said. "Your file says you're gifted with languages as well as with people."

"The file flatters me. That, or it libels me."

"And you *do* deflect a question well. Okay, Brother Putin is one of the dominant figures of our time," Quintero said as they continued down the hall. "He took a Russia that was bankrupt and coming apart at the seams in 2000 and restored it as a world power. No small trick.

Like him or not, and like most Americans I don't, Putin's brilliant, cunning, vulgar, occasionally charming, possibly sociopathic, and probably the most cold-blooded bastard on the world stage since Stalin or Hitler. On top of that, he's much beloved by his countrymen. So he's here to stay unless we get lucky and some Slavic sorehead shoots him. But I never said that, right?"

"Not to me, at least," she said.

"Thanks. God knows, power loves a vacuum in Russia. Any ruler who's soft gets replaced by a dictator within a few months. It's like the Middle East. How do you hope for democracy where they've never had it?"

She let the question fly off into space without a response. She didn't know a short answer anyway.

Quintero arrived at the door he wanted and unlocked it with a swipe of his ID card. The lights went on automatically as he led her into a small viewing room. There was a large screen on the forward wall and a dozen large chairs. Whatever Quintero had to show her, it was going to be shown on a big screen.

"You're going to be dealing with Russians again in the near future," he said. "I'll get you the proper background files. Electronic transfer. Put it on your own laptop, but be careful to keep it behind your own security wall. Okay?"

"Done."

"Grab a seat," he said. "Any seat."

She did.

"No popcorn," Quintero said as he went to a control panel.

"I'll survive."

Quintero flicked a few controls. The lights went down and the screen came alive with encrypted graphics, codes for what they were about to see. Quintero slid into the chair next to Alex with a control in his hand.

"This is from Russian television. December of 2005. Let me know if you've ever seen it before."

An image came alive on the screen. The colors were faded and distorted, as if from bad video tape. There was an empty conference room on the screen.

"Here's what's going on," Quintero said. "Vladimir Putin appears on television in broadcasts to the Russian-speaking people of the world. That way he reminds people who's in charge. *He* is."

On the screen, Alex could see the figures of various men coming into view and taking their seats at a conference table. There appeared to be five men, all in suits. She caught glimpses of faces but didn't recognize anyone.

She shook her head. "Whatever this is, it's new to me," she said.

"It's fairly new to all of us," Quintero said.

"These appearances are daily occurrences on Russian TV," Quintero said. "Putin holds staged meetings in important-looking conference rooms. In reality, the rooms don't exist. They're sets built with government money and kept at various points around the country. So wherever he is, Putin can give a fake meeting."

"When was this again?"

"December 12, 2005. We recognize the conference room. Or the set. This was recorded at Novo-Ogaryovo."

"Novo-Ogaryovo?" she asked. "That's a new one to me."

"Putin's suburban estate outside Moscow," Quintero explained. "Notice the Christmas tree. Nice homey touch, huh? The 'conference room' is a TV set at Putin's estate."

Alex had already noticed the tree. "Seriously. My eyes are getting damp, I'm so moved," she said. "I'm sure there were cookies baking, also."

"Right," he said. "Cookies made out of his enemies, most likely."

On the screen, five men were sitting at a table. Then Putin entered the room, or arrived on set, and all five bolted to their feet. Putin sat as the camera came in close on him. The president addressed the Russian people. Quintero fell silent and Alex tuned in to the Russian. Instantly, she understood at least partially why she had been led into this room.

In Russian, Putin was discussing Russian-Ukrainian relations. At issue was what had at the time been a major international flap over the natural gas pipelines that ran from Ukraine to Western Europe but which the Russians actually controlled.

Alex thought back. From her knowledge of recent political events in Europe, she recalled that the issue had come up right around the time of the so-called Orange Revolution, the events that had propelled a fledgling quest for democracy to legitimacy in Ukraine. These events had transpired more than three years before her own ill-fated trip, but they had also laid the groundwork for the disastrous presidential visit to Kiev.

Putin continued in his crudely accented, clipped Russian. He was thick-shouldered in his dark suit, self-assured, and had a gaze filled with menace. He was stocky, balding, and had the intimidation quotient of a big mean-eyed cat.

"I am sure that the settlement of the complex issue in the gas sector will have a positive effect on Russian-Ukrainian relations," Putin continued in Russian. Alex understood him fluently, but someone had provided subtitles for the CIA, subtitles which in Alex's opinion could have been more accurate. But she continued to listen.

"It is important that Russia's approach to calculating European gas prices is recognized as justified for all free people," Putin said. "But relations between Ukraine and Russia are assuming a new quality and are becoming a truly transparent market partnership for Russian and Ukrainian natural gas. This is good for all free people."

"'Free people,'" Alex repeated, "there's a laugh."

Then the camera drew back. Not everyone listening to the original broadcast had been free, and the agreement Putin referenced was as transparent as a Siberian blizzard. One of the men assembled around the table — identified also by subtitles in Russian and in English — was Aleksei Miller, the chief executive of Gazprom, the state gas monopoly. Another was Viktor Khristenko, Russia's energy minister.

Then there were two other men identified as members of Putin's political entourage. The camera panned to the fifth man.

Sharply, Quintero hit a control button.

The frame froze on the fifth man at the conference table. Alex gasped.

"Recognize anyone?" Quintero asked.

Alex answered quietly. "I certainly do," she said. "I recognized him right away. Yuri Federov."

"It's nothing new that Putin would be keeping company with

gangsters; he's a gangster himself. But it's pretty impressive even for a big-time hood like Yuri Federov to be seated at a staged meeting with Putin. You weren't invited to that meeting. I wasn't either. The president of the United States wasn't invited. The pope was a no-show; so were Brad and Angelina, and so was Santa Claus. But Federov *was* there, and Putin obviously wanted the camera on him. Why? There must have been a reason. And your boy Federov must have had a fair amount of juice to get his butt at that table."

"I'll say," Alex said, still stunned. "Why didn't anyone show this to me earlier? Before the trip to Kiev, for example?"

"Slowness of sifting and interpreting raw material," Quintero said. "This clip has been in inventory for two years, but just came out of 'analysis' three weeks ago. One of our resident Russian chicks went through it and tagged it with the names of all the people in it. When I knew you were coming over today, I ran Federov's name through the records and spotted the new entry. I thought you'd be interested."

"You thought right. Thank you."

"Next time you see Yuri Federov," Quintero said, "maybe you can ask him how he happened to be breaking bread at the top table."

"On the contrary," Alex answered thoughtfully, "I've spent a decent amount of time with Federov. Never once did he ever mention that he had actually met Putin, much less knew him. Doesn't it surprise you that he's never mentioned it?"

"Considering we all know that he's always trying to get you in bed, yes," Quintero said. "Power. The ultimate aphrodisiac. I'm *amazed* he never mentioned it."

"For some reason," she said, "he probably didn't want me to know. That's interesting right there. So when I see him, I'll be sure never to mention it . . . until just the right time."

Quintero let his clip roll again. It neared conclusion as the camera panned in on an unsmiling cobra-eyed Putin. Putin finished his statement, then stared mirthlessly into the camera. Then he eased into a hard, cold smile. Not a smile of joy, more like a landlord finally evicting a troublesome old widow.

"S Roždestvom Khristovym i S nastupayušèim Novym Godom!" the president of Russia finally said from behind his sinister grin.

Then the clip was finished, the screen went blank, and the lights came up automatically.

"What was that at the end?" Quintero said. "Sounded ominous but I didn't get it."

"He wished us all a Merry Christmas and a Happy New Year," Alex said. "The thing is, coming from Vladimir Putin, it sounds like a death threat."

TWENTY-EIGHT

Before leaving Langley, Alex spent some time with a man named Thomas Meachum in the Technical Resources Division. Meachum was in charge of preparing her documents for her trip. Meachum led her through a photo area where new passport and license photos were taken. In keeping with normal procedure, Alex changed her hair and her expression from shot to shot. Tech Resources also had a variety of women's blouses and tops to change in and out of. For her driver's license, she wore a summer tank top. For her passport, an office-style blue blouse with a jacket.

She was equally careful to remove the pendant from around her neck, the one with the praying hands that she had acquired in Venezuela. Then, giving it greater thought later in the day when she returned home, she placed the pendant in her jewelry box. No point in taking extra chances and risk identification through a unique piece of jewelry. For the duration of the case, she would do without it.

The next morning, Alex selected an itinerary to Cairo.

While she would have loved to have chosen a direct nonstop from the United States, she reserved, instead, a seat on an Air Canada flight to Toronto from Washington. From there she found a pair of Alitalia flights that would pass through Rome. She kept her reasons to herself for that specific route. The Agency allowed her to book herself through in business class rather than the dreadful economy class that had recently turned into a form of latter-day steerage.

She left her apartment and went to a newsstand. She purchased fifty dollars' worth of phone cards. Then she walked several blocks until she found a coffee shop where she had never been before. Making sure no one was on her trail or able to listen in on her cell phone, she used a public phone and called Joseph Collins in New York. With regret, she confirmed that her impending visit to Venezuela would have to wait until early the following year. Collins had no issues with that. She also asked, as a special favor, if she could lodge a close friend at the East 21st Street apartment.

"Who's the friend?" he asked.

"A girl who's in a bit of trouble with some bad people," Alex said. "She needs a place to stay out of view."

"Well, as I mentioned, my son is out of the country for another several months," Collins said. "I'm sure it will be no problem."

She then phoned Don Tomás and asked Janet to pack immediately. Alex would be away indefinitely, she explained, but there was someplace safer that Janet could stay.

She had one more call. This one would max out one of her phone cards. The call went to Rome where she arranged to have a dining companion on the evening she would be passing through the Italian capital.

Alex accompanied Janet to the bank, where she withdrew enough money for a month. In the afternoon, Alex purchased a new cell phone and paid cash in advance for three month's service. She gave the new device to Janet.

Later in the day she and Janet crowded into the backseat of her car and kept low to avoid any watchers. Don Tomás drove them to Union Station in Washington where they took a train to New York. In the station Alex visited a locksmith and duplicated the keys to Christopher Collins' apartment. Then they took a cab to 21st Street. Alex installed Janet in the apartment. She also introduced Janet to Lady Dora Rose, the marginally daffy proprietor of the building. Alex explained to Lady Dora that Janet had recently become estranged from a man in another city who was prone to violence. It was not altogether a lie. Then, still working from her own cell phone, Alex phoned Yuri Federov. Federov, when he answered, was just leaving one of his doctor's clinics. He sounded pleased to hear from Alex so soon again.

"I'm in town," Alex said.

"In New York?"

"Is there another town?" she joked. "As it's turning out, I might get transferred here."

"Ah! I envy you. Some handsome, wealthy man will spot you and marry you in a heartbeat. I envy him, with such an extraordinary wife."

"That's the distant future," Alex answered, playing along. "I'm in town with a girlfriend and I need a favor or two in the immediate future. I'm also willing to do one in return."

"Name it."

She asked if she and her friend could have an audience with him as soon as possible, with Paul Guarneri attending also.

"Would this evening work?" Federov asked.

"That would be excellent."

"Paul and I have two tickets to the hockey at Madison Square Garden," Federov said. "New York Rangers against Chicago. There are several Russian players."

"After the game then?" she asked.

"Nonsense. Come with us."

"You said you had *two* tickets. Aren't those games sold out way ahead of time?"

"I have friends," Federov said. "So does Paul. Are you carrying a gun? What is your country coming to? They have metal detectors now at sporting events in America."

"Yes, I have a gun. I also have a federal permit."

"Then you're okay. Paul has a New York permit. I'm walking around defenseless, however. I feel naked. How do you like that, huh?"

"Not very much," Alex said.

"Wear something sexy," he said, "in addition to the gun. Meet us at the Seventh Avenue entrance, okay?"

"Okay."

Two tickets turned into four within two hours of game time. Federov had seats three rows behind the Rangers bench in the $1500-per-seat territory. Janet had never been to a professional ice hockey game before, much less in the "connected" section with a pair of wise guys. The Rangers won 4 – 2 in a game memorable for forty minutes of fighting penalties. One of the Russian stars scored two goals and handled himself well in a brawl. Federov went wild like a kid. Both Janet and Alex savored the experience.

After the game Guarneri's driver, a young man named Anthony, waited in a stretch Cadillac at the corner of Seventh Avenue and 33rd Street. They all piled into the car, which drove south down Seventh, then turned east and crossed the Brooklyn Bridge. Twenty minutes later, they arrived outside a small Italian restaurant in Red Hook named Margherita's. The restaurant's kitchen was closed to the public by that hour but remained open for a selected clientele. Guarneri's car and driver waited outside, parked next to a fire hydrant with the engine running.

The woman who owned the place, Margherita herself, came out and greeted Paul Guarneri with a hug. She was a small gnomelike woman shaped like a bottle of Chianti. She had gray hair and gushed over Paul. She alluded to knowing Paul since he was a boy. She was just leaving.

Over veal and a light red wine from Sicily, Alex eventually got around to what she wished to discuss.

"Against favors past and present that I might do for either of you," Alex began, addressing the two men. "I wonder if either of you could do me a favor while my friend Janet is in New York. I need to be away for what may be a few weeks."

Both Federov and Guarneri settled in to listen.

Alex began. "As you may know, Janet is her real name. But it's all of her name you'll need to know unless she chooses to tell you more. And I've already advised her not to, for her own protection. She's in some trouble and needs looking after. Normally I'd see to it myself, but her situation is so delicate that I don't have time to work out something myself. I need to take a work trip to the Middle East," Alex said. "I leave within a few days."

"So you want us to watch over her for you?" Federov asked.

"Yes. I wonder if you would establish some security around Janet for me," she said. "Make sure nothing happens to her. She has some people who wish her harm. She needs a bodyguard. At least one, maybe a couple."

"I might be able to arrange something," Federov said, "but I am powerless in this city now. I don't live here, and I don't know the right people. Further, I will be going back to Switzerland very shortly."

But Guarneri started to laugh. He had a couple of young men in his organization who specialized at such jobs, he said.

"Your men need to be respectful as well as protective," Alex said. "They should be married men with families and not inclined to socialize."

"I have the right people," he said. "They know better than to mix pleasure with business. They can arrange with her a time when she goes out each day. And they will accompany her. Maybe between the hours of noon and three. Then again in the evening when she desires it. They can also inspect her apartment when she reenters to make sure no one is inside waiting."

"They'll need to be armed," Alex said.

"That goes without saying."

Federov glanced at Janet, then back at Alex. He smiled. "What has this nice young woman done to get in such trouble with so many bad people?" Federov asked.

"She saw something. Or she thinks she did. That's all I can tell you."

"You work for a government security agency," Guarneri said, probing gently. "I would be happy to arrange protection for her. But why can't the government do it?"

"In this case," Alex said, flattering them, "I trust you more than I trust them."

Guarneri's lips parted, and he flashed his expensive teeth. "Why do you trust *me* more? That's a good one."

"I trust you more, Paul, because you want my help in the future with your Cuban situation. I'm prepared to advise you informally on that, perhaps even accompany you to the island. That's not something you can purchase or obtain somewhere else."

She paused and, from his delighted expression, realized that she had pressed the proper buttons.

"Again, I need to maintain certain professional ethics. I won't tell you how to *break* the law, and I refuse to advise you how to *avoid* the law. But I can guide you in ways to attain what you need *within* the law. That has an extra benefit to you since any profit you might obtain you will not have to hide."

Guarneri nodded. Contentment came across his face. Simultaneously, a look of amusement went across Federov's. Janet grinned innocently.

Then, "All right, then. We have an agreement," Guarneri said. Guarneri lifted his wine glass and held it forward. A moment later, three other glasses clicked with his.

After dinner, they walked in pairs the short distance to the curb, Janet and Alex walking ahead, Federov walking several paces behind them with Guarneri.

"I've never been with such dangerous men in my life," Janet muttered, "and never felt so safe at the same time."

"Just go with the flow," Alex said, "and don't get too used to it. Hopefully, if I accomplish what I want to accomplish in Egypt, you'll be safe when I return."

Anthony, the driver, sprang from the car when he saw the young women approaching. He opened the door and ushered them and their escorts into his vehicle. They sat comfortably in the back as Anthony then navigated the traffic to Alex's apartment building where both women got out.

In bidding each other good night, Federov stepped from the back of the limo and stood on the street with the two women. Guarneri remained in the car. Federov embraced Janet as a new friend. Alex clasped his hand and embraced him in a quick hug also, then turned to go.

But Federov held her arm. Impetuously, he pulled Alex back to him and fully surrounded her with his massive arms. He pulled her into a strong embrace. He planted his lips to hers and gave her a long powerful kiss, one she initially tried to resist. Then, for reasons even she couldn't explain, she felt a tremor inside her, a feeling she knew she shouldn't have felt, and her resistance melted. She went along with it. She completely let him have his way until, several seconds later, he drew back from the kiss and released her, astonished, into the cold night.

"See you soon again," he said.

It took her a second to gather herself. "Soon again. Good night, Yuri," she said. "And thank you."

Janet and Alex walked to the doorstep of the brownstone. The limousine stood guard, not moving, till the women were inside.

"I think that big Russian hood likes you," Janet said on the stairs.

"Much too much," Alex agreed.

"Is that cool or is it gross?" Janet asked.

"Both."

Alex stayed over in New York at the apartment on 21st Street. Later the next morning, she slipped off to a small Episcopal church, one she had always liked, near Gramercy Park, to meditate and say a small prayer. She always found churches particularly restful. When she returned to the apartment she noticed that there was a Lexus parked next to the curb in front of the steps to her brownstone.

Alex knew the driver was watching her. He was a rugged-looking guy with a very New York face, about thirty years old.

Just an interested male, she wondered, or something more ominous? This carried an echo of the block surveillance that her apartment building had endured in Washington.

Her hand drifted to her weapon as the Lexus window rolled down. But the man gave her an engaging smile and held up his hands to show that they were empty. He meant no harm. Cautiously, she approached the car.

"Are you Alex?" he asked.

"It depends who wants to know," she said.

He had a Brooklyn accent so thick she could carve it with a knife.

"I'm Calo," he said. "I work for Mr. Guarneri."

"Ah, then I'm Alex." They shook hands. "Keeping watch?"

"Yeah," he said with a grin. "That's what I was told to do. Nice day, huh?"

"Beautiful," she said.

"Don't worry none about your girlfriend. I'm equipped. See?"

He parted the front of his windbreaker and revealed a nine millimeter automatic holstered under his arm. The gun had a massive silver frame. A cannon.

"Just don't get in trouble with the New York cops," Alex said.

He laughed. "Hey, forget about it," he said. With his other hand, he reached to an inside pocket. He produced and flipped open a NYPD badge. "I *am* a cop," he said. "I moonlight in security and doing bodyguard work."

"Beautiful again," she said. "Stay safe."

"Yeah. You too."

She took the train back to Washington, arriving in the early evening. The next morning, she was back in Langley and connected again with Thomas Meachum, the ID expert. From a file in his office, Meachum pulled an assortment of freshly minted new documents, all with the most recent photographs of Alex. On top was a forged Canadian passport in the name of Josephine Marie LeSage. It had been backdated to reflect an issue in 2008. Various travel stamps had been impressed into it from England and Ireland, in addition to Canada.

Alex looked at it and began the process of memorizing her new name and date of birth, as well as her cover story. For the purposes of Cairo, she was a Canadian university professor, a single woman, on sabbatical and spending a holiday visiting the antiquities of Cairo and the Nile.

"I assume this will jibe with Canadian records?" she asked. "In case there's a problem?"

"Canada's a friendly country, so yes," he said. "Usually."

"Thanks for the ringing endorsement," she said.

She carefully examined the passport. She smirked at the new pictures, taken the day before. Not bad. She was now fifteen months older and had been born in Ottawa, eh? Her newest alternative universe took shape.

She sorted through the rest of the envelope. There was an Ontario driver's license and two credit cards along with an ATM card from the Bank of Toronto, all in the name of the fictitious Josephine.

"I think I'll go by 'Jo' for short," she said.

"Whatever, Jo," said Meachum.

He gave her a selection of pens. She signed everything, alternating pens. Using his skilled hands, Meachum then put some scuff and age on all the documents.

"Which passport do I leave the United States on?" Alex asked.

"Your American one," he said. "I cross-checked your travel plans. In fact, your instructions are a little complicated. You're to fly to Toronto first on your US passport. We have a secure mail envelope. After you've gone through Canadian immigration, you'll rendezvous with someone from our consulate in the Toronto airport. He'll approach you and introduce himself as Ken, and he'll say that he works in Detroit. We have an envelope ready. Give him your US passport in the envelope." Meachum showed her the envelope, a padded manila one about four by six. "It will be returned to us via a diplomatic courier. Thereafter, you're Josephine, a nice girl from the Canuck Midwest."

"Go, Leafs," she said.

"That's the spirit. We worked things with the Alitalia reservation, also, so you can check in for the trans-Atlantic flight as the Canadian woman."

"Got it," she said.

The afternoon she spent packing and purchased a few guide books on Egypt, as well as a phrase book. She stopped by her doctor's office. The wound to her arm was checked. It seemed to be healing properly. It was fitted with a new bandage. There was no lasting damage but some scar tissue would remain. That evening, she played basketball and had dinner with Ben at the hotel pub across the street.

Then next morning she was at Dulles International and caught her midmorning flight to Toronto.

She rendezvoused easily with her contact, Ken, at the Toronto International Airport. She gave up her United States passport to him, then killed a couple of hours in one of the airport bars, reading, drinking too many glasses of wine, and waiting for her departure.

The ten-hour Alitalia flight took her across the Atlantic, down across Western Europe, and into Rome, where she arrived the next morning. She had booked a small suite at the Hassler Roma, another upscale lodging on the American taxpayer's dollar. The hotel was situated just above the Spanish Steps in the heart of the Eternal City. After clearing customs and immigration, Alex took a taxi there, arriving shortly before noon.

Fortunately, the hotel allowed her an early check-in. She was able to grab a shower and then lay back for what she hoped would be a short nap.

TWENTY-NINE

She blinked awake several hours later and looked at the clock by her bedside. It was almost 6:00. For several seconds she couldn't figure out which 6:00 it was. Or where she was.

Then gradually she realized. It was evening. The disorientation of trans-Atlantic travel had caught up with her. She came to her feet. There was a coffeemaker in the kitchen area of her suite, and she put it to use.

She sat by a window and sipped coffee. The view of Rome from the Hotel Hassler had taken on the light blues and misty yellows of evening. From her window Alex watched the city grow darker and more vibrant as the evening approached.

She went to the hotel dining room at seven, early by Italian standards, but her dining companion that evening, Gian Antonio Rizzo, had made concessions to Alex's circadian rhythm.

Carlo, the ramrod erect and proper maître d', met her at the entrance to the dining room. She gave Rizzo's name. Carlo managed a low bow and showed her to a reserved table set for three.

She sat. Then, moments later, Gian Antonio Rizzo appeared, arms wide in a gesture of reception. A smile swept across his face. He was dapper in a light brown suit that almost perfectly concealed the ever-present pistol that he wore on his hip.

"Well, well, well," he said, greeting her in English.

She stood and let him embrace her. He kissed her on each cheek, he released her, and they sat.

"So?" he asked at length. "This hotel is usually up to my high standards. Is it up to yours?"

The hotel was lavish, one of the most distinctive in Rome. She took his question with several grains of salt. "It's excellent," she said.

"Ever stayed here before?" he asked.

"No, I haven't."

"But you'll only be here for overnight?"

"That's correct."

"Well, that's a shame," he said. "I have a formula. An equation, as you will. Gian Antonio's Rule of how to stay in a hotel and be remembered forever."

"Leave bullet holes in the walls of your room?" she asked. "Or a body under the bed?"

"Very funny," he said, "but that's not quite the effect I was after. I mean, how to be remembered *favorably*. Here's what you do. You book for a week. On the first day give them your order for breakfast, exactly what you want and the hour you want it. Tell them what kind of jam or mustard you like, what sort of coffee or tea. Tell them which newspapers you want, I suggest the best local newspaper, *Le Monde* in France or *Il Messassero* or *Il Corriero della Sera* here, plus the American one, *The Herald Tribune*. Don't ask for *USA Today*; it's only the American peasants who read that."

"I get my news off the internet," she said. "Maybe three or four sites per day."

"Of course you do. We all do. Don't be silly. That's not the purpose of this. Order the newspapers anyway."

"Okay," she said, laughing.

"Give each doorman a ten-Euro note when you arrive. Learn the name of the room service manager, the concierge, and the desk manager and give each one a twenty when you arrive and when you leave. Take at least two saunas. You're a woman, so be seen at least in one outfit with a daring skirt and boots in the middle of the day. In your case, swim at least once so the staff can get a good look at your fine figure. Have dinner or cocktails prominently with at least three different men. Always order the same cocktail and have the concierge book your dinner reservations away from the hotel. Come back in a year, and they will remember you."

When she stopped laughing, she responded. "Gian Antonio, I don't know what I'd do if I didn't have you to guide me through life," she said.

"Oh," he said modestly, "you would survive most likely. Some people do. Just not as long or as well."

"Who's the third?" she asked, indicating the third place setting. "Who's joining us?"

"Ah!" he said. "Good that you inquired! A young lady. A friend of mine, very close. She was an intern with the police in Rome; now she's studying art, but she might want to do a career in forensic sciences. So I'm teaching her the ropes."

"Lucky her," said Alex.

"Yes, very lucky girl," Rizzo said with mock conceit, or at least Alex thought it was mock. "Knowing me is better than three years at any university. And learning the black arts from me is, I suppose, much like learning piano from Mozart." Alex laughed, to his obvious pleasure. "But, my heavens," he continued, "she's young, so who knows? Even she doesn't know what she wants to do. Her name is Mimi."

"As in Puccini's *La Bohème*," she said, playing one of her best Italian cards and continuing the music motif.

"As in *La Bohème*," he conceded with a nod. "In the future you should come by Rome, and I'll take you to the opera. The greatest opera house in the world is here in Rome. Compared to the Italians," he said with all the humility he could muster, "the French, the English, and the Germans sing like second-rate canaries. And the Americans don't sing at all."

"I'd love to do that with you sometime," she said.

"Sing like a canary?"

"No, attend the opera in Rome," she said, engaging his line of dialogue. "I can't imagine the price of good seats at the Rome opera these days."

"Oh, I never pay," he said. He playfully raised his brown eyebrows. "The tickets don't cost anything if you work it right," he said over the top of the menu as he glanced at it. "It's all a matter of whom you know. And *this* Mimi," he continued, bringing the conversation back to *La Bohème*, "*my* Mimi, is much healthier and more fit than the one who perishes of mezzo-soprano disease in Puccini's act five. I'm happy to report this. And from the appearance of you," he said, examining her as he ran his gaze across her bare shoulders, "you would appear to be, also. Fit and healthy."

"I'm in good shape, in good spirits," she said. "Sorry to have only one night in Rome. I go on to Cairo tomorrow."

"Cairo?" he said with no humor whatsoever, turning over the concept. "*Cairo.*"

"Ever been there?" she asked.

"Many times." He paused. "Officially and unofficially. Noisiest city I've ever visited and I've visited many."

"Noisy?"

"The racket on the street is beyond belief," he said. "Take earplugs."

"Sorry, I don't have any."

"Get some here at the hotel pharmacy. You'll be pleased you did. You'll thank me later."

"I'll try to remember," she said.

"What's your business in Cairo?" he asked, his eyes narrowing slightly. "Don't tell me you're fluent in Arabic now that I haven't seen you for several weeks, and about to run a one-brave-lady operation against the whole bloody jihad."

She laughed. "Not a chance," she said. "Seriously, it's starting to smell more Russian than anything."

"Ha! Well, you're becoming a bit of an expert there if you catch my drift."

"I catch it, and I wouldn't say that you're wrong. So you're 'mentoring'?" Alex asked, going back to the place setting that remained unattended.

"You could say so," he said. "Delightful girl. I'm enjoying it."

"So it's more than professional?" she asked.

"You could say so," Rizzo said again.

"And we can still speak freely when she arrives, if she arrives," Alex said.

"Absolutely."

"I ask because there's a bit of shop talk to get through."

"I reckoned that ahead of time," Rizzo said, "and I asked Mimi to come by at seven thirty. I hope you don't mind."

"Far from it," Alex said. "That's perfect."

A waiter arrived to take an order for predinner drinks. Alex was hardly in the mood for another boozy evening, but allowed Rizzo to talk her into a Prosecco, which actually worked very well. Alex moved to business.

"One of the positives of the operation we just completed in Madrid," she began, "was that for the first time, it allowed me to make some extensive personal contacts in the European intelligence community. Similarly, I had a very good relationship with an agent who worked for the Chinese service, the *Guojia Anquan Bu*."

"I remember," Rizzo said.

"Two days ago in Langley, I was shown a file about an Egyptian spymaster who went to his death out a window in London. One of those 'jumped-or-pushed?' cases."

"What was the man's name?"

"Dr. Ishraf Kerwidi," she said. "He had links to several intelligence agencies."

"I know of him, and I know of the case," Rizzo said.

"In the report that I read, the name of one of the investigators rang a bell with me," she said, "Rolland Fitzgerald."

Rizzo was nodding. "Yes. The young Englishman from Scotland Yard. Pleasant fellow. He didn't contribute much in Madrid, but I rather liked him."

"Would you be able to contact him?" she asked. "Pick his mind a little. I can forward to you by secure internet a copy of the report I'm working with. See if there's anything further he can provide."

"You don't want to contact him directly?"

"No," she said. "Mr. Fitzgerald might be more inclined to share an extra detail with another member of a European service, rather than an American. Additionally, if I'm on my way to Cairo, I don't want to raise any extra flags."

Rizzo stared down at his hands, not answering but thinking. Then his gaze shot back up to meet hers. "And you want me to pass along any extra details that I can discover without revealing that I'm passing it along to you."

"Yes," she said. "Any small detail might be useful. But I also do not want to call any additional attention to myself by inquiring about a high profile spy case that touches upon the Egyptians."

"So Fitzgerald should not know where the inquiry is coming from. Or where his information is going?"

"That's correct," she said. "It's not that I don't trust Fitzgerald, but who knows where his own contacts are compromised? If you make the inquiries, he won't think much of it. Dr. Kerwidi used to live in Rome. If there's a further inquiry from an American, he'll be more guarded."

"I'll contact him for you," Rizzo said. "Send me the information you have and give me two or three days to run things around. Would that suffice?"

"Yes, it would. You're an angel," she said.

"Or a demon," he answered, "to go along with a request like that! What else before Mimi arrives? Anything?"

"Yes," she said. "You're European, you were in law enforcement, and you've worked in the same type of fields as I have. Have you ever been to Russia?"

"Three times in the last five years. Twice on assignment. Once to attend a funeral of a friend who died mysteriously. That should suggest something right there."

"How much do you know about Vladimir Putin? And Russia under Putin?"

"Aside from what we all know?" he asked.

"Yes."

Rizzo's expression went faraway and journeyed back after several seconds. His face grew serious. "I can tell you what Europeans in law enforcement know and are talking about," he said. "A few cases that are discussed in private circles."

"That would be a good start," she said.

"Just recently I was speaking to one of my other contacts at Scotland Yard," Rizzo began. "He tells me that the British are seeking the extradition of one Andrei Lugovoi from Russia. He is to face a homicide charge in the poisoning death of former Soviet agent Alexander Litvinenko. Litvinenko was a former KGB operative who became a prominent dissident opposed to Russian President Vladimir Putin. The people trying to kill him used a radioactive substance called metalloid polonium 210. They broke into his home and hid it there, gradually poisoning him with radioactive contamination day-by-day. Ninety percent of the world's polonium 210 comes from a single facility in Russia. Scotland Yard found traces of polonium 210 not only in Litvinenko's home in Britain but also in Hamburg, at locations visited by Lugovoi's associate Dmitri Kovtun, the day before Kovtun and Lugovoi attended a meeting with Litvinenko in London. It is theorized that Kovtun and Lugovoi shipped the chemical from Russia and infiltrated Litvenenko's home. But this was particularly messy, this case, because maybe another two hundred people came into contact with the polonium 210. These Russian hoods are like that Colombian cocaine gangster who blew up an airplane with a hundred people on it to kill his own victim."

"Pablo Escobar," she said.

"Yes. Human life means nothing to beasts like them. Only terror and death and the ability to get their way mean anything."

"Any chance of the case being resolved?" Alex asked.

"Very little. The Russians and the British have so far not agreed on much about the case. The Russians suggest that Litvenenko's murderer is more probably to be found among London's community of exiled Russian dissidents and expatriates. This is nonsense, of course. Nothing like this happens without Putin's approval."

Alex's eyes drifted from the table she shared with Rizzo. At the next table a roast duck was being carved for what appeared to be a Chinese couple.

"There was a story out of France last year," Rizzo continued somberly. "The well-known Russian human rights lawyer, Karina Moskalenko, found mercury in her car. Moskalenko had pursued the Russian government in international courts for human rights abuses. She works out of France now, Strasbourg, I think, since Russian prosecutors sought to disbar her and destroy her work in Moscow. Before authorities found the poison, Moskalenko had complained of deteriorating health. Does this sound familiar?"

"It sounds similar to the case you just mentioned," she said.

"Exactly. And Litvinenko was once Moskalenko's client. Interesting?"

"Very," Alex said. "We're not too far removed from the era when the Russians tried to smuggle a live body out of Rome in a trunk, are we? Or when they stabbed a Bulgarian dissident in London with an umbrella with a poison tip."

"Not far at all," Rizzo said, finding a perverse humor in it. "Same dog, new tricks. Where's James Bond when we need him, right? *From Russia with Love*. One could do a modern sequel called *From Russia with Lovely Polonium Tablets*," he said. "I dislike the new James Bond, by the way. Daniel Craig. Makes Bond look like a homicidal thug. He behaves like a bouncer in a Corsican mob joint. But what do I know? All I know about movies is that I don't enjoy going to see them anymore."

Still no Mimi, which was fine. A beautiful young waitress appeared wordlessly and refreshed their glasses of Prosecco. Rizzo gave her an adoring smile, then turned back to Alex to dwell further on politics, death, and assassination.

"Moskalenko was a very high-profile target," Rizzo said. "She had won thirty cases of rights abuses against Russian authorities before the European Court of Human Rights in Strasbourg. Her offices and her assistants have another hundred pending. Moskalenko represented the jailed former oil billionaire Mikhail Khodorkovsky whom Putin had imprisoned, as well as the former world chess champion Garry Kasparov, who now leads anti-Putin opposition in the old Soviet. Moskalenko also once represented a woman named Anna Politkovskaya. She was a journalist, but she was shot to death two years ago as she was entering her house in Moscow. Moskalenko was poisoned just as she was set to travel to Moscow to take part in pretrail hearings for the Politkovskaya murder. *Flagrante, no?* If the Putin people go after her like that, they'd go after you or me in half a heartbeat. And where does it come from? It comes from orders right at the top. Putin and his thug gangster friends who run the country."

"How far is their reach?" Alex asked.

"Their reach is everywhere," Rizzo said. "Their reach could be around your neck as you sleep. Even to America. In Europe, they operate with impunity. Rome, Paris. London. Who's to stop them? Putin's killers are quick and devious, and they retreat immediately into a criminal Russian underground and beat it back to Russia before

Western European law can catch up with them. Frankly," he said and then paused, "if I could, if I needed to, I'd use my own weapon to take one out before he could disappear with lawyers and diplomatic cover."

A basket of warm bread arrived. Alex made herself busy with it. What she was hearing was deeply disturbing, but she listened intently and absorbed everything.

"Look," said Rizzo. "Politkovskaya's murder even agitated strong public disgust over what was seen as a blatantly political assassination. Politkovskaya was one of the most trusted journalists on the subject of Chechnya. She had many ties to moderate Chechnyans and wrote scathing articles critical of the way Putin dealt with the secession crisis. Politkovskaya had survived a previous attempt on her life: someone attempted to poison her as she prepared to cover the siege and massacre in Beslan in 2004. So her funeral turned into a powerful outcry against the brutality of Russia's politics. She was buried at the Troyekurovsky Cemetery in Moscow. Before Politkovskaya was buried, two thousand anti-Putin pro-democracy Russians filed past her coffin to pay last respects. No high-ranking Russian officials could be seen at the ceremony. Eventually, there were some suspects charged, but a jury refused to convict them."

"So the police and the judicial system are useless once again?" Alex said.

"Completely. The assassins sent forth by Putin operate with impunity. No one in Russia or Europe or the Middle East is surprised at anything. Saddened, maybe. But *shocked*, no. Listen, this month marks the anniversary of the murder of Dmitri Kholodov. Kholodov was an investigative journalist killed while he was investigating corruption in the Russian army. His attaché case had been booby-trapped. The trial of his alleged murderers ended in acquittal. A colonel charged with the murder won compensation for his forced retirement and pretrial confinement. He was rewarded, in other words, and given decorations by the Putin government. Kholodov's friends complain but nothing will be done. The murder goes unpunished like thousands of similar crimes under Putin and Stalin."

At the next table, a champagne cork popped with all the proper subtlety of five-star dining.

"Five years ago, for a final example," Rizzo said, "my acquaintance Yuri Shchekochikhin mysteriously died. He was a member of the Duma, the Russian parliament. He too was poisoned. Putin's people love poison and give it to people they wish to be rid of because the poisons they use cause slow, horrible, painful deaths. Officially Shchekochikhin died of an allergy, but his body was cremated before an independent analysis could be done of his remains."

For a moment, Rizzo seemed to be thinking of several other stories to add but then preferred to leave them out of the evening's chat.

"The Russian gangsters who now run the country are a blight upon the civilized world," he said. "There is no defeating them because we are limited by our democratic means. Thousands of crimes are committed, never to be resolved. You know, my uncles were Communists in the auto factories of northern Italy. They were foolish in their time, though their foolishness was understandable. They idolized Lenin and Stalin and that pig Khrushchev. They were workers, my uncles, and they reacted against the *fascisti* here in Italy. I loved my uncles, but I was forced to hear quotes from those old red bastards. Here's one I remember. Stalin once theorized, 'No man, no problem.' You see what that means?"

"Eliminate the man and you've eliminated the problem," said Alex.

"Not only are you very intelligent but you understand too well the basest forms of human behavior," Rizzo said. "I don't know if that is good or bad for you, Alexandra LaDuca, but it is what it is. And you are correct. Stalin spoke of killing the man who causes the problem in order to kill the problem. The Putin management style is exactly the same. In the latest government-sanctioned high-school history text, Stalin is described as someone who used 'terror as a pragmatic means of resolving social and economic problems.' Understand that? Russian society under Putin now sees individual murder as a means of social management. Want to call it, 'godless neo-Stalinism'? I would."

Alex nodded. "I would too," she said.

"Putin is Stalin's disciple, just as John, Mark, and Paul were disciples of Jesus. Now," he said, his eyes flicking away for a moment, "have I answered your question?"

"More than adequately," Alex said. "Thank you."

"Good! Here's Mimi."

A smile swept Rizzo's face, and Alex quickly located the indiscreet object of his desire.

A young woman of about twenty had entered the room. She had Technicolor hair, chopped short in a trendy fashion. It was streaked with blue, green, and yellow in a blend of Japanese schoolgirl and *manga* fashion. She was trim and lithe and wore a snug red miniskirt. Most of the male eyes in the room followed her as Carlo, the starchy maître d', led her to their table.

Rizzo embraced her with a long hug and a kiss on each cheek. Then he introduced her to Alex. She giggled slightly, flirted with him outrageously, and Rizzo held her chair as he seated her. It wasn't a matter of her being half his age; she was closer to a third.

"Now," he said. "Where were we?"

The topics of Russia and Putin did not come up again over dinner.

Alex dined amiably with her old friend and his new friend. They switched into Italian after Mimi joined them, but during the meal Mimi demonstrated a thorough ability in English. Alex's instincts told her that she could like the young girl and trust her. She, Mimi, seemed to have one foot in several different cultures, or perhaps one long sleek leg if Rizzo described it, and reminded Alex of herself. Alex brought them both up to speed on her assignment in Egypt. Alex also wondered if there would be a way she would work them into the equation. Mimi could easily be an asset. One never knew.

Rizzo and Mimi listened carefully as Alex briefed them, interrupting occasionally to ask questions. Rizzo offered suggestions about dealing with Arabs and Russians: useful stuff such as, with a smile, "They're cutthroats. Don't trust any of them."

At the end of the evening, Rizzo insisted on paying. He tipped generously and, again demonstrating his *legère de main*, if not his outright kleptomania, pocketed a blue and white porcelain ashtray in front of his headwaiter friend, Carlo, who rolled his eyes and suppressed a laugh. Later, in the hotel lobby, Rizzo gave the ashtray to Mimi as a souvenir of the evening. She made a complex verbal joke out of her previous knowledge of Rizzo's light fingers and deft touch. Having consumed perhaps too much wine, they all exchanged a bawdy laugh.

To end the evening, Rizzo walked both women, their combined age not quite approaching his, to the elevator that led to Alex's suite. He held Alex's hand and had his other arm wrapped around Mimi's waist.

He gave Alex a kiss on both cheeks to wish her a good night, turned, and headed toward where he had left his car as Alex rode the elevator up to the fifth floor.

THIRTY

The next morning, Alex took the elevator down to the lobby. She checked out and was about to ask the concierge to summon a taxi for the airport but instead felt a hand on her arm.

"Alex, my dear," came a smooth male voice in Italian.

Startled, she turned and found Gian Antonio Rizzo next to her. He was clean-shaven, sharp-eyed, and obviously refreshed, even wearing a different suit, this one every bit as impeccable as the last.

"What are you doing here?" she asked.

"I never left. I've been here all night."

"You're kidding!"

"Yes, I am. Of course I went home, but now I'm back. I came over to drive you to the airport," he said.

"That's so kind of you. But completely unnecessary," she said.

"Yes, of course, but what is unnecessary in life and what one does of one's own volition is often a pleasure, as is this. So I insist," he said. "I am a man of leisure these days, or at least give the impression of being one. Come along. I've been wanting to show you my car since the day we met."

He took her bag for her.

"What is it they say in America? 'Pimp my ride.' Well, look at the ride that I've pimped for you today."

Outside the front entrance, gradually drawing a small crowd, was a sparkling white 2009 Maserati GranTurismo, Rizzo's set of wheels.

He held the passenger side door for her, and she slid in to cool leather that made her sorry she was leaving Italy so soon. Rizzo hustled around to the other side and took the wheel. Six figures' worth of Maserati trumped a Fiat taxi any day. A few minutes later they were out on the highway leading to Leonardo da Vinci – Fiumicino Airport. The drive felt like a lift on a magic carpet. One could enjoy an auto like this for getting around town every day.

"How does a career policeman afford such a beautiful automobile?" Alex finally mused aloud in Italian on the journey to the airport.

Rizzo laughed. "The same way that a career policeman might afford such a beautiful woman," he said with a laugh. "*Come se dici in Inglese?* 'You find a way if you are smart.'"

"I suppose you do," she answered with dual meaning to match the Maserati's dual exhausts.

Almost protectively, almost like a big brother or maybe even an uncle, Rizzo revealed another facet of himself. Using his own security passes as a retired member of the *brigade omocido* in Rome, he escorted Alex all the way to her gate. Then, before she boarded the flight to Cairo, he pulled her to a safe distance from the other travelers. He held her hand and spoke to her with urgency.

"Alex," he said, "I must impress upon you: you are not just dealing with criminals now. You are dealing in espionage. This is dangerous, venal, and dirty. It is not fun and games. There is always the chance that an operation will blow up and your career will be ruined in ten seconds. You can be disfigured or killed in even less time than that. In World War II — my *father's* day, your *grandfather's* day — we knew what our objective was: to defeat the Nazis and the Fascists. In the days of the cold war, we knew also a clear enemy, a clear objective: the Russians and the Communists."

Rizzo's eyes were narrowed and his voice was low and succinct.

"Today, the armies are often invisible until they attack," he said. "Our national borders mean nothing. Saudis fly airplanes into the beautiful skyline of New York, and American fighter planes attack weddings in Pakistan in return. There are no heroes, only villains. It is very hard to discern your motivation when the objective is vague, dear Alex. I worry about you so much on this 'adventure.'" He shook his head, and she saw tears well in his hard brown eyes, much as they might at Mimi's death in *La Bohème*.

He put his strong arms around her and hugged her so hard and dearly that her feet lifted from the ground. Then he set her down again.

"Who are you going to be dealing with in Cairo?" he asked. "Arabs and Russians, correct?"

"Probably."

"If hell itself emptied out tomorrow morning we would discover that it was mostly filled with Arabs and Russians," he grumbled. "I do not like this for you!"

"I'll be all right," she said. "Really! I'll be all right."

"Let me go with you," he said. "I can join you in a day."

"I can't do it that way," she said. "I have specific orders from Langley how this is supposed to be done. There will be a team in Cairo and — "

"I don't trust your team in Cairo," he said. "And you shouldn't either."

On the airport public address system, the last call was made for boarding Flight 34 from Rome to Cairo.

"I need to go, Gian Antonio," she said.

"Va bene," he said at length. "And I will contact Rolland Fitzgerald for you. But I know how these things go. One holds to all game plans until the first shot is fired. Then chaos. So when there's chaos, you're allowed to call in people whom you trust. Those are the rules of engagement. I will stand ready. I will be your chevalier, *your* cavalier, when you need one." He paused. "I would not want anything to happen to you," he said again.

He held her as long as he could, then released her to a world he knew to be cruel and calculating. At the last step before the gate, she turned and gave him a smile and a wave. She knew he would still be watching. To Alex's eyes, he looked sad and overly concerned.

Then she boarded another Alitalia jet.

She was seated in 5-H of business class, a window. She had a wonderful view of Rome and Naples as they flew south. Her eyes then followed the bold coastlines of Corsica and Sicily and the boot of Italy in the Mediterranean as the plane banked and turned to the southeast. The geography had not changed since the time of Christ, and with suddenly refreshed eyes, she was thrilled to gaze upon it.

She watched out her window with fascination as the flight traveled southeast and crossed the Mediterranean. She was finally on the final leg of her trip to Egypt.

PART TWO

THIRTY-ONE

Within two hours she saw the topography of northern Africa for the first time. She recognized the contours of the Nile Delta where it met the sea. Far away to the east she could see the ancient land where the Suez Canal had been built a hundred and fifty years ago. Beyond, also within her view in the distance through the hazy sky, she could see the Arabian Peninsula and the Red Sea, the land of so many of the Bible tales of her youth.

For much of the flight Alex had been prowling through files on her laptop and poking through a phrasebook of Egyptian Arabic. Now she leaned back from the window. A strange feeling was upon her, accompanied by a poignant memory.

When Alex had been in her midteens, she had been too good a student for her own school system. One thing had led to another, and she had been sent away on a full scholarship to a private boarding school in Connecticut where she was allowed to excel in all her studies, particularly languages. The summer after her junior year she had won an internship to work in France, and off she had gone again, full of adventure and naïveté, and hiding within her a heavy element of fear and intimidation.

She had been away from home before but had never been so far away, never on another continent and immersed in another culture. Additionally, it was one thing to have excelled in French in the classroom, quite another to be smacked down in it in real life.

She had flown from New York to Paris. Her first night in Paris passed safely and securely. She had registered in advance at a student residence in Paris and had hung out with some other Americans. But the next day had been different. She had taken a train deep into the center of France, a single girl of seventeen traveling alone, with one cramped bag of clothes, three hundred dollars in cash, and a single credit card that would max at five hundred dollars.

She had been scared and had felt lost and vulnerable. She asked herself why she was doing this, whether this was what she had really wanted, whether it might have been easier and more pleasant to have just spent the summer hanging around her mother's home in California.

On the southbound train, Alex fell into a conversation with an older French woman, a woman old enough to remember the world war in which, fifty years earlier, she said, she had lost her husband at Dunkirk. The old woman befriended her, even gave her some fresh fruit from a basket. They both descended from the train at Saint Etienne and said their good-byes. The old woman, whose name was Marie-Claire, gave her a hug, and Alex reciprocated. Marie-Claire felt frail and bony in her grasp and almost unsteady when Alex released her. She reminded Alex—distantly and in spooky kind of way—of her own late grandmother.

Alex had to find her way on foot to a local youth hostel, where she would stay overnight, and then the next morning take another train to the Camargue region where her job awaited her.

She walked down some questionable streets to get to the hostel. She took the wrong route twice and was corrected twice when strangers answered questions. When she arrived at the hostel, early in the evening, it was not the nicest place. Peeling walls, worn linoleum, dim corridors that reeked of age and abuse. Worse, the hostel had been overbooked and there wasn't a room for her. There wasn't even an extra bed in the dormitory. The staff wasn't entirely helpful, and to top it off, the phones weren't working.

She was near tears. Had the trains been running, she might have turned around, retraced her route to Paris, then to New York, then home to California. Who could blame a frightened teenager for wanting to go home?

She sat in the lobby and tried to evaluate what to do. Several minutes later, a young man came over to her and sat down next to her. He was very slight of build, with a mocha complexion. In French he started a conversation and asked what nationality she was.

"I'm American," she said in French. "From California."

"My name is René," he said. "I'm French, but of Tunisian origin."

He smiled and tried to speak English with her, but his was limited, so their conversation ensued in French. He was eighteen and had technical training in computer engineering, he said, mostly self-acquired. He had enlisted in the French Air Force, he said, *l'armee de l'air,* he proclaimed proudly. This was his final evening at liberty. The next day he would take a train in a different direction and travel onward to Nantes in west central France for six weeks of basic training. It was his hope to eventually see the world, to be posted in someplace exotic like Polynesia or Martinique where the French maintained bases. He added that it had always been his dream to visit America, as well.

Alex joined him for dinner. They had soup and bread and cheese in the hostel cafeteria. She waited to see whether the hostel keepers would find a place for her. But while her conversation with René played out in the forefront of her mind, in the back of her mind her worries accelerated.

What would she do? Despite the kindness of the old lady on the train and the gentle amity of René this evening, she had never felt so homesick in her life, so cut off from everything she knew. In her stomach was a knot that wouldn't untie.

After dinner, there was a change at the concierge's desk. The new man told Alex that the phones were up and running again and they had called everywhere, including local homes that might take in an overnight border. But it was early summer and there were no beds to be had anywhere within a hundred miles. Nor was there any way for a single girl traveling alone to get to anywhere else. And it was against regulations for anyone to stay in the hostel's lobby or office area.

There was still some daylight remaining. In midsummer in the south of France daylight remained until almost ten o'clock. Alex walked outside the hostel, stood in the street and tried to decide what to do. She noticed that across the street there was a small Catholic church. It was white stucco with peeling green paint on its front door.

Alex walked to it. She tried the door but it was locked. When she turned around, however, she was surprised to find René standing very close to her.

"I heard what's happening," he said. "You can have my room for the night."

She was shocked. "That's kind of you," she said. They spoke in French, and at this time in her life, hers was halting. "But you're about to go into the military. I couldn't possibly take your room for the final night."

"I wish you would," he said.

"Where would you go?"

"I have a backpack. I can sleep in the park. Among the hobos," he said with a smile, "among *les clochards*. It will be an adventure. I'll be gone before dawn as long as the police don't catch me."

"No, no," she said. "You mustn't take such a risk for me."

"Then let me sneak you into my room and we will share it," he said.

Her expression must have conveyed her confusion, appreciation mingled with anxiety and suspicion. He sought to defuse it. "I warn you, there is only one bed. It is very narrow and there is no space on the floor. But I will be honorable."

She searched his eyes. Sometimes, she thought, angels take strange forms.

"All right," she said.

They returned to the hostel. A friend created a distraction for the concierge and Alex darted down the corridor to René's room. The concierge either didn't see her or chose not to.

The door to René's room was unlocked and the room empty. He followed a minute later, closed the door and locked it. The room was tiny, maybe eight by ten, with a nightstand and a bed, just as René had described. Barely enough room for two people to stand up together, much less lie down together.

The shower and bathroom facilities on the corridor were communal. They took turns so that Alex could have privacy to change and so that he could too. Awkwardly, at 11:00 p.m., they turned off the single room light and lay down together, Alex between the wall and René's body. Around her neck, Alex wore the small gold cross that her dad had given her years earlier, the one she had eventually lost in Kiev. She knew René had noted it, but he said nothing about it.

A moment passed. They both started to laugh at the preposterousness of the situation. Then they started to talk about their homes, their families. They discovered they were both only children raised by a single parent. René had been raised by his very strict father, who worked in a factory. His mother had deserted the family when he had been five. René had been raised as a Muslim but had fallen away from his faith, perhaps as a reaction to the strictness of his father's Islam.

"What would your father say if he knew you were here, lying in bed, with an American girl?" Alex asked.

"Oooh!" René answered quickly. He laughed and pointed to his lower backside in the dim light. He furiously waved a finger to indicate that he didn't even want to *think* about what would happen. He made a moaning sound over the beating he probably would have received. "But my father and I do not agree on many things," he said. "It is one reason I am going away and joining the *armée de l'air*. It doesn't mean I don't love him or respect him. It only means we disagree."

After hushed conversation of nearly an hour, fatigue rolled in upon them. Alex taught René some words and phrases in English. *Hello. How are you? Good-bye. Good luck.*

René reciprocated with some useful words in Arabic.

Marhabbah. Assalaam Alaikim. Maasalaamah.

Hello. Peace be unto you. Good-bye.

"If you greet most Arab people in their language, you break the ice," he said. "They will trust you more and treat you with a genuine smile," he said. "*Assalamou Alaekom* means 'hello' or 'hi' in Arabic. Another word is *Ezzayak*, said as a question. It means, 'How are you?' Learning a few Arabic words will always make a difference."

"*Assalamou Alaekom*," she tried, laughing, garbling it.

"*Assalamou Alaekom*," he corrected. It quickly became a joke between them. They laughed until she felt herself drifting, trying to stay awake but no longer able. The last thing she remembered was René saying something to her that she didn't understand. She was too tired.

The next morning she awoke with a start. It was 8:00 a.m., and she was alone on the bed. She looked everywhere in the small room. René was gone and had taken all his things. She waited for several minutes to see if perhaps he was in the shower or the bathroom. But no. He was gone.

She pulled on a T-shirt and some jeans. She snuck out of the hostel. The new concierge on the morning shift gave her a cursory glance but said nothing. She went outside into a warm summer morning. She was still unsure what to do, whether to go forward with her trip or go back to America. The knot had returned to the pit of her stomach, and she again felt alone, sad, and vulnerable. She had made one friend, or thought she had, and now he was gone too.

The door to the church was open across the street. She had time. She wandered in. There were a few older people sitting in various pews. There was stained glass at the front, a hundreds-of-years-old depiction of Jesus raising his hands to God.

Alex sat for a moment, then closed her eyes and said a prayer. She wanted wisdom. She wanted guidance. She wanted to know how to proceed. She opened her eyes.

Nothing much had changed. She stood, bowed slightly to the cross at the altar, turned, and walked back toward the front door.

She was near her decision. She would return home. The loneliness was too much.

Then something caught her eye.

In the back pew, among the old people she had walked past was the lady from the train. The old woman smiled at her and raised a hand. She signaled Alex to wait, as if she had something to say.

Outside, Alex waited. The old woman came out of the church a few seconds later.

"Today you will continue on to the Camargue?" she asked, recalling the previous day's conversation.

Alex hesitated. "Yes. Yes, I think so," she said. "Unless I change my mind and go back to Paris. I'm thinking about — "

"No, no, no!" the old woman said sharply. *"Il te faut continuer, ma chérie!* You must go on. You must stay with your plans. You are young and pretty. The world is big and wonderful and waits for you. You will make many friends. You are a blessed person, I can tell."

"Merci bien," Alex said.

"If I had a gift, I would give you one," the old lady said. "But I am old and not well off. So I don't."

"I think you just *did* give me a gift."

"I don't understand."

"You remind me so much of my grandmother. It's almost as if you're her."

The old lady laughed. "You flatter me," she said.

"My train leaves in an hour," Alex said. "To the Camargue. Thank you."

"Good luck to you," the old lady said. "May God always bless you."

They embraced again. On her way to the train station, Alex stopped by a small grocery store. From a cheerful shop owner, she bought fresh bread, a packet of cheese, two apples, and some bottled water for the train ride. She had an eye out for René but did not see him.

On the train through the French countryside, in a compartment that seated six, she wondered what guideposts, what angels, had been on earth for her. Across from her sat a mother with a boy of about ten. They were French of Sudanese origin, Alex learned as a conversation developed.

Alex tried her next phrase of greeting in Arabic. They smiled and responded with kindness. Alex engaged the boy in a casual conversation and eventually traded one of her apples for a pear while the mother smiled. The sun was brilliant outside, and there were new vistas beyond the train windows that she had never seen before. She sat in rapt attention and watched a new part of the world unfurl before her young eyes.

She felt older this morning. More confidant. Her French was coming more easily. She realized that she was a more confidant young woman this morning than the frightened young girl she had been twenty-four hours earlier. She would never, for example, have traded the apple for the pear a day earlier; she would have been too withdrawn. And she also suddenly realized that the knot in her stomach was gone. Oddly enough, it had disappeared when she was walking back up the short aisle of the church in Saint Etienne, when the old lady raised her hand and signaled her.

Now, a dozen years later, her flight from Rome leveled out. It followed the Nile River and finished its descent toward Cairo International Airport. Alex stared downward and again surveyed the ancient landscape, almost able to taste the millennia of history that lay along the river. Distantly, southward, beyond Cairo, she thought she could see the Pyramids of Giza.

Alex guessed that the old woman might well have passed away by now. She wondered what had ever happened to René, whether he ever visited Martinique or Polynesia or America. She could never remember his last name and wasn't sure that she had ever known it. But she recalled the first three words of useful Arabic that he had taught her.

Marhabbah. Assalaam Alaikim. Maasalaamah.

Hello. Peace be unto you. Good-bye.

Well, she mused, you could live your whole life bracketed by those thoughts.

And she wondered whether that whole experience with René in the hostel and with the lady on the train and in the small church, whom she might also never see again in her life, had prepared her for this trip to Egypt more than any other single experience in her life.

THIRTY-TWO

Alex passed through Egyptian customs, then immigration. The Egyptian security officer scanned her passport. He waited for something on a computer screen, and so did she.

Whenever she traveled on a fake passport, immigration unnerved her. She watched everything the agent was doing and observed every facial gesture carefully. She even watched his eye movements as he looked at his computer screen. She felt her heart race and felt her blouse moisten with sweat.

Then the agent closed her passport, handed it back, and nodded to her. He smiled. "Welcome to Egypt," he said in English.

Moments later, she retrieved her baggage from a clanking, outdated carousel and soon found a young man from the US Embassy holding a piece of paper with her new name on it. She approached him, smiled, and identified herself.

They shook hands. As it turned out, there had been one other passenger on her flight who was attached to the US diplomatic section in Cairo. He was a man about ten years older than she. The driver was also waiting for him. Once he had found both travelers, the driver took Alex's bags and carried them to a waiting van.

"I'm Mo," the driver said as they piled into the van.

"Short for Mohammad, I assume," Alex answered.

"Mo is fine," the man said without humor.

"Well, at least they didn't send Larry or Curley," the other traveler said *sotto voce* to Alex, who had to suppress a smile.

Mo and Cairo traffic were perfectly suited to each other. The ride into the city was crazy, with hyped-up drivers often passing between two other cars in the actual lanes, as a static-filled radio filled the van. It was not usual to be in a stream of traffic four-cars-across on a two lane highway at sixty miles per hour. Alex and the other American in the van exchanged another glance. She checked that her seatbelt was tight. The driving was worse than what Alex remembered from some of her trips to Central and South America. The only worse traffic that she could recall was during her trip to Lagos two years earlier, where there seemed to be no rules at all.

"I wish I had a helmet," she said to the other man.

He laughed and shook his head.

"Me too," he said. "And maybe some extra life insurance."

Mo either couldn't hear them or chose to ignore them.

The highway passed through several upscale blocks in the northern fringe of the city. Alex noted a number of satellite dishes on buildings, most of them looking as if they hadn't worked for the past twenty years. Gradually the new buildings gave way to some very old ones, and she knew she had arrived in an ancient and picturesque city, a city she read about so many times in her life.

Cairo. *Al Qahirah*, as it had originally been called. The Triumphant City, so named for all the invading armies that had conquered it and then left, defeated by the quirky eccentricities of the city itself. The ancient was intermingled with the new on endless blocks. And even after the highway, traffic was a nightmare.

Their van pulled up in front of one of the better hotels, the Metropole Cairo. The Metropole was a bright modern building with several guards around it, many with heavy weapons. There was a display of foreign flags above the entrance arcade. Alex nodded a good-bye to the other passenger, and she stepped out. A porter picked up Alex's one piece of luggage from the rear of the van.

Alex tipped Mo with an American ten-dollar bill. He grunted in response.

The Metropole stood impressively by the River Nile. The lobby was modern. It gleamed with new furniture and artwork in an Egyptian motif. Alex checked in easily, and a second porter took her to her room.

The room was a small suite, actually, more like a room and a half, a sitting area, and a sleeping area. It was thoroughly air-conditioned and had numerous amenities — multiple telephone lines, internet access, satellite television, a small refrigerator, and a polished marble bathroom with separate showers. It afforded a spectacular view of the

Nile as well as a hotel pool. It was obviously designed for diplomatic and business travelers, a fine base for conducting business or exploring historic Cairo. She had heard the Metropole was considered one of the best business hotels in the Middle East, and her impression on arrival did nothing to undermine that premise.

She knew from her previous "official" visits to Nigeria and Ukraine that every US Embassy provided arrival kits for guests, including maps of the city and phrase books. She found such a kit waiting for her with a card from a political officer at the Cairo Embassy. His name was Richard Bissinger.

She knew from experience that the political officer was often more than simply that. For better or worse, Bissinger, or whatever his real name was, was her CIA contact.

On one of the maps was a notation as to where the embassy was. It wasn't far. She had also noticed on arrival that the entire neighborhood was well policed, even beyond the weapons-toting guards that ringed the hotel. Also within the kit was a cell phone, new and presumably secure.

Alex changed into a knee-length tan skirt, a conservative light blue blouse, and shoes that would allow her to walk or run as needed. She had a linen jacket and threw it over her arm. She carried an extra silk scarf but tucked it into a jacket pocket. She knew that if she wished to enter a mosque or any Islamic holy place, she would need her neck and arms covered. She memorized the short walking direction to the embassy and set out on foot, ready for anything, not wishing to consult a map or guide book and look conspicuously like a tourist.

What struck her immediately on her way, in addition to the remorseless heat, was the din of the city — a confirmation of what Rizzo had mentioned. There was an unyielding background noise to every block. Motor vehicles jammed the streets. The drivers had one hand on the horn and a rules-free way of attacking any intersection. Trucks and cars ducked up onto the sidewalk to pass. Many seemed to have won an uncontested divorce from their common sense as well as their mufflers. Vehicular anarchy reigned. Alex regretted having not taken Rizzo's advice about the earplugs.

Big trucks rumbled by. Pickup trucks hit their air horns at each other. Battered black-and-white taxis honked, and their drivers exchanged profanities with each other. She was secretly pleased she didn't understand Arabic, at least not right now. Men worked on cars in the street. Vendors hawked newspapers, snacks, water, fruit, and bootlegged DVDs from tables on the streets. Butchers hawked meat in stands that overflowed out onto the sidewalks. They blasted radios and cranked up the volume on television sets. As she walked, *muezzins'* calls to prayer wailed from loudspeakers in the minarets of thousands of mosques in the city, as they would five times every day.

Forewarned, Alex could still not believe the din. People in private conversations shouted to be heard. Some blocks were only slightly quieter than standing next to a jackhammer. She wondered how people could live here. It was unlike New York or London or Madrid or Moscow or any other internal-combustion-engine-choked metropolis that she had ever experienced. This was like living next to a lawnmower.

To her relief, she was at the embassy in fifteen noisy minutes.

The American Embassy was a green high-rise of about a dozen stories, next to the Japanese Embassy. Like her hotel, it overlooked the Nile. Ten minutes after arriving in the lobby, she sat in the office of Richard Bissinger on the third floor of the embassy, savoring the silence within the American enclave.

There she waited.

THIRTY-THREE

Bissinger entered several minutes later. He was a thick, compact man of about five-eleven, with slicked-back hair. His brow jutted, his eyes were dark, and his chin receded sharply into his body. He looked like a prize-fighter who'd been knocked out several times but lived to fight again.

"Well," Richard Bissinger said, "welcome to Egypt."

"Thank you, I think."

"So who are you?" he asked. "Other than who you really are, I mean."

She handed him her passport. He opened it, studied it for a moment, curled a lip, gave her a bemused smile, and slid the passport back.

"Nice work, the passport," he said.

"Latest thing, in more ways than one."

"Josephine, huh?"

"That's me."

"Well, I read your c.v. this morning, Josephine. You've been busy in the last two years. Lagos. Ukraine. Spain. Points in between."

"Seriously," she said. "Either a dark cloud follows me or I'm following it."

Bissinger nodded. "That's how most of us feel," he said. "Welcome to the club."

"You know why I'm here," she said. "Reports about a Michael Cerny."

"I know all about that. Transcripts from Langley. Plus local activity. This is a headache. Need to get this wrapped up quickly. Make Cerny disappear and everyone who sails with him. You used to work for him? Cerny?"

"He was my case officer when I was on the Ukraine assignment.

He was involved in a gunfight in Paris in June, and I thought he was shot to death. So did the Agency. Now we're getting sightings."

"Like Elvis," said Bissinger. "Only more radioactive and not in a Walmart."

"What else can you tell me?" Alex asked.

"Not much good," he said. "We've had a lid on Egypt for several years. The place is out of control but under control. Know what I mean?"

"*We* means the CIA?" she asked.

"The CIA. The United States. Western Civilization. All of the above. Right now Egypt is our type of place. Thank God they don't hold free elections here or we'd all be out on our butts."

"Not to split hairs," she said, "but from what I've observed over the last couple of years, you wouldn't be out on your butts so much as you'd be forced to work the same operations with much deeper cover. Am I not correct?"

Bissinger looked at her first with skepticism, then shook his head with approval. "Are you as good in the field as you are with words?" he asked.

"I like to think so."

"I'd like to think so too," he said. "If you are, you're going to like it here. The stated goal is to apprehend Mike Cerny and bring him back in. He looks like he's about to do a deal with some Russians, and we can't allow that to happen. So everything is on red alert here, no pun intended. Speed is important. We have an operation planned, and you're the essential part."

"What's he selling?" she asked.

"Technology."

"Whose?"

"American."

"To the Russians?"

"Maybe to a third party, brokered by some Russians."

"What am I supposed to do?" Alex asked.

"Show yourself, maybe lure some disgusting Russian thug into a bedroom overnight for some really ugly and abusive sex, be vulnerable, maybe get naked and get slapped around a bit and eventually get killed," he said without any glint of humor.

"Just another day at the office," she answered, going with it.

"Yeah, except I'm not kidding."

After a few seconds, *"What?"* she finally said.

She stared at him. *CIA people I have known*, she thought to herself. *Where did the Agency recruit these people? From the loony bins of the world?*

"Oh, it's not as bad as it sounds," he said off her stare. "You'll catch on. I'm going to put you in touch with the main people we have on the streets here," Bissinger said. "As you might imagine, our best sources aren't American. The person you really want to talk to is a Jordanian named Voltaire."

"Voltaire?"

"Rarely see the man, myself," Bissinger said. *"Voltaire* is what he goes by. I'm going to give you the name of a café in old Cairo. It's a place called Fishawi's. Go there tomorrow evening around 7:00. There will be two local women sitting at a table in the rear. They're local assets. One of them will be named Artemiz. They'll have a bouquet of roses on the table. If the roses are upright in a vase, you should present yourself to them. They speak English. Not the roses, the women. If the roses are turned over, lying flat, security isn't perfectly in place and you should leave. If that happens, come back here the next morning. If the roses are upright and it's a 'go' for the evening, the women will then guide you to meet Voltaire. When he approaches you, he'll make a reference to the Zodiac. If you feel ill at ease with anything, don't respond to it. Tell him he's mistaken and reject the advance. If you're comfortable, pursue the Zodiac reference. You okay with all this?"

"I know how the game is played," she said.

"Need me to repeat it?"

"No."

"Good. Voltaire is your key guy. He runs our streets but behind the scenes. His information is impeccable. He's expensive, but we work with him. Think of me for your white intelligence, Voltaire for the black stuff. Dark, dark black. If any shooting starts, duck. It won't necessarily be you they're trying to take out; it'll be Voltaire. The Islamic fanatics would have killed Voltaire years ago if they were smart enough to figure out who he is and if they could shoot straight, two qualities that they have lacked historically, fortuitously for us."

"So I hear."

"That's right," he said. "You just took a few stitches in your arm. How's that holding up?"

"The scab itches."

"Most of them do," he said. "By the way, you never mention my actual name, either, the one you see on my business card. In any conversation with Voltaire or anyone else on this operation, I'm *Fitzgerald*."

"Fitzgerald?"

He nodded. "I'm an educated sort of swine," he said. "My father was in this same line of work. And in my younger and more vulnerable years, my father gave me some advice. He said always use a *nom de guerre* that you respect and that you'll remember. That way you won't get a bullet in your back some night."

"Got it," she said.

"Again, good. How do you like Egypt so far?"

"I just got here."

"So? No opinion yet?"

"Well, you make it sound quite charming."

"I live here. I know how it works."

"I couldn't believe the noise on the street," she said.

"What noise?" he asked. "It's a quiet place."

"Very funny."

"Ah, you get used to the brutal sound effects, and it's the least of our problems," Bissinger said. "People here shout to be heard and shrug because they say there is nothing they can do but join in. That's the biggest city in Africa outside this embassy. In some areas, the density of people is ten times what it is in New York. People here honk, bang, scream, howl, or whatever they need to do to make it through the day or across the street. The noise is the cause as well as the reaction. Fire a gun and maybe no one will notice. If you don't like it, shout back at them. If you're here long enough, you'll get used to it and you'll shout at everyone. But there's an upside: every other place in the world will sound quiet after you leave."

"I'm also not wild about the part where I'm supposed to get killed," she said, backtracking.

"What part was that?"

"What you just mentioned."

"That's good. I was afraid the part about the ugly overnight with the Russian would have you walking out of here."

"When do I hear what the real game plan is?"

"When you meet Voltaire, but what I outlined above isn't far off. So I'll ask again, how do you like Egypt so far?"

"Want to help me form an opinion?"

"Sure."

"Then give me a quick overview."

"Fair enough. Current history begins with the Gulf War of 1991. Egyptian infantrymen were the first Arabs to land in Saudi Arabia to evict Iraqi forces from Kuwait. Know why? The US government paid Egypt half a million dollars per soldier that Egypt sent into the fight. This is all unofficial, of course. But the program worked. When the United States formed alliances to kick Iraq out of Kuwait, Egypt's President Hosni Mubarak was the first to join. Because Egyptians were some of the first to move into Kuwait during the liberation, Egypt suffered more casualties than reported. But after the Persian Gulf War was a success, Mubarak's reward was that the United States, the Gulf states, and Europe forgave Egypt around twenty-billion-dollars' worth of debt. It turned the Egyptian economy around overnight."

"And the average Egyptian doesn't know this?"

"Of course not. There are rumors. Mutterings in cafés. But the government controls the press. Hell, the average American doesn't know it, and we have a free press, so why would the average Egyptian?"

"Point," she said.

"Corruption within the police departments and the Ministry of Interior is rampant here. Don't trust anyone within the Egyptian government or any state agency. As a woman in the Arab world, you'll not only get a hand under your skirt but you'll get a knife in your back or worse. The state security agencies operate unchecked. They execute criminals without trials when they want to, and there are maybe about ten state prisons hidden out in the desert that exist off the record. Any individual police officer can violate any citizen's privacy or rights. They can make unconditioned arrests whenever they want. You run into a police lieutenant or captain, it's a sign of danger, not safety. So if you have to rely on anyone here, use one of us, never one of them."

She listened with close attention.

"As for the president of the country," he said, "Mubarak has been in power for almost three decades. He's survived at least six known assassination attempts and maybe a couple dozen more that got nipped before a shot was fired. Islamic fundamentalists. They don't like him for exactly the reasons we do like him. He cozies up to us and feels he can live with Israel, his public anti-Zionist yammering notwithstanding. Look at his history. He works both sides of the street. He went to their air force academy half a century ago and became a bomber pilot. Part of his flight training he received at the Soviet pilot school in Bishkek in Soviet Kyrgyzstan. In 1964 he was appointed head of the Egyptian Military Delegation to the USSR. So he started out his career as a Soviet guy. In 1972 he became commander of the air force and deputy minister of war. In October 1973, following the Yom Kippur War, he was promoted to the rank of air chief marshal. In April 1975 he was appointed vice president of Egypt, and following the assassination of Sadat by militants in 1981, Mubarak became the president. For half a dozen years he was a loyal guy for the Russians. Then the Soviet Union collapses, and it's all roses and valentines between him and Washington. Suddenly he's our guy. Do we object? Hell no. He might be a hooker, but he's a hooker who knows how to keep us happy, and we can afford him."

Bissinger leaned back in his chair.

"Want some hardware?" he asked. "I'd suggest you carry some."

"Absolutely," she said.

"Come along," he said. "This is usually everyone's favorite part of an embassy visit."

They proceeded to a separate room down the hallway. In a well-fortified storage area, which he used his own pass to enter, he led her to a closet enclosed in steel, which had several shelves of metal boxes.

"Preferences?" he asked.

"Do you have a Baby Glock?" she asked.

"That nifty little German problem-solver?" he asked. "A Glock 27? Can't go wrong with one of those."

"That's the one."

"Excellent choice."

"So? Do you have one?"

"No. No got. Never seen one here. A shame, really."

"What *do* you have?" she asked.

"Here's a hint," he said. "The Egyptians do a lot of business with Italy."

"Okay. I like the feel of a Beretta," Alex said. "Something small and compact. There are a few Colt models that will do."

"Good call," he said.

He scanned the boxes, pulled one off a central shelf, unlocked it, and handed it to her. The box clicked open. There was a small pistol within, with a hip holster. She pulled it out and hefted it in her hand. It was an attractive new piece, a Beretta Px4 Storm Sub-Compact pistol.

"Easy to conceal. I've used one," Bissinger said. "It has large frame firepower. This one packs 9mm, thirteen to a clip. Does that work for you?"

She admired it. "Looks like it should."

"It's a nice weapon for Egypt," he said. "It's corrosion resistant. So you can sweat like a sow all over it with no damage. Sign for it and return it when you leave the country. I don't want to see it pop up on Egyptian eBay."

She examined it thoroughly. It wasn't loaded. She hefted it again in her hand. Slim and sleek, it would indeed pack and conceal well beneath a light jacket. Bissinger gave her two clips, two boxes of bullets, and a two-word benediction.

"Happy hunting," he said.

She loaded the weapon and affixed the holster on her right hip.

"Is that it for now?"

"Not entirely," he said. "I'll walk you down to the lobby; there's someone else I want you to meet."

"Who would that be?" she asked.

"Amjad," he answered. "Amjad is going to be one of the most important people during your assignment here. Come along."

They took the elevator down to the main floor. When they emerged from it, Bissinger spoke again in lowered tones.

"The guy I want you to meet is our top Egyptian security person. By Egyptian, I mean he's one of them, but he's been in the embassy here for years."

"He's a local cop?"

"Yes. Rank of colonel. The police here have ranks similar to army ranks. Holdover from when the British ran the place. Anyway, Amjad is one of the top guys in the city dealing with the diplomatic community. You should know who he is."

Alex was wary.

"I've been told they're not that trustworthy, the local police," she said.

"Ah, don't believe everything you hear, unless it comes from me or Voltaire," he said. "The Arabs are a mixed lot, I admit. But the ones you can trust are the most loyal, steadfast friends you'll make this side of Valhalla. Then there's the rest. Those will cut your throat."

"So this is someone I can trust? Maybe?"

"Ha!" Bissinger said under his breath. "Not a bit. But, hey! There he is. Amjad!"

Not far away stood a thick man in a khaki Cairo police uniform. He was about six feet tall and when he turned, his face was tanned and grave with a moustache. He was a dour-looking big man with a sad expression and dead eyes set back in his head. With his puffy eyelids and sagging jowls, like an old poodle. But he also looked strong and wore a sidearm. He seemed like a man who knew how to get things done and was widely disliked for it.

Then, when he saw Bissinger and Alex, his face transformed. He smiled. "Why, Mr. Bissinger. Charmed," he said with a slight bow. And indeed he seemed to be just that. Charmed.

Bissinger handled the introduction of Colonel Ahman Amjad to Josephine from Toronto.

"I have my car outside," Colonel Amjad said. "I could drive you."

"I really don't mind walking," Alex insisted.

"I insist," the colonel said. "You must be tired."

Alex was about to refuse again, but her feet were killing her and the jetlag was catching up. Then there was the din and grittiness of the walk over, the catcalls from men in trucks and taxis. She thought better of it.

"All right," she said.

The colonel gave her a bow. "I'm honored," he said.

He led her to his vehicle, an unmarked police car. He held the door to the backseat open and she climbed in. He came around, slid in, and started the car. The ignition sputtered and resisted slightly, and for one horrible stretch of seconds, Alex wondered if that was how Carlos's car sounded before it turned into a flaming execution chamber.

The car failed to start. She was ready to bolt.

Then Colonel Amjad turned the ignition a second time. The engine kicked in. He pulled out of the secured embassy parking and into traffic on the motorway along the river. Traffic was moving faster than a crawl now, a propitious sign.

"You are American? From where?" he asked, glancing into his rearview mirror as they drove.

"Canadian, actually."

"Ah! Canada!"

"You've been there?" she asked.

"I've been to America and I've been to Canada," he said proudly. "I have one brother in Vancouver and a half-brother in New York."

"That's very nice," she said. She couldn't get a range on him. Was he snooping or being sincere?

"Maybe next year I go and visit again," he said. "I don't know."

He hit some traffic and started to work his horn, not that anyone paid any attention. Another driver started to give him a threatening gesture but backed off immediately when he noticed the police uniform.

"Well, I'm sure you'd enjoy your trip," she said. "I hope you're able to visit."

He shrugged while driving. Then, seeing an opportunity, he switched on a small blue flashing light on his dashboard. Traffic ahead of him gave way and Colonel Amjad edged through it like a weasel.

"There is a phrase in Arabic," he said. He then gave it in Arabic. Alex didn't understand. Arabic was still beyond her dossier. "The phrase says, 'Let every man eat bread,'" Amjad said. "We are also so busy here. Police. One thing stops and another starts. Very hard for me to travel and get away."

"I understand," Alex said, who wasn't sure if she did.

He found the exit from the motorway, and they were back at the hotel within a few minutes. After her initial reservations, Alex was satisfied with the trip, and with Colonel Amjad. A chauffer was a great thing, a police escort something even greater.

Colonel Amjad pulled into the semicircle in front of the hotel. The doormen knew enough to stay away until the proper moment. The colonel turned around from the front seat.

"May I give you some advice?" he asked. "For your personal safety? About Cairo."

"Please do," she said.

"When walking on the street, walk as far away from the cars and motor scooters as you can," he said. "Bad people, they pull up right next to you, grab your purse, and drive away. Or, with a single Western woman, they force you into the car. Stay close to the buildings. Don't give money to beggars. Some of them will stalk you and send their family members to follow you home and harass you for more money."

"Simple urban precaution," she said. "Thank you."

He nodded politely. "Yes, you could say," he said. "And maybe," he said, giving a nod to her head, "if I am not being presumptuous, you might purchase a headscarf or two. It will help you fit in. Even in Western business clothes, for a woman the *hijab* is a good idea."

She thought about it. "Good advice, Colonel," she said.

"Are you really Canadian or are you American working undercover with the embassy?" he asked.

She laughed. "Got to admit it!" she said, not missing a beat. "I'm a spy!"

"You are?"

She laughed again and shook her head. "You flatter me, Colonel. I'm a visiting scholar and a personal friend of Mr. Bissinger at the embassy. Everything I know about spies I saw in James Bond movies."

"You are very pretty. You could be a Bond girl."

"That would pay better than what I do as a teacher, Colonel. You flatter me again."

"So be it," he said. "It is my pleasure to be at your disposal while you are here."

She gave him a final smile.

"If at any time you feel there is a threat or a danger, please call me. I insist. Here," he said. He wrote out his cell phone number and handed it to her. "I oversee security for the Americans, Canadians, and British. I am often at the big hotels."

She thanked him again. "And I'll get myself some scarves."

Then she was out of the car. He pulled out of the driveway and back into the endless Cairo traffic. From the corner of her eyes, she watched the car disappear.

"What a creep!" she thought to herself.

THIRTY-FOUR

It was past 3:00 p.m. when Alex left the hotel, wearing the Beretta concealed beneath the linen jacket. Anxious to adapt to Egyptian time, she went walking in the city, curious to see what she could while she had a small amount of downtime. On her stroll, she reversed course several times to make sure she wasn't being followed. When she was convinced that no one was trailing her, she relaxed slightly.

She was in one of the more affluent neighborhoods. She could read the streets enough to tell that much. But as a single Western woman alone on foot in Cairo, she had her difficulties. When she stopped and looked at postcards in a souvenir stand, an Egyptian man approached her, stood too close, and spoke to her in English.

"You are American?" he asked.

She tried to ignore him.

"British?"

"*Soy Mexicana,*" she answered in Spanish, stepping away.

He persisted in English. She tried to throw him by crossing the street, but he followed and persisted. "I help you see city," he said. "I can be guide."

Finally she said, "I don't need help," in English.

"We have a drink now," he said. "And I tell you about Cairo."

They stood near the entrance to a café. She turned to him and glared. "All right," she said. "Let's go in here. Buy me a Coca-Cola."

They sat. He ordered. Then Alex made a motion with her hands as if to wash them. "Bathroom," she said. "Wash up."

He nodded. The waiter arrived with their drinks. She took a long sip. Then she excused herself to use the washroom. While he waited, she eased out the back entrance of the café, jogged a block through a crowd, and continued on her way.

By 4:00 p.m. she had arrived in Old Cairo. She spent an hour wandering through crowded markets. The aroma of herbs and spices pervaded the air: cayenne, coriander, saffron, sesame, turmeric, and cinnamon. On the streets, in the public squares, there were beggars, snake charmers, acrobats, rug peddlers, minstrels, astrologers, and would-be medicine men.

She tasted different spices and examined some earrings but was more in the mood to look, not to buy. She did follow Colonel Amjad's advice, however, and purchased three scarves. They were beautiful pieces in tan and green silk with very Egyptian designs, each slightly different. They would help her blend in somewhere later perhaps, or so she reasoned.

She stopped for a tea and was again relieved that no one was following her. Across from her, a row of men smoked hookahs and quietly assessed her as they sipped tea along with their smokes. Finally, in response to their persistent and curious gaze, she smiled back and nodded to them.

She recalled her teenage friend, René, from years ago.

She looked at the men. *"Marhabbah. Assalaam Alaikim,"* she said. Hello. Peace be with you.

They broke into surprised smiles. They nodded respectfully and smiled broadly.

Then, late in the day, she went up to the Citadel, the thousand-year-old fortress originally built to protect Cairenes from the Christian crusaders of Europe. As she stood on a promontory overlooking the city, she could hear the *athan*, the call to prayer, sounding from all angles. There seemed to be a *masjiid*, a mosque, in every direction, each equipped with loudspeakers attached to its minaret. Like the street vendors and hawkers, even the mosques were competing for attention and customers in this small, crowded universe. And yet, in a cramped, sooty, elbow-to-elbow way, the city had its charm — or at least her first view of it. Alex felt as if she were picking up the feel of the place.

The sun was setting. She bought a cheap digital camera, took some pictures of the Citadel, and headed back to her hotel. Back in her room, she went again to her window to savor her new venue. Below her, in the back lot of the hotel, the blue pool gleamed. Tourists with brown bodies frolicked and splashed in it. Beyond, the sun set on the Nile, and she watched a few pleasure craft and sailboats navigate the river.

Toward 8:00 in the evening, Alex had dinner alone in her hotel room. There were three different menus: American, European, and Muslim. She ordered from the European. From her window again later in the evening, she could see the lights of part of the city.

She realized anew how exhausted she was. She made sure her door was bolted properly and, after her experiences in Geneva, examined all the walls for any false entrances or exits to her room. As was her habit, she placed the loaded gun by her bedside. She had no desire to wake up in a place different from where she had fallen asleep. It had happened before.

Toward 10:00 in the evening, Cairo time, she reviewed secure email on her laptop. There was nothing of importance from back in the United States, where it was now midafternoon. Nothing from her contacts in Cairo either.

Then, just as she was about to log off, her secure email came alive again. It was from Rizzo. He had spotted a newspaper article that had just appeared. He enclosed a link.

She clicked on it and read:

EXPERT IN RUSSIAN POISONING CASE IS SHOT

FBI joins investigation,
but officials think it's just local crime

By Evelyn McFedries
Special to The Wall Street Journal

WASHINGTON—FBI agents are assisting Washington, DC, police, who are investigating the shooting of a Russian expert, a man who spoke out on *NewsLine NBC* last weekend and strongly suggested that veterans of the KGB were responsible for the poisoning death of Alexander Litvinenko.

The Russian expert, Grigor Popov, was shot Thursday night as he stepped from his car in front of his house in Bethesda, Md. Police in Prince Georges County say witnesses claim to have seen a lone gunman running away after the shooting. Popov remains hospitalized in critical

condition with a gunshot wound to the lower ab-
domen. He is under police guard at the hospital.

Popov was a longtime consultant on Russian
affairs. From 1990 to 2002, he was director of
security for the Senate Intelligence Committee.

On last weekend's *NewsLine*, he said of Litvinenko's death: "A message has been communi-
cated to anyone who wants to speak out against
Vladimir Putin and the Kremlin: 'If you do, no
matter who you are, where you are, we will find
you and we will silence you.' "

FBI and Maryland police are aware of Popov's
theories regarding the Litvinenko death. But
local investigators are highly skeptical that
this was anything other than street crime. The
FBI, however, has theorized differently.

In an additionally bizarre coincidence, another person who appeared recently on a *NewsLine*
broadcast died of a heart attack last month.
Reporter Howard Dunbar of the *Times* of London,
who had also written about the Litvinenko case,
died Feb. 20, before the *NewsLine* segment was
broadcast. He was 52.

Mr. Dunbar was a veteran British foreign cor-
respondent who had reported from Eastern Europe.
Just before his death, he had been reporting in
Ukraine.

She read the article twice.

Okay, good to know. Continuing background.

Russia. Ukraine. Putin. Mysterious death. Apparent political assassination.

Special significance beyond that? If there was any, Rizzo didn't note it and she didn't catch it.

She yawned. She undressed and showered. She brushed her teeth.

She collapsed into a very comfortable bed and was asleep within seconds.

THIRTY-FIVE

In the 1300s, Cairo had been the crossroads of trade between Europe and the Far East. As Cairo grew as a commercial center, the need expanded for space within the city for traders to gather, open stalls, and engage in commerce. The horse keeper of one of the sultans, Gharkas al-Khalili, seeking appropriate new quarters for Muslim merchants, purchased the land of the old Fatimid royal cemetery. He dug up the bodies that had been interred there, transported them by horse-drawn carts to a place outside the city walls, and dumped them to rot in the heat and sunlight.

So much for early urban renewal.

With the land now cleared, a new market was built in 1382 by the Emir Djaharks el-Khalili in the heart of the Fatimid City upon the old burial grounds. Together with the *al-Muski* market to the west, the new commercial area created one of Cairo's most important shopping areas in the Middle Ages. But more than that, the market established Cairo as a major center of trade, and at the Khan, as it is now called, one will still find foreign merchants where the market was founded in 1382.

Historically, this same market was involved in the spice monopoly that encouraged the Europeans to search for new routes to the East. Indirectly, it led Columbus to sail for the Americas.

On the evening of her second day in Cairo, Alex walked through this shopping district, passing through the narrow passageways between shops and booths, tradesmen and artisans, until she came to an old café named Fishawi's. Cairo remains a city that reeks of age, and Fishawi's is a great part of that aroma.

Fishawi's has been open every day and night for two centuries. It is a dark, noisy place, reminiscent of an old-fashioned Paris café, with gas lights and small tables scattered inside and out.

Alex entered the café alone and surveyed the chamber. It didn't take long to find the people she was looking for. There were two women in headscarves and robes at a table midway back in the café, talking, but obviously waiting for someone. Their eyes were upon Alex from the moment she saw them. They wore no veils. They would have been otherwise unremarkable except Alex spotted the bouquet of roses immediately. That, and the fact that they were the only pair of women within the entire café. There were scores of men.

The roses were upright in a vase. That was the "clear" signal.

Alex walked to the table, conscious of many eyes upon her. The women stopped talking and looked up at her, though the chamber remained noisy.

"I'm a friend of Fitzgerald," Alex said in low tones in English.

"Yes?" one of the women said. "You are Josephine?"

"I am Josephine," Alex said.

"I'm Artemiz," the woman answered. "Be seated. Welcome."

"You are alone?" the other woman asked.

"I am alone."

"You were careful when you came here?" Artemiz asked.

"I'm always careful," Alex said.

"That's very wise," Artemiz said.

The women looked enough alike to be sisters. Dark eyes, round faces, black hair. Mocha skin.

Alex looked for an extra chair. There was one nearby. She reached for it but Artemiz stopped her hand.

"Wait," Artemiz said softly.

Alex looked back at her. She knew enough not to interfere with any safety precautions. As was usual in cases like this, Alex was very conscious of the gun under her jacket, and how quickly she could get at it.

The two women spoke to each other. Alex was surprised. She realized that she had missed something. The women spoke Farsi to each other. They were, it was quickly apparent, Persians, not Arabs, though Muslim nonetheless. They were most likely Iranians in exile.

The second woman got up, went to the entrance, and stepped outside where she could see the street as well as be seen. Artemiz remained in the café. She indicated that Alex should now take the seat. Alex did.

"Sit and relax for a minute," Artemiz said.

Alex watched as the woman on the street flipped open a cell phone and made a call. Then the nameless woman retreated from the café side of the street to the opposite side. Artemiz engaged Alex in a petty conversation, but Alex kept her eyes on the street. She then saw two burley men appear and take positions, like sentries, by the door. They were conspicuous in their size, well over six feet each, and bulked up. Alex assumed they were also armed and part of the security arrangements for the meeting. It was Alex's first clue that she wasn't about to rendezvous with any old broken-down street spy.

Several minutes passed. Artemiz continued a meaningless conversation about tourist sites in Cairo. Alex replied politely to each question and waited. She broke a sweat. The woman on the street stayed within view. Alex felt her anxiety level rise but continued to watch. The woman out on the street took an incoming call that lasted no more than five seconds. She then put her phone away and reached with her right hand to her left elbow, tapping it twice.

Artemiz changed subjects in mid-phrase. She reached beneath her own robe, pulled out a checkered head scarf and handed it to Alex.

"Here. Wear this," she said. "We're going to move. Come!"

"To where?" Alex asked.

"Voltaire is ready. He will see you now," Artemiz said. "Put the *hijab* on."

"I have my own," Alex said.

Artemiz was surprised. "Then wear it," she said.

Alex reached to a pocket and pulled out a *hijab*. She wrapped the new scarf around her head and neck. The Persian woman looked at her and then smiled, as if Alex hadn't donned the scarf just right.

She hadn't.

"Here," Artemiz said. "Let me." She reached to Alex and with a greatly bemused grin adjusted the scarf. "You have a beautiful face," she said, staring into Alex's eyes. "The scarf sets it off. I have a cousin who lives in America, in Los Angeles, and you remind me of her. Now, come with me and walk quickly."

Alex stood. The Persian woman put a hand on her arm and pulled her toward the rear of the café. Alex suddenly was apprehensive and felt a fresh surge of fear.

Was she being set up? Led somewhere to be shot? Had there been a breach of security? She didn't have time to sort out such thoughts. She only had time to go with the moment. Artemiz took Alex's hand and pulled her quickly along. Alex kept her other hand near her weapon and followed. Artemiz weaved past the waiters and a klatch of men standing in the rear of the café, drinking and smoking dark acrid cigarettes or hookahs. Artemiz seemed to know them. She smiled and they stepped aside for her, allowing her to move toward a doorway, curtained with thick beads, that led toward a kitchen.

The two women pushed through the curtain.

Then they were in a kitchen, where several Muslim men in white labored over various dishes and grills while chattering in more high-decibel conversation. The chamber was full of conflicting cooking smells: baking fish, charred lamb, grilled chicken, steamed fruits, and spices.

Artemiz pulled Alex through the kitchen and to a rear door. Then they were out into a back alley where the footing was treacherous.

"Follow, follow," Artemiz said with urgency. "Fast, fast."

They went several paces down the alley. Rubbish and who-knew-what crunched underfoot. Artemiz turned sharply and led Alex into the back office of another café, where another big man sat by the rear door — an armed sentry, Alex assumed — and then into another kitchen. It all happened so fast that Alex could have been being kidnapped and wouldn't have known it until a pistol was placed to her head. Then they were through the kitchen and next arrived breathlessly in the back of the café, this one slightly more presentable.

There was an empty table in the rear. It was in the corner, and there was a bench behind it, big enough for two. The Persian woman led Alex to it.

"Sit," said Artemiz.

"Where's Voltaire?" Alex asked.

"One minute," Artemiz said.

"Where — ?"

"Don't speak. Don't say names. Wait here. Keep quiet."

Cautiously, Alex eased into the seat. Artemiz turned and departed, vanishing back through the kitchen, leaving Alex alone at the small table, quite astonished. Less than two minutes earlier, she had been sitting in another café on a different block.

Alex's gaze swept the room. She saw no one she recognized. Her hand settled upon her Beretta, just in case. Her heart was thundering, and her eyes measured not just the distance to the front door but the impediments to it also. She felt as vulnerable as she had at any time in her life. She didn't even speak the language. The palm on her weapon was pouring forth a flood of sweat.

Then a tall, sturdy man at the end of the bar turned around. His gaze crashed into Alex's. Their eyes locked.

He was a handsome man, Caucasian with blunt features, probably about fifty, maybe past fifty but very fit. He wore a beige Western-style suit and a light blue dress shirt, open at the collar. He was just over six feet, she reckoned, and after turning to appraise her he stood rock still as he looked at her. He too wore a *hijab*, but his eyes were blue and his face more German than anything. Distantly, and perhaps absurdly, he reminded Alex of Peter O'Toole in the old *Lawrence of Arabia* movie posters.

He established eye contact with Alex. Then he walked to her, calmly, without menace, and with great confidence. Alex checked his hands. They were empty. She looked for a bulge under his jacket and found it on the left side.

He came up directly to her table, stood politely but assertively, and looked down at her through keen but saddened eyes. Then he grinned and his face became ten years younger.

"May I join you, my dear?" he asked.

"It depends on who you are and what you want," Alex said.

"I'm a Sagittarian," he said. "Does that make it any better?"

"It might," she said. "I'm a Capricorn."

"So was Sadat, so was Stalin, so is Dolly Parton, and so was Jesus. So maybe then I should sit down," he said.

"Maybe you should."

A moment passed, and a small wave of relaxation washed over

her. "So good of you to come to Cairo," he said in perfect English that could have been from anywhere. "You see, we have a crisis here with someone you used to work with. You might want to consider becoming totally obsessed with it. I know the rest of us are."

"Talk to me," Alex said, settling in.

The spy known as Voltaire reached easily into his pocket and pulled out a pack of Marlboros. "Filthy habit, smoking," he said. "I wish I could kick it. Then again, like a lot of my filthy habits, I rather enjoy it."

He offered one to her.

"No, thanks," she said.

"Not even one?"

"Not even a puff of yours," she said.

"Smart," he said.

But he lit one and blew out the smoke. Then, just as easily, he began to talk.

THIRTY-SIX

You're going to help us bring home a renegade intelligence agent," Voltaire explained. "That's why you're here. But part of the way I work is to be seen as little as possible by anyone who knows exactly what I do. So for our purposes here, you're going to be the point person, the person who's on the front line to bring in Michael Cerny. Does the operation make sense to you so far?"

"From what I know of it, yes," she said.

"This operation has more than one goal, as you'll discover. I'll tell you right now that there's more going on here than you already realize or than you'll perhaps ever know." He paused. "Think of yourself as a colonel in artillery in the D-Day invasion. You have authority, but do you really know what the generals are doing? Of course not."

Alex watched him, his steady gaze, his steady hands, and said nothing.

"I'm not planning to give you a thorough briefing today. We have a little window of time before we close a trap on the individual in whom we have an interest. 'Judas,' I'd like to call him," Voltaire said.

"Judas," Alex answered. "Very good."

"I operate under the assumption that you're fully up to an assignment like this, mentally and physically," he continued. "Otherwise you wouldn't have been sent, nor would you have persevered to find this place. If you had any last minute trepidations, you would have disappeared in the alley. So I won't even ask if you have second thoughts. You wouldn't be sitting here if you did. My condolences on your loss in Kiev, your fiancé, by the way. I know the whole story."

"Thank you," she said.

"I spoke to our mutual friend at the office in Cairo, the gentleman who directed you here. Fitzgerald."

Alex nodded.

"He's your guy for background information, what has already

happened. One doesn't understand the present without understanding the past," Voltaire said. "But I'm your person for what we're going to do, what will happen. Are you ready to get killed?"

"Not really."

"Me, neither. That's good. And I like you," he said. "But if there's a choice between one of us getting killed, I'll choose you in a heartbeat. I'd expect you to do the same. Are you a religious person?"

"I am," she said. "A practicing Christian."

"I'm not anything."

"I can tell."

"That damns my soul to hell, doesn't it?" he asked.

"It's a theory," she said.

He laughed. "You're good. Sharp. Hungry?"

"A bit. Is food an option?"

"Sometimes." He signaled a waiter. The establishment had kebabs, a chicken couscous, and something called a *bisteeya*, which Voltaire suggested.

"What is it?" she asked.

"It's a flaky pastry concocted from almonds, dates, and pigeon."

"*Pigeon?* Like underfoot in New York?" she asked. "Feathered rats?"

"Very similar. Hemingway survived on them when he was struggling in Paris after World War I. Try one."

"I'm not struggling, I'm not in Paris, and I'll have a kabob," she said. "Lamb, not mutton, right? And with rice."

"As you request," Voltaire said. "If they bring salad, don't touch it. That's how you get dysentery."

To be clear, Voltaire translated the order into crisp Arabic. The waiter nodded, smiled, and disappeared.

"Very good," Voltaire said. His eyes swept the room. "You've got some sass to you too. That helps. How do you feel about seducing a man you've never previously met."

"Depends on who he is, what he looks like, and where we are."

"Good answer," he said. "I was in the military for six years. Not with the Americans but with a Western power. I was in a branch equivalent to your US Marines. Whenever one was asked a question of logistics and wanted to hedge on the answer, one would say, 'It depends on the situation and the terrain.' That's the answer you just gave."

"This 'seduction'?" she asked. "This ties in with an overnight with a Russian that Fitzgerald mentioned?"

"It might."

"This seems to be emerging as a sub-specialty of mine," she said facetiously.

"We all have our moments and our skills," he said.

"What are yours?"

"You'll find out as we go along," he said. "As you need to know. But think of me as a Swiss Army knife. I have a lot of functions other than just cutting throats."

"Which armed forces were you with?" she asked.

"If I wanted you to know that, don't you think I would have just told you?"

"Of course," Alex answered. "But I figured I'd give it a try."

"You look like you'd be a real pleasure in bed," Voltaire continued. "Sleep with me later tonight, and I'll tell you about my army career."

"I don't need to know that badly. In fact, I don't really care."

"Good response. How many languages do you speak?" he asked.

"You've seen my file. You know the answer," Alex said. "English, Spanish, French, Italian, Russian, and I can get by in Ukrainian. I have a limited reading knowledge of German and a familiarity with Portuguese almost by default because it overlaps so often with the other Romance languages."

Voltaire nodded. "I speak the same languages as you do, plus Greek and Arabic, obviously, but without the bloody Ukrainian. I mention all this in case it becomes an element in our communication over the next few days."

He paused.

"The German I speak with considerable ease," he said. "My parents were Nazis. My father and both of his brothers were in the SS."

He looked her up and down.

"Are you shocked?" he asked.

"Shocked? No. I'm not even surprised. And I'm certainly not impressed."

"One of them was the commandant of a labor camp in Poland," he said. "Very nice man as long as you weren't a Jew, in which case he was a monster. He escaped here after the war. I rather liked Uncle Heinz, murderer though he was."

"That's for you to live with, not me," she said. "Assuming there's even a grain of truth to any of that, which I suspect there isn't."

He kept a tight gaze upon her, eye to eye. Then he relented and smiled. "All right," he said. "You passed."

"I passed what?"

"Until right now I could have rejected you as a working partner. You didn't know that?"

"No."

"Now you do," he said. "I'm going to talk to Fitzgerald by phone later this evening. He'll send you some further background files, mostly on the intelligence operations of a 'third party' nation that is normally friendly to the United States, but isn't always. Any idea who that might be?"

"I could offer a short list."

"Good. Don't. Fitzgerald will send you files. Read them in the morning. Tomorrow we'll meet again. Have you been out to the Pyramids of Giza?"

"Never," she said.

"Good again. We'll go for an open-air ride. Perfect place to talk. I'll explain what will be expected of you. Be in front of your hotel at 3:00 p.m. Dress a little bit like a tourist if you can. Khaki is good. If you don't have any with you, there are shops around the hotel. It will be hot in the afternoon, then cool in the evening. Khaki is perfect."

"I brought some with me," she said. "Work shirt, slacks, and shorts."

"Good move. Ever ride a horse?"

"Last year in the Kentucky Derby. Finished third."

"Brilliant, but answer me for real."

"When I was a teenager, neighbors had horses."

"In the US?"

"Eastern Ontario. I also worked on a ranch in France one summer. I rode there too."

"Like it?"

"France or the horses?"

"Either," he asked.

"Both."

"Good," he said. "You might be on the back of a camel tomorrow. It's similar, just hurts more if you fall because you're higher up. And God help you if you get kicked with a hoof."

"You're serious about this camel thing?"

"Completely. It goes with my cover. I'm a local businessman. I invite friends and business associates from all over the world and take them out to the tourist places. Wide open air. We can talk in complete freedom. Many of my guests are beautiful single women, so even if we are observed, nothing raises an eyebrow."

"Got it," she said.

"Now, tell me a bit more about yourself," Voltaire said.

"There's very little reason to," she said. "You obviously know a lot about me or you wouldn't have come here to meet me."

"True enough," he said. "But tell me things anyway."

"Such as?"

"Tell me something I might not know," he said, "something that might have escaped your official file or record. And don't bore me with any of that Canadian nonsense, I know exactly who you are."

She thought for a moment. She sipped the chilled tea that accompanied the meal.

"All right, here's something," she said. "I got into this line of work almost by chance. I never had any desire to do it. I was at a desk in Washington working on internet financial frauds. Next thing I know, they put me out in the field on a mission to Nigeria. That was a group effort. But thereafter, I got hooked into a trip to Ukraine. They needed someone who spoke Russian, so they tapped me."

"You never thought there might have been an ulterior reason?" he asked.

"For what?" she asked, slightly surprised.

"For sending *you*. Specifically you, to Ukraine."

"No. I didn't."

"It never occurred to you?"

"Not until now."

"Always consider something like that," he said. "That's a word of good advice for the evening, free of charge."

She pondered the point.

"I'm enjoying this dialogue. Keep talking," he said.

"About?"

"How you never sought your current métier. But like greatness in anything, rather than seeking it or attaining it, you had it thrust upon you."

Plates of food arrived. Suddenly, Alex was very hungry. She dug in, and they retreated to small talk for several minutes.

"Here's something else, since you asked," she said at length. "I tend to take code names very seriously," she said. "The more one examines them, the more they reveal something about the person who has taken them."

"Do tell," said Voltaire.

"The desk-bound intellectual who yearns for action takes the name of 'Fireman.' The outlaw takes the name of 'Sheriff.' The atheist takes the name of 'Priest.' Somehow your code name expresses something about you. A reference to French parentage perhaps instead of the Nazi cover story that you tried to sell me. A coy allusion to the Enlightenment in Europe. You're obviously well educated, I suspect perhaps even in the French language, as you speak it with no accent that I can pick up and with excellent diction and grammar. Or you have a yearning again to be what you're not, vis-à-vis, French. I may never know, but somewhere the name is a key."

"Very, *very* clever," he said. "Maybe as a reward, I should tell you part of it."

"Maybe you should. If you chose to, I'd listen."

"Consider it an expression of opposites. It's an expression of personal philosophy as opposed to anything of action, strategy, or import. You're a rather educated little imp, yourself," he said. "My guess is that you've studied French extensively and probably read it on a university level. So if you read French literature of any sort, you probably read *Candide*."

"I did. And I once saw a production of the musical in New York."

"And what was the key phrase of Dr. Pangloss? Of what was the real Voltaire mocking so bitterly?"

"The concept that this is the best of all possible worlds," she answered.

"Exactly," he said. "And that is exactly the opposite of what I'm making fun of, what I'm alluding to. This world that we live in is, in my benighted opinion, often the worst of all possible worlds."

"Hence your code name fits you completely and gives away a large part of you," she said. "Because that was absolutely the feeling of the real Voltaire."

He laughed. "You're the first person I've ever met who cut right through to the core of that," he said.

"I might be the first person who cared enough to," she said.

"That too," he admitted. "Impressive. It's rare enough to find an American who has read *Candide*."

"I'm Canadian," she said.

"Good catch."

"Nice try."

A waiter came by and cleared their table. They ordered a final mint tea.

The conversation drifted back to Voltaire's long residence in, and expertise about, the city of Cairo. From there he rambled into local politics as he smoked again. Alex found it wise to listen.

"The people of Cairo don't believe their rulers, but they give credibility to every halfwit political rumor that goes around, no matter how stupid and ill-founded. Did you know that Coptic Christians were waging a secret war by going around spray painting crosses onto the clothing of Muslims? Did you know Israel had hired and sent to Egypt one thousand AIDS-infected prostitutes to infect young Muslim men? Did you know that radical Muslim extremists were planning to dump poison into the vats at the Stella brewery? You keep your ear to the ground in this city and you'll hear just about anything," Voltaire said. "Unless you trust your source beyond any question, you believe nothing that you hear and maybe ten percent of what you see." He paused. "Want to experience an example of it for yourself?" he asked Alex. "Right now?"

"Where? How?" she asked.

"There's a little group in a café near here that I join every now and then. People talk. Often in English. I drop by and listen and do some give and take. It helps to keep an ear to the ground."

He glanced at his watch. Alex glanced at hers at the same time. It was 10:45.

"And they don't know who they're talking to?" Alex asked.

"They don't know and they don't care," Voltaire said. "My cover is this: I'm a Monsieur Maurice Lamara, an importer of air-conditioning units from France and Italy. I run a midsized company here. I have a dozen employees and I treat them well. I never go near the embassy, and I collect a nice payment every month from the Americans who put an electronic transfer into a bank in Europe for me every month. Cairenes voice a lot of noisy opinions, but they know better than to ask many questions because they might get a visit from the police. You'll see what I mean."

"Who will you say I am?"

"My *femme du jour*," he said with a trace of lechery in his eyes. "They're used to seeing me with beautiful Western women, one after another. I bring women by, just to show them off. They rather admire me for it in their swinish Arab way. If you're game, I'll take you there."

"I'm your squeeze of the night, huh?"

"So to speak."

"I didn't travel four thousand miles to go home early," she said.

"That's the spirit."

"Am I dressed okay? For wherever we're going."

"You're fine. Keep the headscarf. We'll have some high-artillery backup, anyway. I don't go anywhere without it."

"I noticed. You have at least six."

"There are more than that, but I'm not giving away numbers."

"Eight then? The two Persian women have guns?"

"Now you have it."

"I never for a moment thought you were stupid," she said. "Let's go."

Voltaire turned and gestured to a burley man seated two tables away. The man stood. As his body straightened up to standing position, Alex realized he was even larger than she had guessed. He stood maybe six-four. He wore a white robe and an Islamic skull cap. He came to the table and a grin spread across his face. He had the torso of a Kodiak bear and the face of a cherub with a stubbly beard.

"This is Abdul," Voltaire said. "Abdul and I have known each other for twenty years. He's one of my bodyguards and he'll lead the way."

Abdul held out a hand to Alex.

"Charmed," he said.

"My pleasure, I'm sure," Alex said. Abdul's hand was like a catcher's mitt.

Abdul nodded.

"Where are you from in America?" he asked.

"I'm from the Toronto area," she said. "I'm Canadian. What about you? You're a native of Cairo?"

"I'm Iraqi," Abdul said. "I grew up in Detroit. I was in the US Army for six years. Fort Hood, Texas. Fort Benning, Georgia, stateside, one tour in Afghanistan."

"Surprising place, isn't it?" Voltaire asked. "I assume you have a weapon. Check that it's functioning in case there's trouble."

"Expecting any?"

"I never expect any. And I always prepare for it."

"My weapon is fine," she said. It was where it always was, on her right hip, accessible, the safety catch on.

"Then let's go," he said.

THIRTY-SEVEN

Abdul left the room for several seconds, then came back and gestured that they should follow. They took off. Alex stayed close to Voltaire. They were back in the alley but now headed in a different direction. It was close to 11:00 in the evening, and Voltaire led her into an alley between shops. It was so dark that she couldn't see and so narrow that they had to pass one at a time.

"You're a brave woman, coming here by yourself, Josephine," Voltaire said softly and affably. "You're well educated and attractive. There must be easier ways for you to make a living. Safer too. Why do you do it?"

"Sometimes I ask myself the same question," Alex said.

He snorted a little in reaction. "We all do," he said. "What is it? The adrenaline? The danger of hanging out with disreputable people? The feeling that we're on the side of the angels? A sense of justice? Must be some reason why we kick through back alleys and put our lives on the line. My question is rhetorical, really. I don't know the answer and I suspect you don't, either."

"When I figure it out, I'll let you know," she said.

"I promise you I'll do the same."

They came to an even narrower passage between buildings. No more than two feet in width, jagged nails sticking out from bricks, plus some electrical wires. For a moment, Voltaire took her hand to steady her. "This is tricky here," he said. He eased Alex through sideways for twenty feet until they emerged into a wider alley.

"Tu parles français, n'est-ce pas?" he asked.

"Je parle français, oui," she answered.

For good measure, even though there was still noise from the city in the background, he suggested switching into French. Less chance of being overheard and understood. Alex concurred and agreed.

While French was not uncommon in Egypt, it was nowhere nearly understood as much as a second language as English.

"I'll give you thirty years of history in six minutes as we walk," Voltaire said, still in low tones. "And my history lesson will tell you where we are today. Anwar Sadat, who succeeded Nasser in 1970, was assassinated by his own soldiers in 1981. Several of the soldiers who shot him had had family or close friends who had been displaced by one of his urban renewal projects. Sadat was liked and respected outside of Egypt, but here the poor and the Islamic militants hated him. It was a matter of time before his own people murdered him. And he misplayed his most basic politics at home. He quietly funded some Islamic radical groups, figuring they would combat the leftists who Sadat actually feared. His plan backfired. Some of those who conspired to kill him had been radicalized by the same groups that Sadat had founded. Other leaders of the assassins were people whom Sadat had himself freed from Nasser's jails. They weren't grateful, they were bitter. They hated the government no matter who was running it. They felt the government had betrayed Islam. It was their theory that if someone had betrayed Islam, it is the duty of the individual as a Muslim to right that wrong. So they righted the wrong by murdering the president of their country. Quite a place, huh? Egyptian politics as usual. That's how it's been for centuries. It will never change."

The alley widened.

Abdul was about fifty feet up ahead, and Alex realized one reason he wore white. He was more visible that way. There were no overhead lights, just reflected lights from the windows of the back entrances of the stores and the houses that they passed.

"Were you in Egypt at the time?" Alex asked. "When Sadat was assassinated?"

"I was a young lad," he said. "I was a student at the American University in Cairo. Beautiful place until it got trashed by the unwashed Islamic masses."

They wound their way down several more alleys, each one more serpentine than the previous. Alex realized they were in a different district now. The omnipresent stench of backed-up plumbing was everywhere, as was the scent of stale cigarettes. In the better locations there was a mélange of cooking smells, mostly spices she didn't recognize as well as onions and garlic frying.

"Hosni Mubarak was Sadat's successor. Mubarak was on the reviewing stand when Sadat was assassinated," Voltaire said. "While Sadat turned and glared at his assassins, Mubarak had the good sense to duck when the shooting started. His reward? He became president of the country. Then he did some other smart things too. A quarter of a century ago Cairo was a mess. A million cars. Pollution so thick you could chew on it. Sewage overflowed into the streets. Skyscrapers were overpopulated and poorly constructed. The blight spread practically all the way out to the Sphinx's testicles, and, ironically, the desert was spreading right into Cairo. Sand covered the streets. Sand and garbage. And on top of the sand and garbage, more sand and garbage and the bodies of people who had died overnight, natural or otherwise. The whole place, the whole population, was festering. Work into that the fact that this was one of the most overpopulated cities in the world and you begin to get the picture."

As they continued, Alex could overhear heated conversations from open but barred windows, music from radios, the drone of televisions, and at least one violent argument between a man and a woman. The noise, like a steady irritating disco beat, just kept on going.

The argument descended into physical fighting. Alex and Voltaire kept on walking. *Husband and wife?* Alex wondered. *Prostitute and customer? Mother and son?*

It could have been any.

"Mubarak saw what had happened to his predecessor, getting shot down by his own people, so he was smart enough to attack all the things that were wrong. And he had some success, which is why he stayed in power so long. Mubarak got money from foreign powers for acting as the regional peace broker. He planted trees, built roads and sewers, and gave the main thoroughfares a facelift. He got the Chinese to build a new conference center, got the Japanese to build an opera house, induced the French to build a subway line, and got the Americans to give him just enough military clout so that he could stay in power but not enough military power to attack Israel again. So what happens? All the middle-class Egyptians who had moved to Europe and America started moving back. The doctors. The engineers. The middle-class émigrés. Cairo didn't become Paris, but it was no longer a slum surrounded by sand and camel dung. You'd think that would be a good thing, right?" he asked.

"Maybe," Alex answered.

Alex did a double-take. They passed an establishment that was wide open from the back. It was obviously a brothel, with several half-naked women hanging out in the doorway and in the windows, dark-haired, sullen, and tattooed.

They smiled at Voltaire as he passed. He waved and they waved back. They probably know him, Alex thought. The girls looked disapprovingly at Alex, as if she was infringing on their business. One of them said something to her in Arabic and the others laughed.

"The pseudo-prosperity created its own problems," Voltaire said, continuing in French. "The people in the slums, the people who were in those overcrowded high-rises, and even the working-class people of the city, the people who drove taxis or cleaned the streets or worked in the hospitals, the 'new affluence' never trickled down to them. It was grabbed off by the émigrés who had moved back. And so the poor and uneducated got even angrier. You'd think they would have tried to embrace the new order, run their lives a little differently, try to Westernize their lives the way the successful returned émigrés had. No. Know what they did instead?"

"My guess is that they clung to their own traditions all the more fervently," Alex said. "And that would mean an even more tenacious embrace of Islam."

"That's exactly right," Voltaire said. "The fundamentalist Islamic preachers used the mosques and the television to convince this great struggling mass of people that they weren't doing anything wrong. The problem was the Egyptians who had become Westernized and fallen away from Islam faith, the mullahs said. The people who had returned with wealth and Western wives and cars and credit cards, they were the big problem in society. You'd see graffiti all over the city that said, 'Islam *is* the Solution.' And as an example of proof of Islam being the solution, they held up Saudi Arabia."

"Why Saudi Arabia?"

"Saudi Arabia is one of the most piously conservative countries in the Arab world. Never mind the hypocrisy. Ignore the fact that all the ne'er-do-well Saudi princes go on debauched trips to Europe and America and dissipate themselves in the nightclubs and the whorehouses. We're talking about official Saudi policy and society. It is a tenet of Islam that Allah will take care of the truly devout. Well, the Saudi sheiks from the bloody House of Saud park their camels and their Rolls-Royces right on top of the world's greatest petroleum reserves. What better proof is there of Allah's favor than that? So if you were a traditional young Egyptian, you were impressed by your devout friends who went, not to Europe and got corrupted, but to work in the Gulf in the oil business. They'd do it for three to five years and then come back with a car, gold jewelry, a fat bankroll, and a veiled teenage wife that to all intents and purposes they owned, some poor girl not destined to get an education or a breath of free air in her entire life. But that's just my opinion. Not a bad reward in this life for keeping the faith, is it?"

"A lot of men wouldn't think so," Alex said.

Abdul disappeared around a dim corner. Voltaire suddenly grabbed Alex by the arm.

"Tiens! Attends un moment!" he said. Wait a moment.

He cocked his head, as if to listen for danger. They held their ground; then, when nothing happened, Voltaire indicated with a nod that they could proceed. Alex and Voltaire turned the same dark corner a few seconds later.

Abdul had already vanished. They were in a black dead-end alley. Alex and Voltaire stood for a moment. There were a few doors, back entrances to homes, Alex thought. The doors were wooden and shabby. Somewhere a big dog was barking. Abdul had disappeared through one of the doors, Alex guessed. The only light was a bluish hue from an overhead window, either a florescent bulb or an old television. Sounds of second-story conversations tumbled down into the alley. Somewhere a man was snoring loudly. Alex couldn't tell where.

Alex glanced at Voltaire and wondered if she had been set up. "Are we all right?" she asked.

"We're fine," Voltaire whispered. "Just another few seconds." He shot back to his civics lesson. "Anyway, the influx of wealthy émigrés allowed the fundamentalist mullahs to gain even more influence," Voltaire said. "Not with the government, but with the unwashed masses. Look, one fundamentalist preacher wanted zucchini to be banned from Cairo markets because of its phallic shape. Another one claimed that the Cairo Tower, a big, new, long, narrow building that rises out of a newly greened parkland, should be destroyed. He claimed that its size and shape might sexually arouse a generation of young Egyptian women."

"And people took that seriously?" Alex asked.

"Educated people? No. Of course not! But one Egyptian journalist, a headstrong chap named Farag Foda, was indelicate enough to make fun of that idea and some others at the Cairo book fair one year. The *book* fair, *pour l'amour de Dieu!* You'd think he would have been speaking to people who were at least somewhat enlightened. Instead the mullahs declared him 'a foe of Islam' and he was assassinated. And a local Islamic scholar, a witness before the court, testified that the killers had done nothing wrong since there was no sin in killing a foe of Islam. He said that the murder of Farag Foda was an apostate's punishment that the local imam had failed to implement. The killers were eventually executed, which only made their cause more sympathetic to their followers. It was a time, not unlike now, when assassination was not uncommon. And it wasn't carried out by geniuses, either. A squad of gunmen on motor scooters once assassinated the speaker of the Egyptian parliament right in front of a new Western hotel. No one could figure out why they had hit this guy because he was middle level and not even disliked by the radicals. It turned out later that they mistook him for their real target, Mubarak's minister of the interior, who tended to pass by the same place every day. It was typical. The killers were reckless and ignorant, but they didn't lack for aggressiveness, and they were bent on shooting someone, anyone. So they did."

There was a noise above them as Voltaire concluded. Alex ducked and cringed. Then she raised her eyes to the window from which came the bluish light. A head appeared, silhouetted by the back light. Someone—a pudgy woman in a head scarf—looked down at them and said something in Arabic.

Voltaire gave a smile and waved. He answered in Arabic. The head disappeared.

Then one of the doors opened and Abdul stepped out. He stood in the half-open doorway and motioned for them to join him. Voltaire allowed Alex to go ahead of him.

They stepped into the back of a building. Alex had the sense of being in a private home, but they seemed to be in a storeroom of some sort. There were several packing crates and empty burlap bags. There were boxes of canned food stacked up, as well as a collection of knives and small saws. There was one electric drill that could be converted into a saw. What she was looking at, it occurred to her, were implements for either commercial cutting or the disposal of a corpse.

Or both.

From the next room came a conversation in Arabic — all male voices — and the heavy stench of non-American cigarettes, the type of cheap Bulgarian crap that Russians and Middle Easterners smoked.

Abdul quietly closed the door behind her. He gave a nod to Voltaire. Alex felt trapped, apprehensive. If she had been set up there was no way out. Voltaire took her hand. She didn't like that because it was her gun hand, but at this point she had to go with it.

"We're here," Voltaire said, switching back into English. "Come along. No way to chicken out now."

THIRTY-EIGHT

The evening maid was the first member of the break-in team at the hotel. No point to break down a door or pick a lock when one has access to a key. The maid was a friendly old Arab woman named Mellilah, underpaid as most of the hotel staff were, and went about her evening duties as usual.

Well, almost as usual.

She entered Alex's room at 8:30. She refreshed the bathroom with new towels and new soaps. She tidied the wash basin. In the living room she provided a new note pad near the phone, and she emptied all the wastebaskets in the suite.

In the bedroom, she made down the bed and pulled the shades. She fluffed up the pillows and left mints at the bedside. She turned down the top cover and the sheets and adjusted the air-conditioning for overnight sleeping.

She was finished within five minutes. When Mellilah left, she pulled the door almost completely closed. The door touched the frame of the doorway but did not click shut. She moved along to the next room.

Two minutes later, in the uniforms of porters at the hotel, two men named Hamzah and Mamdouth followed her path.

Hamzah was the hardware man and the lookout. He carried a steel suitcase and entered Alex's room first. He set down the suitcase and stayed near the door. Mamdouth showed up a few seconds later, sliding into the room and closing the door behind him.

They moved quickly to the bedroom. This was a routine job as long as Alex didn't return and no one in the hotel caught them. They set to work.

In Alex's sleeping area they went to the bed and lifted the mattress off its box frame. They eased it onto the floor. Then Hamzah and Mamdouth donned special masks and gloves. Hamzah opened the steel suitcase. The sides of the suitcase were enormously thick, exactly what was needed to carry heavily radioactive material.

They donned goggles and headgear. They wore other protective garments underneath their clothes. Mamdouth stepped back. Hamzah reached within the suitcase and removed a cylindrical container. It looked like an elaborate thermos and was the size of a quart of milk. Mamdouth withdrew to the next room to stay as far away from this part of the operation as possible.

Hamzah opened the insulated container. It contained a mixture that looked like heavy-grained sea salt. It was white with a bluish tint, but Hamzah didn't spend much time looking at it. In fact, he didn't want to look at it at all. He had read about the stuff that he was assigned to plant. It scared him. He had seen what it had done to people. It attacked their immune system and made people violently ill after a few days. Given close exposure — and that's what they were lining up for this Canadian woman — it would kill her in anywhere from five days to two weeks. It was a cruel and vicious tool. Hamzah liked the idea of using it to attack the enemies of Islam.

He leaned forward quickly. Touching none of the crystal directly, he sprinkled them onto the box frame that held Alex's mattress. There was about a cup of the stuff in the thermos and he scattered it evenly. A few hours sleep at night would give just the right lethal exposure. He was clear on what his boss had ordered. No way this Western woman was going to complete her assignment in Cairo.

Then he moved to the bathroom that adjoined the bedroom. He unscrewed the shower head and sprinkled some small crystals into the head. He replaced it. Then, in a moment of inspired venality, he opened Alex's medicine kit and found her toothpaste.

He opened the tube and pressed several crystals into it. Then he found a Q-tip and pressed the crystals down into the paste. He worked the crystal into the paste so that it would dissolve. He closed the tube again, careful not to allow any sign of tampering. He smiled. If this stuff was as mean as he understood it to be, a simple ingestion of the toxic substance would lead to an agonizing death within a few days. It would start with head pain and stomach discomfort and quickly deteriorate from there.

Inch'allah. As God willed it, he told himself.

Hamzah stepped back, breathing heavily within his mask, while Mamdouth continued to watch the door in the living room. The worst thing that could happen would be if the Canadian woman came home early.

There! Done!

"Mamdouth!" he called.

His associate quickly came back into the room. They lifted the mattress back into place and settled it on top of the bed. It settled on perfectly straight, just the way old Mellilah had left it.

They packed up the thermoslike canister and put it back in the suitcase. They clamped the suitcase shut. They walked quickly to the next room and pulled off their masks and gloves.

Mamdouth opened the door a sliver. He looked out and then ducked back quickly. He recognized a nasty-looking figure in khaki. It was Colonel Amjad, strolling up and down the hall, looking at doors.

Mamdouth indicated to Hamzah that they should wait. They did, Mamdouth's hand remaining on the doorknob.

Then the colonel was gone. Mamdouth poked his head fully into the hall. No one. Perfect. They stashed their garments and stepped out. They pulled the door shut. It clicked and locked behind them.

They went down the back stairs wearing their hotel uniforms. The Metropole was a big hotel, and security was nowhere as good as Western guests thought it was. Plus, they had bribed the rear guard, who was a brother in Islam.

They were out the gate within two minutes. This was even easier than planting a car bomb. They were away in a waiting car in four minutes.

It was neater than a car bomb too. The poison wasn't messy for anyone unless you were the victim who slept on it or someone who had inadvertently been exposed to it for several hours. If that was the case, it would be living hell and a horrible death.

THIRTY-NINE

Voltaire led Alex to the next room, which was a smoky sitting area — a shabby chamber with peeling paint, a pair of rundown sofas, some extra tables and chairs. There, a group of three men sat around a small table, on the sofa and on a cushion on the floor. They wore Western shirts and pants and white Arab headgear. They turned toward Voltaire when they saw him, and their faces illuminated in smiles. One man was cleanly shaven, two had bushy firstgrowth beards. Their gaze jumped quickly from Voltaire to Alex, and all three faces broke with even broader smiles and greetings in Arabic.

They stood. They liked Voltaire, whoever they thought he was, and they liked the idea of a female guest. Voltaire introduced her as a family friend who was visiting Egypt and the Holy Land on holiday.

They switched into English. The men around the table could not have been politer. Alex already knew that men in Cairo tended to be very polite, unless they were trying to assault or kill you.

Getting a further grip on where she was, Alex realized that they were in a small café and storefront that was part of someone's home, a common setup in Cairo, much as it is in Central and South America. The front of the place opened onto the street, and there were four other tables, though all of them were empty. The small group that she and Voltaire had joined were the only customers. It was just past midnight now. Abdul, who had led them there, seemed to have disappeared. Alex didn't question his absence.

A waiter appeared. Voltaire ordered in Arabic before Alex could speak. The waiter addressed him as "Monsieur Lamara." Two more teas arrived. And then, before she could object, a hookah.

She looked at him in astonishment.

"When in Cairo, do what the locals do," Voltaire said with a wink.

A single hookah with a double hose sat before them. It was a giant water pipe, decorated in gold and blue, that stood about three feet off the ground. The waiter gave Voltaire and Alex fresh plastic mouth-pieces. Alex looked at the substance being packed into the bowl of the pipe.

"What's in this?" Alex asked.

"Not what you think," Voltaire said. "Maybe not even what you're hoping for."

"Can you be more specific?"

"Ever smoked one of these?"

"No."

"Well, you're about to, my Canadian friend," he said. "I ordered something called *ma'sal*. It's special hookah tobacco. *Ma'sal* is tobacco with honey and other sweeteners added." He paused and seemed to be enjoying this. "You know what the original Voltaire once wrote? 'Once a philosopher, twice a pervert.'"

The Egyptian men watched her with smiles and amusement. In turn, she watched as the waiter packed a damp sticky brown substance into the bowl.

"I don't smoke," she said.

"Tonight you do," he said.

"Unhealthy," she said.

"So is our line of work," he countered. "So don't insult my friends."

"I want to see you smoke it first," she said.

"Oh. With pleasure."

There was a small amount of a special charcoal in the bowl, burning black and red. Voltaire nurtured the flame and drew in a breath. The smoke filtered and cooled through the water. The conversation around the table resumed as Voltaire held the smoke in his mouth and exhaled. The aroma that drifted toward Alex was more suggestive of a fruity pipe tobacco than anything else.

Deftly, Voltaire steered the conversation to politics and to the new American president, who was a great improvement on the world stage the men at the table agreed. But then Voltaire inched the conversation a few years farther back, to the previous administration and the attacks on New York and Washington in September of 2001. Around the table, it was common currency that Osama bin Laden and Al-Qaeda were not responsible for the attacks of September 11, 2001.

The United States and Israel, according to the general opinion put forth, had to have been involved in the planning and execution of the attacks.

"I don't believe what the American government says," one man at the table said. "They don't tell the truth, the Americans. The United States did 9/11 to itself with its own airplanes so that they could invade Iraq for the oil."

There were nods all around. Voltaire gave Alex a conspiratorial glance. He picked up the second hose and handed it to Alex. With some reservation, she put it to her lips.

"Don't inhale into your lungs," Voltaire said, softly and outside the conversation around the table. "Just hold it in your mouth, get the flavor and the relaxation. Then exhale slowly."

"Like Bill Clinton?" she asked.

Voltaire laughed.

"The attacks were part of a conspiracy against Muslims," said another man, who turned to Alex, hoping for agreement. "I do not believe that a group of Arabs could have waged such a successful operation against a superpower like the United States. We are not smart enough. We are not powerful enough."

"But the hijackers were Saudis," Voltaire reminded them.

"Ah, but look at Washington's post-9/11 foreign policy!" the first man countered quickly. "It proved that the United States and Israel were behind the attacks, especially with the invasion of Iraq."

There were nods all around. Alex drew some soft, sweet smoke into her mouth. She was convinced that she was going to cough, but didn't. There was a further glimmer of amusement in Voltaire's eyes and a sparkle in the eyes of some of the other men.

There was also a sparkle in the *ma'sal* concoction. It was infused with honey, possibly with a hint of raspberry also. Alex exhaled the smoke in a long, steady stream. She felt like the smart-ass self-satisfied caterpillar in *Alice in Wonderland*. Oh, if her friends back home could see her now, she thought.

One of the men couldn't take his eyes off her. When his gaze caught hers, he motioned to her headscarf. "Are you a follower of Islam?" he asked.

"No, I'm not," she said.

"Then ...?"

Thinking quickly. "I am a guest in your country," she said. "So I wear this out of respect for your customs."

Good answer, she thought to herself.

"That is gracious of you," he said. There were nods all around. She was okay, they decided. She took a second draw on the hookah pipe and blew out the smoke gently and soothingly. Nothing extraordinary happened. She took another drag and didn't mind it at all.

Voltaire gave her a wink. Tonight, she was one of the boys.

"Maybe people who executed the operation were Arabs," said a third, younger man, joining in politely. "But it had to have been organized by other people. The Israelis, the Americans," he said. "The Mossad. The CIA. Zionist businessmen."

"Jews did not go to work at the World Trade Center on that day," the first man insisted, finding a further thread of agreement.

"Yes. Why is it that on 9/11, the Jews did not go to work in the building?" said the second man. "Everybody knows this. I saw it on TV. Everyone discusses this. It is evidence of Zionist involvement."

Alex drew and exhaled a fourth drag from the hookah. Then, provoked by what she was hearing, she joined in the conversation.

"Much of what you're saying is preposterous," Alex said. "Even if it were true, which it is *not*, how could Jewish workers have kept it a secret from coworkers?"

Momentarily, the men were taken aback, not used to a strong, articulate opinion from a female.

"Jews do things like that," the second man was quick to say. His tone suggested that he was willing to explain the world to a female who didn't understand as well as he did. "They are loyal only to other Jews and their financial interests."

"And to Israel!" said the younger man. "American Jews will do anything to protect Israel!"

Alex felt herself losing her patience very quickly. The monstrosity of all this from apparently otherwise rational people left her momentarily speechless. But the fuse of indignation was burning down.

"I don't agree with you," she said.

"That's because in America where you are from, the government controls the press."

"I'm from Canada," she said.

"Canada is part of the United States," said the younger Arab.

"The Canadian government controls the press too," said the first man.

Emboldened, she was about to respond with a barnyard epithet, something not far from *bolshoi*. But Voltaire, highly amused, picked up on the feeling. He tapped her hand quickly, a reminder to stay under control. He had brought her there to listen and to observe, after all, not to make sparks fly.

"What is important is that this was an attack against the world of Arabs," the third man said. "Why is it that the Americans never caught him, Bin Laden, if they say he was responsible?"

"How can they not know where he is?" muttered another man.

"Because he launched the attacks and then disappeared," Alex said. "That or he's dead." *And burning in hell*, she might have added, but didn't.

Her audience was having none of it. With no malice whatsoever, they ignored her.

Voltaire gave her hand another tap and threw a sharp frown at her. She knew he was reminding her to stay cool.

"Americans know everything," the man who was speaking maintained, dismissing Alex. "They didn't catch him because he hasn't done anything. What happened in Iraq confirms this. The Americans attacked against Arabs and against Islam. They did it to serve Israel."

"How true it is!" Voltaire said. "Zionist conspirators, all of them." He turned to Alex and guided the conversation. "*Comment va ta fumée?*" he asked. "How's your smoke?"

"Better than I thought it would be," she answered in French, "unless you're talking about the smoke coming out of my ears."

"Better smoke coming out of your ears than intemperate remarks coming out of your mouth," he said succinctly. "No point offending my friends when there's no chance to change their minds now, is there?"

Alex retreated into another drag from the hookah.

"The problem is that Americans are brainwashed by their leaders," the first man said. "It makes no sense that Mr. Bin Laden could have carried out such an attack from Afghanistan."

"There are a lot of Arabs who hate America, but this is too much," the younger man said. He was more passionate than the older men. "And look at what happened after the September eleventh attacks! The Americans invaded two Muslim countries! They used 9/11 as an excuse to invade Afghanistan. Then they went to Iraq. They killed Saddam, they killed his sons. They killed tens of thousands of civilians and claimed they were 'liberating' them. They tortured ordinary Arabs in their prisons. They sent hostages to Cuba. How can you trust the Americans?"

"You can't!" Voltaire said sharply. "Never! Filthy infidels!"

Alex felt like launching into them. But she retreated again into the smoke from the hookah and eased back. Voltaire was right and she was learning from him. She wasn't going to change their minds, and they weren't going to change hers.

She finished her drink.

She thought of many things to say and silently swallowed every one of them. Within minutes, the fuel in the hookah had burned down and the conversation had drifted to soccer and Egypt's chances against Cameroon in the upcoming World Cup.

Her temper was easing down too.

"Do you know anything about sports?" one of the Arabs asked her.

"I know that Egypt's national footballers are the best in Africa," she said generously, playing her audience. Football here, of course, meant soccer. The men cheered and applauded. Alex had ended the conversation on an up note and had made friends. She didn't chip in her further opinion that the glorious giants of world soccer — Brazil, Italy, Spain, and Argentina — would, if given the chance, annihilate the hapless Egyptians.

Instead, she turned to Voltaire. "I'd like to go back to the hotel now," she said. "May we go?"

"It's late. I'll see that you get there safely," he said. "Let's find a taxi." He rose to leave. "Come on along."

Voltaire slipped back into Arabic and thanked his friends for their conversation. The men at the table returned his smile. They stood and bid Alex a warm farewell.

FORTY

Incredible," Alex muttered to Voltaire when they were back out on the street. She took his arm as they navigated crowded pedestrian traffic toward a cab stand. It was almost 1:00 a.m. now, and the street was overpopulated with beggars, some ambulatory and others passed out on the sidewalk. "What they were saying was complete rubbish! I could barely control myself."

"I know," he said. "I was watching you. But what they think, what they say, all that is completely predictable."

Then, for security on the street, he switched into Italian. He spoke close to her ear as they looked for a taxi. Alex spotted a couple of taxis and pointed them out.

"No," Voltaire said. "I use a certain cab stand. It's two minutes from here. You think I'd get into *any* Cairo taxi? Certainly not. I value my life more than that."

They walked a few blocks. One or two beggars accosted them aggressively. Voltaire rudely ignored them and at one point physically shoved away a man who had drawn too close to Alex.

"By the way, where's Abdul?" she asked.

"Why? Do you miss him?"

"Just asking," she said.

"Don't worry about it," he said. "I'll get you back to the hotel safely."

In Cairo, the newer cabs were yellow. The older ones were painted black and white, often with mismatched doors and panels, the result of the Demolition Derby aspect of Cairo traffic. They found one of the older cabs parked by itself at a cab stand. The cab was black with one green door and a white trunk. The sign on the top said OFF DUTY. Voltaire opened the door and told Alex to climb in. She did.

The driver turned up a moment later. He looked like a punk, about twenty-five years old with attitude. He wore a Western-style windbreaker and a white baseball-style cap that carried the blue and white logo of a French soccer team, Olympique de Marseille. He had black hair slicked back.

There was no meter in the cab. Fees were always negotiable.

At first, as was his habit, Voltaire sought to negotiate the cost of the ride in English. A noisy, contentious argument ensued in Arabic between Voltaire and the driver as Voltaire insisted on being taken to the Metropole Hotel and the driver loudly refused.

Other drivers, also off-duty and sharing smokes, looked and laughed. The driver massacred his English, and then switched into Arabic. Voltaire followed into Arabic, apparently much to the driver's surprise.

Voltaire seemed experienced at this, however. He knew how to strike the proper deal. He flashed some extra money and the driver acquiesced.

Then they were off. The cab was not air-conditioned and it rattled. The driver smoked, against the recent law, and held his cigarette—another Eastern European stinker—out the window.

"These old cabs are rolling death traps," Voltaire muttered cheerfully to Alex, returning to English. "But they're extremely reasonable in price, even if the drivers are complete idiots like this one—and sometimes can't find the ocean from the end of a pier. One can rattle one's way clear across Cairo for little more than it would cost simply to step into a cab in London or New York. And, of course, there's also the fear factor and the thrill of taking one's life in one's hands. Take this complete imbecile of a driver, for example. Eventually he'll get someone killed. Let's just hope it's not us tonight."

No response from the driver, who seemed intent only on getting this trip done.

Alex nodded. The taxi jockeyed through traffic. Nighttime Cairo fascinated her, in its wealth and its sleaze, the latter even more visible now in the early morning hours. They passed a row of nightclubs. Local wise guys were piling into Mercedes limos and Rolls-Royces, accompanied by an armada of sleek women in short party dresses and the latest fashions from Europe. The driver spotted someone he knew, a chauffeur, and shouted a greeting at him in Arabic.

"I'm still recovering from the conversation at the café," Alex said to Voltaire. "It's one thing to know how people feel. Another to hear it spoken to your own face."

"You'll hear worse than that if you stay here long enough," Voltaire said. "Was that the worst anti-Americanism you've experienced firsthand?"

"Far from it," she said. "I may look young but I've been in the field for a few years. I've heard things. The conversation this evening just stands out as among the most warped."

"That is the problem the United States has in this region," he said. "In order to fight the really bad people, you have to convince people that there really is a real evil. They have to believe it in order to help you. That's a battle we're losing."

"We?" she asked.

"I'm on your side," he said. "I serve America and I root for America. And I deal with the dangers and the misunderstandings here every day. That's why I brought you here. You saw it for yourself."

The driver turned the corner abruptly. Alex watched him.

Alex looked around. "Do they have seat belts here?" she asked.

"Seat belts in the Third World?" Voltaire asked. "Got to be kidding. Why don't you ask for a diet soda, while you're at it?"

"Okay," she said.

"This driver is a complete moron, one of the worst I've ever encountered. Probably doesn't even have a license," Voltaire said. "Do you know the difference between a chimpanzee and a Cairo cabbie?" he asked. "The chimp can be taught to drive a car."

The driver's glowering eyes kept alternating between the road and the rearview mirror. She wished he would just watch the road.

"You know why people think the way they do here?" Voltaire asked a few seconds later as their cab jockeyed through the streets of Old Cairo in the direction of Alex's hotel. "Above and beyond the sorry details of 9/11, this is how many Arabs view their governments. Not just in Cairo, but throughout the Middle East. The people hate their leaders, and they have learned *not* to believe them. The state-owned media are also hated and distrusted. Therefore, they think that if the government is insisting that Bin Laden was behind the attacks on Washington and New York, he must *not* have been."

"A *Catch–22* sort of thing?"

"More like Pirandello," said Voltaire. " 'It *is* so if you think so.' Perverse, is it not? But it's what we have to deal with, you and I who do the work that we do. The average Egyptian thinks President Mubarak says whatever the Americans want him to say, and that he's lying for them because the Americans keep him in power. There's even an element of truth to this. Mubarak wouldn't last a day without US support."

"I've forgotten," Alex said. "Is he elected?"

"Not really. A referendum is held every few years. Mubarak runs and those who vote can vote yes or no. The election is fixed, of course, so the man in power always wins the referendum. Government employees take care of the results. If free elections were held, someone far worse for American and Western interests would be elected. So the United States government doesn't allow it to happen."

"So it's like Saudi Arabia?" Alex said.

"Very similar," said Voltaire.

They stopped at a light. On the street, eighties-style disco music boomed out of another nightclub for Westerners. In this small part of the globe, Donna Summer was still the queen of the night.

"It's the same story all across North Africa and up through the western Mediterranean," Voltaire continued. "Every single country is governed by a bad guy or a really bad guy, so pick your poison and pick it carefully. And I include Israel in my assessment, unless you think Moishe Dayan, Ben Netanyahu, or Ariel Sharon are charm-school alumni. A couple of these guys were almost as crude and lethal as Stalin or Putin. If you want my opinion, and you're going to get it even if you don't since we're riding in the same cab, the whole region is a stink hole, and it's going to blow up the world one of these days if the Western powers misplay their hand. And you know what? They have a long history of misplaying their hands. Look at two world wars, Korea, Vietnam, Kosovo, Somalia — the list goes on and on."

The driver turned another corner with a jerk, skidding tires, and a spewing a florid exchange of profanity with another driver.

Alex watched him. The driver's censorious eyes kept alternating between the road and the rearview mirror. Several times, his eyes focused on hers. She kept her hand near her Beretta. Alex sensed something more than a little wrong with him, maybe something a little psycho. But she couldn't place it.

"Americans might do better to try to understand the Middle East," Voltaire said, easing back. He fished into his pocket, found a pack of Marlboros, and joined the driver in an illegal smoke.

"I'm not even talking about the average Joe driving a truck down the interstate in Iowa. I don't expect those people to understand. I'm talking about the people in Washington, the ones who make the decisions and whose decisions are going to get us all blown up if they make the wrong ones. If only those people listened to what people in the streets and in the cafés in Cairo are saying. I'm the first person to admit that it's an abomination. But the general view here is that even before September 11, the United States was not a fair broker in the Arab-Israeli conflict. Then it capitalized on the attacks to buttress Israel and undermine the Muslim Arab world. And you know what? There remains just enough historical truth to that to fuel every insane conspiratorial theory you hear in Cairo."

The cab stopped for another light, then it came out of it like a jackrabbit on steroids, reeling across three lanes, cutting off the cab behind it.

Accelerator, brake, accelerator, brake.

Cab rides I have survived in the Third World, thought Alex.

Thought, but didn't say. This driver was a piece of work.

There was a long blast of a horn from the rear and the sound of someone screaming. Alex's driver made some sort of gesture over the roof of the car.

"Just get us there in one piece, would you, you idiot!" Voltaire barked at the driver. The driver glowered back and said nothing.

"The greatest proof in the eyes of the average Arab was the invasion of Iraq. Just try to convince people here that it was not a quest for oil or a war on Muslims. Just try! It's like trying to convince many Americans that it was, and that the 9/11 attacks were the first step. It's the result of widespread mistrust, the belief among Arabs and

Muslims that the United States has a prejudice against them. So they never think the United States is well intentioned, and they always feel that whatever it does has some other motive behind it."

Alex had no answer. Her hotel lay up ahead. Voltaire finished his smoke, flicked the butt out the window, and changed the subject, sort of.

"Anyway, I'll phone Fitzgerald tonight after I drop you off. I'll have him send you the merchandise we discussed. Don't worry about it tonight. But start your day with it tomorrow."

The taxi stopped in front of the hotel.

"Uplifting, isn't it, all this?" Voltaire said. "It shows you what the West is up against in this part of the world. You know, it's easy for Americans to dismiss such thinking as bizarre and something that goes on far from their Pennsylvania barbeques and their Wyoming rodeos. But that misses the point. Washington needs to understand. That such ideas persist represents the first failure in the fight against terrorism, the inability to convince people here that the United States is, indeed, waging a campaign against terrorism, not a crusade against Muslims."

The driver waited, scanning the street, looking bored, watching a few well-dressed European and America women on the front promenade of the hotel.

Voltaire leaned to Alex and held her arm. He leaned to her and gave her a kiss on the cheek.

"Want to invite me up to your room?" he asked. "There's still time."

"Nope," she said.

"I'll let you in on a secret," he said. "I'm the most experienced lover that you would ever have."

"Is that right?" she asked.

"It is."

"Then actually you'd be the most experienced lover that I might *never* have," she said. "The answer is still no."

"I didn't think I'd be successful. But I thought I'd ask."

The driver seemed intent on ignoring Voltaire and his advance.

"Good night," she said. "Three p.m. tomorrow, correct?"

"Correct," he said. She opened the cab door and pushed one leg out. Voltaire grabbed her arm to stop her. She turned back to him.

"One other thing, Josephine," he said.

She waited.

"Keep your guard up at all times here. Don't *ever* assume anything. Always question everything you see. Want me to give you another example, how things aren't always how they seem?"

"Go for it," she said.

He released her arm and turned back to address the driver.

"How you doing tonight, Tony?" he asked in English.

"I'm fine, Mr. Lamara, sir," the driver answered in English with a broad smile. "How's it going for you, aside from getting turned down by the lady?"

"Could be better, could be worse," Voltaire said with a laugh. "This is my associate. Josephine. She's going to be working with us on a mini-project."

"Nice to meet you, ma'am," the driver said. "Welcome to Cairo. Hope you liked the crazy ride."

Stifling her shock, Alex only stared at the driver.

"Tony is from New York," Voltaire said. "He's one of our street people in Cairo and one of my bodyguards. He came on duty when Abdul went home."

The driver raised a hand, which now held a massive black pistol. He used the nose of the weapon to push back his Olympique de Marseille cap, giving it a polite tip. He grinned again, then stashed the weapon back under his jacket where it had been.

A beat while it sunk in. "I should have known," Alex said.

"Yes, you should have. See you tomorrow," Voltaire said.

FORTY-ONE

After ordering breakfast in her room the next morning, Alex pulled on jeans and a T-shirt. She sat down at the desk in her suite and opened her laptop. There was a double window open to the daylight, and the sounds of the city — traffic, voices, children, car horns, vendors — were more distant because her window faced the swimming pool and the hotel's private enclave.

She sorted through personal emails from home, answered some, and put others on hold. She opened one from Janet, who was kicking back in New York and had developed a crush on one of her bodyguards. Well, at least things were under control on that front, Alex theorized. Maybe if Janet was really lucky she'd get taken to some velvet-rope mob joint with some of the guys. Who knew? She took Paul Guarneri at his word that Janet would be kept safe and well treated.

Alex's breakfast arrived via room service. She tried to eat lightly in hot countries and stick to bottled water, fruits, and food that couldn't easily contaminate. Looking back to her laptop, she found a transmission from Fitzgerald. Alex opened the CIA file and, wondering what impact it might have on her own operation, began to read.

It was a single document, the result of several other documents merged into one in order to provide her a background briefing. She was tempted to skim, but knew better. So she read carefully.

Israeli espionage efforts against the United States
Document Is/2009/19/07/cia- Esp.hg.7

On June 5, 2008, the US Central Intelligence Agency intercepted a conversation in Berne, Switzerland, in which two Israeli officials had discussed the possibility of getting a confidential letter that then-Secretary of State Condoleezza Rice had written two years earlier to Palestinian leader Yasser Arafat. One of the Israelis had commented that they may get the letter from "Kanga," apparently a codename for an Israeli agent within the US government.

This revelation has again been treated by much of the American and Israeli press as an aberration, as over sixty years Israeli officials have claimed that they do not spy on the United States. Israeli Foreign Minister David Levy once told the *Wall Street Journal* (7/6/2007) that "our diplomats all over the world, and of course specifically in the Unites States, don't engage in such things." Similarly, Prime Minister Netanyahu's office once declared, "Israel does not use intelligence agents in the United States. Period."

Yet this has demonstrably not been the case. From the very infancy of the nation-state of Israel, espionage activities and theft of information have occurred from friends and foes alike, often more from friends than from foes.

For example, in 1954, a hidden microphone planted by the Israelis was discovered in the office of the US ambassador in Tel Aviv. In 1956 telephone taps were found connected to two telephones in the residence of the US military attaché.

The most damning and notable case is the one of Jonathan Pollard, which dates from the 1980s.

Jonathan Jay Pollard, a veteran of US Navy intelligence forces, sold secrets to the Israeli government during the 1980s. Pollard claimed that although he did spy for Israel, he did not conduct espionage against the United States.

Born in 1954, Pollard majored in political science at Stanford University. He longed to emigrate to Israel, imagining himself as a superspy fighting on Israel's behalf. Instead of moving to Israel, however, he enrolled at the School of Law and Diplomacy at Tufts University. At Tufts, he sold information on foreign students to the CIA.

Although he already had his foot in the door with the CIA, the Agency turned him down when he applied for a job. After attending a 1982 meeting between US Navy and Israeli intelligence officers, Pollard was convinced that Israeli security was threatened because the US was withholding crucial secrets from its ally, particularly in the area of poisonous gases manufactured by Iran and Iraq. By that time, Pollard had a security clearance that gave him the authority to check out classified documents and take them home. Soon Pollard was smuggling out suitcases crammed with highly classified material from US Naval Intelligence. The US government claimed Pollard eventually leaked classified information on the layout of the Palestine Liberation Organization's headquarters in Tunisia, which Israel eventually bombed . . .

As an agent with the FBI, Alex had been familiar with the Pollard case. But refreshing herself on the background details, while on assignment in Cairo, had a chilling edge. She continued reading.

Pollard photocopied and turned over to Israel more than fifteen hundred classified messages and more than a thousand documents. The Israeli government paid Pollard $2,500 per month. They also financed trips to Europe and a $7,000 ring for his wife . . .

(Examining officer's note: It is no small irony that Pollard was actually on the payroll of the taxpayers of two separate countries: GHL 12-24-04)

The Federal Bureau of Investigation was finally alerted by suspicious coworkers to the quantities of files that Pollard was signing out. Eventually, the FBI put surveillance teams on Pollard to discover what he was doing with the material, suspecting that he might meet with a foreign representative. Within a few weeks of 24/7 surveillance, however, Pollard apparently became aware of the attention.

(Examining officer's note: It has never been established how Pollard became aware of the surveillance efforts, but it is widely believed that he was tipped by the Israeli service he was supplying: GHL 01-23-05)

In 1985, Pollard and his wife sought asylum in Israel. The two drove to the Israeli Embassy in Washington, DC. Pollard requested political asylum using his own name. But the officer on duty apparently didn't know who his uninvited guest was. Pollard and his wife were evicted from the embassy by Israeli guards. They were immediately arrested by the FBI.

Pollard never had a trial. At the request of both the US and Israeli governments, he entered into a plea agreement. Pollard received a life sentence and a recommendation that he never be paroled.

The CIA claimed that another highly placed Israeli spy in the US had to exist in order to give Jonathan Pollard his highly specific tasking orders. The CIA and FBI both code-named this individual as "Mr. X" but his/her identity was never discovered.

(Note of examining officer #2: No cooperation was ever forthcoming from Israel on the subject of "Mr. X." No surprise there. JGF 02-15-06)

In November 1995, Israel granted Jonathan Pollard Israeli citizenship. To the US, this signaled Israel's willingness to accept full responsibility for Pollard. His potential release in order to return to Israel became a hot-button item. Israel threatened to cease peace talks with the US until the issue was resolved but failed to gain Pollard's release from prison. Pollard's case was considered by Presidents Reagan, Bush, Clinton, and Bush 43, all of whom denied him clemency . . .

As of September 2009, Pollard is in the twenty-fifth year of his life sentence.

Alex stopped reading because she felt mildly nauseous.

Was there something about this tea that disagreed with her? She had slept well, but there was suddenly a queasy feeling in her stomach. It went away in a moment. Last night's tea? Airline food from the other day? Something in the sooty Cairo air that had compromised her immune system?

The discomfort was sharp, like a pang. She had once contracted food poisoning in Mexico and it had started this way. She winced. Then it felt as if something was wrong with her head. Her forehead throbbed as if she had a migraine. Then that went away too.

She read carefully and quickly through the summary paragraphs of the remainder of the files. A few stood out:

Item: "The Lavon Affair": In 1954, Israeli agents attacked Western targets in Egypt in an apparent attempt to upset US-Egyptian relations. Israeli Defense Minister Pinchas Lavon was removed from office, though many think real responsibility lay with David Ben-Gurion.

Item: In 1967, Israel attacked the USS *Lib-*

erty, an intelligence-gathering vessel flying a US flag, killing 34 crew members. See *Assault on the Liberty,* by James M. Ennes, Jr. (Random House).

Item: In early 2007, an Army mechanical engineer, David A. Tenenbaum, told investigators that he "inadvertently" gave classified military information on missile systems and armored vehicles to Israeli officials (*New York Times,* 2/12/07).

Item: In ·May 2008, the US ambassador to Israel complained privately to the Israeli government about heavy-handed surveillance by Israeli intelligence agents, who had been following American Embassy employees in Tel Aviv and searching the hotel rooms of visiting US officials . . .

The FBI knew of at least a dozen incidents in which American officials illegally transferred classified information to the Israelis, said former Assistant Director of the FBI Mr. Raymond Wannal. The Justice Department did not prosecute.

She concluded her reading. Okay. She got the point. Normally the Israeli intelligence services worked with the Americans. Sometimes they worked against them.

Why was Fitzgerald sounding this theme so sharply? She considered his age again and thought of the Suez crisis of fifty years ago in which the English, French, and Israelis sought to lash back at Nasser without the Eisenhower administration knowing their intentions. The mission had been a failure and had made Nasser a hero in the Arab world.

Her mind fiddled with the sound of it.

Nasser, NASCAR. Just two letters apart. She broke a mild sweat. What was going on? Suddenly, another surge of pain in her stomach. She really didn't feel good.

Well, she had taken some precautions before this trip. She had some Ciprofloxacin in her medicine kit for just such emergencies. She went to the bathroom, found one, scored it, and popped half a tab.

She looked at her clock. She suddenly felt lousy. Bad jetlag, she figured. That didn't help.

Heck, she didn't have to be anywhere until 3:00 in the afternoon, when she needed to be in front of the hotel to meet Voltaire. Might as well get some extra rest. She went back into the bedroom and lay down again on the bed.

FORTY-TWO

Alex's eyes opened at half past two in the afternoon. She felt better. Either the turbulence within her had settled or the medication had helped.

She found the bulky khaki jacket that she could wear over a navy tank top. Maximum coverage. She packed a bag to carry on her shoulder. In it, she threw her weapon, which she kept loaded with the safety catch on. She also took her passport, some cash, and a credit card. She was wary of the sun, so she threw an American baseball cap into the bag too and was careful to take sunscreen and sunglasses.

She was in front of the hotel within a few minutes. Voltaire had a BMW X5 SUV in the hotel driveway. He was waiting for her. Alex climbed into the passenger's side of the front and, as they pulled out, flipped down the vanity mirror.

She watched a car pull out behind them.

"Friendly, right?" she asked. "The car that's trailing us?"

"Bodyguards. Abdul and one of his pleasantly unsavory people. They'll be with us most of the day."

"Good," she said. She pushed the mirror back upward.

"So if we get shot in the back it'll be by our own people, not the opposition. Isn't that reassuring?"

"Seriously," she said. "You have quite a sense of humor."

"Oh, relax," he said. "This is your tourist day. We talk a little and discuss what's going to happen. Tomorrow you work."

"Sounds like a plan," she said, easing up a little. Her stomach rumbled, then was steady again.

On the drive from Cairo to Giza, Alex saw row after row of endless tenements, much as she had noticed on the trip into the city. Their vehicle passed miles of redbrick buildings built illegally, according to Voltaire, and by hand.

"The bricks come from the local mosques," he said. "The people who live there have only recently received running water and electricity. The buildings grow in height as the families grow. One generation builds a floor above their parents and so on. Then you realize brick buildings can only go so high before gravity takes over. Buildings crumble all the time. The people living there are usually crushed to death."

"I don't suppose the government does anything," Alex said.

Voltaire laughed. "Why would they? It helps control the population problem. There are too many people already. But it's in these same slums that Islam is most fervent."

They arrived in Giza in less than an hour.

They parked the X5. There was still urbanization all around them. Alex had imagined the pyramids in a remote desert, somewhat farther away from Cairo. But the stretch of desert where the Pyramids of Giza stood was surrounded on all sides by city. The location was more like a national park than a remote wonder. Alex brought her shoulder bag containing her weapon with her.

Voltaire led Alex to a stable run by some Bedouin tribesmen whom he knew personally. The Bedouins rented out horses and camels by the hour. Alex was tempted by the camels, but opted for a horse. Voltaire did the same. The Bedouins put them up on a pair of beaten-down old horses and cracked the whips behind them, sending them off.

They entered a sandy patch that led to the pyramids, which Alex could distantly see up ahead — three immense structures reaching toward the hot blue sky. Alex had never completely understood the magic and majesty of this place until she saw the Great Pyramids of Giza rise before her as they approached.

"I've lived in Egypt for most of my adult life," Voltaire said. "I'm not very religious in a traditional Judeo-Christian sense. But this is a place where spirituality can be felt almost anywhere. The country is full of discovered as well as undiscovered ancient burial sites. No matter where you go you're sure to fall on pyramids, temples, or *mastabas*, which are tombs. I've visited Saqqâra and all its temples. Ever been there? It's not far."

"No," she said.

"Saqqâra has the oldest pyramid in Egypt, that of King Zoser. Then there's the city of Luxor and the Luxor Temple, then the Valley of the Kings, and the Valley of the Queens. There's the Hatshepsut Temple, and the Karnak. Do you know anything about Queen Hatshepsut?" he asked.

"No," Alex said, walking her horse briskly. She glanced behind her and, as expected, saw Abdul and the other bodyguards following at a discreet distance with a second pair of horses.

"She was more powerful than Cleopatra or Nefertiti," Voltaire said, sounding now more like a professor of history than a spy. "Hatshepsut stole the throne from her stepson. She dressed as a man to assert her power and declared herself Pharaoh. Her reign was prosperous. But Hatshepsut's legacy was systematically erased from Egyptian history, historical records were destroyed, monuments were torn down, and her corpse was removed from her tomb. The Egyptians don't like the idea of women having power. Never did and never will. It's a historical aberration when it happens."

Up ahead lay the Giza Plateau and the three Great Pyramids. As Alex gazed ahead, she felt a surge of excitement. She had the sudden sense of watching a dream unfurl before her, of being transported to a time twenty-five centuries before the birth of Jesus when these great burial vaults were built by three generations of pharaohs: the father, Khufu; the son, Khafre; and the grandson, Menkaure. Voltaire kept quiet, letting her savor the moment.

The Sphinx was the guardian of the pyramid of Khufu and remained the center of superstitions because of its mysterious appearance. Known in Arabic as *Abu al-Hol*, the Father of Terror, the statue was called the Sphinx by the ancient Greeks. He resembled their mythical winged monster with the woman's head and lion's body who posed riddles and killed anyone unable to answer them.

Voltaire grinned as a couple rode past them on a pair of camels, barely in control. The woman seemed to be hanging on for her life. Voltaire, genial soul that he was, shouted after them in Arabic and everyone laughed, whether they understood or not.

"When I was a kid," Voltaire said in a revelatory moment, "I went to a school in Lausanne, Switzerland, for a few years. We had a schoolboy game. We would rename the airlines. British Airways at the time was called BOAC. The British Overseas Airline Corporations." He paused. "We called it 'Better On A Camel.' To this day I can't look at a camel without thinking of that."

Alex laughed. "Any other good ones?" she asked.

"SABENA. The Belgian Airline," he said. " 'Such A Bad Experience, Never Again.' "

She laughed harder.

"Here's the best," he said. "TAP, the Airline of Portugal. 'Take Another Plane.' "

She laughed again.

The horses began a pleasant trot, which created a slight breeze. Alex's stomach had settled and she felt good again about the world.

"Thank you for coming out here with me today," Voltaire said. "I don't like to talk business with walls and telephone lines around."

"My pleasure," she said. "As well as my assignment."

He reached to a shirt pocket and pulled out a small device about the size of an iPod. It was common currency between them that it was an anti-bugging foil. He entered a code and replaced the device in his pocket. "There," he said. "That should wound the fragile feelings of anyone who might try to monitor us." There, in the open desert, under God's blue sky, they were absolutely free of any possible electronic surveillance.

Alex savored the beautiful silence around them, the rugged natural beauty of the Sahara, and the sweep of the sky. The only sounds were from the horses, including the swish of hooves on the sand.

They came near the first pyramid, the tallest of the three, Khufu Pyramid, called Cheops by the Greeks. It rose to a summit of nearly five hundred feet above the desert. Khufu had ruled Egypt twenty-five centuries before Christ from 2589 to 2566 BC.

As they approached it on horseback, the tone of Voltaire's voice changed. "I suppose we should talk business," he said.

"Please do."

"A few weeks ago this young American girl, the one you know personally . . ."

"Janet," Alex said. "She's the niece of a friend of mine."

"Apparently she was here in Cairo with a boyfriend. They made an unfortunate discovery," Voltaire said. "A former agent had gone to ground here. Michael Cerny, he was known as, though he seems to like his own code name of Ambidextrous."

"That name was mentioned back in my briefing at Langley," she said.

"Ambidextrous. Judas. Cerny. Whatever we wish to call him," Voltaire said. "He has a past so complicated that to recall it or understand it would be like attempting to memorize a chess game and re-create it in reverse. Suffice It to say that he was supposed to be listed as dead and continuing to operate for our side. Instead, your Janet and her boyfriend happened across him while he was trying to do a deal with the Russians."

"An officially sanctioned deal?" she asked. "Or his own deal?"

"As it turned out, his own," Voltaire said. "And she and her guy just about queered a major financial score for him."

"In what way?"

"Mr. Cerny had no brief to be dealing with any Russians," Voltaire said. "Not after the Kiev fiasco. The Agency sent him here to do some business with Arabs. But he got greedy. Oh, I'm jumping ahead. When Cerny knew he had been spotted by a couple of young Americans who recognized him, he realized that his whole charade was compromised. Or, he reasoned, it was compromised if Carlos and Janet lived long enough to get back to their employers in the United States and file a convincing report of what they had seen."

"So the bomb here was meant to kill them both," Alex said.

"That appears to be the case," said Voltaire. "But the bomb failed. Or, on the other hand, it was only fifty percent successful. Janet gets picked up by the police here, who didn't know what to do with her. She's an American citizen, so they go easy on the rough stuff and just make sure she gets out of the country. Plus, by now she's too high profile for them to just make her disappear." He paused. "The Egyptian police are a curious bunch of apes, as you've probably already noticed. Their job is not to protect the innocent or even apprehend the guilty. Their mission is to protect the dictatorship. The most fundamental tenet of Anglo-Saxon justice, habeas corpus, is considered a quaint indulgence of the British and the Americans. Nonetheless, the Egyptian police don't know what to do with Janet, so they pack her up and send her back to Washington."

"And she starts telling people in Washington and Langley what she saw," Alex said, picking up on it quickly. "But Cerny is supposed to be in deep cover. So they can't admit to her that what she thought she saw was exactly what she did see."

"That's correct," Voltaire said. "And even worse, she reported to Langley that Cerny was speaking Russian to a couple of men in towel-style headdress. You can imagine how that had hearts fluttering in Langley."

"I can imagine," she said.

"Cerny's brief was checked, his logs were examined, his cell phone and home phone records were destabilized and decoded. His emails, official and personal, were downloaded and analyzed. They found Russian contacts and Israeli contacts. This place, Cairo, is crawling with spies and various other intelligence and counterintelligence agents the way Casablanca was during World War II, like Berlin was in the 1960s, like Warsaw was in the 1980s. So then the geniuses in Langley do a reverse search on all of the directories and e-files that Cerny has had access to in the last five years, and they come out shaking their heads. Aircraft, warheads, fighter planes. The man was saving up files for a rainy day, and you know what? To him, it's suddenly monsoon season. He must have downloaded fifty thousand pages of sensitive military documents onto a box full of flash drives, and he's running his own flea market. You read about the Jonathan Pollard case?"

"This morning, yes."

"Do you remember it when it happened?"

"I do. But I was still in grade school."

Voltaire gave her a double take and shook his head. "Yes, of course," he said.

He laughed. So did she.

"You know, Josephine," he said, "if I were thirty years younger I'd put another move on you. But I can't imagine what a fifty-nine-year-old man — even a fit one — looks like to a twenty-nine-year-old. The ruins of Pompeii? Vienna after the world war? Stonehenge?"

"Maybe the Sphinx's younger brother," she said. "But keep in mind I'm traveling a long distance to see such a sight. So be consoled. There's hope for you yet."

"Ouch," he said. "Well, anyway, think of Cerny as another Pollard case, except on steroids and even worse."

Farther on, coming into view, was the second of the three Great Pyramids, that of Khafra. As Alex eyed it, it looked taller than the first pyramid, but she realized that was because it had been constructed on a hill.

"Is Cerny selling to Israel?" she asked.

"Possibly. But we don't even know," he said. "He has contacts with the Israelis as well as the Russians. The two Russians he was dealing with are freelancers also. They'll make deals with the Putin government, and they'll make deals with Tel Aviv, and they'll be very happy to have their little brown brothers, the Arabs, help them murder anyone who gets in the way."

"Okay," she said. "I follow it."

"All of that leads us to here. You and me, on a couple of pathetic old horses, in the cradle of civilization. And our assignment is to apprehend Mr. Cerny before he can complete any transactions, or any further transactions, and make sure his Russian friends go home empty-handed."

"Who were the Russians?" she asked. "Do you have names?"

"Boris Zharov and Victor Kharniovski," he said. "Nasty couple of characters, every bit as foul as that disreputable retiree you hang out with in Switzerland."

"I consider Yuri Federov one of my assets," she said.

"And a wonderful asset he is. But here's the thing on Zharov and Kharniovski. Kharniovski isn't our problem anymore. Victor took a silk rope around his throat in a back alley in old Cairo two weeks back, courtesy of Abdul, Tony, and a few of their friends. Careless of him, don't you think? You should never step into an alley in this city with someone you don't know."

"I did that with you the other night."

"Oh, but I'm okay," he said blithely. "But at least it's a mistake Kharniovski won't make twice. And we managed to keep it out of all the newspapers so Boris doesn't know. He thinks his Kharniovsky buddy is back in Moscow selling the deal."

"Then what *about* Zharov?" Alex asked

"Staying at the Radisson Cairo," said Voltaire, "under the name of Engstrom. He's waiting for his dead associate to return from Moscow, and then he can get Cerny to come forward and close the deal."

"Why don't you just go in and grab him?"

"He's wary," Voltaire said. "He's heavily armed. And he knows who all of our supporting cast is here in Cairo. And there's no room for a slip. But like any Russian, he has his weaknesses. So this is where you come in. Follow?"

"Follow," she said.

They continued to Menkaure Pyramid, the smallest of the three, and by this tomb there were three smaller pyramids, those of Menkaure's children. Alex tried to conceptualize how long five thousand years was. When they reached the three smaller tombs, Voltaire turned to her again. "Want to go in?"

"In where?" she asked.

"The Great Pyramid," he said, turning and pointing, indicating the first and largest of the three. "This is as far as we go. Have to go back, anyway. Not much in it. A lot of stone. Unmarked walls. The mummies and the treasures have all been removed to the museums. But it's still an experience."

"I'm game," she said.

"Good," he said. "Now let's be tourists for a few minutes."

She pulled the horse's bridle to the right, and they turned their mounts together. They rode back to the tallest of the three pyramids. There was another Bedouin with a hitching post near the Pyramid of Cheops. They turned in their horses. Alex had to stretch out her legs to feel right walking again.

They walked from the hitching posts and stood in line. Alex put her hand to the exterior stones and found them cool, like a bottle of chilled water, even though they had been baking in the sun all day. Then she and Voltaire entered the massive edifice of stone. They began to walk down a short descending corridor and then followed a steep passageway up into the center of the pyramid. The tunnel was narrow and short. With a tremor, she flashed back to her experiences in Madrid and the claustrophobic fear from when she had been pinned in an old passageway under the city. But her movement here was free, even though she needed to proceed single file and a bit bent over. She followed Voltaire, who had made this trek many times before, he said. And the place hadn't caved in on him yet.

The passageway was about a hundred feet long and led to what the guide called "The Grand Gallery," a vaulted and arched staircase of about the same distance that led to the King's Chamber. The chamber was empty. Below it lay the Queen's Chamber. No king, no queen, either. Not even a bishop, a knight, or a rook.

They were in a small group of people climbing up into the pyramid, following one of the guides who must have made this trip a hundred times per week. From somewhere, Abdul, Voltaire's bodyguard, had reappeared. A German woman behind Alex became claustrophobic and insisted the walls were closing in on her. She insisted on turning back and did. Alex was sympathetic but continued onward and downward.

The inside of the pyramid was undecorated. No reliefs, no carvings, and other than small graffiti from modern-day vandals, no marks at all. High up on the walls above the King's Chamber, however, there were hieroglyphics about the work gangs building the pyramid. The guide attributed it to Cheops, who had conceptualized his own tomb.

In the evening, they stayed and waited for the light-and-sound show of the Great Pyramids. They sat on a terrace of a restaurant, enjoying a drink. Abdul was again visible, chatting up some tourists at a nearby table. The heat of the day had turned to a desert chill but there was still some glow from the Sahara sunset on the horizon. Watching the Pyramids and listening to the peaceful sound of the desert before and after the light-and-sound show, Alex got goose bumps.

When it was sufficiently dark, the extravaganza began. The commentary did not impress Alex, but the dazzling light show and awe-inspiring backdrop of the Sphinx and Pyramids surely did. Red, blue, and gold strobe effects flashed across the timeless architecture of

Giza, matched with, perhaps inappropriately, the grandeur of the score from Beethoven.

The Sphinx played the role of storyteller. Even though in reality the Sphinx never spoke, tonight a creative conceit was allowed and the old stone lion-woman narrated the history of ancient Egypt in English, French, Spanish, Italian, Japanese, Russian, and Arabic. Fragments of many languages floated up from various handheld speakers in a bizarre audio mix. It was hokey and touristy, but it worked.

Alex and Voltaire ended the evening by taking a riverboat back up the Nile to Cairo, a ship modeled on the *bateaux-mouches* of Paris. Once again Voltaire knew exactly which shots to call. The food on the ship was traditionally Egyptian, tasty but heavy, and Alex started to feel ill effects in her stomach again. But she didn't mention it. Her head pounded from time to time also. Then it would stop. She wondered what she had eaten or what she had been exposed to. Or maybe it was just the heat. She tried to ignore it, to will it away.

"I wonder if you could set something up," Voltaire said midway into the voyage back to Cairo. "A meeting between you, me, and Fitzgerald from the embassy. We need to get together face-to-face at least once. We both have information to convey to each other and to you. I don't want any electronics involved. Sometimes it's difficult for me to access Fitzgerald. So can you set something up?"

"I could do that," Alex said. "How soon?"

"Tomorrow?"

"It could be done, I'm sure," she said.

"Needless to say," he said, "I never set foot in that embassy or any other. In my persona of Monsieur Lamara, why would I? So we need to have a neutral site, someplace above suspicion."

She thought about it for a moment. "We were surrounded by desert today, right?" she said.

"As I recall," he said.

"Then tomorrow we'll be surrounded by water," she said. "How would that be?"

"I like the way you think," he said. "So we're going to meet on a papyrus raft on the Nile?"

"I was thinking more prosaic," she said. "The pool area of the hotel."

"That would work for me," Voltaire said.

There was entertainment on the boat, planned and unplanned. They had live music, and then a belly dancer appeared when they were halfway to Cairo. Alex, who had never been to a belly dancing show before, looked at it with great amusement, and wondered if the dancer was enjoying it as much as she seemed to be. The Egyptian girl flirted with every man in the place, getting reams of dollar bills tucked into the waistband of her skirt and getting her exercise as well.

Voltaire fell into conversation with some wealthy Egyptians who had brought relatives from Europe to see Giza. This dancer was better than average, the Egyptians said. And at the same time, Alex noted Voltaire's technique. He was always striking up conversations, keeping his ear to the ground, being friendly with everyone. He must have picked up tons of information and scuttlebutt that way. He was good at what he did.

In any case, Voltaire liked the dancer a little too much. He enjoyed playing the buffoon tourist instead of the master spy. He got up and danced opposite her and then rewarded her by sticking a US twenty-dollar bill in her skirt. In doing so, he had set a tone for the evening and loosened up the crowd for even heavier tips. She would go into the crowd and grab other victims and drag them up to the stage to dance with her too, which caused most of the excitement. She seemed to specialize in victimizing Americans and did well at it, innocent as it was. She gave Voltaire a wink and a kiss on the forehead when she finished her show and swept past.

Later on the boat ride, Alex and Voltaire talked with an Egyptian man who spoke nearly flawless English. He was berating everything from Mubarak, to Obama, to the captain of the ship, to the French woman standing next to him who seemed to be his wife.

Ever the diplomat, Voltaire agreed with everything he said, except that he offered high praise to the bearing and patience of the French lady. As the ship docked, the day seemed to have acquired a surreal tone to Alex. In some ways, she was a little kid again. She couldn't believe that she had seen and touched and even entered the Great Pyramid of Khufu, the oldest and largest pyramid in Egypt.

Off the boat, Alex spotted a familiar face waiting for them.

Tony with his cab and, presumably, his artillery.

Abdul ducked away into the chilly night, and Tony was back on duty.

FORTY-THREE

Like any fine hotel, the lobby of the Metropole boasted an arcade of overpriced specialty stores catering to the hotel's international clientele. Alex visited the shopping area the next morning and found what she was looking for. A plain navy-blue maillot to use in the hotel's vast swimming pool. A size ten was a perfect fit and the suit flattered her. Not too sexy, but not too demure. It would work.

Toward 1:30, she went to the well-guarded pool area behind the hotel. She entered the water on the shallow end and began doing laps, a small fresh bandage on the scar on her arm. At least she could combine some exercise with business. Despite showering and washing well the night before, the parched atmosphere of the desert remained upon her. The water soothed her.

She completed a brisk ten laps, watching the other visitors to the pool as she swam. She saw Richard Bissinger enter the hotel's pool area, using the guest pass that she had left for him at the front desk. She continued to do laps as Bissinger, or Fitzgerald, disappeared into a bathhouse at the far end of the pool.

Voltaire, she noted, didn't need a pass. He apparently had whatever access he needed to anything he wanted all over the Middle East. He arrived a few minutes after Bissinger but, wearing a pair of shorts suitable for swimming, was faster at getting into the water. He stood at the shallow end and waited for her.

Bissinger emerged from a locker area and slipped into the pool. He moved to the area where Voltaire stood. Alex did a final lap, then emerged and grabbed a towel and a pair of sunglasses off her deck chair. Then she joined her two visitors in waist-deep water.

It was midday and the pool was otherwise deserted, other than children and nannies. The children, splashing and screaming, formed a perfect acoustical backdrop to make electronic eavesdropping on them impossible, even via a rifle mike aimed from a hotel window.

"I've been to meetings that were all wet before," Bissinger said. "But to actually be *in* a pool is a first."

"You should thank me for getting you out of the office," Alex said, standing and pushing back her hair. She toweled her shoulders and let the towel hang across them.

"I do," he said.

"Everyone knows everyone," she said. "I already know that. So what are the signals we need to get straight?"

"It seems that a certain someone in whom we have an interest," Bissinger said, "'Judas,' has just made a move."

"What sort of move?" Alex asked.

"As I understand it, he smelled danger here in Cairo, or maybe a better opportunity somewhere else, and departed from this wonderful country."

Against her normal habit, Alex swore emphatically. She had traveled all this way for no resolution?

"Where is he?" Voltaire asked.

"Tel Aviv," said Bissinger. "Or so we think."

"Ha! Well, that's not far, is it?" Voltaire asked. "Although the jurisdictional problems just increased."

"So is our operation scuttled?" she asked.

"No, I don't think so," Bissinger said. "Look, here's what else we know about Judas. In addition to his actual passport under his real name, he has at least four others. Two are Russian, a pair of solid forgeries that he seems to have picked up from his business associates. Then he's got a British and a Hungarian."

"Impressive collection," Voltaire said.

"I posted an alert for all the passports and their numbers," Bissinger said. "We have an internet apparatus now. Works through Homeland Security and all the airlines."

"How so?" she asked.

They all fell silent as a pool attendant passed by with chilled containers of purified water. They each grabbed one. Bissinger tipped the man with a wet US five-dollar bill, which was appreciatively received.

They drank liberally. The sun pounded down on them.

"When a passport moves in which we have an interest," Bissinger said, "whoever posted the alert gets an update. As long as we have passport numbers, we can keep track of anyone in the world."

"Impressive software," said Voltaire, who was more of a street-level guy.

"We had analysts review the images on the airport security cameras at Ben-Gurion Airport in Tel Aviv. We checked the passengers disembarking for the flight from Cairo. The images we got are not a hundred percent conclusive, but we think that Judas arrived."

"So?" Alex asked. "What if he continues onward with a different passport?" Alex asked. "A fresh document. Presumably a man who has access to four fake passports isn't going to get weak-kneed about finding a fifth."

"We're sunk if he does that," Bissinger said. "We would just have to wait for him to surface again. But the odds are that he won't do that. Whenever a new passport goes into the system, there's always the chance it will bounce from improved security software. The other thing is that if Judas has no reason to be wary other than normal precautions, he'd tend to use an ID that has already worked."

"What's the rest of it?" Alex asked.

"Judas has got some deals cooking for the information he swiped from the US Defense Department, but it's all fairy gold to him until he can close a deal. And we know he needs to close a deal ASAP because he knows that Langley is officially listing him as a defector. We suspect Judas won't move again, wherever he is, until he's given the heads up. It's a one-two punch. He has to hear from his first contact here by email, then he needs to get the voice go-ahead from his number-two guy, his security guy here in Cairo. Only then will he move. Then there's the problem with the apprehension point. Let's say he's coming from Moscow or Ukraine. If he flies to a neutral point, like Athens or Rome, we have no brief to pick him up. Quite the contrary. Certain host countries in Europe would be furious if we did. Too much rendition during the Bush administration. We did it but never told the host countries we were doing it. Over the back channels they're still screaming, and the new administration in Washington wants to distance themselves from the Guantanamo mentality. So we have to sit on our hands and wait for him to connect. We can monitor him, say in the airport at Athens, but even that's risky. He'll be looking for a tail, and if he sees it, he'll cut bait, head back to Russia, and that'll be the end of our ball game."

"Or we can lure him back here," Voltaire said softly.

"What's here that he wants?" Alex asked.

There was a soft splash nearby. A child's wayward Frisbee had skimmed to rest near Alex. She picked it up and deftly sailed it back, with a smile and a wave.

"One of his Russian friends is still here," Bissinger said. "Boris Zharov. Boris is one of the two men Carlos caught him with. Judas is anxious to get his deal with Boris done. *Overanxious*, perhaps, which could work in our favor."

"Tell me more about Boris Zharov," Alex said.

"Boris is still ensconced at the Radisson Cairo," Bissinger said. "He goes down to the hotel lobby every evening around nine. He sits there and glowers for about an hour, smokes like a Soviet-era factory, and waits for instructions from Moscow. He's got a wife back in Moscow, but he's always on the trawl for Western women. If he doesn't get lucky, he goes out to the clubs. Dances with every young girl he can find. Brings them back to the hotel when he gets lucky. He's careless. He builds most evenings around a skirt and a bottle-long consultation with Dr. Stolichnaya. Sometimes he pays for both."

"Well," Alex said. "We all agree on how to target him. This is what you've had in mind for a while, right?" she asked Bissinger.

Bissinger allowed that it was.

"You want me to seduce him, right?" Alex asked.

Bissinger and Voltaire looked at each other.

"Well, if you wouldn't mind terribly?" Bissinger said. "We promise to break in just as you're pulling your dress up over your head."

"Maybe thirty seconds before that would work even better," she said.

"We'll try," Bissinger said.

"I assume Boris can access Judas by email," Alex said.

"That's pretty much what we had in mind," Bissinger said.

She looked to Voltaire, who was squinting behind sunglasses.

"Can you put a couple of guns in the room as backup?" she asked.

"I was going to offer Tony and Abdul for the snatch operation," Voltaire said. "They like to get their noses punched from time to time. Makes them feel good about themselves."

A moment passed as Alex thought it through.

"Okay," she finally said. "But if I'm going to be the centerpiece of that exercise," she said, "I want to bring in at least one of my own people and maybe a laptop tech."

"How long would it take to get them here from America?" Bissinger asked. "If Boris gets bored and goes home we're out of luck. Ditto if Judas scores with the Israelis and sells his wares there."

"My contacts are in Rome," she said.

Bissinger looked at Voltaire. "That'd work," Bissinger said.

"Okay with me," Voltaire said.

Alex turned back to Bissinger. A welcome breeze swept over the pool. "You said he also needed a voice okay before he returns," she said. "How do we work that?"

"That one's trickier," Bissinger said.

"How are you feeling today?" Bissinger asked, seeming to shift the subject.

"I'm okay," Alex answered.

"Head? Stomach?" he asked.

"I think I ate something a little tainted on the flight," she said. "Or maybe it's been the heat. Today I feel better. How did you know and why do you ask?"

"You were poisoned."

"What?"

"Or an attempt was made to poison you. See here's the thing—Judas got wind of the fact that someone had been sent from the US to spot him. He reasoned it was you. Something about some shootout in an American drug store. So he got out of Cairo until you, who could identify him, have been successfully killed. They planted some radioactive crystals in your hotel room. You've been bathing in them and sleeping on them. You should be able to illuminate any room you walk into by now without even turning on a lamp."

"Are you—!"

"Not to worry," Voltaire said. "Some of my people intercepted the plot. We have a young man named Masdouth as an infiltrator. He was part of the team that planted the crystals in your room. They switched some harmless stuff for the poison."

"How on earth did they get in?"

"Same way that Judas knew who had come from America. A traitor in out midst."

"Who?" she demanded.

"Who got a good look at you and would have been able to describe you to Judas?" Bissinger asked. "Who knew exactly where you were staying, right down to your room number? The same individual has been compromising our embassy for years and stood guard while the crystals were being planted in your room. He kept the hallway clear for the intruders. As soon as he departed, it was their cue to get out."

She sighed and seethed with anger. "Colonel Amjad," she said.

"There will be a day of reckoning for him too," Bissinger said. "But first we need to play the colonel along and he needs to report that you're dead. Game?"

In Alex's mind, it all fell into place. "Game," she said. "How does that work?"

"It works with you posing on a slab in a filthy Egyptian morgue and letting the colonel get a look at you," Bissinger said. "With you out of the way, there would be nothing stopping Cerny from making a quick gambit back to Cairo."

"So I'm supposed to play dead."

"If you wouldn't mind."

"If you think we can get away with it, I'll go for it," she said.

"Then I think we're finished here," Voltaire said.

"I think we are," she agreed.

"Thank you, Josephine," Bissinger said.

"My appreciation also," Voltaire said. "What a trouper."

"Some day in the future," she said, "you guys owe me big time."

First Bissinger left, then Voltaire. Alex tossed her towel back on a deck chair and gently flipped her sunglasses on top of the towel. As events, past and future, swirled in her head, she wore off her nervous energy with another ten laps. Then, after drying off and getting five more minutes of sunshine, she went back upstairs and phoned Gian Antonio Rizzo in Rome.

That same afternoon, Bissinger arranged to have a network of rooms rented at the Radisson Cairo where Boris was staying.

FORTY-FOUR

The next morning, without checking out of her own hotel, Alex had gone to the area of central Cairo known as Zamalek, where most of the embassies were located, along with the fashionable shops. There, in one of the French boutiques, she purchased a very short cocktail dress in smooth black satin. It was the type of dress that a young woman could wear to a private party or in one of the Western hotels, but which could never appear on the street. She bought a pair of heels to go with it and a purse that was big enough to pack her phone and her Beretta. It was a come-and-get-me outfit, and Alex was wearing it for work. Amused, she wondered if she could deduct it on her tax returns.

Then, that evening, Alex sat at the end of the hotel bar at the Radisson Cairo. She nursed a glass of wine and had a pack of Marlboros on the bar in front of her. Boris entered the hotel bar at about 9:00 p.m., as was his habit. He went to a table in the corner and sat down where he could survey the whole room. Alex had positioned herself where she would be directly in his line of view. She reached to her pack of Marlboros and lit one. Her first cigarette in ten years. She didn't look directly at Boris but felt his eyes on her as she smoked.

Patience, she told herself. *He's going to assess me very carefully before he makes a move, if he makes a move at all. He may be careless, but he has to be at least a little bit cautious.*

She engaged in a small conversation with the bartender, who brought her an ashtray. Then an American couple came in. She didn't know them, but she had a drink with them. Alex spoke with a slight Latino accent. She sold herself as a wealthy Mexican lady waiting for a no-good boyfriend, loud enough to allow Boris to overhear, as well as to advertise what language he could use if he wanted to make an approach.

The American couple was from Illinois, and they congratulated her on her wonderful English. She hoped they wouldn't kill the potential sale to Boris. The Midwestern couple left, and Boris was still there. He was looking at her, which was fine, assessing her from head to toe. She glanced his way, gave him a friendly smile, and looked away. She was showing as much leg as she ever had in her life, and she knew Boris liked what he saw.

A few moments later, she reached back to her pack of smokes. She picked up the pack of cigarettes and tapped one out. She muttered to herself in Spanish, as if in anger. She fumbled with a cigarette and dropped it, as if soused. Then she felt a presence next to her. She feigned surprise when a gold lighter snapped open and a sharp yellow flame rose in front of her.

Boris. The lighter was one of those five-hundred-dollar Dunhill ones. That or a fine counterfeit. The flame could have served as the Olympic torch.

"May I?" he asked in English.

His hand was frightening. It looked like a small anvil. She assumed he had a second one that matched. Yuri Federov looked like a poster boy for the Boy Scouts compared to this thug.

"Sure. Why not?" she answered.

She leaned forward and let him light her smoke. She inhaled and blew out a long steam of puffy white carcinogens as the lighter clicked shut.

"I'm sorry," she said. "I'm feeling slightly lonely and very angry. And I'm getting very drunk."

"No need to apologize," he said.

She stayed in English. Russian would scare him off.

"I can join you?" he asked.

"I wish someone would," she answered.

He slid onto the bar chair next to her. "You're very pretty," he said, turning back.

"If I'm so pretty, why did my boyfriend stand me up?"

"He doesn't appreciate you," Boris suggested.

"Ha!" she said. "You tell him that when and if he gets here," she said with inebriated inflections. "Will you tell him that?"

"I will," Boris said, ever the gent.

"I'm getting old," she said with self-pity. "Almost thirty. I guess I'm losing it."

Boris laughed. "Not at all," he said.

She eyed him up and down, as if to see him for the first time. He was a big man, maybe six-three, and broad—bigger than she had thought.

"Nobody appreciates me tonight," she said sullenly. "So I'm just here getting plastered. I hate to drink alone."

"So do I. You'd permit if I joined you?"

"Sure," Alex said. "Drink as much as you want. Just make one promise."

"What's that?"

"If my boyfriend comes running in more than an hour and a half late," making what sounded like a joke out of it, "punch the SOB out for me."

Boris laughed. He held up a fist the size of a small pumpkin. His hands were cushioned with muscle and crisscrossed with scars, one-shot knockouts waiting to happen.

"I'm good at that. Punching out," he said. "If that's what you wish, I will do. You tell me when, and you don't be afraid of anyone when you with me."

"Thank you!" she said drunkenly. "I appreciate a gentleman."

Boris gave her a nod.

"I hear an accent," Alex said. "Where are you from?"

He held a hand to her. "I'm Boris," he said. "I'm Russian."

She feigned surprise again. She held her hand to his. He took it. He had the grip of a professional fighter. Iron. She guessed further Russian ex-military. She uncrossed and crossed her legs to pique his interest.

"I'm Maria," she lied. "I'm from Mexico." And deep inside her, she admired her own personal best: Alex, Josephine, and Maria, three IDs in five days, spanning all of North America.

"If you're from Mexico," he said, being cautious, "let me hear you speak Spanish."

"Well, that's easy," she laughed. *"¿Le apetece tomar algo conmigo? ¿Qué toma?"* she said.

"I don't talk Spanish," he said. "What did you say?"

"I asked if you wanted to have a drink with me," she said. "And if so, what?"

He laughed. "I'm Russian. There is only one thing to drink."

He turned to the bartender and ordered a triple shot of vodka. Stoli all the way.

Conversation ensued. The vodka arrived, three generous shots of about two ounces each, arranged in a tray of crushed ice. Boris toasted her and knocked back the shot with a quick gulp. Then the second.

"Want to see one of my favorite party tricks?" she asked.

"Sure," he said.

She reached to the third glass, picked it up and held it to her lips. "May I?" she asked with a twinkle in her eye.

"I dare you," he said.

"Watch closely," she said.

Intrigued, he watched as she grabbed a book of matches on the bar.

She struck a match and lit the vodka. She let the flame blaze until it receded beneath the rim of the shot glass. Then she slapped her right palm on the glass and held it tightly there. The flame extinguished and formed a vacuum. She used the suction to pick up the glass without closing her fingers on it. She whirled the drink around to Boris's delight, defying gravity. Then she used her left hand to pull the glass free. With an upward motion, she tossed the vodka up out of the glass into the air as one would throw a piece of popcorn into one's mouth. She caught the shot in its entirety and swallowed it in one gulp. Her throat, for a few seconds, felt as if it were on fire. But Boris was, she could see, impressed.

"I have seen soldiers do that, but never women," he said.

"You have now," she said. "Hang around and you'll see me do a lot of things you've never seen a woman do." She snuffed out her cigarette after another drag. "I'm flying," she said. "I mean, I am *really* flying. Too much alcohol." Idly, she wondered what her late Robert would have thought if he could have seen the Slut Girl 101 role she was playing in a hotel bar in Egypt. Then she put it out of her mind. So impressed was Boris that he ordered another set of three shots. Then he took out his matches. He lit all three vodkas. He drew a breath, took a drink of some cold water from the bar. He stood and stepped back.

Then Boris repeated the trick, but using the vodka while it was still flaming. He tossed it high into the air, quickly positioned himself under it and caught it in his mouth. The second shot, the same. Then the third, which was a slight miss and splashed him across the jaw.

He staggered slightly, laughed, and wiped his face with his sleeve. Alex applauded as if drunk out of her mind.

More small talk. The room started to sway a little for Alex, but not as much as her body language tried to show. She wondered how much booze she had consumed in her life for the overall security of the United States of America. She kept crossing and uncrossing her legs. She knew that the fire had been extinguished from the top of the booze, but she had lit one in her target's gut.

Two shots later, Boris got around to what he wanted to know, "Are you staying here with him?"

"Here with who?" Alex asked.

"Your boyfriend."

"Oh. Him. No," she said.

Good, she thought. *He's inquiring about my room arrangement.*

In the periphery of her view, she watched Rizzo, who had arrived that morning, walk into the bar and sit down at a table.

"No," she said to Boris. "He's at another overpriced hotel. The Hilton. He was supposed to meet me here, and then we were going to go out. But he's stood me up, you know that, Boris? You know how much it hurts a woman to be stood up?"

She took on a dispirited expression. "He probably went chasing after a younger girl," she said. "So why should I care?"

"You're here alone?"

"On business. For three days. Then I go on to Athens, then back to Miami. That's where I live. Miami. The new capital of Cuba."

Boris was more than intrigued. Alex slurred slightly, then took another sip of the wine that still sat in front of her. Her hand was shaky, and she spilled a few drops.

"I'm sorry," she said. "I'm bothering you. I should leave."

"No, no, no," he said, amused. "You're not bothering. Please stay."

"I don't want to make a fool of myself."

"You're very beautiful," he said again.

She looked away. "I don't feel beautiful. I feel rejected. That's how I feel. I hate being alone. I'm almost thirty," she said.

"You could pass for five years younger." He placed a hand on her bare thigh to steady her. The touch went through her like a shock, but she went along with it. His hand was every bit as strong as it looked. If things went the wrong way, this was going to be real trouble.

"You're kind," she said.

He glanced at the small bandage on her arm, the one that covered the vestiges of the bullet grazing.

"What happened to you?" he asked.

"My boyfriend gets rough with me sometimes," she said. "He's a pig."

That seemed to turn Boris on. Alex looked him in the eye. She had had her experiences with post-Soviet Moscow-style hoods, and this was another one. In a previous generation, Boris's station in life would have been as one of the thick-browed KGB security gorillas who would stand by the door in a leather jacket to keep the trade delegates from going AWOL. These days, in the buoyant Putin-era consumer culture of workers-of-the-world-shop-till-you-drop, the same tough boys developed a taste for Swiss watches, German cars, and French cologne, while they pursued North American women.

Her gaze drifted away. She knew she had him. She wondered if Rizzo was getting jealous with the hand-on-the-bare-thigh stuff. She also wondered how much of this the bartender was taking in. The bar was otherwise quiet.

She looked back to Boris. His eyes were not on hers but rather on her breasts, or what he could see of them in a moderately low-cut dress. She caught him looking at her neckline. He grinned when detected.

She straightened up and withdrew slightly. She put her hand on his hand, the one on her leg. She made an effort to push it away, but he wouldn't budge. He was grinning like a lecherous gargoyle.

"You're a fresh boy," she said.

"Yes, I am," he said proudly.

"You're coming on to me," she said drunkenly.

"Most certainly," he said.

"But we just met."

"I don't care."

"Didn't your mother warn you about strange women in hotel bars?" she teased.

"I like strange women in hotel bars," he answered.

He wasn't very smart, Alex was thinking. Occasionally, she liked that in a man.

"Maybe I'm offended," she said.

"If you were offended, you'd walk away. You're not doing that."

She laughed slightly. "Are you always so sure of yourself?" she asked.

"Often," he said. "I'm drawn to beautiful women."

She said, "I'm much too drunk. Before I fall off this stool, I should go upstairs."

"I would like to join you," he said.

She didn't answer. She took a final swig of wine, rose from the bar stool, and turned. "Do what you want, Boris," she said. Then she leaned forward and whispered in his ear. "Follow me but be discreet. The 'towel heads' are terrible prudes," she said.

Boris smiled and nodded. He lifted his hand from her leg so she could stand.

She took a tentative step to leave, played the drunkenness just right, and steadied herself with a hand on his massive shoulder. She turned toward the bar exit, struggled a little on her heels, and headed out. From her peripheral view, she saw him knock back another shot of vodka. He then reached to his pocket and dumped a fistful of cash on the bar.

Alex passed directly by Rizzo. She left the bar and crossed the lobby with another wobble. She went to the elevator. She turned.

Good. He had followed. Now Boris was about ten feet from her, trying to make a decision. She gave him a smile and then, to seal the deal, a wink.

The elevator door opened. There was no one else in it. She stepped in and he followed again.

"My room is on the sixteenth floor," he said.

"Mine is on the seventh," Alex said.

"We will go to mine," Boris said.

"I need to stop at mine first," she said.

She wondered if she had somehow alerted him to danger. His expression suggested that he didn't like that idea, her room. In the Russian services, or any services, survival was contingent upon the continuing talent for suspicion. And so far, Boris had survived very well.

"I will wait for you upstairs," he said.

"If I lie down in my room I might never get up," she said.

The elevator arrived on the seventh floor. The door opened.

"So if I don't come upstairs, I've gone to bed alone. Don't wait."

Impulsively. Boris stepped out of the elevator behind her. But she could pick up the scent of suspicion from him. He didn't like this. Something about this was setting off alarms.

"Why do you have to go to your room first?" he asked.

She held his hand and gave him a wink.

"Never ask a woman too many questions," she said. "But if you really want to know, I want my toothbrush and a few overnight things. Is that okay?"

He didn't answer. She moved to her door. Everything was going the way she wanted it to so far, but it was essential that she bring him into her room, if only for a moment. If he held out for his own room, she was sunk.

But he followed her to her door. She felt his body hulk behind her. She could smell the bad cologne and imagined that she could feel his breath on her neck.

"I have a negligee that I was going to wear for my boyfriend," she said. "But now, tonight, I don't care. You'll be my boyfriend, and I'll wear it for you. Two days from now I'll be back in Miami and no one will ever know about us. Except us. How's that?"

"That's good," he said.

"Will you wait outside my room for me?" she asked. "Do you

want to wait here? Or would you like to come in and watch me get undressed?"

He didn't answer. She ran her room card through the proper slot on the door above the doorknob. The little green light came on. She placed her hand on the doorknob and began to push the door open. She felt his powerful hands on her shoulders. She wondered how he would try to kiss her. Then, quickly, she found out.

His slid his hands roughly down her and surrounded her body with his arms. He pulled her back closely to him until her body was flush against his. His lips came down on the right side of her neck and he began to kiss her bare shoulders. He held her in one of the strongest and most powerful grasps that she had ever encountered.

The grasp didn't thrill her. It scared her.

She managed to turn around in his arms, but only because he let her. He could have overpowered her in an instant. He could have choked her to death in a few seconds. She looked up to him and he smiled. She knew she had him.

His lips came down on hers. His lips were firm and warm, and she realized it had been quite some time since she had allowed a man to kiss her like this. Then one of his hands was busy behind her back. He had the zipper to her dress in his fingers, and he was working it downward.

She professed shock, even when he had it down a few inches and the shoulder strap of her new dress was loose. Her body was pressed firmly against his. She managed to move a leg and push the door open behind her.

"You're a very bad boy," she said. "I don't think we're even going to get upstairs."

He grunted. "Maybe not."

"My room is very comfortable," she said. "The bed is big enough for two. Follow me?"

Alex pulled away from him. She had a sense that the booze had caught up with him, and his reactions might be dulled. She hoped she was correct.

Flirtatiously, she smiled and took his necktie in her hand. "This is going to be fantastic," she said. "Come along." She gave him a quick kiss on the cheek.

She felt the door open inward behind her. She pulled him along and whatever hesitation he had felt now dissipated. Boris followed her into the room. As they took the first steps inside, she leaned back to him, cupped her hands behind his head to block his view, and kissed him again.

Their lips were still touching when the blackjack in Abdul's hand came from the right side and smashed across Boris's temple. The blow landed with more of a clunk than a crack. It split open the skin and bounced off.

With exquisite timing, Alex released her prey and pulled her hands back. Tony, crouched low behind the door, came from the left with a small iron club that went straight at Boris's knee from the left side. The club smashed into the side of the kneecap with a resounding crunch. A second harder blow to the same spot staggered Boris more than the first.

At the same time, two of Voltaire's other local people rose like phantoms from behind a sitting-room sofa. They rushed toward Boris, who was now screaming profanely in Russian. Alex ducked out of the way. Her four backup men tried unsuccessfully to drag Boris to the floor.

Alex kicked the door shut as the men wrestled violently. Voltaire's men hit Boris hard and shoved him forward until he crashed onto the carpet, knocking over a table and a lamp.

Alex moved too close and caught an elbow to the side of the face. She staggered from it. In the melee, other fists flew wildly. One of them grazed her under the chin. Half of her face stung, and Alex realized that she was right in the midst of the brawl herself. She had lost a shoe and a shoulder strap had ripped.

Boris fought like a wild man. He threw his powerful elbows at the men on top of him. He caught one in the jaw and one in the gut. The room was alive with crashes, thumps, and profanity. Boris clenched one of his huge fists, threw a massive backward punch at one of Voltaire's men and caught him in the testicles.

The man howled profanely and loosened his grip.

Boris lunged for his right ankle, and Alex realized she had been correct. That's where his gun was. "Pin his leg! Pin his leg!" she yelled.

Abdul sat on the leg, and the other men managed to yank Boris's hands upward behind his back as Alex knelt and lunged into the fray, grasped at Boris's ankle, and struggled to take the gun from him. Abdul shoved a Taser to the base of Boris's neck and let fly with several seconds of current. The electric charge shot out of the Taser with a cracking, zapping sound.

Boris's body jumped like a great fish on a line. He howled again. His body convulsed, then the howl ceased, and a guttural near-choking sound followed. At the same time, Tony and Abdul continued to work his hands upward behind him. Finally they succeeded in handcuffing him.

Alex accessed the gun on Boris's ankle. She pulled it out.

Voltaire stood nearby, arms folded, surveying calmly. A few seconds later, it was over.

Boris lay stunned but not unconscious on the crumpled and torn Iranian carpet that covered the floor. Tony grabbed him by the hair, lifted his head, and slammed it down again.

He was still breathing hard, clinging to consciousness, blood flowing from his brow and skull. He was probably wondering how he could have been so stupid as to follow a woman into a hotel trap.

"Very nice," Voltaire said. "Dare I say, this is almost an art form."

Abdul and Tony unleashed a strand of duct tape. They wrapped tape firmly across Boris's mouth and looked to their boss for further instruction.

"Give him a lot more," Voltaire said with more feeling than was necessary. "He'll need it."

The assailants stood him up. Tony caught him again with a fist to the midsection, then another. They Tasered him again and watched his body convulse. Then they picked him up and shoved him awkwardly down onto the sofa, his wrists still manacled behind him.

The sofa was bolted to the floor and from somewhere someone produced a chain. They wrapped the chain around the captive, locked it to the sofa, and then stood back.

"Nicely done," Voltaire said again.

Boris came out of his stupor slowly. His eyes were wide and delirious, like a beached shark. But he was a prisoner and he knew it. Alex stepped back, her hand to her face where she had been hit twice.

"Are you all right?" Voltaire said evenly.

"I'm fine. I got grazed. No big deal."

"I'm so glad," Voltaire said. "At least you don't have to undress and go to bed with him. That might have been even worse."

"Very funny," Alex said. It wasn't.

"Ouch," Voltaire said. "But I assure you I've done worse in the call of duty."

Voltaire reached beneath a jacket and pulled out a Glock. He stepped forward until he stood five feet away from Boris, with his arm extended and the business end of the Glock trained at Boris's head.

"Okay," he said to Alex. "Talk to our guest."

Alex pulled a chair into a position a few feet from Boris. She sat down and crossed her legs to get comfortable.

She spoke in Russian.

"We're very sorry to inconvenience you, Boris," she said. "But we need some cooperation from you."

Boris looked at her with surprise and then hatred. But her Russian was so sharp that night that it corralled Boris's attention immediately. He stopped struggling and was very still.

"Cooperate with us, and we will make it worth your time. Cooperate and you'll be out of here in twenty-four hours. No one will ever know what happened. You'll be free to go, and my employer will even reward you with a few thousand Euros for your trouble. *Fail* to cooperate, and I'm afraid my friend here will grow impatient and shoot you."

She let it sink in.

"Unfortunately," she continued, "time is very short. So you have only ten seconds to decide."

Boris searched the room. Voltaire removed the clip from his weapon so Boris could see it was full, then slapped it back in. He whirled it in his hand with a sadistic flourish and moved the weapon closer to its mark. He squinted with one eye as if to bring the aim to the center of Boris's head.

"Such a beautiful carpet in this room too," Voltaire said. "It would be a shame to stain it. Let's see what our boy has to say now."

Abdul reached to the duct tape and ripped it off Boris's face.

Boris responded with a torrent of obscenities in Russian, Putin-style. Then he spit at Voltaire.

"Oh, dear," Voltaire said. "Insubordination."

Boris turned back to Alex.

"Who are you?" Boris asked. "Americans?"

"It doesn't matter, Boris. You're our prisoner until we get what we want."

The hostage continued in Russian. "What do you want?" he asked.

"Cooperation," she said. "Now. What will it be? Please make the wise decision."

Boris spit again. This time the expectoration contained parts of a tooth. But at least it was the beginning of a dialogue.

FORTY-FIVE

Ten o'clock the next morning. There were six of them now in Room 734. No one was particularly cheerful.

Boris sat on the sofa, chains still across his feet and his waist, a large white bandage covering the purple bump and gash across his forehead. There were bags under his eyes. His captors had seen to it that he had been up all night.

Alex sat on a chair several feet away in a pair of jeans, a T-shirt, and her Beretta on her right hip where it now lived. She had changed since the previous night, and while the cocktail dress had been fun and served its purpose, the jeans were a better fit.

They had been joined by a young Swiss who went by the name of Leonardo — after DiCaprio, not Da Vinci — a lad who was the resident cybergeek who worked for Voltaire in Cairo. A wiry young girl named Rebecca had done an impressive break-in of Boris's room. She had filched Boris's laptop and brought it downstairs.

Now Leonardo picked his way through it. Mimi, Rizzo's friend, teamed with Leonardo to work on hacking Boris's encryption. Mimi had graduated from her colorful Sailor Moon period that was so-two-months-ago and had now suddenly gone Goth, a drastic overhaul from just a few days earlier. Black nail polish, black boots, soft powdery makeup, a black miniskirt, and two silver rings on each internet-savvy finger. She had also roared past Leonardo and was taking the hacking of Boris's machine to new levels.

She had been at it for an hour when she leaned back, satisfied.

"He's using Advanced Encryption Standard," Mimi said, staring evenly at the screen and continuing to work the keypad. "It's a symmetric 128-bit block data encryption technique developed in 2007 by the Van der Waal brothers, a couple of insane Dutch cryptographers," she said.

"So?" asked Alex. "Can you penetrate it?"

"Oh, yeah, yeah," she said. "It's not a bad program. There's back-door access to it, but difficult to achieve. The US government adopted the same algorithm as its encryption technique in 2008, replacing the DES encryption it used to use. I'm surprised to see a Russian goon using this stuff," she said.

Boris's eyes, all one and a half of them, were wide with rage.

"The Van der Waal brothers were psycho, like I said," Mimi continued, "so the logic of their program is elliptical. It doesn't follow any traditional encryption logic. That's what's so severe about it. It goes by the rules of 'Mondo van Waal,' which is to say it's completely unpredictable and follows no logic at all, more like a counterlogic, but it's still kinda cool."

"So can you crack it, Mimi?" Rizzo asked, exchanging a glance with Alex.

"Hell, yeah," she said.

"You rock, Mimi," Rizzo said. "Doesn't this girl rock?" he asked the room.

The room admitted that Mimi rocked. All except Boris.

Alex glanced to the battered and unhappy camper on the sofa.

"You should warn your people," Mimi said to Voltaire, Alex, and Rizzo. "Someone was drop-dead careless exporting this encryption technology. You could apply this program to a different platform and break into existing GSM codes all over North Africa. I don't think Boris here is smart enough or computer-savvy enough to do that, but, for example, if terrorists gained these same encryption codes for your own laptops, they might be able to impede your abilities to track them."

She worked the keypad intensely. Leonardo had bailed.

"They could also apply a GPS application," Mimi said, "and monitor your movements. That way," she said cheerfully, "they could know where you live and be there to meet you. They could put broken glass in your bathwater, arsenic in your coffeemaker, or just an ice pick in your ear as you slept. Someone needs to be more careful with this crap. Anyone got a cigarette?"

Alex looked at her.

Rizzo gave her one of Boris's disgusting Russian smokes.

Mimi lit up. "This thing's gross," she said. She snuffed it after two drags. "What is it?"

"Bulgarian tobacco," said Rizzo.

"Yuck," she said. "No wonder people fled to the West for fifty years. Anybody got a Winston or a Pall Mall or even a Nakla or anything that doesn't taste like horsesh — ?"

Abdul had a pack of Winstons, which kept Mimi calm.

"So, young lady, you're telling us that most of the police agencies of Western Europe and North America are sharing the same encryption technology as this hood?" Voltaire asked.

"That's pretty much what I'm telling you, Einstein, yes," Mimi said, smoking.

"Great," muttered Voltaire. "That's a whole separate report to Langley."

"I'll let them know," Alex said.

Alex turned back to Boris. "Why don't you earn yourself a few extra points here and tell us where you got your encryption system?" she asked in Russian.

Boris shrugged. "Moscow," he said unhelpfully in a muffled voice from under the tape across his mouth.

"Most likely that's true," said Mimi. "It was already programmed into the laptop when it was given to Boris. I don't think he's smart enough to program it or apply it himself. I mean, just look at him."

"Strong as a bear, but only half as smart," Rizzo suggested pleasantly.

"Do you hear what my technician and my associate from Rome are saying about you, Boris?" Voltaire said. "They don't think you're the sharpest knife in the drawer."

By now, Boris was wondering why they were talking about knives.

"Okay," Mimi finally said. "I'm into the program. What now?"

"We need to send something," Bissinger said.

"That'll be a problem too," Mimi said, "unless you get your prisoner to do it."

"Why?" Alex asked.

"There's an extra encryption layer," she said. "The laptop has been textured to recognize finger touch, keystrokes, and speed. It's like it's looking at your handwriting and telling who you are. So anyone important who he sends to is going to be alerted that it's another sender. Unless Boris does the typing."

Bissinger and Voltaire looked to Boris.

"That's not going to be a problem, is it, Boris?" Bissinger asked.

Another low profanity from the Russian indicated that it wasn't.

Alex leaned forward. "Here's what Boris should send," she said. She leaned forward and handed her notepad to Voltaire.

On it, there was a message that purported to be from Boris to Michael Cerny. Voltaire eyed it, made no changes, and passed it along to Boris. Rizzo walked to Boris and, with a quick yank, again ripped the adhesive duck tape off the Russian's mouth.

Boris, not having much choice in the matter, took the pad in his hands, which were still shackled together. For a full minute not a word was spoken in the room.

Then, "Read it to us," Voltaire asked.

Boris drew a breath and began.

"Direct message from Department of Interior Management, Moscow, for Ambidextrous," said Boris. "Superiors require further final visible samples of product before meeting your price. Second meeting in Cairo with representative is essential before completion of transaction."

"Now send it," Voltaire said.

Mimi turned the computer around and pushed it to the Russian.

"He'll never fall for it," Boris said. "You would need me present, and you would need to set a place."

"You *will* be present," Voltaire said, "and we'll set a place when he responds. Now send it."

Boris gave everyone in the room a final glare. He leaned over the keyboard and tapped out the message. It took less than a minute, and then he hit SEND.

He leaned back.

"Good," Voltaire said. "That was the easy part."

FORTY-SIX

The highway that led south from Cairo to the morgue at the "new city" of Bahjat al-Jaafari was four lanes, two in each direction, and as gray as the sandstone buildings that were visible beyond the highway's edge. High walls ominously enclosed the roadway. To Alex's mind the walls gave the road a claustrophobic air, even though the desert beyond was long and flat and stretched into the hazy sky. Traffic was intermittently either very fast or very slow. The road was cratered with cracks and potholes.

Alex had traveled this road once before, the day she went to see the pyramids and the Sphinx, but that had been a pleasant day and this one was not. The best she could ask for was to get through it and survive.

Operations I have known, she thought to herself. *Lulls before storms. Somewhere almost all of them blew dangerously off course. The chainsawed car in Lagos. The RPG attack in Kiev. The near-death in a subterranean tunnel in Madrid.*

And today?

Alex's driver was an American Marine named Len, a twentysomething and one of the usual guards from the embassy in the capital. He was not in uniform but instead wore a gray shirt and black slacks with a military sidearm on his right hip. His foot tended to be heavy on the floorboards, and he didn't miss a bump.

As Len drove, he spoke with a deep-Dixie accent and took an immediate liking to her, much as a man would take a liking to a woman who reminded him of an older sister. Man of the world that he was, he boasted about the German girlfriend he had in Munich whom he visited a few times a year.

"My fraw-leen," he called her. Alex listened indulgently.

They rode together in a black Hummer with deeply tinted windows and doubly reinforced panels and windows. There was a third person in the vehicle too, another Marine, also in plainclothes, which in his case was a white polo shirt and jeans. He went by his last name, which was McWhorter. He was a lieutenant from Virginia, and he sat with an automatic submachine gun across his lap.

They drove on the highway that went out toward the pyramids, then exited the main road and accessed a tributary road that led east over tougher terrain. Alex felt her anxieties heighten. About two miles behind them, another vehicle followed, this one an unmarked van with three more Marine bodyguards, all disguised as laborers.

McWhorter spoke little the whole ride but chipped in when a settlement came into view down the road. "That's Bahjat al-Jaafari," he said. "The tallest building in the settlement is the hospital. The morgue is attached to it."

"I recognize it from the pictures," Alex said. She felt her heart race. Her sweat glands started to misbehave. What if this operation some-how had been compromised? Was she at greater risk here than she had previously imagined? Would there be a final irony that attempting to *play* dead would end with her being dead for real?

As she did in such circumstances, she spoke a small silent prayer. It had never hurt before. She was sure it would do no harm now.

The SUV turned from the tributary road onto an uneven, bumpy stretch of sand and gravel. The roadway passed for the access route to the hospital and the morgue. Len cut the speed out of self-preservation.

Alex was dressed in the garb of a middle-class Egyptian woman, in an ankle-length linen dress. She wore a beige *hijab* on her head. She had a veil but it was not yet in place.

She pulled out a cell phone and hit Rizzo's number. They had fresh phones but had worked up this charade for whoever might be listen-ing. One never knew. She spoke in Italian.

Two rings. A third.

That's right. He's waiting, she thought to herself. *No need to sound as if he were waiting for a call. He'd pick up after three but before—*

"*Allo?*" he answered.

"*Signor Rizzo?*"

"*Si.*"

Alex assumed the role of a clerk calling from a Fiat dealership back in Rome. She cheerfully conveyed the bad news that Rizzo's 1987 Spider needed a new gearbox. Rizzo responded with a graphic obscenity, designed to sully the ears of anyone eavesdropping.

"How long will a repair take?" he asked in a vexed tone.

"Maybe three weeks," she said. "The part needs to be special-ordered from Torino and the inventory is already backordered."

Another salty profanity. Then, "How much?"

"About three hundred Euros. I could call back with a specific sum if we place it on order."

"*Si, si.* Go ahead," he said with exasperation. "Do the blasted over-priced work."

"*Grazie, signor.*"

She rang off. The call meant they were safely accessing the hospital. The three meant she expected to be there in three minutes. Her two solders listened in like a couple of terriers, but if they understood Italian, she wasn't aware of it.

Next, they were driving on sand, then fine gravel. They arrived at a semicircle in front of the hospital at Bahjat al-Jaafari. Alex scanned for trouble. So did her soldiers. Did she see any or not?

She couldn't tell. Their vehicle slowed but didn't stop. No one in the Hummer spoke. Alex moved her hand under her dress to grip her pistol. It was awkward. She had to pull the window side of the dress all the way up to where the gun lay on her lap. But the Beretta was her final line of security.

Near the entrance was a solitary man leaning against the building. He was in Arab garb, moustache, soul patch, and dark glasses. Six-two maybe, she guessed. Unusual height, potentially one of their thugs. He was smoking and he carried a small canvas bag. A weapon within or overnight clothing? A bomb or his dinner?

Not far away was a small van. No one in the driver's seat. Were there gunmen in the back, assassins waiting?

Then again, they thought she was dead, didn't they? They had announced her missing and then her body found. So why would the opposition be here? Or then again, why *wouldn't* they be here? And why didn't the thuggish man glance their way? If he were waiting for arrivals, would he be curious?

Why was he now walking away the way he was? Shouldn't a black Hummer have attracted his attention, his curiosity? There was also a gaggle of women sitting by the bus station. No problem there — they looked fat and middle-aged — unless they weren't women, had weapons stashed and were going to spray the vehicle as soon as a door opened. They had bags with them. Big bags. Ominous. The tall Arab threw his cigarette away. A sign?

There were two other small knots of Arabs, all men. Alex took a quick census. Four in one group, three in the other. Good Lord, if she was walking into a trap and there were five to eight guns out there, she didn't stand a chance. They wanted her dead, and they wanted to make sure, so, again, why *wouldn't* they be here?

"Our instructions are to take you to the rear entrance," Len said. "The morgue, not the hospital."

"I know. Follow the instructions. Do everything by the book."

"Yes, ma'am," he said.

The SUV rolled through the semicircle. No one paid them much notice. She heaved a long breath, then assumed — or hoped — they were clean.

McWhorter turned in his seat and looked at a vehicle behind them. He smiled.

"Our backup is on our tail," he said. He raised a hand and gave a slight wave.

Alex pulled the veil up onto her face. It felt strange, like a mask she would use to examine toxic evidence. She wished she were back on the friendly beaches of Spain, wearing almost nothing. Or maybe back in Washington at her desk. Or anywhere but here right now — not that there was any turning back.

"I thought they were two minutes behind us," Alex said.

"He must have hauled ass and caught up," McWhorter said. "Anyway, he's here. That's good."

"We're going around back," Len said.

"Good thing," she said.

On the side of the building, at the base of the wall, a man was lying down. Dead? Rotting in the sunlight and heat? Sleeping? Faking? She didn't know.

Len turned the corner. The back of the building was void of people and vehicles. A good sign. She scanned. Nowhere to take a shot from either.

No trees, just sand.

She looked carefully, keeping the Beretta in her palm.

She checked her veil to make sure it was secure.

Len came in close to the building. Then they rolled to a halt. She flicked a glance through the car's rear window. The backup vehicle came around the corner and stopped about twelve feet away. She glanced at it carefully, then turned to McWhorter.

"Are the right people in that car?" she asked.

He looked, squinting. The driver gave a thumbs-up signal.

"Yeah. We're cool," he said.

McWhorter put a hand of support and caution on her shoulder.

"I know it's not in the plan, but do you want me to go through that door first?" he asked.

"That would give us away, wouldn't it?"

"It might, but — "

"I'll be okay," she said, hand on the door.

"Good luck," Len said.

"Yeah," McWhorter added.

She gave him a nod. Then she was out the door, prim and proper, like a middle-class Arab woman calling on a medical facility.

For some reason, her feet felt strange on the sand. Must have been her slippers. The heat radiated upward. She carried her bag. A change of clothes. The gun remained in her palm. The steel door was a few feet away. Somehow she felt more vulnerable out in the open, even though if this operation were tainted, a volley of bullets might lurk on the other side of the door.

She moved quickly. The Egyptian sun pounded down. Ra the sun god wasn't a benign spirit.

The service entrance was unlocked, a dull steel door that could have been pulled off its hinges by any strong man or woman. She pulled it open and glanced back. The Marines gave her a final wave.

Suddenly, she liked them a lot and missed them. They weren't hillbilly tourists with guns anymore. They were big brothers-in-arms.

She entered the morgue. Stench assaulted her nostrils. Formaldehyde, disinfectant, rotting flesh. The aroma of ugly death.

She hadn't been ready for it. She gagged.

Okay, memory. Don't fail on me.

She steadied herself. She had memorized the directions to the office of Dr. Badawi.

End of the corridor, turn left. Follow that corridor about ten feet, turn right. Ignore everyone. If spoken to, don't talk. What the heck could I say, anyway? "Loved your pyramids? Hated your radioactive crystals."

She traveled through a warren of dingy corridors. She picked up signs that would lead her to the medical examiner's station. There were voices and sounds from adjoining rooms. Mostly in Arabic. Nothing good. Some wailing. Some fool was playing music.

Supplies were stacked up in the corridor. There were two body bags, both looked full. Cadavers on top of each other. Small. Probably children. She shuddered. It was hot. Humid. Fetid.

She passed two nurses who eyed her strangely but didn't speak. Proper ID? She noticed quickly. No one had anything. What was proper ID in a place like this? A scalpel? Bloodstains? A pulse?

Then she arrived. An office, door opened, just where it was supposed to be. Cluttered. Much noise from adjoining chambers. Some piece of heavy equipment was rumbling.

A heavy saw? Were they cutting a body? She cringed again. She couldn't wait to get out of here.

She found Dr. Muhammad Badawi at the desk in his office. He looked up when she arrived at the door but said nothing for a moment. Then, "Yes?" he asked in English, suspicious.

"I'm Signora Ijerra from Rome," she said. "I believe you know my brother."

"I believe I do," he said. A long pause. "You're alone?" he asked.

She glanced over her shoulder up and down the corridor.

No one.

"I'm alone," she said.

He made a motion with his head, indicating that he would follow and she should lead. He passed her and entered the corridor, bringing her along.

"I believe your brother is en route," he said. American educated, she could tell instantly from his accent. Her feverish nerves eased slightly. He spoke good English and, even better, spoke it softly.

"I believe so. Brother Gian Antonio."

"Yes," he said.

Dr. Badawi led her to an adjoining chamber two doors down. They went through a door and entered the room together. It was an examining room of sorts, combined with storage. Supplies and a sink, a couple of guttered tables in a disgraceful state of nonhygiene. On a shelf above a side table were three jars with bodies of stillborn human infants floating in amber liquid. She gagged and tried to keep her thoughts on the task at hand.

There was a gurney in the middle of the room and a beige body bag on it. There were also two sheets, white and folded.

He closed the door. "You know what to do?" he said.

"I know."

"You're very brave."

"I just look that way. I'm terrified."

"That's how I feel every day," he said. "You prepare yourself. I'm going to leave to give you privacy. When I come back in, I'll apply some fine powder to your face and then some wax. I apologize but it will be necessary."

"I understand," she said.

He nodded. Then he turned and left the room. She drew a breath, then pulled off her dress. She stepped out of her slippers and removed her bra. Why, oh why in instances like this did she always absurdly think of her mother's advice from twenty-five years ago:

Always wear clean underwear in case you're in an accident . . .

She grabbed the first sheet and wrapped it around herself. She kept it snug, but not so tight that she couldn't keep her gun in her palm.

She pulled herself up onto the table and slid into the body bag the way she had slid into a sleeping bag as a twelve-year-old kid at camp. She lay back. She heard voices in the hall and then a hand on the doorknob. She heard the door open but couldn't see it.

Someone said something nasty-sounding in Arabic, and then the door closed. She hoped it was Dr. Badawi.

More footsteps. They approached the gurney where Alex lay flat and motionless, her eyes closed.

A hand settled on her shoulder. She was careful not to flinch.

"It's all right, Josephine," an Arab voice said. "Open your eyes."

She opened her eyes a third of the way, then the rest. Dr. Badawi stood over her. "Your friends, Rizzo and his two cohorts, they've arrived. They will be viewing your body in a few minutes. You're calm?"

"As much as possible under the circumstances," she said.

"I'm going to dress your face slightly now," he said.

"Go ahead," she said.

"Keep your eyes closed, breath evenly and lightly."

She closed her eyes. She tried to ease into almost a light trance. The doctor ran a brush with powder across all parts of her face, from the hairline down across the neck. He adjusted the sheet to shroud her neckline, then readjusted it.

"I'm going to put a piece of gauze in here also. That's standard." He pulled it over her face.

"You can breathe?" he asked.

She gave a slight nod.

"Good," he said. He pulled it away.

Then, distantly, she heard voices in the next room. She recognized Rizzo's. It sounded as if he were arguing with someone. Not unusual. Dr. Badawi told her he was going to get an attendant to wheel the gurney. The attendant, he said, was a technician who was not in on the ruse. Alex would have to keep still.

She remained silent. The doctor zipped the bag. Alex felt the zipper slide over her face and head. She opened her eyes just enough to see a crack of light from a six-inch gap where he had left the bag open.

A wave of claustrophobia was upon her, almost as bad as the time she had been trapped in old tunnels under Madrid. She fought the feeling. She suppressed the deep desire to push her way out of this bag. Yet she had disrobed, wrapped herself in sheets, and climbed in voluntarily. And if everything went right, this would be over in ten minutes.

And if it doesn't go right? she asked herself.

Don't go there! she answered.

She heard Dr. Badawi walk away, leave the room, and then return a few moments later with a second pair of footsteps. She heard them talking. The doctor was with a woman and they spoke Arabic. Alex guessed that the woman was a nurse, maybe one of the suspicious ones she had passed in the corridors. Alex felt deeply vulnerable. She was in darkness but kept still.

Then the gurney began to move. She knew that she was going on display before Rizzo and two other men in the next room. She tried to steady her minimal breathing. At the same time she felt that her heart was kicking so loudly that they could probably hear it in Cairo, even above the din of traffic.

Then her gurney was moving on the uneven floor.

FORTY-SEVEN

She heard a steel door to the visiting room rattle and felt her gurney being pushed forward. The room tone changed.

She heard voices. First Rizzo. Then Colonel Amjad. Then the embassy guy whom she hardly knew.

She heard the door close, and she knew she was on center stage. The room fell silent, and the gurney stopped moving.

The doctor spoke in English as she heard the clinician step back and keep her distance.

"Which of you is — ?" Dr. Badawi began.

"I'm Rizzo," she heard Rizzo say, his voice slightly muffled and disembodied, listening as she was from within the bag. The interpreter from the embassy explained who everyone was. He spoke in Arabic and English, and Alex wished she could understand the Arabic.

"Who will do the identification?" Dr. Badawi asked.

"I will," said Rizzo. "So let's get it done."

"As you wish."

The doctor reached to the zipper. He pulled it gently open, lengthwise across the body. He stopped just past Alex's chin. She held her breath. She kept her eyes closed as someone lifted the thin gauzy fabric away from her face. She felt a hand land on the gurney and assumed it was Rizzo's.

"Oh, my dear Lord," she heard him mutter low and in Italian. "Oh, no ..."

"This is the woman you were working with?" Dr. Badawi asked. "The American woman who was missing?"

Several seconds of silence. She wondered if she could sneak a breath. She tried not to. Another moment passed. She heard Rizzo answer.

"Yes," he said. "It is."

"You're certain?" the doctor pressed.

Come on, she thought. *Get it over.* She couldn't hold her breath forever.

"Yes, yes," he said. "I'm certain."

"You knew her personally?" the doctor asked. "Or professionally?"

"Both," Rizzo said.

Please, please, please. Close the canvas. At least put the gauze back.

"Oh, dear Lord," she heard Rizzo say. There was more silence. She knew everyone was staring at her. Then something happened.

There was commotion. Colonel Amjad must have done something because she heard Rizzo getting very angry, and she could feel the vibrations of some sort of scuffle.

"Have some bloody decency, would you!" she heard Rizzo shoot back. "You keep your hands off this woman's body or I'll rip your arms out of their sockets! Understand me?"

There was an ominous pause.

"You tell him that!" Rizzo snapped to someone, she assumed Ghalid, the interpreter. "And make bloody well sure he understands!"

Ghalid urgently spoke Arabic to the other man.

"I was only making sure," Colonel Amjad said.

"Making sure? Making sure of *what*? We're in the blasted morgue!" she heard Rizzo roar. "What more do you want? A severed head? A bullet hole you can put your fist in?"

Zip the bag. I can't keep holding my breath. Zip me back in!

"All right," Amjad finally said to Rizzo.

"Too bloody true, 'all right,'" Rizzo said. "Let's get out of here."

Someone swiftly rezipped the bag. The hand pulled the zipper all the way shut. Alex was in near darkness and a second surge of claustrophobia hit her. But other hands reached to the bag and pulled the zipper back down six inches and left it there.

"There is some paperwork," Dr. Badawi said in English to his visitors.

Rizzo spoke softly. "Of course," he said. "Paperwork. Always. The world could come to an end but there would be paperwork even if no one were left to complete it."

The doctor turned to his assistant. "I'll take it from here," he said in Arabic, dismissing the technician. Alex heard the technician walk away. She heard the steel door open and clack shut.

"You've done a good thing by coming out here," Dr. Badawi said, presumably to Rizzo. "A quarter of the deceased out here are never identified. The medical authorities tell me they had to bury six hundred unknowns since January of this year, unidentified and unclaimed."

"Typical," Rizzo mumbled.

The doctor answered, "This had been a fairly routine day until you arrived."

"I'm honored," Rizzo grumbled.

Her heart started to settle slightly. The worst was most likely over. Now if she could just get out of this horrible sack of death. Rizzo seemed to be rustling some papers.

"The United States Embassy in Cairo has started procedures to retrieve her body," Ghalid explained softly. "However, it might take several days. So — "

"We're taking the body with us today," Rizzo said. "I'm not leaving without it."

"That would be quite impossible, sir," the doctor said.

"Nothing's impossible," Rizzo said. "Make it happen. We owe it to this woman to get her physical remains back to her country of origin. I'm acting on behalf of the Italian government and the government of the United States. I'm not leaving without her," he said again. "And Mr. Bassiri from the American Embassy has brought the proper paperwork."

"True?" Dr. Badawi asked.

She felt a toe twitch. Hopefully, no one saw it. Her face started to itch from the powder. She knew she was starting to sweat, and corpses aren't supposed to sweat. God forbid if she had to sneeze!

They must have been shuffling documents.

Come on! Hurry up! This is a nightmare in here!

"All right," she heard the doctor say softly. "This would seem to be in order. We won't miss one more set of remains. Less storage, less digging — no disrespect intended." A pause. "Will you call for the proper van to transport her?" he asked.

"Immediately," Rizzo said. "I wish to see the body back to Cairo personally. Then I wish to come back here and visit the place where she was killed."

She heard the doctor collect the documents. "Then we are finished here," the doctor said. "Under the circumstances, I'll see that the body is ready to move today."

"Grazie mille," Rizzo said. *"Choukran."*

"Âfowan," the doctor answered.

And thank you from me too! she thought.

"I'll stay with the body," Rizzo continued. "We owe it to her that she is returned to America. I want to make sure the body gets there."

"You do not have any reason to think — ," the doctor said.

"I have every reason to think something could happen," Rizzo retorted sharply. "I said I'd stay with the body! What language do I have to say that in so that you'll understand?"

"Very good, *ya-effendim*," the doctor said. All a big show for one piggish, corrupt cop. "If it pleases you, you may wait here in this chamber. Over there, perhaps."

More conversation. Several more seconds.

Her face was really starting to itch now. And some sweat mixed with powder had leaked into her eye. It was stinging. Beneath her backside, the sheet was soaking with her sweat. It was turning cold and making her shiver. She started to fight off a sneeze.

"Should we wait with you?" she heard Ghalid ask.

"No." Then Rizzo went off on Amjad. "Get *him* out of here before I shoot him. We're already in the morgue and I'm starting to think it's just too convenient to pass up."

A few more seconds. A sneeze that was harder to put a lid on.

"I'll be at the embassy if you need anything else," Ghalid said to Rizzo. "Be advised, transport for the body back to the US will probably have to go to Frankfurt first, then New York or Washington."

"Just get the paperwork done," Rizzo said. "It's bad enough the way it is."

Then she heard what she most wanted to hear. Doors closing. She heard no new voices and no alert from Rizzo. So Amjad was maybe out the door. Then she heard more steps, and the door opening and closing again.

More steps. No voices.

She lost track of who was where.

Then she heard a final set of footsteps. Rizzo's? It had to be his. She doped out the scenario. He was going to the door where Amjad and Ghalid had exited. She heard him open it. Then she heard him close it and bolt it from within.

The footsteps came back to the gurney where she lay. She felt a presence hovering over her.

It's you, Gian Antonio, yes? It has to be you! I pray to God Almighty that it's you!

She cheated. She opened her eyes very slightly to where she could see through narrow slits and through the gauze across her face.

It was Rizzo. She was sure. He placed a hand on the bag and gave it an affectionate touch, almost a caress. She felt it on her right shoulder. Then with both hands, he reached to the zipper and pulled it downward lengthwise again.

With a cryptic, stoic expression on his own face, he stared down at her, unaware that she could faintly see through eyelids that were so narrowly open.

"Oh, my Lord . . . ," Rizzo said softly. "What have we done now? Oh, my Lord."

Then Rizzo laughed. With that, Alex fully opened her eyes.

"Extraordinary," Rizzo said calmly.

She felt fine cracks in the wax on her face. She smiled a long smile of relief and exuded a long breath.

"It's over?" she asked.

"It's over," Rizzo said.

He drew the zipper down completely. She held the sheets to her, wearing little or nothing under them but still with the Beretta in her palm.

"Welcome back from the dead," he said.

"Nice to be back," she said. "I can't wait to get out of this bag."

"I'm sure," he said. "Most people never do."

"How did Amjad take it?" she asked.

"I'd say he bought it completely," he said. "But who knows?"

Throughout the following days, returned to Cairo and ensconced in a new hotel under a new name, Alex sought to recover from her own death. She stayed off the streets and emerged only in a veil. She dined with Rizzo one night and with Voltaire at his home the next. She met Voltaire's wife as well as his two young children. His wife, it turned out, was a stunningly beautiful Japanese woman named Mieko. She was his third wife, he said, and was about thirty. The family brought Alex no closer to figuring out Voltaire's origins than she had ever been. Alex wondered if even his wife knew.

But that was neither of the questions that raged before her.

In her quiet moments, in the many hours that she spent alone, she wondered two things. First, had their gambit been successful in feigning her death, and would the man she had known as Michael Cerny now emerge from whatever cover he was under? Would he attempt to finish his deal with the Russians or the Israelis or whoever was buying these days? She waited for a signal from Bissinger at the embassy in Cairo that would alert her of such movement. Alex would need to be present for the identification and the apprehension.

But then second, there was the larger enigma. Mentally shaking the pieces of the larger puzzle, she kept trying to work Yuri Federov into the equation of all that had transpired in the last year. There was a connection somewhere between Federov and Cerny, but no matter how much she racked her brain, she couldn't locate the proper geometry of it. No matter how much she rearranged the angle and the pieces, she couldn't nail the logic.

She went out for lonely walks as days passed. She kept her own counsel. Rizzo returned to Rome by way of Monte Carlo, Mimi in tow, where they tried their devious hands at *chemin de fer* and, according to an email, apparently came up big winners.

And all this time Alex remained in Cairo, laying low. A week passed. Then part of another. On instinct, she started again through the minefield of her laptop, accessed everything, backtracked, and marched forward. She reviewed all the salient events of the last year, ranging across Kiev, Paris, Venezuela, Spain, and Switzerland.

Then, expanding the venues somewhat, she started a handwritten list of all the places that had figured into her three operations. When she included the previously overlooked, Novo-Ogaryovo, Vladimir Putin's suburban estate outside Moscow, there was a flash of light, almost like a little flare of ignited gas.

Suddenly she had it.

Words from William Quintero, the CIA case officer she had met with most recently before embarking on this trip, came back to her.

"Notice the Christmas tree. Nice homey touch, huh?" he had said.

Homey, indeed!

She reopened her laptop and went to the internet.

Yes, indeed. Alex was certain now. She had it.

She booked a flight to Switzerland immediately to seek corroboration of her final theory.

FORTY-EIGHT

When her flight landed in Geneva, rain was falling. She noticed the drops on the window of the aircraft when it taxied to a halt and then again on the windshield of her cab as she took it to her destination.

She didn't go directly to Federov's house. She knew better. She was traveling light, with only an overnight bag that was good for three days maximum. Worse, she had had to leave her gun with Fitzgerald in Cairo.

To the cab driver, a Senegalese in a camo field jacket, she gave as an address one that Federov had given her over the phone. It was a corner in one of the better residential districts of Geneva, a corner that led to a quaint cul-de-sac of lavish homes behind high walls and gates. She was tempted to think of it as a gated community, but then again the entire Swiss confederation was a gated community. She put that thought out of her head and stepped out of the cab.

The cab pulled away.

Two children on bikes glided easily past her in the mist. She hung her overnight bag over her shoulder. Across the street a sturdy young man was standing at a rare phone box, appearing to be in conversation, and down the quiet street there were two men walking.

More importantly, she had no followers.

The man at the phone box hung up and again Alex waited. She looked back and forth in each direction. Then, about a hundred feet ahead, maybe more, she saw a hulking figure all in black, standing in the road in the twilight. The man was wearing a cap and a scarf, and something about him looked very Russian, even from a distance. Then again, she decided, from three thousand miles away, the man would have looked Russian.

He raised a hand and waved to her. She turned toward him and waved back. The man at the call box walked in a different direction without ever directly looking at her.

The man in black stood his ground. Alex walked toward him. It wasn't Federov, she knew, but one of his entourage, one of the tough boys whom he kept employed around the clock. That was fine. She figured he was armed, and, for that matter, she felt better that he was.

He seemed larger as she approached. He stood maybe six-four, a block of granite, with beautiful facial features: a Slavic Adonis. And idly — not that it mattered currently — Alex wondered whether he was one of the men who had so unceremoniously abducted her from Federov's hotel a few months earlier. If he was, he gave no such indication.

"Hello," he said, managing half a smile as she drew within a few paces.

She answered in kind. *"Dobry den'! Dobry den'! Ya govoryu po ro-osskie.* Hello. I speak Russian," she said.

He looked at her, grinned, and sniffed.

"I speak Russian too," he said. "Follow me."

He said his name was Nick but didn't say much beyond that. Nor did Alex ask for more. Nick led her for a block and then turned down another side street. They followed a high brick wall until they came to a gate. There was no number outside, no name, no marking, but Alex recognized it from her previous visit. Beyond the iron gate stood Federov's house, window shades drawn in every room, lights blazing almost everywhere. Sometimes she thought the whole world was unmarked to her, a series of ominous enigmas to be decoded as she went along.

The man in black pushed a buzzer and waited. A voice came on in Russian. Alex's escort mumbled something into a speaker. The two doors of the gate came heavily apart. The mist was thickening to a light rain and flirting with becoming sleet. Welcome back to winter and the darkness of a European November. Thank heaven they were at Federov's doorstep and on their way indoors.

She remembered quite well the first-floor landing of the house, the grand entrance hall, the study to one side, the living room to the other. Nick unwrapped the scarf around his neck and Alex unwrapped hers. He led her to the salon, a room she had been in before, and Alex was thinking how different her arrival was here this time as opposed to last.

Inside the room, Federov sat in a leather chair in a corner, a light blanket upon him. Logs were burning in a fireplace. Yuri smiled at the sight of her and got to his feet with an effort.

"Hello, Yuri," she said.

"Ah, my angel," he said. Raising himself to his feet, she realized suddenly, was more of a struggle than it should have been. He had a heavy steel cane nearby on his left side. For a moment she needed to stifle a gasp. He looked maybe ten or fifteen pounds lighter than when she had last seen him in New York.

When she was near to him, he took her arm. His grip was nowhere nearly as strong as when they had first met. In the nightclub in Kiev, his arm had been like a vice, the strongest and most ominous arm that had ever wrapped around her shoulders. Since then there had been others, but she would never forget his strength that first night in Kiev. Tonight, his grip was tentative.

He drew her closer. She allowed him to kiss her on both cheeks, gallantly in European style. Then she drew back and he released her. There was a thin line of sweat across his brow. The room was cool, even though the fire was going nicely in the fireplace.

"You're not well," she said in English. "I'm sorry to bother you."

At best, he was a man in recovery; at worst, a man in steep decline.

"Ah," he said, raising a hand dismissively. "I had some bad elements inside me. Not just my personal nature, my soul, but my body too," he said, trying to make light of it. "I had some surgery and am having some treatments. The doctors. Russian. American. French. In the end, what do they know, what can they do? If they're not treating you like a pincushion with their needles, they cut you up like a piece of meat."

He slid back into the chair, landing heavily.

"Will you be all right?" she asked.

"I will be fine. No disease is stronger than Yuri Federov."

"Don't lie to me," she said.

"You've traveled far. Would I lie?"

"Yes, you would. May I ask you what's wrong?"

"You may ask, but I will choose not to answer. We can talk today of many things, and I will answer honestly. But my physical condition is off limits, hey. Maybe at a later date. So now, what else?"

A woman appeared in modest uniform. Yuri introduced her. Her name was Marie-Louise. She looked very Swiss in a white blouse and a trim black pencil skirt that went to just above the knee. Not surprisingly, Marie-Louise was very pretty. She seemed to be Federov's housekeeper and her obligations were probably limited to only that because these days he didn't look fit enough to be keeping a live-in paramour.

In fact, Alex hated to admit, he looked like a shell of himself. She reckoned if it wasn't from illness, it was from medications. Heavy ones. She had always thought of him primarily as an evil man, perhaps beyond forgiveness, but now she felt sympathy and sorrow. Sometimes she didn't understand her own emotions, her own sense of decency, just as at other times she had trouble understanding people who lacked the same. But the vision of him today was like getting punched in the stomach.

"May we serve you some tea?" Federov asked.

"That would be wonderful," Alex answered.

"And you'll stay for dinner?"

"That would be excellent too."

"I assume you have a hotel reservation?"

"I do."

"Good. We will cancel it," he said. "Your former room has been readied for you here—I insist. Unfortunately, this medication has left me very weak today, so I can barely even dream of pursuing you amorously. So you will sleep undisturbed."

"That will be a change," she said.

"My regret," he said.

"I'm sure."

"Then you'll stay?"

She drew a breath. "I'll stay."

The tea arrived with biscuits. As Marie-Louise served them, Alex moved to the point of her visit.

"I want to talk to you about Vladimir Putin, Yuri," Alex said.

Federov laughed cautiously. "Normally you want to talk to me about Chekhov or Dostoyevsky. Now you want to talk to me about Putin. How would you say it in English? Your interests have declined several notches."

"Degenerated?" she suggested.

"That's it."

"But for professional purposes, I need to ask some questions," Alex said. "There's something so obvious, so apparent, it was in front of me the whole time, you with your company, the Caspian Group. You used to sell energy, right? And your power and influence in Kiev."

Federov shook his head. "So what about all this?" he asked.

"I want to put a theory to you. About Kiev, what happened. And you. And Vladimir Putin."

"All hail the great Putin," he said sourly, an echo of the 1930s propaganda posters that hailed "The Great Stalin."

"You can hail him all you want, Yuri," she said, "although I'm not going to join you. Putin is taking the country in ominous directions, is he not? Much of what has happened recently is a great departure, isn't it? Fifteen years after Boris Yeltsin's standoff with the Soviet Union from a tank turret in Moscow, Russia isn't just turning away from democracy, it's sprinting full speed in the opposite direction and redeveloping its nuclear arsenal."

"If you say so," Federov said.

Then he waved his hand in a dismissive gesture.

"Things are much better than they used to be in Russia," he allowed. "Now there is food in the supermarkets. There are many privileges. There were so many unsuccessful changes that what goes on now is justified. Putin's priority is order, order, and more order. This comes as a relief to most Russians." He paused. "But you are also right. Putin wishes to be the new czar. He rebuilds the Russian empire not on Western ideals but in his own image."

"As with many images of the past," Alex said, "Putin brought back the Communist flag as a military symbol. He also restored the Soviet national anthem. In a recent speech, he referred to the collapse of the Soviet Union as 'the greatest catastrophe of the twentieth century.'"

Federov shrugged. "So, hey? Putin only says what many Russians think."

"But when you watch the antidemocratic alliances he's building with Islamic countries like Iran and Syria, you also see how that worldview is playing out," she said. "And at home, his rule is as ruthlessly effective as Stalin's, or Peter the Great's. Putin has his grip firmly upon all aspects of Russian life. Political speech. The press. Religion. The Russian Orthodox church enjoys favor with Putin officials, but most other religious groups draw harassment and threats. Other Christian churches are viewed as subversive. And then there's the economy. The state took over the major Russian oil companies, businesses that operated with free market boldness during the Yeltsin years. And what about the Russian oil tycoon, Mikhail Khodorkovsky? I had some conversations with one of my associates in Rome about Khodorkovsky."

"What about him?"

"He was sentenced to nine years in a Siberian jail."

"That is Khodorkovsky's problem, not mine or yours."

"Let's backtrack," Alex said. "Vladimir Putin is a national hero to many Russians, a man who stepped from shadows to resuscitate a Russia that others had run into the ground, looted, and left for dead. He has been the vital link amidst the chaos that followed the fall of Communism. But he is also a cunning strongman atop a clique of robber barons. He was a career officer in the KGB, an organization whose members never leave. Worse, Putin is anti-Western, undemocratic, and comfortable with criminals. Civil liberties he sees as societal weakness."

Federov shifted uncomfortably. His hand fidgeted with the handle of his cane.

"Many people underestimated Putin right from the beginning," Alex said. "Gorbachev provided the collapse of the old Soviet Union, and then Yeltsin became the shaky steward of the new democracy. But when Yeltsin introduced Putin to the world in the summer of 1999, announcing that Putin was his sixth prime minister in a year and a half, no one expected Putin to have any shelf life. Why would he? His predecessors had all failed to bring stability to Russia. So what would be different about him?"

Federov snorted. "Quite a bit," he said.

"Obviously. And look at the mess he inherited. Chechnya had exploded and become an international Islamic cause. Crime and corruption were rampant, and a new class of billionaire gangsters controlled the nation's resources and were becoming a major voting bloc in the parliament. Then there was also Yeltsin's bumbling manner, a white-haired figure atop the government, midway between a butt-pinching clown and a benevolent drunken grandfather. Nothing in 1999 suggested that Putin would last more than a few uneasy months. And the available information on Putin, a career KGB operative, was almost nonexistent. As a former spy, what defined him was his own obscurity. One prominent Western newspaper described him as standing six-five. They had it backward. He stands five-six. He's a tiny man, Yuri, unlike yourself but like Napoleon or Stalin. And like Napoleon or Stalin, a successful commander does not have to be large in physical stature, only large in intellect and in the art of confrontation and intimidation."

Federov grunted anew.

"So what did Putin do next?" Alex said. "He directed a new military campaign in Chechnya. The war had compromised Russia's self-esteem. Putin did not just promise to restore Russian rule. He used violence as an instrument of governmental policy. So Russian troops destroyed much of Grozny, the Chechnyan capital. They launched murderous sweeps through the Chechen countryside that were reminiscent or the old Soviet or German sweeps of World War II. If you were in the way, you got killed. Putin's language in speeches in Moscow was bellicose, vulgar, and unapologetic. He knew no rules in his efforts to reestablish Russian sovereignty over breakaway provinces. Russia's losing streak was over and his popularity climbed. In 2000, Yeltsin resigned, and Putin was elected president in one of Russia's rare modern elections."

"All this is known by both of us, hey?" Federov said. "Where do you go with this?"

"To you. And to Ukraine."

He seemed uneasy for the first time. "How?" he asked.

"You'll see," Alex said. "Putin took advantage of events over which he had no control. Russia's oil and natural-gas reserves are the world's largest. Russian coal, mineral deposits, and timber were gigantic assets as well. So suddenly the country that not long ago could not afford to fuel its air force and army was now swimming in petroleum and cash. The Russian stock market soared. Personal incomes quadrupled. A society that endured food shortages adapted to a consumer culture that bought what it wanted. French clothing, Belgian chocolates, American CDs and DVDs, Chinese electronics, Finnish cell phones, Italian shoes, Cuban cigars, and single-malt scotches. Rates of car ownership multiplied. Moscow's roads, cluttered during Yeltsin's time with pathetic old Zhigulis, were now packed with BMWs and Ford Mustangs. All of this was due to the stunning increase in energy prices. Petroleum. Natural gas. What was the name again of that conglomerate that you used to run, Yuri? The one where you kept all the records in your head. The Caspian Group."

Federov nodded. "That was it," he said. "As you know."

"Wasn't energy one of your main products? Something you sold? Gas, mostly. In Ukraine?"

He nodded.

"In 2004, Putin fixed his own reelection just to be sure," Alex continued, "even while the Russian economy roared ahead. People in power were making millions. So Putin was seen as the steward of the new wealth, and the country was stable again, although dangerous and run by armies of bandits. And meanwhile, Putin cashed in on another world event, one that he opposed but which worked well to his benefit: the American invasion of Iraq."

Federov laughed. "Bush's folly," he said.

"Of course. The war in Iraq was a great success," Alex said, "for Putin, not necessarily America. By 2005, Russia had demolished the ragtag Chechnyan army. The few insurgent warriors who remained were either being captured and executed or, in many cases, coerced to join a pro-Russian government led by Ramzan Kadyrov, the rebel-turned-Putin-loyalist who replaced the chaos of conflict with a local dictatorship. Two underground Chechen presidents were killed. Pro-

Islamic foreign fighters had been a radicalizing presence in the war, but now they had all fled to Iraq to join the war against the Americans. What had been a persistent problem for Putin was now a problem for George Bush. American soldiers got to fight the Islamists instead of Russian soldiers fighting the same Islamists."

She paused.

"By this time, Putin's approval ratings at home exceeded seventy-five percent," she said. "That meant he could turn his attention to his next problem."

He grinned. "*Ukraine*," he said with a homesick smile.

She nodded. "*Ukraine*," she confirmed.

"In 2005, a peaceful revolution in the old Soviet republic of Georgia had overturned a pro-Russian election result much in the style of Putin's reelection. A pro-West government was in power, eroding Russian influence. And then the tide of democracy spread. A Ukrainian opposition was organizing in Kiev. In the elections of 2004, Putin had supported a pro-Russian candidate, Viktor Yanukovich. Yanukovich had been convicted of robbery but had the support of the creaking old pro-Russian political machine built by Leonid Kuchma, the widely hated departing president. Putin jumped in as if the race were a domestic affair. He presided over a Soviet-style military parade in Kiev and committed Russia to an energy deal that pledged to sell natural gas to Ukraine at a deep discount through 2009. Natural gas is the lubricant of the Ukrainian economy. It heats Ukrainian cities and powers electrical plants and factories. Putin's deal — to sell gas for less than a quarter of the market rate through Yanukovich's first presidential term — was a subsidy-for-loyalty exchange, and promised Ukraine's elite ample opportunity for graft. Right?" she asked.

"Right," Federov laughed. "Reselling subsidized Russian gas at high profits is a common way of doing business in Ukraine," he said.

"It's a common insiders' swindle, is what you mean," she said.

"That is what Westerners think," he said, "but it is how business is commonly conducted in Ukraine."

"Maybe so. But here's where Putin had a problem. Yanukovich was not elected. His rival, Viktor Yushchenko, survived dioxin poisoning and emerged as the symbol against post-Soviet rule. And the next thing you knew, the 'Orange Revolution' was under way. Kuchma's government falsified an election victory for Yanukovich. But this time the government couldn't sell the big lie to the population. Hundreds of thousands of demonstrators took to the streets all over Ukraine. The demonstrators were out in all of the cities and towns demanding that their voices be heard. In response, seeing an impending civil war, the Ukrainian courts, newly open and anxious to show their independence, demanded a new vote. Putin was on the defensive again. What to do? How to keep his man Yanukovich in power? Send in tanks? The army? Ukraine was a big place compared with, say, Hungary in 1956 or Czechoslovakia in 1968, and the mood was explosive."

Federov nodded.

"But you know the story better than I do, Yuri. Putin is nothing if not a brilliant strategist. What was his weapon in Ukraine?"

"Gas," Federov said, his eyes narrowed. "Gas, and the deadly cold of the Ukrainian winter."

"Exactly. And what did he do?"

"Putin announced that the gas agreement with Ukraine was now void," Federov recalled. "Ukraine would have to pay competitive market rates, now more than five times the previous offer." He paused. "That meant Ukrainians could freeze to death because they couldn't afford heat."

"That's correct," Alex said. "Gazprom, Russia's state gas monopoly, set a deadline for late 2005. The threat's timing was carefully chosen, and the many ironies were inescapable. Ukraine faced the prospect of gas shortages in winter. And Putin, the KGB man who had given a Soviet-style energy subsidy to a nation to buy its loyalty, was now lecturing Europe about the need for market rates." She shook her head. "Brilliant, but unconscionable," she said. "Ukraine had been the breadbasket of the Soviet Union in the 1930s but faced the *Holodomar*, the fake famine of the Stalin years when the Soviets exported all food and grain from Ukraine. And now Putin had raised a similar specter. Now there would be a shortage of natural gas, never mind that Ukraine had a surfeit of natural gas and should have been self-sufficient."

Federov nodded. A gangster understood another gangster.

"The reformer, Yushchenko, resisted Putin's deadline," Federov remembered. "So Putin increased the crisis more, hey? The Russians cut the pressure in gas pipelines feeding Ukraine. Then the same pipelines that fed Europe started to fall in pressure too. Putin was squeezing everyone. It was early winter. No one in Berlin and Paris and Vienna wants to be cold."

"I've done my homework, Yuri," she said. "Most gas that arrives in Europe travels through lines that pass through Ukraine. Every elected leader in Western Europe was furious with him. What was he thinking?"

Federov laughed.

"Ukraine had overturned Putin's falsified election," Alex said. "Putin was furious. So he cut off gas to Western Europeans so that Western Europe would pressure Ukraine and Yushchenko." She paused. "And if my theory holds, Yuri," Alex said, "that's where *you* came in! You and your phantom company, the Caspian Group. You were the most powerful local man in the underworld. You controlled everything from black-market munitions, to sea-going merchant vessels, to stables of women. But energy, natural gas, was a big item in your stock, wasn't it? You had your own huge supplies stashed away at depots in Odessa and Sebastopol. So Putin and his people came to you and so did Yushchenko. You brokered a deal. I have a CIA memo all about it, and I finally learned of the televised press conference that you attended but never mentioned to me. But the deal wasn't known in the West until about six months ago, about the same time that Michael Cerny went underground."

"Yushchenko was trapped by Putin's power play with the gas," Federov confirmed.

"If Yushchenko stayed in power," Alex continued, "millions of Ukrainians would have frozen to death. A new Ukrainian genocide. They would have been begging the Russians to send tanks in to remove Yushchenko and reopen the pipelines. But if Yushchenko resigned, Ukraine would be back in the old Soviet sphere of influence, Gazprom would have controlled the energy, and eventually the country would have been doubly at the mercy of Russia again, first on energy production and second in terms of political domination. There's no secret that the old band of crooks and criminals from the Kuchmar regime would have been back. Correct?"

"Correct."

"So you offered both sides a way out: the new reform government could buy gas through the Caspian Group at a compromise price. It was just enough to override the Russian shortages. But as a deal, it was a stinker. Insiders were greatly profiting. Such as you, such as the Putin regime, such as Yushchenko's people. But most of all, the deal that you engineered was to Putin's advantage in two significant ways. He had compelled Ukraine to accept his terms. And he had dirtied Yushchenko with a gas contract that sullied his government and image as a reformer."

"There was a third too, hey?" Federov said.

"What was that?"

"Putin had shown Europe that he could stand up to Western pressure and spit in their eyes," he said. "His predecessor, Yeltsin, the white-haired old capon, never did that. Putin made Europe fear Russia again. Fifty years ago, East Germany, Czecho, Poland, Hungary: the Russians ruled with tanks. Now, not necessary. Putin rules with energy pipelines and petrodollars."

"There's an expression in English attributed to the artist Andy Warhol," Alex said. "Everyone will be famous for fifteen minutes. You got yours out of the gas deal, didn't you?"

His brow furrowed. "In what way?" he asked.

"You got to sit in that fake conference room on television with Putin and his minister of the interior and the head of the oil company," she said. "By making you visible it was clear you had brokered the deal. That made you a very powerful man in Ukraine, didn't it?"

"I already was."

"But it made you *more* powerful, particularly in Ukraine. All hail the great Federov, right, if you don't mind me giving you a variation of the old saying."

"Sure," he said with half a laugh. "If you want." He licked his lips and smiled.

"Which brings us back to Mikhail Khodorkovsky," she said. "The

one-time oil baron of the old post-Soviet years. Where is Khodorkovsky today?"

A dark expression overtook Federov. "You know as well as I do. He
is in a labor camp near the town of Krasnokamensk. It is a hellhole
out near the Chinese border."

"Seriously," Alex said. "And the labor camp is attached to a ura-
nium mine and processing plant, isn't it? During the Soviet era, it
was the type of place from which no one ever returned. A gulag, like
Solzhenitsyn wrote about."

"There are such horrible places," Federov replied with another
shudder. "If your benevolent God is real, you and I should be spared
from ever going to such places."

"And so should anyone else," she said. "Khodorkovsky was a
young man similar to you. Modest background, but highly ambitious.
He used family, Communist party, and overtly criminal connections
to grow very wealthy very quickly. He moved aggressively into what
had previously been the state oil company, and founded a Russian petroleum company named Yukos. With deregulation, in the Yeltsin era,
Khodorkovsky became so powerful that as of 2004, Khodorkovsky
was the single wealthiest man in Russia, as well as one of the most
powerful. And that didn't sit well with Vladimir Putin, did it?"

"No."

"So Khodorkovsky was arrested on charges of fraud. A bit later,
Putin took further actions against Yukos, leading to a collapse in the
share price and eventual bankruptcy. Khodorkovsky was sentenced
to eight years in prison. The sentence was seen as a warning, wasn't
it, as to what happens if an individual other than Putin gets too
powerful? In fact, an aide to President Putin once admitted that the
Khodorkovsky prosecution was a warning to the Russian business
community. And all of that, Yuri, brings us back to you. You too were
too powerful. All by yourself you were able to broker an agreement
between the established and the reform factions in Kiev. You worked
both sides of the Orange Revolution. Who knows exactly whose side
you were on when those RPGs started to fall near the American president, but I am sure you had a lot to do with it, much that you've never
even confessed to me."

"We all have our dirty secrets, hey?" he said. "Maybe someday you forgive me for mine."

"Some of us have more secrets than others," she said. "You more than me, for example."

Alex knew she had him just where she wanted him. She had marched him through unpleasant recent history for almost an hour, feinting in her line of questioning, darting one way and then the next, revealing casually what she knew that he didn't know she knew, interspersing it with an accurate recap of what had gone on in Kiev.

Federov's eyes were riveted on hers now, but he was like an abused dog. He didn't know whether he was about to get a treat or a kick in the ribs.

"I'm going to tell you the end of my theory now, Yuri," Alex said. "In response, I want the truth. I'm only going to do this once. Our relationship depends on your being more forthright than you've ever been. Understand?"

"Maybe," he said with a quick, nervous smile.

"After you solved a problem for Putin, you also created one for him. You were just a little too big in Ukraine. Maybe too popular, maybe even too powerful. After all, you were another hand on the gas lines, and Putin wanted to control those himself."

Federov didn't flinch.

"He could have had you arrested in Ukraine. For what? Who knows? He could have done away with you the way he did away with Khodorkovsky. But for you he would have wanted to make the exit more complete. So, through one of the back channels between Moscow and Washington, he started feeding information on you to the Americans. To the CIA and the FBI. Putin was brilliant at such things. In the same way he pawned off on the Americans his problem with the Islamic freedom fighters in Chechnya, he decided to pawn you off as well. The CIA became involved, and Michael Cerny became the point man for the operations. They tried to assassinate you two or three times but it didn't work. Then the US president was going to Ukraine, and I was sent to keep tabs on you and see where and when you might be vulnerable. I'm sure there was a plan to take you out in Kiev, but with the presidential visit going on, there was too much activity, so it wasn't possible to do anything at the time."

She paused.

"I noticed that you went underground after Kiev," she said. "You pulled out of your businesses in Russia and Kiev completely and rarely set foot in either place. In fear of your life?"

"I live in Switzerland and never go back to Ukraine," he said. "I'm forty-nine years old and do you know what my goal is? I'd like to celebrate my fiftieth birthday."

"And I can't imagine why."

"Can't you?"

"That's irony, Yuri. You say one thing to mean the opposite."

"Like when Putin says *uvidimsia*. The word means, 'I'll see you.' But when he says it this actually means he wants to cut your throat."

She paused again.

"Who called in the rocket attack on the presidential visit?"

"Filoruski," he said again. "Pro-Russian dissidents in Ukraine who feared an alliance with the West."

"Your answer hasn't changed from last time. Is that it?"

"That's it," he said.

"Then answer two more things for me," she said.

"Sure."

"History as I related it from 1999 to present, vis-à-vis you and Putin and the gas crisis in Ukraine. Do I have it correctly?"

"Yes," he said.

"And your relationship with Putin," she said. "You did business, you knew each other well, you both profited from the gas crisis in your own way. But then you were too big for Putin's liking. So you needed to be taken down. I'm correct?"

"It's a good theory," he said.

"So I can take that as a 'yes'?" she asked.

He made an expansive gesture with his hands.

"It's a 'yes,'" Federov said.

She leaned back. "Excellent, Yuri," she said. "Our business is concluded for the day. Now we can relax and have dinner."

Federov seemed relieved that the inquisition was over.

"Oh! And, sorry, there *is* one more thing," she said as an afterthought.

She extended a hand to help Federov to his feet. In the doorway, Nick loomed. She reasoned he had been listening the entire time. But it didn't matter.

"This propensity for poisoning people with radioactive material," she said. "That seems particular to Putin."

"It is," he said. "Very!"

Steadied, he used his cane to take a first step toward the dining area. Nick appeared close by, offered an arm and shielded him from a potential fall.

"So it would only be done on Putin's orders?" she asked.

"You would need access to the materials," Federov said. "Even in Russia that would be difficult without the help of officials. But you see, look at the bigger picture. Nothing like that happens without the say-so from the top man," he said. "So if you have some radioactive poison, you follow it back. It all leads to the same place."

"So if poison were planted against someone, the order would have come straight from the top," she said, not as a question but as a statement. "And whoever was doing it would be linked to Putin."

"That's how it works," he said. "Hey?"

"Hey," she said softly.

The aroma of a roasted chicken filled the downstairs. Obviously, Marie-Louise earned her keep in more ways than one.

"Thank you, Yuri," she said. "You've been more than helpful. That really is all."

"Then I have one question for you," he said.

"What's that?"

He paused. Fatigue was all over him. "What is your favorite color?" he asked.

"My favorite color?"

"That's what I'm asking."

A moment. Then, "Blue," she said. "Why?"

"I'm like you," he said. "There are things I have always wanted to ask."

FORTY-NINE

Alex awoke early the next morning to the vibration of her cell phone. She answered it while still in bed and found herself talking to "Fitzgerald," who was still in Egypt. He gave her a moment while she sought to clear the early morning mist from her brain.

Then, "How did your visit go?" he asked.

"I got what I needed," she said.

"I hope you didn't bother to unpack," he said.

"I'm traveling today," she said.

"You're not the only one, we think," he said.

"Uh-oh," she said, sitting up in bed. "Do tell."

She looked at her watch. It was 7:36 a.m. in Geneva, an hour later in Cairo. Across her bedroom her overnight bag hadn't been touched, and beyond the window was another cold, gray Swiss morning.

"One of the license plates we discussed the other day," Fitzgerald said. "The car is apparently out of the shop. It's moving again."

By license plates, he meant passport numbers. One of the five. And by car, he meant Michael Cerny.

"I believe it's one of those old Zil limousines belonging to a Mr. Constantine," he said. "That would be one stop before delivery here."

The Zil meant that the voyager, Cerny, was flying on a Russian passport. Constantine was code for Constantinople, meaning he was most likely on Aeroflot, stopping in Istanbul before continuing on to Cairo.

"Do you happen to know the color of the vehicle?" she asked.

"Blue and white," he said.

Blue and white meant El Al.

"Was he unable to find a buyer on his trip?" Alex asked.

"It appears unlikely. Not sure here that he had any actual buyers for a blue and white vehicle," Bissinger said. "It's like the art market in New York. Russian buyers all the way."

"Understood," she said.

All of that meant that Cerny had most likely taken the bait from Boris and Colonel Amjad. The timing suggested it. The Israelis were out of the picture and probably had never been in it. It had been a feint to entice his Russian buyers, or so it looked.

"Moving as part of a larger shipment?" she asked.

"It would appear so," he said. "We checked all the manifests. No other items connecting, but there's always the chance of acquiring more merchandise along the way. Constantine is like that."

"Constantine is, indeed," she agreed.

She had the context. Cerny was on an Aeroflot flight out of Tel Aviv to Istanbul. Fitzgerald explained further that the old car would then be shipped to Cairo via Kuwaiti Air.

"Very good," Alex said

"I'll see if some of our inspectors can give it a look in transit," Fitzgerald said. "There's always the chance that more merchandise will be gathered. But I know you'll wish to be here for delivery."

"Absolutely," she said.

"Do you think you can make it?" he asked.

"If I take an earlier train," she said. "Yes."

Train, of course, meant plane. And merchandise suggested that Cerny could pick up a bodyguard or two as he connected in Istanbul. The passenger manifests would be closely watched for any indication of that.

"That would be good," Bissinger said. "You are, after all, the only one among us who can tell the real item from a counterfeit. So we're relying on you to be here."

"I wouldn't miss it," she said.

"You need to identify the item," Fitzgerald concluded. "Then we'll purchase it."

"Got it," she said. And from there, Alex was in motion. She rose from bed, washed quickly, dressed, and was downstairs.

Nick was sitting in the living room in jeans, a T-shirt, and a power-house of a Russian pistol nestled into a shoulder holster. He was hooked up to some music on an MP3. He grinned slightly when he saw her.

"Is Mr. Federov awake yet?" she asked.

"He had a difficult night," Nick said sullenly, removing the ear buds from his ears. "He won't be up for a few hours."

"Medication?" she asked.

Nick grunted. He stood.

"Could you get me a taxi?" Alex asked.

"I'm told to keep watch on you," Nick said.

For a moment, Alex interpreted that to suggest that she wouldn't be allowed to leave. Then Nick refined what he meant. "If you need airport, I drive," he said.

"That would be excellent," she said. "Thank you."

She did not see Federov that morning. She was out the door in another fifteen minutes, at the airport within sixty. She exchanged her ticket for the next flight back to Cairo.

Two hours after that, her flight broke through the heavy cloud cover of central Europe, hit the sunshine, and began a smooth flight back to Egypt.

FIFTY

The man traveling under the Russian passport of Benjamin Schulman put his paperback novel across his knee as his El Al flight descended into Istanbul. He could have caught a direct flight to Cairo, but precaution ruled against it. Anyone moving back and forth on El Al between the Egyptian capital and the Israeli capital drew extra scrutiny, and extra scrutiny he did not need.

He still sensed something strange about Boris's email and Colonel Amjad's mildly garbled phone call. But he also knew that he had to take some chances. Some days, *everything* was a chance. He had placed a price tag of two million dollars on the merchandise he was currently peddling, and for two million bucks and a cozy retirement in Paraguay or Argentina, well, why not? Besides, for anyone to know who he really was or what he was about would mean that his passport numbers were blown. And how could that be?

He had ninety minutes of turnaround time in the airport in Istanbul. He watched his own back carefully, spent time in shops and in the washrooms. He didn't expect trouble in Turkey, but if he had a tail or any sort of surveillance, this was where he could pull out a second passport and board a plane to a safe third country. Syria, for example, was just two hours away.

Schulman, or Cerny, knew that the law-enforcement bastards behind the two-way mirrors and the digital surveillance cameras were busy and active even though he couldn't see them. But he saw no street-level activity to suggest he was being followed. So he continued to the boarding gate for Kuwaiti Air and continued his trip.

Benjamin Schulman on Kuwaiti Air. He enjoyed his little joke.

The Kuwaiti Airbus arrived punctually at the gate in Cairo at 6:15 in the evening. The airport was busy. Like the rest of Cairo, it was noisy and overcrowded.

Cerny proceeded from the exit ramp to the baggage carousel and waited. The delivery of baggage to disembarked passengers was bad enough in the First and Second Worlds, Cerny grumbled to himself. In the Third World it was an instrument of psychological torture.

He wasn't that fond of Arabs. Of the Middle Eastern people he knew, he vastly preferred the Jews, which is why he was always willing to do business with them — or at least offer to. They were smart, modern, and learned, and they paid well. What more could he want? The best that could be said for Arabs, in his opinion, is that they hadn't adapted very well to the twentieth century, much less the twenty-first. So he was often standoffish when Arab men crowded too closely to him, as they did here in the baggage area. He kept finding himself pulling away and repositioning himself.

Arab women were different, however. He liked the demure mystery of the veil on younger women. He had no objection, in fact, when one particular woman stayed close to him at the carousel. He turned and looked at her eyes. She looked away quickly, as Islamic women often do. He liked to pursue them, so when she stepped a bit farther away, he moved closer to her.

She wore a headscarf of blue, gold, and green silk. A very pretty new one. He gave her an eye-to-eye gaze again and then a smile. She looked away. He loved this cat-and-mouse game. She was wearing an Islamic gown over Western clothing. It was a shame to him that all the very pretty Islamic females were so prudish, but maybe this one, with some Western habits, could turn into some fun.

He dismissed his desires. His thoughts returned to business. He spotted his bag and plucked it from the carousel. Good luck — none of the crooks in baggage handling had broken into it. It was his lucky day.

He proceeded to immigration. When he got there, he noticed that the same woman had fallen into line just in front of him. He watched her progress as she went through the line. He eyed her carefully. Under all that clothing, she had a nice shape.

The strangest thing, he noticed as she passed through immigration, was that she had a Canadian passport. Who would have guessed?

He lost track of her as he passed through immigration himself.

Everything went smoothly. It was time to look for a cab. He went through the glass doors that led outside to the taxi stands.

He joined the line. There was some sort of commotion going on where the cabs were being routed to the end of the line. He became wary. Anything unusual put him on alert. But he settled himself and stood in line with his bag. He tried to discern what was going on.

A sense of paranoia gained on him.

Then a Cairo taxi, a van with its off-duty sign turned on, pulled out of the regular cab line and, with the assistance of the local police, pulled up to the line of waiting passengers. It stopped right in front of Cerny. The rear door opened. *What was this?* he wondered.

Cerny felt a tap on his shoulder and heard a woman's voice.

"Michael?"

He felt a flash of anxiety. He turned. It was the woman in the veil again, the same one that had been at the luggage carousel, the shapely woman in Islamic garb over Western clothing.

"Nice to see you again," she said.

Cerny stared. He didn't like this. Not at all.

Alexandra LaDuca reached to her veil and removed it quickly so that he could see her full face. She could see the look of horror when he recognized her. In that instant, Michael Cerny knew that his operation had crashed.

Cerny threw a fist at her. But she parried it expertly and threw her own shot into his face. She nailed him directly in the nose. He staggered and would have fought more, but four powerful hands came out of the back of the van. They hauled him backward. He shouted profanely, but no one came to his rescue. Struggling and shouting, he was pulled into the van.

People in line yelled, screamed, and broke away as the commotion spread. But as usual, the police protected the public order. Inside the van, a cloth rag wrapped across Cerny's face and smothered him. He felt an incipient buzz. Then he felt a needle in his shoulder.

Alex picked up his bag and threw it in.

She climbed into the van with him and pulled the doors shut. Tony pulled away, the police clearing a corridor for them to escape.

FIFTY-ONE

On the third day after Cerny's apprehension, Alex's cell phone rang in her room at the Metropole. She answered quickly, thinking it was her arrangements to return to America. She had an evening flight that day and was anxious to get home.

But the call had little to do with travel. It was Bissinger at the embassy. Her request had been granted, Fitzgerald told her, and she could have thirty minutes to speak directly to Michael Cerny, one-on-one in his cell. But he was about to be moved, Bissinger explained, so it would have to be today.

"Moved to where?" she asked.

"Just moved," Fitzgerald said.

"Right. When do I get to see him? I have a flight tonight to Rome."

"Now," Fitzgerald said. "There's a man in the lobby waiting for you. You'll recognize him."

"Thank the powers that be for me."

"Personal courtesy of Voltaire himself," Fitzgerald said. "Call it professional courtesy. The best of all possible worlds."

"I'll thank him when I see him."

"You won't see him. Unless you do. But I'm told you'll see his handiwork — and have some closure."

For some reason that gave her a little cringe. "Why does that sound so ominous?" she asked.

Bissinger ignored the question. "It's a rough place where you're going. Proceed accordingly," he continued.

"Is my visit with the prisoner official or unofficial?" she asked.

"Unofficial. No notes. No recording devices. It's strictly off the books. Don't sign in. There's a window of twenty minutes. The prisoner is supposed to be alone in his cell; you're going to keep him company."

"Got it," she said.

"I hope so."

"Gun?" she asked.

"Bring it along, but you'll have to check it before you go onto the dance floor. I need it back here anyway, and you can't take it on the plane no matter who you know or work for."

"Good point," she said.

She threw on a pair of jeans and a jacket, kept her Beretta in her shoulder bag, stuffed the rest of her belongings in a travel duffel, and went down to the lobby. An SUV was waiting for her. She recognized Tony, who had by now become her favorite chauffeur in all of North Africa, and possibly the entire continent.

Tony drove her to yet another seedy area of the city, and soon they were going through checkpoints — first police, then military. Before long they were going down a remote highway through the sand, the scorching road seeming to go from nowhere to nowhere.

Along the sides of the road were trenches, with wire and an occasional sentry post. They were in a no-man's-land of some sort, and Alex was already looking forward to leaving. Scenes like this made her love America and its freedoms all the more.

Then they arrived at a final gate, which was manned by soldiers. Tony seemed to know them. Alex looked at them carefully. She saw rank and insignia on their uniforms, and they appeared to be Arab. But she couldn't tell exactly what they were, and she knew better than to ask. They were on a paramilitary site of some sort, one of those official unofficial brigades one finds in certain nondemocratic countries.

Everyone, everything, was unmarked. There were sentries and soldiers all over the place. Most of the buildings looked like guardhouses, tan walls set on sand with high barred windows. It looked like something from the cold war, but when the SUV pulled up to a stop and she stepped out, it wasn't cold at all. It was easily a hundred and ten degrees in the broiling sun.

Tony said little, though he did ask her for her gun. She handed it over, holster and all.

"Can you have it returned to Mr. Fitzgerald at the embassy?" she asked.

"I'll give it to my boss," he said. "I think that would put it in the right channels." His "boss" meant Voltaire.

"I think it would," she agreed.

He walked her to one of the guardhouses and knew exactly where he was going. He led her past three guards with automatic weapons, into a building where a distant air-conditioning unit rumbled and kept the heat down to about ninety, plus the humidity. The architecture reminded her of the morgue where she had posed as dead. She cringed.

She went through two more locked gates and then into a cell where Michael Cerny was sitting on a cot. There was a steel table bolted to the floor, a plastic chair, and a pair of rings on the wall that could accommodate wrists. The area below the rings was stained. Alex had to tamp down her disgust when it dawned on her that the stains were from many years of blood.

Cerny saw her. First he looked at her in surprise, then fear.

Alex sat down on the chair.

Cerny continued to stare at her. He was sweating as if someone had opened an invisible faucet above him.

"Hello, Michael," she said.

"I have nothing to say to you," he said. "I don't know why you came."

"I'm here to talk anyway," she said.

"It's not you who worries me," he said.

"Maybe it should."

"It still doesn't," he said. After another empty moment, he said. "I understand they're moving me."

"I don't know anything about it," she said.

"Where to? Do you know that?"

She shrugged.

"Figures," he said.

She had been thinking, as she entered this chamber, on what she really had to say to him — how she might have lectured him on a sense of decency or blamed him for the death of her fiancé. But none of those words came to her, and the clock was ticking from the time she sat down.

"Quite a difference between here and when we first met, isn't it?" she asked. "Or even between here and the last time we saw each other."

"Nothing personal, you understand," he said after several distant seconds.

"No. Of course not," she said. "And I'm not an official inquisitor. The local man allowed me a few minutes with you, just to satisfy myself."

"Pretty generous of him," Cerny said. "What did you have to do in return?"

"Ask nicely," she said, dishing it back. "What occasions this is that I saw an old friend of yours the other day. And after a conversation with him, almost everything fell into place."

"What old friend?" he asked, as if surprised to learn that he had any.

"Yuri Federov."

Cerny shook his head.

"He's still alive? I'm surprised." He snorted.

"I'm going to describe to you my sense of the big picture," she said. "I don't suppose you'll want to comment, but I'm going to entertain you with it, anyway."

"Suit yourself."

"It was the Russians who put you up to getting rid of Federov, didn't they?" she began. "They sent you to the United States many years ago, back when Vladimir Putin was holding together remnants of the old KGB. Sell a little bill of goods here, another one there. You were Putin's man in Washington and Langley — or more likely *one* of Putin's men — going all the way back to the 1990s when you first appeared hawking your bag of tricks. Didn't much matter who you were selling out to start with, did it? Langley was always buying the act. But then, as years went by, and the goals got bigger, every person you compromised was in some way inimical to Vladimir Putin."

He shifted on his cot. There seemed to be some swelling on the side of his head, and he kept touching it.

"I even reviewed all the cases you worked, right up to the one about Dr. Ishraf Kerwidi, the fellow who went out the window in London.

That served a whole host of interests, didn't it, Michael? Putin. The Israelis. Maybe even the Americans."

"Kerwidi had it coming," Cerny said.

"By your way of thinking, I'm sure he did," Alex said.

"You might want to watch out for open windows yourself," he added, "if you keep making enemies all over the place. Got to be people who think you have it coming too, Alex."

"Just like the people around here think you have it coming as well."

"What does that mean?" he asked.

"I just wouldn't want to be you right now," she said.

"Who would?" he asked with a final dash of irony. "Certainly not me."

"So then I would be correct?" she said, glancing at her watch and backtracking. "You were a Russian agent, going back at least a decade. And the whole operation in Kiev was put forth primarily to take Yuri Federov out of the picture for Putin. I talked to Yuri about this. He's not well, by the way. Federov, by his own admission, had become too powerful following the Ukrainian gas crisis of 2005. So in a strange way, American interests and Russian interests — Putin's interests — merged. He was on the US hit list for gangsterism, arms dealing, and tax evasion. But worse for him, he was on Putin's hit list for just being too powerful. So you came to the CIA with a plan to take him out. First by an assassin in Rome who hit the wrong person. And then later in Kiev."

Cerny exhaled a long breath, one of resignation.

"It was an easy sale," Cerny said. "The CIA wanted Federov gone. Who really cared if Putin wanted him gone too?"

"Poor me. Poor Robert. Poor everyone else who got killed in Ukraine that day. We were all caught in the middle," Alex said. "Do you remember a Colombian cocaine lord named Pablo Escobar?" Alex asked.

"Sure, I do," Cerny answered.

"Escobar once planted a bomb on an Avianca-jet — just to kill one specific person," Alex said. "The plane blew up and eighty-six people died. Collateral damage. That's what we've all been. Collateral damage for the games nations play."

"That's how life is. You'd do the same if you were assigned to do it."

"No, I wouldn't," she said. "I'd like to think, in fact, that there's a special place in hell for people who do things like that."

"Well," said Cerny. "I told the inquisitors everything, so why shouldn't you know too? So I serve a few years in prison. Putin'll get me back. They always do. That's all I'm going to say."

"That's all I'm going to ask," she answered.

By then, time was up and Alex had had quite enough. Two military men in blue berets were at the cell door. They clanked the door noisily and said something in Arabic that Alex didn't understand. She was more than ready to leave. The door opened with a metallic groan.

She left the cell without saying anything further. If Cerny had anything more on his mind, and she was sure he did, he wasn't going to talk about it.

FIFTY-TWO

One of the guards accompanied her back down the hall. Alex had the impression that the guard spoke none of the languages she knew, so she didn't attempt conversation. Tony was sitting on a desk in the entrance area, his jacket off, his shoulder holster and weapon exposed. Once again, Alex knew the drill. By this time, it seemed to her, she knew too many of the drills. Tony would continue on with her and deliver her to the airport. Operations were like that. As soon as one was rolled up, the CIA liked all the players out of the country as quickly as possible. Once she got back to Washington, there would be a lot to talk about. Yet most of it she wouldn't be able to even mention — not to her friends anyway.

Outside, two SUVs were waiting in the scorching sun, both with their motors running. Tony walked her to one of them. He opened the back door for her. As Alex stepped up to slide in, she saw the form of a man in the back seat. He was bare-headed with sandy-hair and sunglasses. He wore a beige linen suit. He had been waiting for her.

Handsome devil, he was. Voltaire.

"I didn't think I'd see you again," she said. "On the other hand, I was sure I would."

"Oh, I wasn't sure myself," Voltaire said. "But you were of great value here in Cairo, so I wanted to see you off personally. There's a final bit of business, then we'll get you to the airport."

She waited. "What sort of business?" she asked.

"You'll see."

He engaged her in small talk for several minutes, and she gained the impression that he was stalling. Then she saw why. While her SUV and the neighboring one were poised and ready to go, a third vehicle swung into the driveway. It was an armored car. Green, the color of Islam, but with no markings.

"Welcome to the world of espionage," Voltaire said softly. "And what would the world of espionage be without payback?"

"I'm not sure I like it," she said.

"What? Payback?"

"No. The world of espionage."

"Ah! Who does? Often it's like a disease. You didn't choose to have it, it found you. And you're in it now, my dear lady," he said. "And you *do* excel at it. You have your own assets, your own nascent network. I'm very favorably impressed. Back and forth you went to Europe. You used the database in Washington as you worked; you helped us reel in some troublesome people here. You really did a formidable job. I'd work with you again any day."

"Is that a compliment?"

"It could be construed as one. How's that? Take it as an expression of praise only if you wish."

Voltaire motioned to the armored car. The rear door opened. No one got out. Two security people stood around the vehicle with machine guns, however.

"What am I watching?" she asked.

"The final act. We have our instructions from Washington."

She kept silent. Half a minute later, two guards brought Cerny out in wrist manacles and leg chains. They frog marched him to the armored car and roughly pushed him into the back. One of the guards went into the back with him, presumably to chain him to a seat. After a moment, the guard came out.

Then they were underway, a small cortege of three vehicles, traveling at about twenty miles an hour down the paved road, through the sandy landscape of the barracks, through the gates, and into the outside world. Alex's SUV was the second in the progression, and the third SUV followed them.

"You have your luggage, your passport, everything you need for your return to America?" Voltaire asked.

"I have everything," she affirmed. For a moment, she started to relax.

"Good. In a short while you're going to feel very lucky to be leaving this dreadful place."

"Why?" she asked. "Where are they taking Cerny?"

"Not far," Voltaire laughed. "Remember those five agents of mine who were murdered? I did mention that, correct?"

"No, I don't remember that," she said.

"Oh. Dreadful oversight on my part," he said in a voice that indicated that it wasn't. "See, that's part of my personal tab with Mr. Cerny. I've lost people here in Egypt thanks to him. Same way you lost someone in Kiev, same way that girl lost her boyfriend via the car bomb at the hotel. *Compris?*"

"Oh, Lord," she said.

Watching over the shoulder of Tony, the driver, through the front windshield, Alex saw the armored car accelerate and pull away from them. It went from being fifty feet ahead of them to one hundred feet, and then to maybe one hundred and fifty. And as the armored vehicle pulled away, she felt Tony ease up on the gas. He allowed the interval between cars to grow.

Then the SUV from behind them did something that at first appeared crazy. It overtook Alex's vehicle and went speeding beyond them. Everything played out as if it were slow motion. The armored car up ahead pulled to the side of the road and its driver and its guard jumped out. They walked with a leisurely pace away from their vehicle as the trailing SUV pulled to an abrupt halt behind it.

Two executioners stepped out, their feet hitting the ground almost before the car had stopped, Uzis across their chests. Tony eased to a crawl, and they continued to approach the scene of the stopped vehicles. But Tony didn't overtake them. He slowed almost to a halt and stayed distant.

The armed men went to the gun portals in the armored car and pushed their own automatic weapons inward. The van wasn't so much a security vehicle now as much as it was an execution chamber. As Alex watched, she knew that Cerny was a dead man this time. And he probably even knew it himself. She didn't hear him scream, but she was sure he did.

Even over the air-conditioning of their van, Alex could hear several seconds of gunfire. There must have been fifty shots all fired into the armored car. The man in the back, no doubt chained into the most vulnerable position, had no chance at all.

The gunmen followed with a second burst and stepped back.

They gave Tony a wave and he accelerated. Seconds later, they passed the armored car. The gunmen were masked with light camouflage kerchiefs, and Alex could not see their faces. Nor would she have wanted to. The armored car was surrounded in a small noxious cloud of gun smoke, and the men waved to them as Tony's vehicle slid past. Then Alex looked away, feeling nauseous.

"There," Voltaire said calmly. "That's done. Excellent."

Alex was silent.

"Which airline again?" Voltaire asked her. "Swiss International? That's a good choice. Can't go wrong with Swiss International. I understand the *hors d'oeuvres* are excellent."

Several minutes passed before Alex answered.

FIFTY-THREE

On December 24, Alex observed her thirtieth birthday. The event was a bittersweet occasion, considering the events of the year. But she celebrated with a small group of friends in Washington. As was frequently the case with her birthday, falling on the day it did, it was a half-Christmas half-birthday celebration. Friends from work filtered in, as well as friends from the gym. Don Tomás dropped by to speak five languages and keep everyone amused. And once again, Alex missed Robert horribly.

She went to a Christmas Eve service at her church in Washington and then went home alone. On Christmas morning, she did something unusual. She slept.

Over the next two days, she packed. The job in New York had been offered to her, and she had accepted it. The moving men arrived on the twenty-seventh. Her personal bags were packed and stashed in the trunk of her car. The listening devices she had personally disabled. One morning when she was out for a walk, she threw them into the Potomac.

As the moving men worked, she dropped by a few of the establishments that she had patronized in the neighborhood. She said her good-byes.

When she went back to her apartment, it was empty. She stood and looked at it for a long, cold moment. An instinct told her to take a walk through and then another instinct warned her not to. Enough was enough. She closed the door.

She rapped softly on Don Tomás's door to say good-bye.

He answered. She gave him a shrug and tried to keep her eyes from welling. He did much the same. Then they embraced in a wordless hug. He had been as close to family as anyone in the last days — older brother, uncle, and advisor. She would miss him.

Then she went down to her car.

She turned the key in the ignition, came up out of the garage, and left her block for the final time as a resident. She drove past the monuments again and then watched them recede in her rearview mirror. Thus, on an otherwise ordinary Tuesday afternoon, Alex moved out of Washington and drove north to New York.

By this time, Janet, her protégée, had found her own friends, her own apartment, and a new job. She was happy, living in Brooklyn, and anxious to introduce Alex to her new boyfriend, who — against Alex's best advice — was one of her former bodyguards.

PART THREE

FIFTY-FOUR

Six weeks later, Alex was at her desk in her new office in Manhattan when her cell phone rang. She glanced at the LED and read the incoming number.

She recognized the country code: 39. Italy. She also recognized the number.

She smiled. She picked up. "*Ciao*, Gian Antonio," she said.

He laughed. "I should be used to the technology by now, but I'm not," he said in English. "You know who's calling before you answer."

"Consider yourself flattered," she said. "I knew it was you and I picked up."

"I'm deeply humbled, *Signora*," he said with evident amusement.

She glanced at her watch. "What time is it there?"

"Evening," he said. "So *buona sera*,"

"*Buona sera.*"

Within a minute, he moved to the objective of the call. "Your Russian has lost track of you," Rizzo said.

"Which Russian?"

"There's more than one? Federov. He's been quite ill, you know."

"I knew he was ill," she said in a more somber tone. "I didn't know how ill he was. Where is he?"

"Geneva," Rizzo said. "He's residing in a place called Le Clinique Perrault."

"What's that?" she asked.

There was a heavy pause. Rizzo's voice assumed a grim tone. "He's in a—What do you call it in English?" he asked. He switched to Italian to be clear. "*Uno ospedale per i malati in fase terminale. Un ospizio.*"

"A hospice," Alex said, her chair moving forward. It took a moment for it to sink in. "*Terminale?*" she asked, making sure she had heard right.

"*Terminale,*" he said again.

"Uh-oh," she said.

"He phoned me. He says there is something enormously important," Rizzo continued, changing back to English. "And he will only talk to you."

"Give him my number," she said gently. "He can phone me anytime that he—"

"No, no. He wishes to speak to you—*and only you*—in person," Rizzo advised.

She sighed and felt the weight of the news. "Gian Antonio, I'm beat. I just started a new job in New York. I don't know whether I have another trip in me right now. Know what I mean?"

"Yes, I know, I know," he said. He paused. "Advise me what flight you will be on. I'll meet your flight in Geneva. Would that make it any easier?"

"I didn't say that I was going."

"Not yet, you didn't, no," Rizzo said. "But I know you very well by now, Signora Alex," he said. "I doubt if you'd turn down the request of a man who is so gravely ill."

"I see," she said.

"Alex?"

"*Si*, Gian Antonio?"

"You should come as quickly as you can."

Two mornings later, the February sky in Geneva was gray and grim, much as it had been almost exactly a year earlier in Kiev on a similarly fateful day. Alex had taken a direct flight from New York. Gian Antonio Rizzo was at the airport in Geneva waiting reliably for her.

Their taxi drove them through the center of the city, past the Hotel de Roubaix from which Alex had been abducted. Then, five minutes later, they arrived at the Clinique Perrault on the rue Joffrin in central Geneva. The cab pulled onto the gray gravel of a wide semicircle driveway that formed the front courtyard of the medical clinic.

The driver hopped out of the cab and hurried to open the door for Alex. A small flock of startled pigeons fluttered upward from the driveway as she stepped out. The birds took roost within the crevices of the ornate façade of the Clinique, where they lurked and watched her arrival. It was all inconsequential to them.

Alex reached for the wallet in her purse, but Rizzo, ever a gentleman around those he respected, waved her off and paid for the ride from the airport. He tipped the driver generously. They both carried only overnight bags. Then another sense of déjà vu was upon her—an unwelcome flashback to Kiev again—as a slight snow had begun to fall.

Always, in her mind, there had been a light snow in Kiev. At Robert's funeral there had been a light snow. When the RPGs had been incoming at Mihaylavski Place there had been a light snow. What might God be trying to tell her? She didn't know.

She shivered, not from the temperature. The cold had been much worse elsewhere recently, and so had the sense of doom and foreboding and sadness.

A few moments later, they were in a starkly modern but serene lobby. They presented themselves to the visitors' desk, showing their passports. They registered properly as visitors and were directed toward a bank of elevators that would take them to Federov's room on the fourth floor.

Rizzo continued to speak Italian. "It might be better if I waited down here," he said.

"I think it might." Alex agreed.

She gave Rizzo a nod. He gave her hand a squeeze. Alex continued to the elevators, and Rizzo went toward the sitting area in the lobby.

Moments later, she was on a floor of the Clinique where a middle-aged nurse named Naomi directed her toward Salle 434. The signs on the floor were in four languages. Very Swiss. French, German, Italian, and English, tacked on almost as a conceit. Every letter and word was perfect.

In the back of Alex's mind a little spark of absurdity danced forth: Naomi had also been the name of one of the girls at the nightclub in Kiev where Alex had knocked back too much vodka and had allowed herself too much time within Federov's grasp. This was a day, it was clear, for heavy ironies.

Well, she decided, she had come a long way from there. They both had, and it didn't seem to matter much anymore, did it? Or did it?

She proceeded down the hall. She was on an expensive wing of the hospice.

Only the best for Federov, she mused. He had earned it, but in some ways he hadn't. The door to Salle 434 was open. Moments later, her mind teeming, Alex peered in.

She suppressed a gasp. The vision shocked her. The man in the bed was Yuri Federov, but not the Yuri Federov that she remembered. The man she remembered was strong and vibrant. This was an extremely sick man, attached to tubes, wires, and monitors. He lay in the bed with his eyes closed, his mouth open, his head tilted at an angle as he appeared to sleep, his face pallid.

Across his chest was an open book with a Russian title. She couldn't see it clearly yet. The book was positioned as if it had slipped from his hands when he fell asleep reading.

With a shudder, and a conscious summoning of willpower, she stepped into the room. She moved quietly. Like a giant cat, however, Federov woke instantly — first one eye opened, then the other.

It took a moment for his gaze to register an identity to go with Alex's presence, but when it did, some of the fear and sadness washed away from his face. Under the circumstances, he looked pleased.

"Ah!" he said in English. "Bless you, Alexandra!"

"Hello, Yuri," she said.

"Heaven exists for me after all. My angel has arrived."

"It's just me," she said. "Just an overgrown American kid from California."

His smile widened.

"You're the person I most wished to see," he said. "Thank you for coming."

He motioned to the book that lay open across his chest. "I'm taking your advice, you can see, hey?" he said. "Catching up on the classics."

She looked at the jacket of the book.

Анна Каренина
Лев Никола́евич Толсто́й

He smiled, as if in a small victory.

"Tolstoy's *Anna Karenina*," she said. "Very good, Yuri. I'm proud of you."

"I'm told it is the greatest of Russian novels," he said. "And I'm told I should read it before I die." He laughed. "Well, it might be a close call," he said. He motioned to all the wires and tubes and monitors.

"It started with lung cancer," he said dryly, as if announcing a losing football score. "That's why I was in New York. Then it spread. Rather than being a typically slow and pokey cancer, mine was pure and aggressive. Presurgery Gleason scores of 9 or 10. Do you know what that means?"

"It's not good," she said.

"The higher the number on this scale of 10 the worse the news. So I had ten."

Despite everything, she felt a caving, tumbling feeling within her. She bit a lip as she settled into a chair beside the bed.

His gaze traveled the length of her, up and down, toe to head, taking her in. Then it settled into her eyes.

"I'm very sorry. I'll pray for you," she said. "And anything else you'd like."

Somehow he had the energy and nerve to raise an eyebrow, almost flirtatiously. "Anything?" he asked.

"Within reason," she said.

He managed a sad smile and a laugh that was so weak that she was appalled. A rasp in his voice made him sound like a much older man. She had been ready for this but not *really* ready. Then again, what might one expect in a hospice? Not stand-up comedy.

"Well, I don't necessarily listen to the doctors," he said. "I know I have more time than they tell me. And as for the book, I've already finished it. But I don't think I understood it, hey? So I'm reading some sections again. Seems to me in the book, everyone is very unlucky with trains and train stations. Even the brat with the toy trains at the beginning. And then there's the part you'd like. This 'Lev,' he's not a Jew, even with a Jew name, or maybe he is. He ends up accepting the Christian God at the end."

"That was a recurring theme of Tolstoy," she said.

"What? Tricky Jews?"

"No, the acceptance of Christianity," Alex said. "Tolstoy was greatly influenced by the Sermon on the Mount. Much of his philosophy of peace followed from it."

"And you know this from your study of literature or from your knowledge of your faith?"

"Both," she said.

He tapped the book. "You've read *this*?" he asked.

"Nine or ten years ago. When I was in college."

"And you remember it?"

"I remember it. It's a book everyone should read. Whoever told you to read it was correct."

"You told me. Several months ago."

She thought back. "So I did," she said.

"Did you like it?"

"I did when I read it. I'd like to reread it."

"Why would you read it again if you've already read it? It will turn out the same way."

She smiled. "Books can mean different things to you at different stages of your life, Yuri," she said. "Read things at different times and you may come away with different understandings."

"So if I read it on Monday I might think differently than on Wednesday?"

"Maybe," she answered, aware that he was playing with her, "but I suspect the time frame there is too close."

"But this is the end of my life," he said. "So I hope I get the good and true meaning."

She searched for words and didn't have the right ones.

"Yuri," she said. "Don't do this to me."

He laughed. He reached to the book, closed it, and set it on the bedside table.

"You're quite extraordinary, Miss Alex LaDucova," he said, playing again with her name. "I wish I had your memory. And your breadth of knowledge."

Federov managed a laugh, which made them both feel better.

"That's good," he said. "Within reason. And again, very kind of you to come all the way to Geneva. Where were you when my message arrived to you?"

"New York," she said. "That's where my job is now."

"Ah, New York. It was a long trip."

"As it worked out, it wasn't that difficult," she said.

"You're very kind," he said. "I find that quaint. And ironic maybe. You're one of the few people I've met in my life who I've had to thank for their kindness."

"Maybe if you had thanked more people your life would have turned out differently," she said.

"And maybe if kindness had been shown to me more often I would have turned out a different person," he mused. With a free hand, he used a paper towel to mop his brow. "But we'll never know, will we? Two theories maybe, hey? One is I was born a mongoose. So I would always be a mongoose. And you can't blame a mongoose for killing a cobra, because a mongoose is a mongoose."

She was aware that he was heavily sedated, sailing along on some synthetic morphine, she supposed, which probably had his central nervous system in chaos. The drugs made him ramble, but she found it not difficult to travel along with it.

"The other, of course, is that events made me what I am," he said. "My father used to beat me without mercy when I was a boy, hey. So did my uncle. You know when it stopped? When I was big enough to hurt them back. Hurt. That's the only real law in life, isn't it? Don't hurt me or I will hurt you. Nations, people. It all works the same."

In another time and place, she might have taken exception. She might have found the right words to say about love and the search for it, about God, about the spirit, about human kindness instead of violence, and a system of morals based on one's faith, or any faith, or respect for other people or the sanctity of truth and life. But that was not a discussion for here and now.

"Are we on fire?" he asked next.

"What?"

"It's very hot," he said. "I wonder if the building is on fire."

"The building is fine, Yuri," she said, realizing that the sedatives were gaining some ground. "But I can call a nurse if you're feeling—"

"No, no!" he said, raising a clumsy hand and halting her. "Enough of nurses and enough of doctors." She sat still and his hand went to the sheets again. He closed his eyes, and Alex wasn't sure whether he was about to drift off. But the nano-nap helped because the eyes opened again in a flash. He seemed to have regained some lucidity.

"Hey," he said. "Time is short. We have things to talk about."

"Go ahead," she said.

He motioned to the second drawer of the bedside stand. "There's a small package in there," he said. "Would you please take it out?"

She reached to the drawer. There was a small blue bag in it. It bore the name of Tiffany & Company, the jeweler. She frowned slightly, not knowing where this was going.

Federov nodded. She closed the drawer and opened the bag. She reached in.

"I bought this in New York," he said as she turned over in her hand a small blue box tied with white ribbon. "It's for you."

"Yuri, you didn't have to buy me a present," she said. "And you shouldn't have."

"It's something very special," he said, watching intently now. "Please open it."

She thought for a moment, but was in no position to decline a kindness. She pulled the ribbon open and set it aside. She opened the box and glanced up at him as she dug through the tissue paper. His eyes were suddenly very happy and almost very young, like a boy on Christmas morning.

Her hand settled then on a smaller box within the larger one. It was in dark blue velvet and was unmistakably a ring box. With reservations, she pulled it from the paper and paused for a moment.

"Yuri?" she questioned.

"Please . . . ," he said, "see this day through to the end."

"As you wish," she said gently.

She opened the box and almost lost her breath. The box contained a diamond engagement ring. It was exquisite and dazzling, a sturdy, bold, brilliant diamond set in a platinum gold band. The center stone was the largest diamond she had ever held in her hands. She was no expert, but she guessed it was eight karats set in a traditional clasp, surrounded by two rows of smaller melee diamonds, alternating with sapphires.

He smiled.

"Blue," he said. "When you came to see me in Geneva last time, you said you liked blue."

Yes, *blue*. She now recalled and better understood his question from several weeks earlier.

Blue, like the Nile. Blue like the sky. Blue like sapphires on the most stunning engagement ring she had ever seen in her life.

"I don't get it," she said. "I didn't know there was a woman in your life again. Who is this for?"

Her eyes rose to meet his and her mouth opened to speak, but his words preceded any she could utter.

"It's for you, Alex. Will you marry me?" he asked.

"What?"

"I'm asking you to marry me," he said. "It is a serious proposal."

Almost gasping, almost angry, thoroughly flummoxed, she struggled to answer. "Yuri . . . I . . ."

"Please say yes," he said. He moved a hand to her and settled it on her knee. He touched her with obvious affection. He was too sick for lechery and time was too short for games.

She looked back down to the ring.

It was jewelry more befitting a movie star or a member of European royalty, not a working woman from southern California who had gone through college on scholarships and now worked in law enforcement. Again, she was no expert, but in the past she had had enough experience on a professional basis with jewelry to know that this piece probably clocked in at seventy-five to a hundred thousand dollars.

She sat before him nonplussed. The reality of the moment was sinking in upon her, the realization that he was not kidding and the offer was indeed serious.

"If you say yes," he added with surprising gentleness, "it would be the most joyous moment of my life."

"Yuri, I don't know what to say."

"Then say yes. I will call a priest whom I know here in Geneva.

And we will do fast paperwork and make it official. We could do it here in the hospital as early as tomorrow. I have paperwork that has been prepared. All you would have to do is sign and—"

"My reaction isn't so much yes or no," she stammered, "as it is that such a proposal is completely out of the question."

"Why?"

"For more reasons than I could explain."

"Give me *one* reason," he said.

The words came out almost reflexively. "I'm not in love with you," she said.

He snorted a little laugh. "At this point," he said, "what does that matter, hey?"

She groped for more words, more of an explanation, but instead was more at a loss for them than any previous time in her life. "I couldn't possibly marry you," she finally expanded.

She abruptly closed the ring box and set it back on the side table.

Federov was, however, neither hurt nor perturbed.

"Be realistic," he continued. "This is my gift to you. If I am in love with you, what does it matter whether you love me? What would—?"

"Yuri, please. Stop this or I'll leave."

"How much time do I have left on this earth?" he pressed. "No one knows. You believe in God? Well, your God is in the process of taking me. So you give me a small gift before I die, and I will give you tremendous gifts that will last your lifetime."

He paused and moved a hand to the ring box. He fingered it but didn't open it.

"Let's be honest," he continued. "I am a very wealthy man. See that drawer?" he asked, indicating the same drawer that had held the Tiffany bag. "All my financial information is in there. Bank accounts. Some in Ukraine, some in New York. Most of them safe here in Switzerland. You will also see letters I have on file with lawyers here in Geneva. You would have access to everything I own if you were my wife. I have a will. I have already named you as a beneficiary."

"I don't want your money, Yuri," she said. "When it comes down to it, I can only be honest with you. I am appalled by the way you acquired your wealth. How many people did you betray? How many did you kill?"

"A small number compared with how many tried to harm or kill me," he answered. "I have taken care of my daughters who live in Canada," he said, "although they do not know it."

"They should inherit your wealth, not me," she said. "They're your flesh and blood. They suffered because of you. They deserve whatever you can give them."

"They hate me," he said matter-of-factly. "Do you hate me?"

"I don't hate you," she said.

"There then, you see?" he said, attempting to close an argument around her. "I want to leave my fortune to someone who doesn't hate me. Do you understand what a wealthy woman you would be, what a wealthy widow you will be in a short period of time?"

"Yuri, I don't think like that. And it was about a year ago that I had to get myself past the death of my fiancé in Kiev. So — "

"I believe I'm worth more than twenty-five million dollars," he continued. "Most of it in cash."

She blew out a long breath. "Yuri, that's not my idea of marriage," Alex said. "Material wealth is not what motivates me."

"What motivates you, then?" he asked. "I'm not sure I understand. Wealth is wealth. Wealth is power. Think of all the charities you could finance, if that is your goal. You would never have to work again in your life. You are young. After my passing, which will be soon, you would be free to do as you wish. You — "

"Yuri, I hate to be so brutally frank. But I'm *not* in love with you! I couldn't marry a man I didn't love. It might seem quaint and old-fashioned to you, but that's how I am. That's *who* I am."

"The man who died in Kiev . . . ? The man you just mentioned . . . ?"

"Robert."

"Did you love him?"

"Of course I did!"

"And you still miss him?"

She opened her mouth to answer yes, but her voice broke before she could find the words. "Of course I do!" she said again, almost indignantly. "Why do you even ask me that?"

Several seconds ticked by. Finally, he spoke again.

"You know, my precious Alexandra," he said, "my whole life, whenever I have tried to show my best innermost desires, to be generous, to be a morally good man, I have faced contempt, scorn, and disbelief. And whenever I gave in to my most base desires I was praised, respected, and encouraged. It is no different now."

"I will not marry you," she said. "I will not even consider it. The discussion is over."

"All right," he said after a pause. A flicker of a smile and, "But then, please allow a grievously ill man a final fantasy. If you would."

"What would that be?" Alex asked.

"Put my ring on your finger. Let me see you wear it, if even for a moment before you say a final no to my offer and hand it back. Before the darkness arrives and the long night claims me, let me hold in my head the image of you wearing my ring, even if the reality of a marriage will never come to be. Let me die with that vision."

"Yuri, I don't know — "

"Please," he said softly, from dry lips below beseeching eyes. "What does it cost you to give me this small amount of comfort?"

To his question, she had no immediate answer. So, "All right," she said softly.

She removed the ring from the box under his careful gaze. Fighting back second thoughts and with a little voice within her screaming that she should know better than to do something as wildly inappropriate as this, she slid the ring onto the third finger of her left hand, where Robert's ring had once been.

Not surprisingly, Federov had chosen the band size perfectly. The ring felt exquisite and repugnant at the same time.

She looked up and her gaze met his. He was looking back and forth from her hand to her eyes, then back again. He reached forward and took her hand, the one with the ring.

"You're sure," he said, "the answer is no?"

"The answer is no," she said. "I'm sorry."

He pulled her hand to him and brought it to his face. He pressed his lips to the back of her hand, then released it. She withdrew her hand from him.

"Very well," he said. "I didn't expect you to accept."

"Then why did you ask?"

"One never knows."

With her right hand, she pulled the ring off her finger. Respectfully, she replaced it in the ring box, closed the box, and handed it back to him.

"Be careful with this," she said. "It has a great monetary value. You don't want it to disappear."

He took it and returned it to the drawer. "It barely matters," he said. "Maybe I'll give it to the nurse." Alex wasn't sure if he was kidding. "She might like to sell it."

He dropped it in the drawer and stared at the drawer. He looked lost again. Alex noticed a fresh line of sweat across his brow. She waited for him to come back again. In time, he turned to her.

"I wonder then," he said. "When the time comes, there is another thing that needs to be done. And I have no one else I can ask. No one else that I can trust."

"Tell me what it is," she said.

"My instructions are that my body is to be cremated," he said. "Then, afterward, there is a place nearby here," he said, "a very pleasant, peaceful place, a section in Geneva, just to the south of the center of the city. It's called Plainpalais." His voiced trailed off for a moment. "Do you know it?" he asked.

"I'm familiar with it," she said.

"I have all that paperwork in the drawer here too," he said. "I have made all the arrangements. So when the time comes ..." With a weak smiled, he added, "Not before."

She nodded. "Not before," she said. "I'll make sure that everything is done properly."

"And you will be there?"

"If I can be," she said. "I promise."

"Thank you. You are more kind to me than I deserve," he said. "Will you also forgive me?" he asked.

"For what?"

"For my greatest sin, my greatest malefaction ever."

"I'm not following," she said.

"No?" Federov asked.

"No."

"I thought you might have figured it out by now."

A deep feeling of unease began to creep over her, as if deep within her she knew what was coming next.

"No. I don't know what you're talking about," Alex said. "Figure what out?"

"Robert's death," he said. He held a long beat, and then he said very clearly, "I was the person responsible."

"What?"

"And the attack on Barranco Lajoya, also," he said. "Completely responsible."

An extraordinary silence crashed down upon the room.

"I ordered the attack in Kiev," he continued. "I ordered it, organized it, and financed it. Then I did everything I could to blame it on my opposition, the *filoruskies*. I wanted to get back at your government for the war they waged against me, for expelling me from America, for siding with that swine Putin, for driving me out of business, for making me into an exile in my own land."

With wide eyes and a sense of disbelief, Alex listened to him, his familiar voice, now racked with pain that was as severe spiritually as it was physically. He was assuming complete culpability for the carnage in Kiev that had shattered her life as well as so many others, the attack that had rewritten in blood one of the worst atrocities ever aimed at her country.

And then he moved along to Venezuela.

"In Venezuela," he continued. "I had the local fascist militia come to try to kill you. I felt you were the instrument of the government, the representative of all my enemies. So they came for you; they murdered some other people, but you escaped again. It was only later that I understood that you were only doing a job. That Comrade Cerny was my enemy. And the disgraceful Putin as well."

A long apologia followed but the words barely made any sense. After a few moments she was not hearing it.

Disgust. Resentment. Fury.

It all welled up inside her, those emotions and more. The monstrosity of all this brought her close to despair, a despair modified with rage, and almost a wish that this conversation had never happened, that she had heard none of it, that she might have lived a happier life never knowing the truth, never having heard this rambling deathbed confession.

And although one wave of angry doubt was in mutiny against another, her heart fought against what she had always known, always somehow suspected, yet found a way to deny until this moment, that Federov had taken Robert from her, that the man now dying before her had shattered her life and left it in small pieces that had been nearly impossible to piece back together.

"So I ask you now," Federov finally said. "Where is your faith? What is it to you? What did your Jesus Christ teach you? Do you forgive me?"

She was angry. Resentful. Fearful. Every foul and vituperative emotion welled inside her.

Somehow she managed words.

"Forgiveness is not mine to give you, Yuri. Forgiveness is for God to give you."

"Will he?'

"Ask him."

"But *will he?*"

"You'll find out."

He took a moment, his strength almost gone. "But do *you* forgive me?" he asked.

She stood in silence, tears welling, not knowing whether she wanted to answer, to flee, or — as one horrible instinct urged — to shoot him herself in revenge, except something about that would have seemed both wrong and too good for him at the same time.

"Please answer me honestly," he said. "Don't give me the answer you wish me to hear, but the one that has the truth. I have little patience left for anything except truth."

Federov paused. "So, I ask you again. *Do you forgive me?*"

Several seconds passed. Somewhere deep in her soul, in something that seemed to her too much like a spiritual abyss, she found an answer that she didn't know was there.

"I think in time," she said, "with the proper strength, I will be able to. Yes. Because I need to. Because everything in my faith tells me to. Because I don't choose to live a life burning with hatred. So with time," she said, "with time, maybe, yes. Right now, I do not know why God has put me on this path. I hope that eventually I will understand."

He nodded weakly. "That is good," he said. "That is as good as I could hope for, hey. In its way, it's a gift. So thank you."

Words had departed her.

"Look," she finally said, her insides raging, "that's really all there is here. There's nothing more to discuss. We're finished here, right?"

He nodded and his head eased back.

"You're a good person," he said. "I wasn't always. I regret."

He closed his eyes. He was dozing within seconds, transported to wherever the dreams, illusions, and drugs took him, his memory leaping through the past.

Alex stood, turned, and went to the door.

She pulled it open, but then, responding to some inner voice, looked back one final time at the now-quiet man in the hospice bed. Dying was sometimes an eloquent act, she mused. Men and women often died in accordance with their lives: in battle, home with their families, in transit, wracked with disease.

Federov's body was very still, and despite her insides being in turmoil, she tried to assess him once more. And almost before her eyes, he shrank to something very small and mean, and something very mortal, flawed, and harmless. She tried to develop a hatred for him, but couldn't.

His eyes opened a sliver and his hand came up almost imperceptibly. "Hey," he said in a near whisper. Then he was quiet again, breathing lightly.

She stared for another several seconds. In the end, he was just a man. More flawed than most others, but just a man.

She gently closed the door behind her. It latched in complete silence.

FIFTY-FIVE

In the lobby of the hotel, she spotted Gian Antonio Rizzo not far from where she had left him. But she did not go to him, not immediately. She wasn't ready to talk to anyone.

She spotted a small chapel in the hospital lobby and slipped into it. Like the doors to the hospital room upstairs, the chapel portals closed quietly. She wanted time to meditate and calm down. The chapel of the hospital was as good a place as any.

Her emotions were all over the place. Her spirit was exhausted. Taken as a whole, Federov's confession contained the most monstrous words she had ever heard in her life.

Robert's death . . . I was responsible . . . Do you forgive me?

It was too much to bear. For the first time since the dark days after Robert's death, she put her head in her hands and cried. Long, hard, deep tears, tears she had fought back every lonely day for the past several months.

Several minutes passed, her mind awash in confusion, her entire soul lost in thoughts and prayer and spiraling images, all the way from the death of her grandmother and her funeral in Mexico, up through Kiev, and into the present. She tried to replay events and determine what she could have done differently, what might have put her in a different place today. But she was unable. She tried to push it all aside and tell herself that what was done was done and that it was God's path for her, but she was unable to do that either. She wondered if she was on the right path or if she was a miserable failure.

And once again she felt very alone. Even in the chapel, she felt very alone.

At length, she realized that she wasn't.

It was a sensation at first, a rallying of the spirit, perhaps, as she continued to lean forward, her face in her hands, her eyes closed.

Then a small amount of additional time went by and she felt a spiritual presence, and then a physical presence to complement it.

It wasn't something she heard or saw. It was something she could sense.

Moments after that, she felt the weight of another person settling onto the pew next to her. For a mad hallucinatory moment, she thought that it was Robert back beside her and that she had imagined all the horrid events of the last year. Then she thought it was Federov, that he had somehow managed to resurrect his energies, came down here, and found her. And then with an equally surreal jolt images came back to her, and she remembered how she and Robert had shared pews together in DC, back when she was several decades younger than she was now, just a year and a half ago. All of that seemed like a previous lifetime — and in a way it was, and in a way it wasn't.

An arm wrapped itself around her shoulders. She didn't resist. She knew who it was. She lifted her head and turned.

"You must have had quite a conversation," Gian Antonio Rizzo said. "Quite a confession."

"It was," she said.

"Deathbeds will have that effect."

She nodded.

"Life's funny," he said. "No matter where you are, *there* you are. So here *you* are."

"Yeah. Thanks for being here with me," she said.

Rizzo kept his arm wrapped around her. It was warm, comforting, and supportive. So were his eyes. She leaned to him and allowed herself to luxuriate in his embrace.

"You were wrong," she said.

"About what?"

"I did manage to turn down the request of a dying man."

"Oh. I see," he said. At length, he asked, "Would it be vulgar of me to ask what the request was?"

"Marriage."

"Marriage!" He seemed as stunned as she had been. "You and him?"

Alex nodded.

"You'll excuse me, but, *ha!*" he said. "The man was more of a deluded dreamer than I thought."

"And that wasn't even the worst of it," she said.

"What *was* the worst of it?"

She told him. All of it. From Kiev through to the jungle of Venezuela, to Paris, back through recent days in Geneva, New York, and Cairo.

"Wow," he said, blowing out a long breath.

"I'm wondering," she said after a long, heavy silence, "if I had known along the way, if I had known for a fact what he just confessed to, that he was responsible for Robert's death, for the slayings in Barranco Lajoya, for every single venal, hateful thing he's done, I wonder if at some moment I might have just killed him myself."

"But you didn't," Rizzo said. "You didn't know and you didn't kill him."

"But should I have?"

"Killed him?"

"Yes."

"Probably not." He paused. "Did you ever *suspect*?" he asked.

There was a long silence.

"And would *you* have?" she finally asked. "If you knew that he'd taken the person you most loved away from you? Would you have just shot him?"

Rizzo's gaze went far away and came back, much as Federov's had several minutes earlier.

"I'm a religious man," he said, "and maybe a little bit superstitious as well. So I'd prefer not to answer that in a place of worship."

"I'll take that as a yes," she said.

"Take it instead as a maybe," he said. "A definite maybe."

She nodded. He took his arm away.

"And you?" he asked.

"What about me?"

"If you'd *known*, would you have killed him?"

She looked away from him and maintained another silence. When he looked back again, her eyes were moist, but something in them had changed—the compassion had changed to anger, or maybe something deeper.

"That's what I thought," he said.

He stood. He offered a hand.

"Come along," he said. "I think it's my duty right now to get you out of here."

"Thank you," she said, accepting his hand and standing.

By then, they had both had enough, so Alex and Rizzo slipped out of the Clinique Perrault without a further word to anyone.

They went for dinner at a small French place on the Place St. François. Alex was still in a mode of deep decompression after the visit with Federov, but Rizzo knew how to guide the events.

They split a bottle of wine and talked about life. Gian Antonio rose to the occasion as a gentleman par excellence and talked her out of her anger and depression and fury. The staff of the restaurant sensed that the two needed space and time and, for that matter, a second bottle of wine, so they provided one, a good Swiss one from the Rhône Valley.

She got back to the hotel shortly after midnight, moderately drunk, which was probably a good thing this evening. She crashed into bed and slept fitfully, unable to come down completely, unwilling to pop an Ambien or any other sleeping aide on top of the wine. She was victimized not by nightmares but by bad feelings about all the events of the last year and a half.

The stint in Madrid, the pursuit of the Pietà of Malta, was a small vacation in terms of the larger picture. But looking back on it, she could see the hand of Federov once again making the first moves toward forgiveness and contrition.

She wondered again: If she had known earlier, might she have killed him? Out of pure whim one day, might she have just drawn a weapon and shot him? She pictured herself doing it, probably when she was one-on-one with him in his magnificent study in Geneva.

But in truth, she would never know. It was the road not taken.

She fell into what passed for sleep around 5:00 a.m.

The phone woke her less than three hours later, exploding rudely at her bedside like a fire bell in the night. In a fog, she answered.

It was Rizzo. He asked if she had heard, and if not, he had news.

"Heard what?" she asked.

Federov, Rizzo explained, had slipped into a coma late the previous evening about the time that Alex had tipsily lurched from the restaurant while hanging on Rizzo's strong arm. In the early morning hours, Federov's heart had fluttered and then failed. Efforts by the Clinique to move him onto life support had also failed.

There had been no relatives listed with the Clinique. No friends, either. Aside from a solicitor, Rizzo was his only contact. So it had been Rizzo's cell phone that the Clinique had called at six minutes past seven that morning when Yuri Federov had been pronounced dead at age forty-nine.

FIFTY-SIX

Over the course of the fifteenth century, terrible epidemics of plague, the black death, ravaged Europe. Switzerland was swept by the pestilence as much as any country, and in Geneva, the leaders of the city — in an attempt to quarantine the dying — built a hospital away from the city center. The building sat on a stretch of pasture land called Plainpalais, between the rivers Rhône and Arve.

The surrounding land took the name of the hospital — the plain palace — that stood on the site. And since death from the plague was almost inescapable for the afflicted, it was only a matter of time that the vast fields surrounding the building became burial grounds.

Plainpalais Cemetery, also known as La Cimetière des Rois, was located on rue des Rois in the center of Geneva. Over the centuries, it had also become the largest cemetery in Geneva. As Federov had indicated, and as Alex had already known, Plainpalais was a peaceful, quiet place, filled with a small settlement of old burial vaults and tomb markers. The pathways within the cemetery were lined with large, aging trees, and there was a bittersweet air to the place, somewhat like the famous Cimetière Père Lachaise in Paris.

Some of the gravestones dated back to the late fifteenth century, and notables of Genevois history had been laid to rest here. Here lay John Calvin, the Protestant reformer; Augustin de Candolle, the botanist; Guillaume-Henri Dufour, the engineer and general; James Fazy, jurist and statesman; Emile Jaques-Dalcroze, composer; Charles Pictet de Rochemont, diplomat; as well as many others who, in the course of five centuries, had played a major role in Geneva's history.

More recently joining them were Jorge Luis Borges, the Argentine author of fantastical short stories, and Sergio Vieira de Mello, the former UN High Commissioner for Human Rights who was murdered by a terrorist bomb in Iraq in 2002.

It was bitterly cold on the day that Federov's ashes were to be

interred. True to her promise, Alex had made certain that the crema-
tion had taken place and that the urn containing Federov's ashes was
transferred to the funeral parlor that Federov had designated. The establishment seemed to have an Eastern clientele, as she dealt in Russian with a crafty funeral director named Rodzianko. In keeping with
Federov's wishes, she also ordered a headstone in black granite with
Cyrillic letters and, in Russian style, an engraving bearing his likeness.

"That," she mused with ironic detachment as she signed the papers, "should scare passers-by for another century or two."

Alex attended the funeral ceremony with Rizzo. They walked a
long, cold pathway and arrived punctually at the designated gravesite
where a small knot of other attendees also stood. Alex didn't recognize any of them. Unlike many such ceremonies that Alex had attended in her lifetime, there was no family and there were no tears.
There was again a light snow falling, just as there had been for Robert's interment.

She was in a somber mood, but it was more associations than a
sense of loss for the man being buried. As the ceremony began, she
wondered if Federov had willed himself into dying, or tinkered with
his drugs, while she was still in Switzerland. That way he would make
certain that Alex would be in attendance. She was convinced that he
had followed one of those courses. Similarly, when she declined to
marry him, she was convinced he had released his tenuous grip on
life.

The pastor was a young man named LeClerc. He was tall, reed-
thin in a heavy coat, and absurdly Harry Potterish with round glasses
and an owlish gaze. He conducted the ceremony in French and Russian. His words were brief. A bronze urn rested above an open grave.

It was minus 4 degrees Centigrade. It felt that cold in Fahrenheit.

LeClerc spoke softly, rapidly muttering a prayer that no one could
hear. Words on the icy air, brief and appropriate, but impersonal. The
knot of people shuffled uncomfortably. Alex counted them. There
were eleven — a strange number, but an even dozen including the
pastor.

The snow thickened. Then the service was over.

Alex had ordered a bouquet of roses for Federov's send-off. She took one and laid it on the urn. The flower was frozen but it didn't matter. Out of decency, Rizzo added a second. Other attendees pitched in, also. No one spoke to anyone else.

Alex and Rizzo turned and started to retrace their path through the cemetery to the exit. They had gone several meters when Alex heard a voice from behind her, a man chasing after her and calling out.

"Mademoiselle? Mademoiselle?"

Alex turned and saw LeClerc hastily pursuing her.

She stopped. So did Rizzo, who remained close. LeClerc arrived slightly breathless and reached to an inside jacket pocket.

"Vous parlez français, madame?" he asked. *"On peut parler français?"* he asked.

She answered, yes, of course. *Bien sûr*, she spoke French.

LeClerc was a little breathless and a little befuddled. He searched several pockets and then found what he was looking for.

"There were some special arrangements today," the pastor explained in French. "I was asked, or I should say, the deceased requested before his death, that if you arrived here on this day, I should give you something."

"How did you know who I was?" Alex asked.

"He described you."

"And what if I hadn't been here?" she asked.

"Well, I asked that too," the minister said. "But the deceased was insistent. He said he knew you would come."

"Then what is it that you have for me?" Alex asked.

"I was asked to give you this."

He handed her an envelope. It was addressed simply, in Federov's shaky handwriting from his final days, perhaps even the final one.

On the front of it was simply written Alex LaDuca.

She felt the envelope. It was too thin to be the ring again; she could tell even with a gloved hand. "My condolences in any event," said the young priest.

"Thank you," she said.

LeClerc gave her and Rizzo a nod, then turned. He trotted back toward the gravesite where workers from the graveyard were readying to lower the funeral urn to its final resting place.

Alex glanced to Rizzo. "Shall I open it now?" she asked.

"Why not?" Rizzo shrugged. "If it explodes, then he'll get us both."

"Very funny."

"It wasn't a joke."

They stood in the cold graveyard. Alex pulled off her gloves. She tore away one end of the envelope. She pulled out a letter-sized sheet of paper which also bore Federov's handwriting, but before she could manage to read it, a small golden chain with an attached pendant slid into her hand.

It landed perfectly in her palm. It had a strange warmth to it, having been carried within LeClerc's clothing.

Alex gasped.

There, in the open day, under a grayish white sky, in the center of her palm with snow falling on it, was the small golden cross that her father had given her years ago. It was the cross that she had worn so many years, up until the horrible day of the RPR assault in Kiev. It was the cross that she had somehow lost that day. Now, almost inexplicably, it had come back to her.

She opened the brief note and read it.

My Dearest Alejandra,

> *Following the horrible events in Kiev, after the snow of February had melted, I walked the ground where the assault had transpired. By the hand of fate, or God, or of some force that I do not understand, I looked down and between my boots saw a faint glitter in the mud.*

> *I reached down and retrieved this, which I recognized immediately, not just for the woman it belonged to, but for what it meant to you. I held it with me for some time. I held it to remind me of what I had done, how I had hurt you and so many others so much, and because I wished to have something of yours. But over the last months, I wished to return it to you. I prayed for a proper time and in God's strange way that time arrived. So that time is here and I return it to you today. May my last act in this world be one of Christian kindness to someone I cared for and may I be judged by my Maker accordingly.*

> *Affectionately,*
> *Y.F.*

Her eyes rose to Rizzo's. She showed him the note and turned away as he read it.

"Sentimental old bird, wasn't he?" Rizzo said. "Typical Russian. Stabbing you in the back one minute, weeping into his samovar to gypsy violins the next."

"Like anyone else," she said, "I suppose he was trying to make his peace. With himself, with the world. With God."

"Sounds like you're sympathetic," Rizzo said. He folded the letter and slid it into the pocket of her coat. "Do with it as you wish," he said.

She took a moment. She studied the cross and chain in her hand.

"Here," Rizzo said.

He reached to it and took it from her. He loosened the scarf around her neck. With two hands he reached around her and put the chain in place. He gave her a gentle kiss on the forehead, as a brother might. Then he stepped back.

"Perfect," he said. "It's back where it belongs."

She glanced at her watch.

"Let's get to the airport," she said. "I'm finished here."

Several hours later, Alex sipped from a glass of whiskey that was on the folded-down tray before her. She sat in the seclusion of a business-class window seat aboard a Swiss International Airlines Airbus. Midway into her eight-hour flight from Geneva to New York, there was a consistency to the drone of the aircraft's engines that was both unreal and therapeutic.

Sometimes it seemed as if all of the humanity had been sucked out of her over the last year. This was a crazy way that she was going through life, she knew, and yet she didn't know how to throw the switch to reverse courses, to go in any other direction.

She searched herself and the sum of all knowledge she had learned to date. She still had her faith, but she knew she sometimes wrestled with it. She knew she probably always would. Like a cathedral, it was never complete, never finished.

She searched the literature she had read over a lifetime. She didn't know whether it was because Russians were on her mind, but here in this aircraft the metaphor that she kept returning to was that of a train.

Long ago she had read *Anna Karenina*, the same as Federov had done on his deathbed. The story had started with children playing with a toy train and then ended with a train wreck and a conversion to deep Christian spirituality.

Well, that Tolstoy had obviously known a few things about the hazards of travel, she mused with a smile, as well as the comforts of spirituality.

She thought back to the train ride she had taken just a few months earlier across central Spain, and how from a window she had seen a small rural funeral that had reminded her of the funeral of her grandmother in Mexico many years ago. She thought about the first time she had flown into Kiev and the last time she had flown out. Then she was ten years into the past, a more innocent time, when she was playing soccer at UCLA. Then there was the summer she had spent in France and the summer she had spent in Russia, the experience that had taught her Russian and paved the way for her being assigned to a spiritual shell of a man named Yuri Federov.

The aircraft banked left at Greenland. The flight became bumpy and the seat belt signs came on. She ordered another whiskey, her third, sipped it, and then, exhausted, slipped easily into a short dream at thirty-five thousand feet. She drifted farther into the Russian psyche.

It would have been absurd to suggest that she had any inklings of love for Yuri Federov. So what was it that she felt?

A strange Christian sense of compassion?

The forgiveness that was a foundation of her faith?

The notion that within every human being there is some shred of decency, even if one sometimes needed to search hard to find it?

She supposed that might have been it.

Could she bring herself to say a prayer for his soul?

Silly question: she had already said many.

In time could she forgive Federov, as he had begged her?

In time, she decided, maybe she could forgive anything. But no one ever said it would be easy.

ACKNOWLEDGMENTS

The author is grateful to many sources for background and research in this book and the entire trilogy, which is now complete. Among them, *The New York Times*, *The Washington Post*, The United States Department of Justice, *Wikipedia*, *The Columbia Encyclopedia*, and *The Encyclopædia Britannica*. The author is also grateful to *Esquire* magazine and author C. J. Chivers for the excellent article "Power: The Vladimir Putin Story" (*Esquire*, October 2008) for further background on the current Russian leader and permission to use that article as a source here.

I'm also once again grateful to my good friend and retired diplomat Thomas Ochiltree for his endless insights on international politics and diplomacy and to my wife, Patricia, for her help, advice, and support in more ways than I can ever calculate.

At Zondervan, Andy Meisenheimer and Bob Hudson saved me as usual from my own verbal excesses. Thanks again, guys. But while I'm at it, I should also mention Christine Orejuela-Winkelman, who did the wonderful interior design for this book as well as my two previous ones. Art director Laura Maitner-Mason did the eye-catching cover design here, and Michelle Lenger was the creative director. Thanks for making my words look good on the page. Thanks also to Kathleen Merz, who did the original copy edit on this manuscript; to Karen Statler, editorial manager, who somehow keeps my books on schedule; and also to my friends Jessica Secord and Karwyn Bursma, who make sure I don't turn invisible after publication. It takes a good team to publish a book, not just an author, so your solid work and efforts are very much appreciated.

Conspiracy in Kiev

Noel Hynd

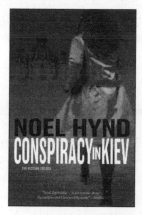

A shrewd investigator and an expert marksman, Special Agent Alexandra LaDuca can handle any case the FBI gives her. Or can she?

While on loan from the U.S. Department of the Treasury, Alex is tapped to accompany a Secret Service team during an American Presidential visit to Ukraine. Her assignment: to keep personal watch over Yuri Federov, the most charming and most notorious gangster in the region.

Against her better judgment — and fighting a feeling that she's being manipulated—she leaves for Ukraine. But there are more parts to this dangerous mission than anyone suspects, and connecting the dots takes Alex across three continents and through some life-altering discoveries about herself, her work, her faith, and her future.

Conspiracy in Kiev — from the first double-cross to the stunning final pages — is the kind of solid, fast-paced espionage thriller only Noel Hynd can write. For those who have never read Noel Hynd, this first book in the Russian Trilogy is the perfect place to start.

Softcover: 978-0-310-27871-9

Pick up a copy at your favorite bookstore or online!

The Russian Trilogy

Midnight in Madrid

Noel Hynd

When a mysterious relic is stolen from a
Madrid museum, people are dying to discover its secrets. Literally.

U.S. Treasury agent Alexandra LaDuca
returns from *Conspiracy in Kiev* to track
down the stolen artwork, a small carving
called "The Pietà of Malta." It seems to be
a simple assignment, but nothing about this job is simple, as the
mysteries and legends surrounding the relic become increasingly
complex with claims of supernatural power.

As aggressive, relentless, and stubborn as ever, Alex crisscrosses
Europe through a web of intrigue, danger, and betrayal, joined by
a polished, mysterious new partner. With echoes of classic detective and suspense fiction from The Maltese Falcon to The Da Vinci
Code, *Midnight in Madrid* takes the reader on a nonstop spellbind-
ing chase through a modern world of terrorists, art thieves, and
cold-blooded killers.

Softcover: 978-0-310-27872-6

Pick up a copy at your favorite bookstore or online!

Share Your Thoughts

With the Author: Your comments will be forwarded to the author when you send them to *zauthor@zondervan.com*.

With Zondervan: Submit your review of this book by writing to *zreview@zondervan.com*.

Free Online Resources at
www.zondervan.com

Zondervan AuthorTracker: Be notified whenever your favorite authors publish new books, go on tour, or post an update about what's happening in their lives at www.zondervan.com/authortracker.

Daily Bible Verses and Devotions: Enrich your life with daily Bible verses or devotions that help you start every morning focused on God. Visit www.zondervan.com/newsletters.

Free Email Publications: Sign up for newsletters on Christian living, academic resources, church ministry, fiction, children's resources, and more. Visit www.zondervan.com/newsletters.

Zondervan Bible Search: Find and compare Bible passages in a variety of translations at www.zondervanbiblesearch.com.

Other Benefits: Register yourself to receive online benefits like coupons and special offers, or to participate in research.

ZONDERVAN®

ZONDERVAN.com/
AUTHORTRACKER
follow your favorite authors